Winter Kill

War With China
Has Already Begun

By GENE SKELLIG

Publishing and marketing enhancements provided by
Flea Circus Books. "Flea Circus" is a registered trade mark.

Buy as e-book: www.amazon.com/dp/B0050D7E06
$3.00off : www.createspace.com/3537111 Code FJEHR84S

ISBN: 0986883107
ISBN-13: 978-0-9868831-0-1

DEDICATION

This book is dedicated to my four children, to my future grandchildren, and to all the children whose future we sacrifice each and every day. If major decisions were in their hands, I doubt they would squander the air, water and life of our planet.

After all, they are going to need it.

DISCLAIMER

The characters and events portrayed in this book are fictitious. Any resemblance to real world events or persons living or dead is purely coincidental or used fictitiously.

FORWARD

Winter Kill was written as a military techno-thriller, which means that there is more detail provided than would be the case in other genres. However, in this case, there are a couple of chapters ("Architect", "Sewing Shop", "Stocking Up") which delve far deeper into the details than is strictly necessary for the story. I believe that many readers will enjoy going into these details about the design and construction of the HOTH facility, so rather than placing them at the back in an annex these details were woven into a few of the early chapters. This makes for a slow build before the accelerating action of the second half of the book. If you find yourself bogging down in details to an extent that you find annoying or distracting, simply skip ahead a few pages or even to the next chapter. You may miss something, but at least you won't give up before the action really takes off.

- Gene Skellig, author.

CONTENTS

CONVERSION TABLE :

1 inch = 2.54 cm
1 foot = 30.48 cm
1 yard = 0.9144 meter (metre)
1 mile = 1.609 kilometer
1 pound = 0.454 kilogram
32.15 troy oz gold = 1 kg gold
1 troy oz gold = 31.10grams (troy) gold
0.10 rem = 100 mrem = 1 milisievert
10 halving thicknesses = $1/1024^{th}$ radiation level

RADITION TERMINOLOGY:

The Roentgen (R) is now obsolete, however it has been used throughout this book due to the long familiarity which readers may have. The current Systeme International (SI) units are the Gray (GY) and the Sievert (Sv) as follows:

1 R = 0.119 Sv   and   1 R = 258 microcoulomb/kg

ACKNOWLEDGMENTS

Thanks go to my wife, Irina, for giving me time to write; to my ruthless editor, Ted Clarke, for helping me carve out the extraneous material and keeping all the details straight; to Zhamil Bikbaev, illustrationist, for contributing the cover; to my "Anvil Chorus": Alan James, Tom, Sasha, Nikolai, Svetlana and others for reviewing and commenting on various aspects of the book; to my mother, Vera, for being my first and most enthusiastic reader; to my late father for using such big words around my childhood home, and to the many people who inspired and guided me along the way.

Thanks also to serving and former members of the Canadian Air Force and the Canadian Forces. To have served with you has been a precious gift. True, the military may not be a very good place for a philosopher, and I have put some of you through hell along the way, but I will always cherish the fellowship and "Team Canada" sense of purpose that is our bond. This can never be overstated, diminished nor forgotten.

I am grateful to everybody who has cajoled, encouraged, discouraged, inspired, frustrated, provoked and challenged me along the way. My life has benefited greatly from these experiences. A great many people have tried to shape me, whether as a pilot, an officer, a writer or as a person. At times it may have seemed fruitless; however, I appreciate the effort and patience of my original mentor, Gary (The Great Gatsby), bosses like Frank, Sharon, David and Merrick, and friends like Albrecht and Mark.

ENHANCED SELF-PUBLISHING

This book is the product of a new paradigm in self-publishing. Winter Kill will take you on an adventure, and introduce you to a whole new world, the Flea Circus world. Authors and readers now have a better alternative to the expensive and at times predatory landscape of a publishing industry in transformation.

Laptop publishing, e-Book and Print-on-Demand (POD) technologies are the root cause for many of the problems faced by authors, however these powerful toos also create enormous opportunities for increasing numbers of people to get involved in the world of books..

The problem is that as many as one million new titles are released by independent and self-published authors each year, with millions of back titles compounding the situation. We self-published authors can feel like insignificant little fleas who have bitten off more than we can chew. Our books are quickly lost in the avalanche of new titles - and that is the elephant in the room for the vast majority of us. Many of us spend thousands of dollars in an attempt to improve our books but statistically we're only going to sell only about a hundred books each – and that's mostly to family and friends. That is an unacceptable outcome.

The solution is as elegant as it is simple. We need to embrace the notion that most of us will not sell tens of thousands of books so spending thousands of dollars is not warranted. We need to lower out cost structure, elevate the quality and reputation of our self-published books, and find a more effective way to connect with a book buying public who are overwhelmed with choices. The Flea Circus solves all three of these problems.

The Flea Circus provides authors, content collaborators, subject matter experts, illustrators, cover artists and niche marketing entrepreneurs with an ethical predator-free interchange. With a break-even point on the order of just a few hundred books due to the royalty-based structure of the Flea Circus Interchange, self-publishing authors are able to set realistic and attainable goals. This is the pathway to success.

Get involved at : www.fleacircusbooks.com

PROLOGUE

LAST THOUGHT

<u>20 May Year 00 ANEW : Day of Nuclear Extinction War</u>

After going back to look at the TV in the coffee room, Triona Hobkirk finally understood why the young woman, Amy Arnott, had rushed out of the office in such a panic. Feeling as though she was lost in a world that no longer made any sense, Triona made her way to the conference room and walked over to her husband. At first annoyed at the interruption, Mr. Hobkirk saw the look on Triona's ashen face. She looked as though she was about to collapse, so he got up out of his chair and reached out to her.

Leaning into her husband's embrace, she told the men in the conference room what was happening. The men turned on the wall-mounted television and became transfixed by what they saw. While they argued about what to do, Triona quietly left the room.

She went into a corner office and then simply waited by the window. She could see people walking out on the tidal flats at Spanish Banks, windsurfers at Jericho Beach, and sailboats plying the waters of English Bay. With just a few puffy clouds in the sky, it could have been a beautiful day. But looking out over the water, she knew there was little time left.

Ground Zero was one km from the office. The fireball expanding outward tore apart all but the strongest structures

1

and carried the contents of the shredded buildings along with it. Every volatile object within three km received enough thermal radiation to spontaneously combust.

In an instant, downtown Vancouver erupted in a massive sea of fire. Millions of tons of toxic smoke and radioactive debris mushroomed into the sky. Like a monstrous dragon spawned in the firestorm below, the obscene cloud reached fifty-five thousand feet before it began to settle on greater Vancouver. Over two hundred thousand people died instantly. Hundreds of thousands more received a lethal dose of penetrating radiation that would kill them within weeks.

Unlike the walking dead whose organs were slowly cooking from the inside, and those who would soon inhale lethal particles of radioactive fallout, Triona Hobkirk did not have sufficient time to register any fear or pain. Before being flash blinded and then vaporized milliseconds later, her last thought was: *Would Amy reach safety in time?*

1

CULVERT

21 August: 3 Months After NEW

He had never been more terrified in his life. Wet, cold, and exhausted, 'Boss Callaghan' craned his neck so he could look back at the entrance of the culvert he had just scrambled into. He felt the icy cold water flowing past his hands, under his stomach and between his water-soaked legs. Beyond, he saw wet snow falling into the barren forest. Snow in August no longer seemed strange to Casey; so much had changed in just three short months.

Casey knew that it would not be long before the dogs led Constable Walker to his hiding place. He had to keep moving to keep the blood circulating in his numbing limbs. Over six feet tall and weighing two hundred and twenty pounds, Casey Callaghan barely fit inside the thirty-inch culvert. The corrugated steel pressing against him on all sides made him feel increasingly claustrophobic and panicky.

They had been on him since shortly after he left his meeting with Don Erickson, head of the Qualicum Beach Volunteer Fire Department. The Fire Hall had long since stopped responding to calls and had been thoroughly looted.

Even so, Don was still a key member of Boss Callaghan's network.

With the phone lines no longer working, Casey had been visiting Don every other week to exchange information. Casey would update Don on the global situation and Don would tell Casey what was going on in town. Each time they met, Casey would offer Don a place at The House on the Hill, or "HOTH" as it had become known; and each time, Don would refuse. Don wasn't ready to give up on his community regardless how dire the situation had clearly become.

The weather had changed dramatically since the war began three months ago. From the weekly climate briefings at the HOTH, he knew that the skies over the Pacific Northwest had taken longer to darken than in other parts of the world. It took several weeks for the shroud of dust and smoke to spread across the Pacific Ocean. Now, with the atmosphere having settled into a persistent dismal gloom, there would be no more blue skies for years to come. Even knowing this, it was still strange to see snow in the middle of what should be summer.

The latest dump of snow had largely been washed away by another bout of unbelievably heavy rain. That made traveling a bit easier. But the constantly gray skies really dampened his spirits, especially when Casey thought about their implications.

On these trips, Casey always brought a full pack of food for Don. This time it was one kilo of corn-meal, a half-kilo of sugar, some salt, tea bags, a few cans of sweetened condensed milk, a couple of dehydrated meals, a small bag of dried fruit, three cans of Spam, several packets of dehydrated soup, the small luxury of a can of sardines, a dozen OXO cubes and a tin of tobacco for Don's goofy old pipe.

Carrying this five kilogram load on his back for the four km hike down from the HOTH had not been too strenuous for Casey. He always got full value from the intelligence that Don provided and it felt good to help out a friend in need. That much food would be worth about 1 gram of gold or twenty liters of gasoline these days.

Don's cupboards were essentially bare. His home had been ransacked more than once in the recent madness so the help provided by Boss Callaghan was a real lifeline. It supplemented the ration of durum wheat that Don collected once a week from the wheat distribution center at the French Creek Marina. A man can only eat so much boiled wheat, but the OXO cubes would give a tasty meat-flavor to the wheat-berry gruel that he had been living on for weeks.

The trip down to visit Don was best done on foot. Using anything motorized would draw too much attention. Casey had taken the normal precautions for going so far from the HOTH. He had set out early in the pre-dawn darkness, taking his time as he followed the forest paths to town. He had his Bowie knife on his hip, as always, and his grab & go pack on his back. He wasn't carrying any fire-arms because he firmly believed that any trouble he couldn't negotiate his way through would be made worse by being armed. But he did have the Motorola XPR 6500 2-way radio in case he needed to call for help from the HOTH. By moving stealthily and taking his time, he hoped to avoid unnecessary interaction with people. It was a strategy that had worked very well in the past, but not this time.

As he struggled through the frigid stream flowing through the culvert, he wished he had some of the high-energy food and change of clothes from the "grab & go". But the pack had been lost in his frantic flight from the dogs.

Constable William Walker had ambushed him at a bend in the road. Casey had been surprised to hear Bill Walker's nasally voice:

"So, if it isn't my old friend, Boss Callaghan!" Walker was holding a shotgun and had the drop on Casey. Bill's side-kick, Frank, was also aiming a hunting rifle. Knowing that he had no good moves at this point, Casey's best option was to wait for them to make an error. So when Frank ordered him to slowly drop his day-pack on the road and to kneel down with his hands raised, Casey obeyed. After removing Casey's Bowie knife and finding no other weapons, Frank yanked Casey to his feet and shoved him towards a foot-path leading away from the road.

Casey tried to look meek as he complied, waiting for a chance to make some kind of desperate move. Bill and Frank had by this time mastered the art of highway robbery. They kept Casey at a safe distance as they shepherded him behind a row of stumps and brush piled alongside the road. Casey knew he had only a few minutes before the situation became much worse. When they got to wherever they were taking him, they would search him and find his other knife, then bind his hands and probably beat him severely before getting into some serious torture. Casey knew how Bill felt about him, and why. He had to make a move soon.

For the moment, it seemed that Walker wanted to take him alive, for the intelligence value if not for the hostage value. After all, Bill Walker had some idea what Boss Callaghan had back at the HOTH. Bill had tried to get inside the HOTH during one of his phony "weapons security" inspections last winter, but had been turned away by Casey at the door. The damage was done, however, because Bill had taken in the smell of real food.

It was all about the food. Food had started to become scarce during the financial collapse of the previous winter, when the arrival of trucks became sporadic. With the dysfunctional supply chain, stores began to run out of goods. With only a few weeks of food on hand when the war began, people quickly turned to hoarding and, ultimately, to looting. Now, three months after the war, all the stores and warehouses were empty. The only "real" food available was what could be stolen from somebody else. No more trucks would ever come.

The ambush site was intended to pick up any vehicles or people coming down on foot from Coombs or off the Island Highway at the Highway 4 exit. Casey knew the danger, but had wanted to make good time getting back to the HOTH with the information Don had given him. He should have stuck to the forest paths and not taken the shortcut across the loop on Hillier's Road. It was a mistake that had now become a matter of life and death as much for Casey as for everybody else at the HOTH should Casey be captured.

And then his chance came. They were walking past a pile of brush pushed up by a bulldozer years ago, making a wall between the trail and the road. Casey had gradually lowered his hands to waist level and Frank had not reminded him to raise them back over his head. A few meters ahead there was a small gap in the maze of branches, rocks and logs. Casey figured he could step lively on a few of the larger branches just firmly enough to get some momentum to propel himself to the crest of the brush pile, and then dive through the gap and roll down the other side. Just before he got to the gap, he snagged a root coming off a stump leaning precipitously on the pile beside him. He tugged on it just enough to start it tumbling down behind him.

By the time Walker realized what was happening it was too late to warn Frank, who had his rifle leveled at Casey's back. As Frank turned his attention towards the sudden whirl of motion coming down at him, he didn't see Casey gingerly tip-toeing his way up through a gap in the brush a few meters ahead. As Frank reacted to the tumbling stump, Casey stepped on the strongest of the branches as fast as he could without slipping in the process. Casey was almost as big as Frank, but Frank was much younger and fitter. In an open fight, it would have been no contest. But Casey had one advantage over Frank – he was truly scared for his life.

When Frank realized that the spinning monster was just a stump and saw Casey disappearing over the top of the brush pile, he knew he'd screwed-up royally. He was unsure if he should fire off a few rounds or start climbing over the branches.

In the second or so that Frank was frozen in doubt, Walker smashed into him, slamming Frank across the shoulder blades with his shotgun as he yelled at Frank, "Get moving! Get him!"

Frank sprang into action and started picking his way over the logs and branches. Just as he neared the top, Frank was startled by the sudden "BOOM" as Walker fired his shotgun, and the "shyuh-chung" as he cocked the shotgun for another blast - "BOOM!" Walker was shooting into the air to get the attention of the rest of his men, who were just a few hundred meters down the trail.

Walker's shooting had two immediate effects. First, Frank was startled by the blasts so close to his ear. His right foot slipped on a wet log covered with leaves as slippery as soap. A sharply cut branch tore a deep gash in his calf muscle. He shrieked in pain and fell back. He wound up hanging backwards and upside-down. His right leg was stuck in the branches and his left leg was awkwardly bunched-up underneath him.

The second effect was to start the dogs barking. They were tied to a tree near three of Walker's men who were sitting by the fire pit warming themselves and having coffee. Walker had ordered that the dogs be kept away from the road so they would not alert any approaching people with their barking. Now he regretted having them so far from the ambush site.

With Frank blocking the only path through the brush wall, Bill couldn't go after Casey right away. It took him a minute to get his men and dogs organized for the pursuit.

By this time Casey had managed to roll down the other side of the brush pile and run across to the other side of the road. He leapt over the guard railing on the other side and went sliding down the gravel embankment to the stump dump below. He regretted it immediately.

Now, rather than being able to run up the road and put some distance between him and Walker, he was faced with the prospect of being exposed in the open. He would be a long way from any cover as he picked his way through the stumps.

Recognizing that moving forward into the stump dump

was a bad idea, he paused. It may have taken him only twenty seconds or so to get his breathing under control, but to Casey it seemed much longer. He expected shots to ring out from up on the road at any moment.

But no shots came. Only the sound of dogs barking and what sounded like a man moaning in pain. Maybe Frank had gotten tangled and hurt in the branches, Casey thought. Good, that'll buy me some time. But the dogs! That's a bigger problem.

Casey knew the dogs would be given his scent from the grab & go pack that Walker had taken. The dogs would lead Walker right to him. He had to get moving in a way that would confuse them. He got an idea, and started to move.

Walker's men extricated Frank from his predicament. Frank's face was beet red from the blood rushing to his head and from the embarrassment of letting Boss Callaghan get away. The pain in his leg was the least of his worries. In these dangerous times, Frank knew, life was cheap. Bill Walker could quite easily throw Frank out of his gang.

Bill did not say a thing to Frank. He just gave short, concise instructions to the other men. He had them give the dogs the scent from Boss Callaghan's back-pack, and set them after Casey with two men and Bill Walker on their heels, the third man was left to help Frank.

All of this only took a few minutes, but it was enough time for Casey to make his way along the bottom of the hillside below the road until he was adjacent to the spot where he had first been intercepted by Walker. After climbing up to peer over the railing he quietly stepped over and out onto the road. His plan was to get his scent trail mixed in with his original path. That might confuse the dogs long enough for Casey to get away.

After reaching the ambush site, Casey skulked along the path beside the brush pile. He felt his pulse racing and his breathing seemed to be very loud. His senses were heightened by his fear as he made his way slowly along the path. He could smell wood smoke in the air from a fire not far away. That meant that he was down-wind. Good! he thought to himself.

A commotion on the road told him that Walker and his men were just across the wood pile from him. Casey could hear the excited barking of the dogs not far off.

When Casey reached the gap where he had first made his escape he saw that it had been trampled down quite a bit. And there was blood. Frank had been hurt after all.

Casey froze. He could hear Frank cussing, somewhere down the path to his left, presumably near the source of the smoke. Then he heard Bill talking to his men on the road to his right. The dogs sounded like they were far off now, probably down in the stump dump following Casey's scent.

"Not that way, go left, to the Highway!" shouted Bill.

"But the dogs picked something up, going to the right!" shouted someone else, a bit more distant.

"OK, you two follow that down there, I'll give you top cover from here on the road," called out Bill.

Casey understood what they were doing, and saw an opportunity. Bill would follow the road bending back to the right, so his line of sight would be cut off by the wall of brush. Casey stealthily picked his way over the blood-smeared logs and through the gap in the brush and came out on the other side. He couldn't see anybody to the right. Casey figured that Bill would be at the ambush site soon, and the dogs would then follow the scent back up the foot-path.

Casey quietly stepped along the road to the left, keeping to the side and trying to be silent. Once he put the first fifty meters behind him he broke into a fast jog and then a steady running pace. He had only a few minutes head start.

Bill didn't hear anything back on the road. His attention was fixed on the dogs now trying to climb the slippery side of the embankment back up to the road.

"What are they doing? They can't climb that! Make them go around!" Bill shouted.

The dogs were really excited because they could smell

Casey's trail very well now. Casey had been sweating profusely when he climbed up the steepest part of the bank, grabbing on to slippery roots and branches. He had hoped that the dogs wouldn't be able to climb the nearly vertical hillside and that their handlers would lose time getting them to go another way. The two men leading the dogs had to put the leads back on the two Shepherd - Rottweiler crosses, Zeus and Adolph. They had to fight with the dogs to get them to move further along the cut.

The dogs were confused and they resisted as they were being pulled away from the scent trail. Eventually the men got Zeus and Adolph to a place where they could climb back up to the road. Once on top, the dogs ran straight at Bill.

Bill was momentarily afraid for his life as the two lathering dogs rushed right at him. He backed away towards the guard-rail at the side of the road only to watch as the dogs suddenly stopped in the middle of the road and started circling and sniffing at the ground. Bill realized that the dogs had stopped exactly where he and Frank had first captured Boss Callaghan. Then he was pissed.

"That son of a bitch! – He's lead the dogs in a circle! Now they don't know which way to go!"

The dogs were excitedly circling one way and then the other. Bill realized that they could smell where Casey had come from as well as where he and Frank had lead Casey towards the campfire. He was certain that Casey would not head back towards town; Casey would head towards the campfire because that would throw the dogs off.

"This way!" he yelled, and got the pursuit moving again.

As the dogs started scrambling over the brush pile for the second time, Bill smiled in admiration. He understood what Casey had done and expected to see the dogs confused once again when they found two different scent paths to follow. This time, however, Bill anticipated that the correct path would be to the left, up the road towards the highway. He was at least ten minutes behind Casey now, maybe a bit more if

Casey had been running hard.

And Casey had been. He had run at a full tilt, or as fast as a 49-year old, heavy-set man scared out of his mind could run. He was at the short path from the end of Hillier's Road up to the embankment of the Island Highway when he heard the dogs again. Now he had a difficult choice to make.

Casey considered his options: Go down to the overpass, the faster route to the HOTH; go up the exposed hillside and cross the highway; or cut along the low side to the east.

But what to do? The dogs are going to be on me shortly! Casey thought quickly as he caught his breath for a few long seconds. He knew that he was up against some very tough guys who would also be good with their rifles. All the dogs have to do is to delay me, and I'm done for! he thought bleakly.

Dogs! That decided it for him. With his mind racing ahead of him, Casey headed off to his left. He moved east along the low side of the Island Highway. He had just fought through a mess of plastic bags and other garbage and worked his way into the culvert under the divided highway when the dogs arrived. The dogs didn't even look down the road towards the overpass. They simply followed the fresh scent leading directly to their prey. They soon closed the distance and reached the entrance to the culvert, barking up a storm.

Casey figured he was about half-way through when he twisted his neck to look back. He could hear the dogs but couldn't see them. Beyond the circle of light at the end of the culvert, he saw wet snow falling into the darkness of the grey forest.

He was exasperated. I'll never make it through in time, he thought as he shuffled along. Suddenly he felt a surprising nothingness on his right and almost fell over into the void. He had been alternately bumping up against the left and right sides of the culvert as he made his way along, but now there was nothing on his right side. He stopped to figure it out.

Recognizing what he had stumbled upon, Casey felt a

wave of relief. It's a junction! He moved his body into the smaller sized feeder-culvert that had joined the larger one he had been crawling along. It was just two feet in diameter and came slicing down into the main culvert at a steep angle.

He struggled a few meters into the much smaller space. Once he was sure he was all the way in, Casey wormed his way over until he was on his back in the smaller culvert. He couldn't see anything as he looked down over his shoes. He imagined that he could see the occasional flicker of light coming off the water at the bottom of the larger conduit, but he was not sure if it was real or imagined in the inky blackness.

As he felt the sides of his new prison with his feet he reassured himself that he was all the way in and would not be visible from the end of the larger pipe. Craning his neck back to look upwards, he saw an intake grate which presumably intersected the ditch between the two sides of the divided highway. He was wet, and weak. But he was alive and just maybe invisible to the dogs. The question is, would they come into the culvert and find him?

As the dogs started sniffing into the large drain, their handlers and Walker came around the corner and saw that the dogs appeared to have found Casey's route. Bill ordered one of his men to climb up the embankment to get to the other end. Big Joe didn't waste any time. Bill and the other man pushed the dogs back so that they could look inside. They saw a perfect circle about sixty meters through the darkness, like the gun-barrel view in the opening credits of a James Bond movie.

Once their eyes adjusted to the darkness they saw light playing off water flowing through the bottom of the large tube of metal. Even with the culvert clearly empty, Bill tried to get the dogs to enter, but they refused. Possibly out of instinct or perhaps due to some bad experience entering a bear's den or a fox warren, something about this space scared the dogs. They stubbornly refused to enter. Bill tried to push Zeus in, but he spread out his front paws and resisted strenuously. Bill then tried to get Adolph to go in, and smacked him on the rump when he refused. Both animals now became despondent Walker took another good look through the culvert and saw Big Joe step into his view of the other side of the highway.

"Stay there, we're coming over," hollered Bill.

"OOOO - KAAAY!" replied Big Joe.

"What's wrong with the dogs?" asked Joe when the other men joined him on the high side a few minutes later.

"They got freaked out at the culvert," replied Bill.

"What do you mean, 'freaked out'?"

"Even when we pushed, they wouldn't go in," said Bill.

Good thinking, Joe sighed under his breath while rolling his eyes. "Bill, you never push a dog into something he's afraid of. Now these guys are ruined for days."

The men decided they'd lost Casey. They certainly wouldn't go looking on the Callaghan side of the highway, so they headed back to the Lodge. After several skirmishes with the Callaghans and other well-armed groups in the region, William Walker had learned not to stray from his own turf, centered on the property he had confiscated.

"We'll get him next time," muttered Bill.

Casey heard none of this. He stayed holed up, terrified and shivering until dark. When he finally crawled out three hours later he was exhausted and extremely weak. He knew he was severely hypothermic because his teeth had stopped chattering and he no longer felt much of anything. Casey knew from his survival training that he had maybe one or two hours left before he would become unconscious and then die of exposure.

With his fingers whitened from lack of circulation, he weakly reached out to grasp hold of some roots as he crawled his way up the embankment. He felt some strength returning to his limbs when he disappeared into the forest above the highway, determined not to give in to the beckoning abyss.

2

DEPRESSION

06 September: 8 Months Before NEW

She was tired when she got home, but tonight she was more than tired. As she opened the door to her family's home in Aurora, Colorado, 37 year old Agatha Jasmine was carrying a heavy load. With a large bag of groceries in each arm, she stumbled on the shoes and boots strewn around by her three sons.

"Ron, I'm home! Come help me with the groceries."

"Hi Honey." When Ron saw the look on her face, he knew something was terribly wrong. "What happened?"

"I'm sorry. This is the worst day of my life!"

"Sit down. I'll get you a glass of water, and you can start at the beginning." Ron took the groceries from her.

"Thanks." She sat down, and took a deep breath. "OK. Here it is. I was let go from the jewelry store. I don't have a job; we have no source of income!" The tears started to flow. "And that's not the worst of it. When I was at the Hi-Lo at the mall, the debit machine rejected both of our bank cards, so I had to use some of the rent money to buy groceries."

Ron knew intuitively that all the strength and perseverance that Agatha had shown these last few months was missing. The family had relied on Agatha's income. Now even that was gone. He knew that she must be devastated.

"Oh, honey. Don't fret. Everything's going to be OK." Ron Jasmine felt like a liar. They were in debt up to their eyeballs, with no source of income. They were already two months behind on the rent and David had warned them that once they were three months behind he would have to evict them.

"Jerry said he was so sorry, but he couldn't even pay my final paycheck. They're broke and the bank seized all their assets. They've lost everything. They're moving back to C-Springs to live with Julie's family." Agatha was on the verge of breaking down. "What are we going to do, Ron?"

After holding Agatha in his arms for a while, angry and powerless to do anything about their plight, Ron began to smile as he suddenly knew what must be done.

"OK, my love, here's what we're going to do. First, we're going to watch a movie with the boys. After that, we'll have a family meeting."

"What movie?" Agatha questioned.

Five days later, the Jasmines headed west in their Dodge Caravan. They felt excited about the adventure to come, even if they looked like a 21st century version of the "Joad" family in "The Grapes of Wrath."

The minivan pulled a small utility trailer filled with camping gear, a few spare tires, some jerry cans of gasoline, the family's bicycles and Ron's tools. On the roof-rack was a heap of suitcases and boxes strapped down and covered with a tarp. Inside the minivan were plastic containers and coolers containing as much food as the rest of their rent money could buy and the available space would allow.

David would not be receiving any more rent from the Jasmines, but he could take what he wanted of their furniture and possessions. Agatha and Ron had sold what they could in a garage sale and left the rest for David to cover their debt.

After watching "The Grapes of Wrath" and hearing their mother's quiet weeping that evening, the boys understood how much trouble the family was in. They were to be homeless, and Mom and Dad had decided they would pack up everything they owned and head out west looking for a better life.

During the family meeting, Ron had done most of the talking. Agatha had figured out his plans during the movie, and sat quietly as she listened to him lay it all out. Agatha was proud of her man as he spoke with an even voice which the boys respectfully listened to. They were scared, Agatha could sense, but they were mature enough to understand what was going on.

For his part, Ron was excited. He knew that there was no hope for the family to survive the global depression by just sitting around in Aurora waiting for something to save them. The past four months of fruitless job-hunting and the occasional day or two of labor he could get had shown him that so many decent men these days couldn't even provide the essentials for their families.

That nuclear attack in Israel last year had been a sign of things to come, Ron believed. The world was going to get very dangerous and Colorado was probably the worst place to be.

Being homeless in Colorado in winter with no food or money would be suicidal. Not only would it be impossible to find work, but the NORAD complex would certainly be attacked if there was a war. On the Oregon coast, Ron reasoned, no matter how bad things get, there should be some place to camp out and not be at risk of being killed by the weather. He figured that with his skills as a mechanic and handyman he should be able to find a way to support his family. And the boys could also work.

As they made their way along the northern route, taking Highway 30 through Salt Lake City and then on to Portland, they saw a few other families that looked as much like the Beverly Hillbillies as they did. They came together as a family to face the crisis, and started to feel an excitement at the prospects for adventure on the West Coast.

As Ron drove, Agatha read the Oregon section in the AAA atlas which provided a general description of each town along with its history, economy and climate. By the time the family reached Portland, they had decided to explore some of the smaller coastal towns along Highway 101.

They had no idea where they were going, nor how they would feed themselves, but believed they had been smart to flee before the coming storm.

When they reached the Oregon coast they were quickly rewarded. The economic crisis had taken its toll on the lumber industry, but there was a much better community spirit in the small towns. To the Jasmine family it appeared that the America they loved was alive and well in the small towns along the coast. In sharp contrast, the larger cities were economic disaster areas full of people depending on assistance programs.

Cities across America had become increasingly hopeless and alien places. Well educated adults couldn't comprehend what had caused the land of opportunity to change so drastically that they suddenly couldn't find ways provide for their loved ones. In fact, with unemployment standing at 35% or higher in most cities, things were worse than during the great depression of the 1930s. To make matters worse, the failure of global commerce had reduced the flow of food and trade goods to only a small proportion of what was required to keeps any large city functioning. As a result, some of the more enterprising communities tried to promote "Victory Gardens" like those that sprang up during the Second World War.

This proved to be difficult because people no longer had the basic agricultural and handcrafting skills to provide for themselves. The cities were filled with educated but completely redundant, essentially useless people.

3

SETTLED

08 October: 7 Months Before NEW

While the Jasmine family and many others sensed that things were going to get much worse, and took steps to find a more viable way of life, the Callaghans moved into their new home.

Casey no longer felt that strange feeling you get after first moving to a new house. After having moved to the HOTH that July, the family had settled into new routines and the HOTH started to feel like home. The school year had started, and the girls, Hope and Tara, were excited about their new social lives. They had become popular. Their exotic Irish – Russian roots helped, but it was their confidence and spirit that other kids were drawn to. Casey put it down to the excitement and energy the entire family felt, having moved into such a beautiful permanent home after so many short-term military postings.

The older boys, Liam and Justin, were doing well too. Liam found his own group of friends in his grade eight class at Kwalikum Secondary. He stayed clear of his sisters during school hours, meeting up with them only after school when Mama would pick them up each day. Liam was always greeted by the happy smile of his baby brother, Donny strapped into his car seat in the middle row of Mama's minivan.

Justin was fitting in well at middle school. He hung around with the boys he had met in 4-H Junior Members Club.

Things were not so rosy for many other children. As more and more economic problems began to filter through the community, school children were being affected. Some families were in real hardship and had been ashamed to ask for help.

When Tanya Callaghan heard that some children were showing up at school without a proper lunch, she personally intervened and organized a "free lunch" soup program at all the schools in the Oceanside region. Recognizing the need, the families of the Oceanside community rallied around Tanya's call for support. Donations of farm produce came pouring in. People volunteered to help with cooking and serving, and the children felt that they were actually part of a larger, supportive community. It also helped Tanya settle in and get to know people on her own.

The communities of the Oceanside area were undergoing other changes, also caused by the depression. There was a greater emphasis on local food production. More and more families had taken up gardening and, to various degrees, hobby farming.

Casey had negotiated with the 4-H coordinator, Klara Rekert, to begin a customized program for his children. They would be responsible for a variety of animals through every stage in the breeding cycle, from insemination to birthing, and the care of calves, foals, piglets and so on.

The "Breeding" project was meant to be a valuable life experience for his children, and a shakeout of the barn that Casey had built and outfitted. Casey felt that going through the life cycle in their own barn would be a great way to really put theory into practice. Mrs. Rekert, for her part, was glad to have the facilities to work with, and the cash.

After each successive animal project was completed, Casey wrote up his observations as "Lessons Identified". Then he modified the layout, equipment, or supplies so that the "Lessons Identified" became "Lessons Learned".

His goal was for his family to be able to care for horses, chickens, pigs, and dairy cows at some future date. And as the economy continued to deteriorate, Casey ramped up his purchases of feed, nutritional supplements and other supplies that he was learning about in the family's initial foray into hobby farming. If a total economic collapse happened, Casey reasoned, obtaining animals would be easy. The hard part would be finding the feed and other supplies that would suddenly become scarce.   Inside the HOTH, as the family enjoyed the extra space, they engaged in other projects. Casey and Tanya designed databases to record the energy used in various household activities. This would later prove useful.

The family experimented with hydroponic gardening in the barn/greenhouse complex. They started with just one tenth of the available space, growing a range of vegetables, fruits and herbs. They became less intimidated as they learned to manage the chemistry, humidity and lighting. The Callaghans were soon enjoying tasty salads made entirely from their indoor garden.

This helped Casey determine what needed to be stockpiled, in terms of the primary nutrients of Nitrogen, Phosphorus and Potassium, such as "20-20-20"; and the secondary nutrients of Calcium, Magnesium, Sulphur, Iron, Molybdenum and Boron. Controlling the lighting was more complex than Casey had expected, but he soon understood which plants worked best with High Pressure Sodium light bulbs and which with Compact Fluorescent. Casey and Tanya discovered that CFL was very good for spinach, carrots, beets and lettuce, while HPS was best for tomatoes, cucumbers, zucchinis, potatoes, corn, and melons.

That night in early October, when Casey and Tanya had their cup of Russian Chai by the wood stove in the kitchen annex, they discussed how well the family was settling into the HOTH and how well the overall design had turned out.

4

ARCHITECT

Casey was uncomfortable with the idea of lying about everything, but it was necessary. After getting off the Skytrain at the last stop of the Canada Line into Richmond, he walked the two blocks to a five-story building on Minoru Boulevard. After finding the information board, he headed up to the fourth floor and 'Winston Brothers' architectural firm.

"Hello, I have an appointment with Rob, at three. I'm Dave McKenzie", Casey lied to the receptionist. To him, she had a remarkable resemblance to the actress, Meg Ryan, with a sparkling kindness in her eyes that made Casey feel welcome.

"Oh yes, Mr. McKenzie, Mr. Mynarski is ready for you in the conference room. It's down the hall on the right."

The firm seemed just about right. It was large enough to handle his commission but small enough to be discreet. The pictures on the wall showed residential and commercial projects, mostly in concrete, and some using the ICF system that Casey had chosen for the facility. And it was a facility more than it was a home.

The project had been his main focus for the last three years. It was more than just a personal dream; it was a necessity. Casey had concluded that survival in the near future required him to follow the example of his ancestors in Ireland and Scotland and build what was, in essence, a *keep*. A well fortified structure, made of stone, and designed to withstand a long siege. The HOTH would be a keep equipped with sophisticated technology, based on a well thought-out design, and built with modern materials.

When Casey completed his overview of the project, Rob Mynarski began speaking, slowly at first. "Well, Mr. McKenzie, I think I understand what you have in mind. However, there seems to be some uncertainty about the project location, timeframes and, possibly, names?" Rob said this with a mischievous smile. "So to be consistent with the emphasis you have placed on security, you will understand that our own policy in such a case would be to require payment up-front for the work you require."

Casey nodded, indicating that Rob had read him correctly, and that Casey was willing to proceed on that basis.

"So this is how it works. You pay us nine dollars a square foot. We provide you with the design work and the associated engineering, but we won't put our engineers seal on the plans until you allow us to carry out on-site geotechnical work. As you don't appear to want to do that, what we'll be doing for you will be up to code, according to industry standards, but will be 'notional' from our point of view. The plans will be labeled: "NOTIONAL – FOR PRELIMINARY DESIGN PURPOSES ONLY'. If you want our seal on the engineering you'll have to pay another $5 per square foot, give us full access to the property for any tests we need to conduct, and we'll need full disclosure from you.

If you go ahead and use the notional plans we generate for you, that's your business." Mr. Mynarski explained all this with a calmness that indicated to Casey that he had gone through this sort of discussion with other prospective clients.

"We will provide you with as many sets of the plans as you like, including our full suite of three-dimensional renderings of all interior spaces as well as the exterior views, of course."

Mynarski then paused, moved his chair a bit closer to Casey, and looked meaningfully into his eyes as he continued.

"We are a bonded institution, Mr. McKenzie, quite capable of keeping your secrets safe. Banks use us to design their vaults for God's sake; you can trust us with the specifications of your panic room."

"Thanks, however I would like to proceed as you say, on a discreet consultation basis at this time."

Casey wanted to trust Rob but he had security in mind. He would not trust all the details to anyone who was not a long-time personal friend with proven loyalty. Too much was at stake. With this understanding with the architect in place, over the ensuing six weeks Casey had several productive meetings with Rob. As they went over the smallest of details, Rob rapidly built up the computer-based design of the facility. Rob's architectural firm had clearly mastered the art of building with concrete, and incorporating Insulated Concrete Foam, or ICF, into more traditional suspended-slab designs. This made for rapid progress.

Rob confirmed where Casey's initial sketches and assumptions were correct and explained where a particular concrete beam had to be larger or have a shorter span. He explained technical details that left Casey with no doubt that he had chosen the right firm. In most cases the changes to the plan were quite simple and logical. Casey had taken the design a long way on his own, but Rob really surpassed Casey's expectations in the details of the mechanical systems, such as air handling, air filtration, hydronic heating, geothermal heating, and panic room design.

"Why do you need to be able to get from the basement mechanical room to both of these panic rooms AND onto the roof level?" asked Rob. "It makes more sense to leave this one in the master bedroom closet, and take this one out through the exercise room."

"No, in this case, I'm sticking with the vertical connectivity here, here, and here. That's firm, Rob," responded Casey, without explaining how the interconnected aspects of the panic rooms and hidden mechanical spaces were actually intended for fighting off the scale of home invasions that Casey was concerned about.

"With all of these security cameras and computer network linkages from your office to this Panic Room, this storage area AND the room up in the penthouse level, why don't you link these into a security company and police alarm systems?"

"Because, Rob, and I'm straying from my principles here a bit, the purpose of this facility is for problems much larger than a simple home invasion."

Rob reflected back on how the elusive Mr. McKenzie had first described his project. He had stressed that the house had to be designed to withstand the extreme heat and dryness of a sustained drought or an unprecedented heat-wave, as well as stand up to massive snow accumulations and extremely low temperatures. Rob considered these to be completely ridiculous conditions, but he mentally bowed to his client and engineered for them.

They had worked together on the finer points. Rob was confident that he was adding value to the project. He had to doff his hat to the customer. Mr. McKenzie had thought a few things out in considerable detail.

The facility would have a drilled well, with the pumps located in the mechanical room in the basement. There would be a back-up, hand-powered pump in the event of a failure of the electrical grid. So whatever happened there would be fresh water. The plumbing system would include a grey water system, keeping laundry chemicals, bathtub and dish soaps separate from the biologically active sewer water from toilets. So there would be one septic tank for the toilets, and a secondary one dedicated to the grey water system.

The design called for the septic distribution field to be covered with an incredible three meters of overburden material. The overburden was to include as much clay as possible from the materials available at the construction site. This was clearly intended to protect the distribution field from freezing up in extreme cold conditions over a long period of time.

A geothermal field was to be the heat source for the facility. Two four-tonne heat pumps would heat boilers for an extensive hydronic heating system. Total heat demand and scale requirements of the heating system, along with the associated thermostats, zones, pumps and control valves were easily calculated once Rob had the baseline heat-loss calculations, window design and sizes, and environmental assumptions.

Insulation would clearly be a major expense in this project. All exterior walls were to be constructed using ICF. In addition, there was to be ten centimeters of sprayed insulation on the inside walls once the metal studs were installed and the electrical, plumbing, and other services were roughed in. This would be an exceptionally solid and well insulated structure.

Rob had wondered why Mr. McKenzie was not going for any mass effect, whereby concrete walls are used to store heat from passive solar heating. The idea would be to insulate on the outside and allow the mass to transfer heat into the interior spaces during the dark hours. Rather, in this case, the concrete mass of all the perimeter walls seems to be for other purposes. The use of concrete, therefore, must be primarily for the purpose of strength and perhaps fire-resistance, certainly not for cost savings.

Fire protection was clearly important to the customer. There would be a roof-mounted 1550 gallon tank. The tank would be topped-up from the drilled well down in the mechanical room.

The electrical system was conventional in one sense, as the facility would be wired for the normal range of electricity-hungry devices. But there would also be a duplicate electrical circuit for essential systems, scaled for minimal electrical consumption. The two electrical systems came together in the mechanical room, where there was also a bank of batteries which were fed by a pair of five meter helical wind turbines, mounted on the roof.

Each turbine would be capable of generating up to 5

kilowatt-hours of power when the winds were at least sixteen km per hour, well in excess of the 1.3 kWh normally consumed by an average house. Not counting recharging loads, the calculated load demand of this facility would be as high as 6 kW-h if fully inhabited and facing extremely cold temperatures. By switching to the duplicate electrical system when winds were calm, the draw on the bank of batteries would be minimized.

Similarly, the electricity-hungry pumps of the geothermal system were to come on automatically whenever wind power was high. This would bring up the boiler to maximum heat for the hydronic heating system in the concrete slabs, which would serve as a form of heat storage. This residual warmth would last for several days, until the winds picked up and the boiler and hydronic heating lines were cranked up again. It would take some management on a day-to-day basis, but in the extreme cold scenario all heat sources would be closely monitored.

At first Rob had thought it strange that no consideration was given to solar power. But now all of these features made sense. It was with the clarity of a sudden and complete understanding that Rob realized that *this structure is designed to survive a nuclear winter.*

"OK, Mr. McKenzie, now I think I understand what you are trying to achieve. I'll need some time to go over the scaling of the electrical and hydronic systems again on my own. I'll need to recalculate your heat loss numbers based on a longer, *nuclear*, winter. That is your reference scenario, isn't it?"

Casey nodded, grimly accepting the fact that his architect might be the sharpest tack in the room.

"And I think the electrical system should also incorporate a trickle-feed option for a solar power array, even if you don't plan to install one," continued Rob, now highly energized by the new dimension that this project presented to him as a systems engineer and designer.

"OK, Rob, but don't put too much into that. I suppose you should also provide me with a few recommendations for solar panels which could be bought and stored for later installation. I am not saying that there will be a nuclear war. I am saying that I want a facility that can stand up to the worst environment imaginable. I want this facility to have every advantage that money can buy. So now that you completely understand my reasoning, please don't judge me, just do the job I hired you to do."

After that point, the weekly updates with Rob were extremely productive. Rob's technical skills were working in unison with Casey's vision for the facility. Then one day Rob said something that made Casey very alarmed. "You know, Mr. McKenzie, I have another client who may have some things in common with you. And I wonder if it would be OK if I arranged a meeting?"

Casey froze. Rob had crossed the line. With his near paranoia regarding security, Casey was not sure how to respond. Rob had done a first rate job of evolving and refining the concept of the facility, and Casey had come to enjoy working with and trusting Rob; but now everything had suddenly been moved to a different and much riskier level.

"Well, Rob, I'm not sure I'm comfortable with this line of thinking. After all, this is all very confidential, right?"

"Yes, and I'm sorry to have brought it up, but the other client is working with some of the same technical questions you are. Although he has not said so, I think that his project and yours could be mutually instructive," Rob answered sheepishly.

Then Casey realized that this was the first test of some of the security protocols he had been working on, in developing his *Contingency Plans* and *Branch Plans*.

Recognizing that these plans were now being triggered by the unexpected comment from Rob, Casey thought all the way back to when his planning for the project had first started. *Information Security* and *Operational Security*, INFOSEC and

OPSEC, were necessary elements in his planning. They flowed from some of the core *Factors and Deductions Analysis* that he had identified in his original planning cycle.

This was why he had paid such attention to various forms of security. Security would be enhanced by the cameras he had planned for key locations around the facility, the observation posts he would establish in the forest, the specialized communication systems, the hidden walls and even weapons and food caches that would be created. But planning and technology alone would not guarantee security.

Casey believed that the only real security was going to come from people. Being part of a community, rather than being isolated from it, was going to be the *Operational Centre of Gravity*. This would go along with the *Strategic Centre of Gravity*, that of *Information Collection and Analysis*.

With these deductions in mind, Casey was clear that what was needed was to make meaningful connections with the right people in the right places. He began a detailed analysis of the personalities and capabilities of key people in the expected *Area of Operational Responsibility*, AOR, and the friends and family members that could be expected.

We need other people in life, Casey believed, even if the number of people we need could be counted in the hundreds and thousands and not in the hundred of millions. We also need to be free from interference. We need security of person and property, and we need to stay below the radar screen as much as possible. Others must not know what you have, if your intention is to hang on to it and use it in the manner you choose.

Casey did not want anybody to have a list of the contents of his home. He did not want some desperate but powerful person to identify his home as an attractive target or potential source of needed supplies.

With this in mind, a considerable emphasis in planning had been placed on information security, intelligence gathering, and networking. So the problem raised by Rob's suggestion of talking with the other client was a philosophically important one to Casey. As Casey sipped on his water and considered what Rob had said, all of that flashed through his mind.

Casey decided to treat this as he would a potential *Emerging Threat* while still remaining open to the possibility that it could work out in a positive manner.

"OK, Rob, here's what I'm prepared to do. I'll meet with your client, but on my own terms. Here is what I want you to do, and I'm sorry if this feels a bit cloak and dagger. Why don't you get his phone number. Then we'll go out for a walk, and you can call him from another location." Casey said this as he got to his feet and moved to the door of the conference room. Looking very startled, Rob awkwardly complied and led Casey to his office, just across the hall.

Rob retrieved the phone number. Casey smiled to the Meg Ryan look-alike as he led Rob out of the office.

Casey thought to himself. Maybe I'm being paranoid, but now I have the initiative. If this supposed client is legit, I can set up a meet with him and ask a few questions right now, without him having had a chance to talk to Rob. If he's fishy in some way, he'll be less prepared and easier to catch in a lie.

But when Casey got Rob to dial the number on a payphone outside the 7-11 near Rob's office, the other client didn't seem fishy at all. His name was Henry Davidson, and Casey liked "Hank" from the start.

"Hey, man, it's alright that you called me right away and cut out the middle man," said Hank. "I would've done the same thing. You can't trust strangers, and why should Rob have told either one of us about the other anyhow? But I'll tell you one thing, the kid's done a great job on my warehouse, and he didn't ask too many questions. I take it that your project and mine share some features that we may not want to have widely known?"

"Yes, but I'm not so interested in the details of your project as I am in having an opportunity to know something about who you are, where you're coming from," replied Casey.

This short conversation resulted in both men agreeing to set out immediately from opposite sides of Vancouver to meet in front of the giant crab sculpture at the H.R. MacMillan Planetarium, at Kitsilano Point. That way, both could be assured that the other would be busy getting through traffic, and the meeting would be candid and genuine, and hopefully unobserved.

When they met, they soon discovered that they had a lot in common and were talking up a storm as they strolled randomly through the park connecting the Planetarium with the Maritime Museum, and then on past Kitsilano Beach. Both men were concerned about the difficulties they saw coming and wanted to have a safe haven that could help them through what could be some very difficult years ahead.

Both men had large families, with Casey leading his family of seven, and Hank with his wife, two teenage sons, a pregnant daughter and a son-in-law. Both men were gold bugs, financing their projects with gains made from the gold junior sector. Gold was surging, as the worldwide currency wars continued to devalue all major currencies against each other, and against gold. The money-printing of the central banks and the sovereign debt crisis was spiraling out of control.

Differences between the two men were notable. Hank was a fisherman; Casey didn't like fish. Hank was a very religious man whereas Casey was not. Casey noticed that Hank didn't talk about any extended family or friends, while Casey had a large number of people he was concerned for. But they both agreed that they could cooperate and be in contact, and ultimately agreed that it would be better if they did not actually look at each other's plans, as that could create a security risk. They agreed to meet occasionally to discuss technical aspects of their projects, and to share information on the best places to buy materials and technical equipment that they both had an interest in.

Hank was an avid amateur radio operator, in addition to having a marine license to transmit on the marine FM frequencies as part of his business operating a small coastal supply tug & barge operation. Once Casey learned this, he suggested that they agree to each have an identical copy of a randomly chosen book which they could use as an encoding reference for open voice transmissions.

Hank understood immediately what Casey was talking about and the two men simply walked into a small bookstore near Kitsilano Beach, and selected a suitable book.

Hank chose "The Forager's Harvest: A Guide to Edible Wild Plants" which would be a useful addition to their libraries. The two men sat at a park bench and discussed how they would use page, line and word numbers to encode their radio messages.

At the time, Hank and Casey didn't realize how instrumental their newfound friendship would prove to be.

5

"h" RECESSION

08 August: 33 Months Before NEW

It was after losing his father to a heart attack that Casey Callaghan really took stock of his life. In doing so, he realized that there had been a generational shift. He could no longer talk to his dad about politics, economics, or philosophy. His father had been a very astute observer of these subjects, and had been a great man in his own right. But now he was gone, and Casey had lost a great source of insight and guidance.

His father's death was a profound loss for the Callaghans. Casey realized that he would have to step forward and become the leader of the extended Callaghan family. He had maybe thirty years of very active life left in him before he himself became an old man and died in his turn. What would he do in that time?

Working through this, Casey had a very difficult few years indeed. It was a mid-life crisis, and it took its toll on his relationship with his wife, Tatiana, or simply "Tanya" . First and foremost, Casey determined that he would leave the military, where he had served as a pilot with the Canadian Air Force. Secondly, Casey decided to move to the West Coast, where he and Tanya could raise their children in a stable, permanent home.

Frequent moving from one military post to another would be a thing of the past, as would the steady paycheck. The couple fought about it for two years, all the while Casey delaying his ultimate goal in favor of keeping his marriage intact and his family together. While he was caught in limbo, Casey had an insatiable fixation on the problem. It was constantly on his mind. He made several trips to the coast, to visit family and talk through issues of his father's passing. He also looked at real estate, thinking about where they should settle.

Casey started to formulate his plan. At first he thought all he needed was about a million dollars to build a home and be debt free, accepting any odds job he could get to keep himself active as he enjoyed retirement. But in those two years, where he spent much of his time thinking about his dream of building a better life for his family, he also became more concerned about the worsening economy.

He had always been a gold bug, so while the global financial crisis unfolded Casey invested every penny he could get his hands on into a developing gold mine up in Yellowknife. He had once been posted there and knew of the region's once prodigious production of gold. While flying a DHC-6 Twin Otter for the Air Force he had landed on an airstrip used by a gold exploration company. The other pilot told Casey about the exploration going on there and how much gold the original mines in the Yellowknife Gold Camp had produced. Casey made contact with the exploration company's CEO and was given a comprehensive tour of the camp, drill core shed, and other workings. This began Casey's long and profitable relationship with Trophy Fish Gold, TFG on the Canadian Venture Exchange.

As he watched the price of gold continue to rise, and got deeper and deeper into his exploration of the financial crisis, Casey watched hundreds of videos on the internet. He was fascinated with concepts ranging from peak oil to how fiat currencies work, and how currencies and economic systems ultimately fail.

One particularly terrifying thing he learned was that there is a mathematical truth called "The Rule of 70", which says that anything that grows exponentially will double at a rate of 70 divided by the growth rate. So if something grows at 3.5%, it will double in 20 years.

What was terrifying about that simple mathematical fact was made clear to Casey in a video he watched on You-Tube. The video was made by a professor who explained the public policy implications of exponential growth. The crazy looking old teacher gave a series of examples of how we fail to apply the simple mathematical truth that for something to continue to grow exponentially, it will keep on doubling in a predictable manner. He illustrated this through the metaphor of a bacterium in a pop bottle, growing at an exponential rate.

In the bottle analogy, consider a microscopic organism in the bottom of a pop bottle. It's multiplying exponentially, doubling every minute. At 11:00 am there is just one bacterium in the bottle; but by noon, 60 doublings later, the pop bottle is 100% full!

Each doubling consumes an amount equivalent to all that was consumed in every prior doubling *combined*. Even if the first several doublings were not noticeable, it is not until the last few doublings that we realize that there is a problem and that the system is about to fail. So in our final minute, we consume the rest of our bottle and then become extinct.

And then the old professor said that this is the central issue facing the global economy. The modern economy is a system where exponential growth is considered to be good, as though it can go on forever. The examples about peak oil, inflation, urban sprawl and human population were scary, and the take-home truth for Casey was what it told him about how little time humankind had until its own extinction.

That hockey-stick shaped graph from those exponential growth videos started to appear more frequently in the economic data. As Casey followed the unfolding economic crisis he recognized that the growth in public debt had become a run-away scenario that ultimately would come to a crashing halt. Casey intuited that the world would become a much more dangerous place.

Whether by wars, exhaustion of resources, or climate change, Casey believed that the world was fast approaching that 11:59 moment. A big die-off is coming, much like the winter kill of a crop after an extremely harsh winter. Casey knew in his heart that this would begin to play out long before his children became adults.

After scaring himself with that realization, Casey knew that the day-to-day responsibilities of providing for his family and enjoying the prime years of his own life were about to become very different indeed.

A few years before, Casey was intrigued at the impact made by a simple flood cutting off a small town in rural Ontario.

The simple event took the community by surprise. Nobody was prepared for it. So when the trucks and trains stopped bringing fuel and food into the community, people quickly found themselves in trouble. The gas station ran out of fuel, and the grocery stores ran out of food. Emergency relief had to be flown in until the road and rail access was restored.

We would all be in a lot of trouble if the trucks, trains, fuel, and ships stopped coming into our cities. And that, Casey had realized, *is exactly how it would happen.*

Something in the system that is the human version of that pop bottle would break. Our exponential consumption and growth rates would come crashing down towards zero. It could be happening already. The economic tea-leaves seemed to be saying that the new normal should be a zero or negative growth rate.

Casey realized that with human nature being what it is, all those talking heads on TV could not get their heads around the simple fact that zero growth may be what we need at this juncture, rather than to employ desperate measures to re-stimulate a logarithmic growth rate of 3% or so. So rather than recognizing the need for sustainable consumption the powers that be were going to fight the slow-down with everything they had. They would print more and more money; try more and more desperate measures to keep the growth going. So the chances for a deliberate, gradual reduction in consumption were long since lost, perhaps as far back as the 1970s. Now there could only be the one, harsh systemic failure.

And that could lead to war.

Casey thought, from what he had experienced in Afghanistan and Eastern Europe, that war was ultimately pointless. He wanted no part of a war that had nothing to do with keeping his family safe. He wanted no part of a regional war, which could escalate into an all out world war.

A nuclear war.

Even with the disarmament and modernization of the world's nuclear forces, there were still sufficient stockpiles of weapons to destroy ourselves several times over.

Perhaps all of his internet roaming had made Casey a bit paranoid but he could conceive of a disintegrating world where a nuclear war would become more likely. A limited nuclear exchange between rivals on a regional basis seemed possible.

A conflict between Iran and Israel was made that much

more likely when Iran admitted that they had achieved the capability of enriching uranium. It would only be a matter of time before Iran would enrich sufficient uranium to that 90% level necessary for an atomic weapon. Add that to the missile capabilities that Iran had developed over recent years and you would have a new nuclear power with the capability of achieving their avowed goal of obliterating the state of Israel.

Once the nuclear genie was out of the bottle, its use would be less restrained because it will be *familiar*. This will be very destabilizing in a world challenged by economic dislocation and shortages of essential commodities such as food, water and energy. The security provided by the cold war doctrine of Mutually Assured Destruction, MAD, would break down.

In the past, the nuclear powers would never use nuclear weapons in war because the massive number of atomic weapons would loft so much soot and fine particles into the upper atmosphere that the world would be thrown into a decades-long nuclear winter.

Casey had read several studies on the subject. The consensus was that there would be considerable cooling in all continental areas of the northern hemisphere. It would only take a few hundred detonations, such as a regional nuclear war between Pakistan and India, to have serious consequences.

A larger nuclear war, with thousands of detonations, would have a much larger effect on global temperatures as well as on how much sunlight would be able to reach farmland. This, on top of the stresses already placed on our environment, would lead to crop failures on a massive scale. Casey believed that the world was on such precarious economic footing that the likelihood of wars in the future was increasing. He decided that this was a personal danger to his family as long as they lived in Winnipeg.

If a large-scale war occurred, then Winnipeg would be one of the key command and control centers that would be taken out by the enemy. Winnipeg was, after all, the alternate headquarters for the North American Aerospace Defense Command, NORAD. Since NORAD was a bi-national agreement between the United States and Canada, an enemy would target both the headquarters of Continental NORAD region, CONR, at Colorado Springs and also take out Winnipeg in an attempt to take out NORAD's ability to provide the United States and Canada with aerospace warning, the monitoring of man-made objects in space, and warning of attack by aircraft, missiles or space vehicles.

Casey concluded that he had to move his family away from Winnipeg, away from the center of the continent, to an area that had a good chance of coming through whatever lay ahead.

Given the direction that global economic conditions seemed to be headed, and the extreme interventions of the world's central banks, printing excessive quantities of fiat currencies, Casey saw that gold would be the means to this end.

When Casey began talking about making a drastic change of life, it led to conflict with Tanya, his stubborn Russian wife.

One of the things that he found most attractive about Tanya was that she was strong enough to resist him. She never let him steam-roll her into doing anything she did not agree to. This had made for a successful marriage, where her caution and thrift were fused with his risk-taking and spontaneity. But when it came to Casey's determination that they had to leave the military, move to the west coast and prepare for a terrible future for humanity, Tanya resisted him fiercely.

To Tanya, Casey's vision for the future was pure fantasy. She believed that the world would keep stumbling from one crisis to another with nothing really changing for average people, just as the world had done for centuries before.

The more Casey pushed, the stronger she resisted. It took Casey an extra two years before he convinced Tanya that it was the right thing to do. The extra two years, however, actually worked out very well. First, by sheer luck, the delay saved them a fortune as the gold junior that Casey had been investing in, Trophy Fish Gold up in Yellowknife, was pulled down in the economic crisis. By the time Casey was finally out of the military and able to invest his nest-egg of severance pay and transferred pension contributions into shares in Trophy Fish Gold, the share price was extremely low due to a collapse in lending. So Tanya's resistance had greatly improved their timing.

Casey was able to pick up over 450,000 additional shares in TFG at just 12.5 cents, to add to the 260,000 he had already accumulated. Soon after his retirement in September, while the Callaghan children began another school year in Winnipeg, the share price of TFG blasted off and quickly rose to $2.50 per share on the news that the Government of the Northwest Territories finally approved the Environmental Assessment and granted TFG the Water Use and Mine Operating Permit.

With the price of gold approaching $3,000 per ounce, the more influential gold stock analysts were suddenly giving "buy" recommendations on TFG with a 12-month price target of $15. Even at $2.50 or so, the Callaghans now had an extra 1.7 million dollars to seriously begin to look at real estate and discuss the features they wanted in their dream home.

Waiting the extra two years also gave Casey the time to scour the internet for information he could agglomerate into his plans. He consumed information ranging from architectural details he liked for the home he planned to build, to technical information on the special equipment he hoped to install, to the volatile state of the global economy, to geopolitical trends and bits and pieces of information of a military nature.

One such tidbit was a file he came across at a think tank in Washington, the *Center for Strategic and International Studies.* CSIS was Casey's favorite source of geopolitical and international military information. He had been visiting their website for more than ten years and had noticed that when key diplomats and academics appear on short media clips on CNN for some major news breaking in Washington it was usually preceded, by at least a few days, by an appearance of the distinguished visitor at CSIS discussion workshops. This inside track aspect of CSIS gave Casey a great deal of confidence in what he read through the CSIS website.

When he came across a CSIS report on a possible Israeli

strike on Iran's nuclear development facilities, he immediately tore into the report. He was amazed at the level of detail that the author had put into the report, and that it was freely available in the public domain.

The report convinced Casey that Iran would soon have enough centrifuges to produce enough Highly Enriched Uranium, HEU, to not only manufacture a nuclear device, but to be able to begin to build up a nuclear arsenal by producing five or more such devices per year – depending on the number of centrifuges that Iran had in operation. But what brought a cold chill to Casey's spine was the thrust of the report, which included the timelines and tactical details for a variety of attack scenarios.

Seeing it all laid out there for all the world to see made it seem so real, so obvious, that Casey felt a sense of history. To him, it was like being in Europe in the late 1920's and hearing of the risks of Germany drawing the world into another Great War. Such warnings had certainly existed, but the vast majority of people failed to act on the warnings and held fast to the hope that the world would not go insane. A very few others, who heeded the signs, were able to do whatever was necessary to flee before the catastrophe unfolded.

As Casey read about the capabilities of the Iranian ballistic missiles, the hardened facilities in which they were building up their atomic infrastructure, and the critical benchmarks and associated timeframes in the report, Casey became certain that Israel would soon have no choice but to attack Iran. The report went so far as to lay out the likely attack scenarios, weapons packages required to achieve the necessary effects, and the geopolitical fallout of such an attack. These details stood up to Casey's experience as an air campaign planner, and made the report that much more credible.

This, along with Casey's prognosis for the global economy, made him redouble his research into another type of fallout, and what he must do in order to be in a position to survive it.

For the rest of the year, while talking heads on TV spoke

of green shoots and a modest economic recovery, Casey positioned himself to exploit the next leg of the economic crisis. It was clear to Casey that rather than a V-shaped recession, it would be more of an "h" shape. Not an "L". Not a Square-Root sign. Not a "W", but a small letter "h": going down, then up a bit, then down *and staying down.*

There would be no recovery after that, Casey believed, only a continued descent into chaos. Casey reasoned that he had perhaps a year or two in which to spend his fortune in gold while the economy still functioned. After that, Casey believed, it would be a "come as you are" struggle and Casey wanted to be ready for it. But what should he build? Where should he build it? How to approach it? All of that would take considerable time and effort to determine.

Casey needed a plan, and Casey knew how to plan.

6

FABRIC SHOP

19 April: 1 Month Before NEW

Tanya was not sure if she should take any of the children with her this time. She often took at least one of her teenage children with her on her shopping trips to Nanaimo but this time she was not sure if it was a good idea. She wanted to be able to really concentrate as this could be her last opportunity to visit her favorite sewing and fabric shops in the small city 45 minutes down-island from Qualicum Beach. Casey said that it was going to get dangerous in town because the currency crisis had taken a turn for the worse. The shortages of last year were back with a vengeance as the supply of everything from consumer goods to gasoline and food had become erratic once again.

It had looked like the Parker administration had solved the currency problem when she brought in the New US Dollar a few months ago. These "New Dollars" were backed with gold, and Canada had followed suit a few weeks later with the "New Canadian Dollar", also backed by gold. That seemed to stabilize things after the global currency collapse of last October. Things began falling apart once again, however, when banks in the US began refusing to exchange the

"Nudies" for physical gold.

It turned out that the quantity of gold held in Fort Knox and the other vaults of the reformed US Treasury was less than what the Treasury had claimed to have. So even this New US Dollar was actually just another fiat currency. The government was talking about confiscating all privately held gold in order to restore international confidence in the currency and yet operate it as an absurd *domestically irredeemable* gold standard.

But Tanya did not concern herself with those pesky details. She had a good sized wad of new Canadian "G-Dollars" and some gold and silver coins in her purse. Despite the shortages, Tanya enjoyed shopping a lot more lately, ever since Casey stopped trying to get her to economize. He seemed to be encouraging her to spend like there's no tomorrow.

Tanya decided to go alone and headed out in the family's spanking-new plug-in electric-hybrid. She loved to drive the Prius Hybrid-Diesel. She especially liked to smoothly slow down to a stop using the regenerative breaking. Then, when the light would go green, Tatiana would accelerate gently while other cars madly rushed past. Her little "Priyusha" got fantastic fuel economy. It could also run entirely on electrical power for the first 150 km of driving, thanks to the increased storage capacity of the new generation of batteries.

The family had an enormous garage at the HOTH. They could fit as many as five vehicles in if they wanted to, but usually kept some parked outside under the cover of the open-sided carport opposite the main entrance to the HOTH. Keeping Priyusha charged-up was a simple routine of plugging the battery charge-cord into the customized 220-Volt wall socket. The receptacle was also used to recharge a small fleet of electrical riding-lawn mowers, roto-tillers, snow-blowers and other machines that Tanya would have expected to run on gasoline. She knew that Casey had ordered these machines as custom-built diesel machines, and that very few of Casey's other machines ran on gasoline. As fuel shortages began to appear, Tanya understood how important it was to keep her car fully charged and filled with diesel.

As she pulled the car into the parking lot at "Annie's Sewing Cabin", Tanya took care to install both of the anti-theft devices that Casey insisted she use every time she went into town. She installed the long metal bar through the steering wheel and then punched in the 4-digit number on a dash-mounted keypad to arm the electronic anti-theft system.

As Tanya walked across the parking lot she had a strange feeling that something was wrong. Instead of following a direct path, she walked in a big curve so that she would have more time to look around before she arrived at the entrance to the store. Casey had taught her to look at her reflection in the window and discretely take in the parking lot in the reflection. Once she confirmed that nobody was walking behind her or near her car, she felt more at ease.

As she got close to the entrance, she looked inside the store and saw that two or three people were lined up at the cashier. Others were browsing in the aisles. It appeared that nothing bad was going on inside the store. Good, she said to herself, two out of three "Safety Checks" completed.

Tanya entered the store and did a quick loop through the main aisles just to take in the mood within the store. Everything was calm except that a few of the ladies seemed to be a bit tense, which Tanya attributed to the shortages. Even this rather expensive sewing shop had lots of empty shelves. But fabric shops were never this bare; they always had heaps of materials, Tanya thought to herself.

After completing the loop, Tanya knew that her third Safety-Check item, after *Transportation Security* and *Venue Security*, was *Exit Strategy*. This Tanya understood very well from her youth in Moscow. You always had to know which way you would run. So Tanya took a few moments and stood just inside the entrance to the store, pretending to read the notices on the bulletin board. She discretely peeked out through the glass entrance door to confirm that there was nobody hanging around her car. Then she did that "We Were Soldiers" thing.

Casey had made her watch a war movie about Air Cavalry in Vietnam. Their Commanding Officer had been doing what Casey called a "Battlefield Assessment", getting his "Situational-Awareness". While his soldiers were running around reacting to whatever was happening or keeping their heads down as she would have done, the leader had been focused *outside* of whatever was happening right then and there. As Casey explained, that Colonel had been listening for *what was not happening*, allowing his intuition to speak to him.

To Tanya it simply meant taking a couple of minutes to stop before engaging in whatever task she was about to do, pausing to allow her senses to pick up what was *not* happening, and to be wary.

As she looked out and across the street, she sensed that something was wrong with the area. *It looked absolutely normal*. And normal, for Tanya, would always be the mean streets of Moscow, not any place in Canada.

It was the driving behavior of the people she observed around the fabric shop that her intuition had picked up on. *People were driving like Russians*. She could see that people were not stopping at the traffic lights. Some would stop, look around and see no other cars, and then just drive on through the red light. When she saw that cars were parked in front of fire hydrants and on sidewalks, she knew that something important had changed. People had stopped following those rules that kept North America such a safe and secure wonderland.

To confirm her assessment, she turned her attention to the few people she could see on the streets. At one building, she saw two men hanging around the entrance to a grocery store. They were not openly armed, but their coats had that distinctive bulkiness that indicated concealed weapons of some sort, and one of them was holding a base-ball bat. They seemed to be looking new customers over in considerable detail. After leaving the store, customers carried their bags to their cars with a sense of urgency. Tanya noticed that they were clutching their bags like you would if you were carrying a baby or something very precious. Then they would quickly get into their cars and drive away in some kind of panic.

It all came together in her situational awareness. Tanya knew what she had to do. She dumped her empty basket and walked out of the store empty-handed. Casey had drilled it in to her a hundred times: "When you notice law and order start to break down, stop whatever you are doing and go home immediately!" She felt only the slightest regret as she calmly drove out of the parking lot, accelerating her Prius smoothly into the traffic flow. Feeling the other cars rushing past on her left further validated her conclusion that things were on the verge of getting out of hand in town.

Nothing in that fabric shop was worth risking her life for. Being cut off from home by getting mixed up in any kind of uncontrolled situation was to be avoided at all costs. After all, they had spent the last few years preparing for a way of life that did not depend on shopping malls. The plan was to be in a perpetual state of preparedness for the worst while at the same time enjoying a normal life. If the world held itself together, wonderful; if not, then the HOTH was always well provisioned with everything they would need. Anything else, if it became difficult to get, they would have to live without.

So as much as Tanya would have liked to pick up a few more rolls of elastic for use in children's pajamas and fitted bed sheets, she would have to get by with just the rolls she already had. Besides, her sewing room was already fully outfitted.

That was one of the many things she loved about her man. From the earliest days of their marriage, and after each military posting, Casey had always provided her with a great sewing room. True, when money had been tight in the first few years, he would complain about how much she spent on fabrics and all the little things she accumulated. However, Tanya loved to sew and it always made the children so happy when they tried on the various outfits that she had made especially for them.

For this final house, Casey had built Tanya a veritable sewing apartment. He had allocated over two hundred and fifty square feet on the lower level of the HOTH for her sewing room. She had bolts of just about of every kind of fabric she could ever want, and Casey had custom built tables for her sewing machines and sergers.

There was also a large cutting table and a few areas of wall-space equipped with Styrofoam sheets for her to pin her patterns to. There was a large library, with hundreds of folded cardboard book-ends into which she had organized her collection of sewing magazines in different languages like German, Russian and Spanish. There were lots of shelves and drawers for Tanya to organize her sewing notions, and there was a full wall devoted to fabric bins. There was also a wall of shelves for commonly used fabrics and lining material. If she ever ran out of room in her sewing room, she would ask Casey to give her some of the extra storage space available in the bunker.

Tanya knew that her sewing room was adjacent to the survival bunker under the garage. She had been shown the bunker in detail but had also been encouraged to stay out without Casey's knowledge. The children had no knowledge of the actual bunker, and assumed that when Mama and Papa talked about the bunker they were referring to the eight by ten room accessible from the mechanical room. That room was stockpiled with cans, jars, boxes and packages that were occasionally rotated up to the pantry and then replaced with new supplies by their Papa, once every six months or so. Tanya liked the self-rotating can racks which kept the oldest goods to the front of the shelves. The children did not know that this smaller bunker was the "Deception Bunker", to be used as a staging place that, if discovered, would leave the main bunker undetected.

Casey had shown only Tanya, Yuri and Danny how to open the hidden wall. It made a lovely bookcase when closed, housing a complete Encyclopedia Britannica, a variety of K through 12 school textbooks, and a wide range of university textbooks. Casey and Tanya were adding more to the "Brainiac Bookshelf" all the time, but there were still some empty shelves in the floor-to-ceiling movable wall. Custom ordered for this very application, the smooth stainless steel roller system built into the solid bookcase made it possible to slide it into the hidden recess with just a gentle one-handed push to the right, revealing a 44 inch wide entry portal to the bunker. You just had to know it was there and how to access it.

Because her sewing room was so well established, Tanya had no regrets as she abandoned her shopping plans and carefully drove out of the parking lot of the fabric store. She stayed in the right-hand lane to avoid the faster, panicky traffic buzzing about. She wondered if she would ever see the shop again. As Tanya drove the forty minutes back, she reflected on how much they had accomplished in the last six months since moving in.

Casey had promised her that this move, unlike some of the moves in the past, would be into a finished house. They would never again move into one of his renovation projects. Their last renovation project had been a disaster. Casey had moved the family into the basement when the main floor and bedrooms were all in various stages of completion. It had only been a matter of repainting the bedrooms and refinishing the floors before she could settle the children into their bedrooms, but the main floor had been a much bigger project. When they moved in that August the kitchen had been completely gutted by Casey and his trusty Russian helper, Yuri.

Casey had been working on that house for all of July and most of August while Tanya had been back in Yellowknife seeing to the final packing and arranging the move to Winnipeg. But even with the military-provided moving contractors, it had been a big job for Tanya. Combined with caring for their three children at that time, and Tanya had had enough of moving. Casey had made the family move four times in the last eight years, after all. So this time, he had promised, he would get the HOTH to completion before moving the family from Winnipeg to Vancouver Island.

This meant that Tanya would be alone with five children for weeks at a time while Casey spent three out of every four weeks in British Columbia, returning for monthly one-week visits to Winnipeg. When in Vancouver, Casey would source materials in the lower mainland, but he spent most of the time out at the job-site on the Island, getting things done. When back in Winnipeg, he would spend as much time as possible with the children and then be up late into the night researching all manner of topics on the internet.

Tanya stayed involved in the construction by demanding that Casey give her all the receipts, invoices and bank statements so that she could try to keep the costs under control, and rein in Casey's spending as much as possible. So even though she was not out at the HOTH site, she could understand the construction process. She already had a very good understanding of the acreage that the HOTH was built on.

They had chosen the actual HOTH site together when Casey took Tanya and the children for a walk in the forest acreage he had bought. The site had spoken to both of them. It was a rock bluff overlooking a nice flat area with creeks in the gulleys on both sides of the bluff. The two creeks demarcated the sides of the property and the rear of the property disappeared in the rising forested terrain behind the bluff.

The low side of the property, where the road access had been cut into the forest, was at the end of a paved road. This road was at the edge of a semi-rural area of small properties not far up the hill from the Island Highway, just above the town of Qualicum Beach. The nearby properties were attractive and well-built homes. Many of them were that type of hobby farm that had nothing to do with farming and had everything to do with a comfortable quality of life.

Tanya had discovered that many of her new neighbors were wealthy enough to not require an income. They wanted a lifestyle where they could grow old watching their children ride horses, or they could get their hands dirty playing in their gardens, or they could keep chickens or llamas or whatever was their retirement dream. It was a very eclectic and energetic area that she had quickly come to love.

After each of Casey's stints out in BC, Casey would come home and excitedly show his latest pictures and talk about what had been accomplished. The pictures told the story of how Casey was bringing their dream into reality. The smile on his face in many of the pictures, as he stood near some large machinery or construction scene, revealed how much fun he was having.

From the videos and pictures, and the excitement in Casey's voice each time he had come home to Winnipeg, Tanya had started to be more and more envious of his time away working on the HOTH. So Tanya had broken her own rule and suggested that they move the family out west before the HOTH was completed. Casey had already anticipated that she would be willing to move soon and had given the relocation personnel at the base in Winnipeg the 30-days notice required to activate the move entitlement of the Captain Callaghan (retired) family. The paid move was the final gift that the military was to give them, after Casey's 20 years of military service.

He had retired a year earlier, and taken a cash-out of his pension. He promptly invested much of it in that gold mine in Yellowknife. Not long after that, Tanya remembered with pride, they had purchased the acreage and started working together on the details of the house plan.

The investment of their nest egg in the gold mine, while very risky, had turned out beautifully. Then Casey began spending money like a drunken sailor. At first it was on survey and geotechnical work, and then on design work. But the gold mine was now in production, with every ounce being sold at ever increasing prices. Their investment was gaining equity faster than Casey could spend it. It was as if they had hit that perfect timing, when a synchronized succession of traffic lights switched to green and sped you along nicely.

The House on the Hill itself was not a house at all. Even though it had seemed silly to her when Casey first showed Tanya the initial sketches of the HOTH, Tanya had gone along with him.

She thought of herself like the wife in that film "The Mosquito Coast". It was a story about a creative man who went a bit crazy and took his family on a risky adventure into a jungle only to have it all end in disaster. The wife in the story had appealed to Tanya as the kind of woman she saw herself as. She had stood by her man, helped him as he pursued his vision, and then tried to mitigate the damage that his risk-taking brought home to their family. He had died in the end, but their love had never faltered. That's what a wife should do for her man, no matter how goofy his vision was, Tanya had decided. Tanya would never forget the way that the wife had looked at her unfinished dishes as she took one last look at the kitchen sink she left behind, at the start of their adventure.

Tanya was confident that her adventure with Casey would not end in disaster. Casey's crazy vision was to survive disaster, after all, not seek it. From Tanya's point of view, Casey was going about it in the most suitable way. He was using his military planning skills, spending countless hours researching on the internet, but most importantly, Casey was welcoming the advice of his wife and partner in life.

In fact, thought Tanya, in the last few years as Casey had come to the conclusion that the future did not look good for humanity, and Casey had shared his thoughts with Tanya. He had told her bits and pieces of his vision as he worked it through in his mind. As he developed the essential design elements of the HOTH, he had incorporated many of her ideas. In the end he had designed and built a facility that would enable a way of life that she was in full agreement with.

The plan was to outfit their home with every advantage that could be of assistance in the worst disaster imaginable. Tanya had no issue with his obsession of designing a way of living which could be sustainable in a hostile environment. As long as Casey lived his life with energy and a positive outlook that things may not go to hell after all, Tanya would allow him his obsession. After all, a man with purpose, no matter how ridiculous it may seem, is a man in full.

There were many side benefits to this particular obsession, Tanya knew. She would have a wonderful house that combined some of her own personal vision with Casey's. Tanya believed that the world would not come apart at the strings as she liked to say in her delightfully Russian-accented English. Rather, life might become more difficult, but would never end in disaster.

Nope, her dream was to live in such a way that when she was an old woman with grey hair she could still have her children and her ten or so grandchildren living with her. Her vision for the Callaghan family was more like a Russian *derevniya*, or old style village. A large extended family should live together on family land and yet be tied to some nearby village where they could find husbands and wives for their children, and trade in the community marketplace. The fact that Tanya had never lived in such a village, coming from an urban way of life in Moscow, was not important. She knew that some families, particularly in her favorite European countries like Spain, Italy and Germany, still lived in extended families and not as isolated individuals in suburbia.

Casey's design for a "house" that could cram in and support forty or fifty people during a crisis was just fine. Thinking of so many guests in her home made Tanya imagine that it would be close quarters in the HOTH, like those conditions her father experienced in the Russian Navy.

Tanya knew, or at least hoped, that Casey's worst case scenario would never happen. So she would never have to deal with so many strangers in her home. She believed that life would keep going on just as it had before. There would be no calamity or war. Their children would probably not want to live in a crappy suburban way of life when they could live with Mama and Papa in an enormous home on a very nice acreage.

It was important for Tanya to infuse Casey's design with some practical touches that would lend themselves to her vision of the future, yet still be consistent with his. She had insisted on a full 25-meter single-lane indoor swimming pool, and Casey had relented. He had the pool incorporated in the lower-level under the greenhouse & barn complex adjacent to the HOTH. It would be accessible from the interior of the HOTH through a connecting hallway from the rec-room in the basement.

By putting it on the down-hill side of the large barn structure, under the feed and equipment storage areas on the opposite side from the animal spaces, there would be enough extra space. With Rob's help, they were able to include a fitness room with a large mirror wall for the girls' dance and fitness workouts, space for the hot-tub and sauna combination, and still have a decent glass wall overlooking the lower terrace. The pool and recreational spaces were important quality of life issues for Tanya, and "must have" items.

Casey and Tanya also added a large area of concrete just outside the fitness rooms, for tennis and basketball. Casey went so far as to install a field of Pex lines in the concrete, so that he could use the Ground Source Heat Pump to freeze this surface into a small outdoor skating rink in the winter.

Tanya also ensured that the HOTH could be evolved to suit the needs of their children when they become adults. Perhaps the children will move away for a few years and then come home to live with her and Casey when their children had learned for themselves what was really important in life. Even if they come back with spouses and children, Tanya had decided, the family home should be able to accommodate all of them with as much privacy as possible. She dreamed of the

HOTH being filled with their large extended family with lots of screaming children and chaos, with her and Casey at the center.

The bedrooms were designed large enough to hold a couple or a small family, like a small apartment. She and Casey could rent the rooms out during the summer as a type of very comfortable bed and breakfast, with suites designed for visiting families. Then, when the need arose, she could stop running the bed and breakfast business, and welcome home her children and grandchildren. Yes, Tanya had long ago decided, let Casey make it a survival facility for the worst case scenario imaginable. As long as it can also stand up to the mess their grandchildren will make when she serves them Russian "bleni" for breakfast!

Perhaps this duality of roles, between her vision and his, accounted for the unusual nature of the House on the Hill. It looked like a fortress. The way it seemed to grow out of the rock outcrop gave it a sturdy appearance. With its rough-textured granite finish and the bastion-like footings towering over the terraced lawn below; the HOTH looked like some kind of ancient Irish keep.

In fact, some of the features had been inspired by the family visit to Scotland and Ireland two years before. In particular, the fortified appearance of the overhanging roof features, the stone wall around the roof-top deck, and some of the decorative walls and structures here and there on the grounds made a powerful statement. The matching log-work and pervasive use of granite stonework around entrances made for a consistently heavy architectural theme. The theme was also applied to the various outbuildings.

The entire complex reverberated with a timeless strength and permanence. But the modern windows, the external lights and lamp posts, and the tear-drop security cameras revealed that this Keep was also built with the most modern of technologies.

There was warmth in the architecture as well. It started with the striking visual impact of the lovely curved road swinging around through the low area in front of the impressive structure, after following a serpentine path through the trees from the main public road. The entry road had been built with security in mind, however. It was subtly designed to keep the HOTH invisible from the main road while making any visitor immediately observable form the HOTH and from every outbuilding and activity area of the complex.

As so many visitors had commented upon their first visit to the HOTH, it was a beautiful setting. The house itself, while large and unusual, seemed to be at home in its surroundings.

There was a variety of well-conceived activity areas, each with its own functional identity but all following the same general style. There was a field-sized lawn area in front, an orderly fire-wood cutting area in front of a large wood-shed, a small orchard just beginning to grow in, and a large chain-link fence-enclosed garden area with a few small sheds associated with it. The property was all about a large family enjoying an active life in a beautiful, natural setting.

Some of the more delightful features included an unusual chicken coop that looked a bit like a prison designed to keep animals in, but was in fact designed to keep hungry predators out. The roof-tops of the outbuildings, as well as the unusual penthouse level of the HOTH, were steep metal-clad roofs much like you would find in areas of heavy snow. This was one feature that did not suit the local climate, as the east coast of Vancouver Island rarely saw any heavy snowfalls.

All of the buildings were built of brick or concrete, or ICF covered with stucco. The pervasive heavy grey color, along with the granite stonework here and there, went well with the green metal roofs. The decorative cedar logs used as posts and beams adorning the entrances to all the buildings put a nice touch on the consistent, although eclectic theme. It all came together in a rugged, yet warm and harmonious, way with just a touch of craftsmanship to lighten the Spartan functionality.

In April of the previous year, when Casey had flown the family out from Winnipeg for a pre-move orientation trip, not all of the finishing touches had been completed. When Tanya first laid eyes on the nearly completed HOTH it surpassed her expectations. What captured her attention after taking in the way the HOTH dominated its landscape was the half-dozen or so fruit tress planted in what looked like a promising little orchard on the right side of the property. The newly established trees were located on a knoll above the lawn area. A few trees sported cherry blossoms in full bloom.

As the Callaghan children got out and ran around with the family's Blue Healer, Limbo, going berserk chasing a Frisbee on the fresh looking lawn on that perfect sunny day, Tanya stood still for several minutes taking it all in. She could smell the soft aroma of the coniferous forest, feel the cool breeze coming down from the mountain, and hear small streams on either side of the clearing.

It was simply breathtaking, like a dream.

7

GUNS GOLD & GRUB

15 March: 26 Months Before NEW

For Casey, the fir and cedar forests of the Sunshine Coast brought back memories of childhood visits to his grandparents log house in Central Saanichton, near Victoria. For Tanya, the forest reminded her of her family's dacha outside of Moscow, where she and her father spent countless afternoons collecting mushrooms for the "gribii" soups and "gorshochki" meals that were a staple in Russian cuisine.

They visited the region on several camping trips, with Casey dragging Tanya and the kids up and down both sides of the Sunshine Coast. Tanya decided that the Oceanside area of Vancouver Island had the most to offer the family, and had all the shopping she really needed in nearby Nanaimo. As long as their new home was on at least five acres and had that lovely forest smell, Tanya was not too particular. Her focus was on her future garden and the home that Casey would build, not on Casey's complicated military factors.

Casey, however, could not rely on his personal preferences. He had to research it all again from scratch, and carry out the full *Environmental Assessment* stage of the *Operational Planning Process.* He arrived at the same conclusion as Tanya, but for entirely different reasons.

Casey established a set of criteria, researched the attributes of the Sunshine Coast communities and plotted the scores in a weighted decision matrix.   The most heavily weighted factor was the *balance between isolation and accessibility*. Other factors included: *distance to a source of hydro-electric power, local food production, capabilities of local contractors, vulnerabilities of the region's geography, local micro-climate, access to fresh water*, and *proximity to military facilities and other strategic nuclear targets*.

Casey's review of census data amounted to an in-depth analysis of the economic, social and cultural information. He also spent a lot of time on "Lines of Communication", in the military sense, referring to the logistical infrastructure of road, rail, airports and port facilities used to move people and supplies into the region. Telecommunications were also assessed, but eliminated from the scoring because they were universally available but also very fragile, and probably unavailable in a major crisis.

Qualicum Beach scored highest, with neighboring Parksville a close second. Casey's evaluation revealed that the Oceanside region got its power from a series of modest sized dams in central Vancouver Island where rainfall amounts were ideal. The transmission lines passed through accessible terrain, bringing power through Oceanside and then on to Lantzville and Nanaimo.

There was some local food production and a surprisingly capable local contracting and light manufacturing base. The census data revealed that it was largely a well-to-do and well-educated collection of Anglo-Irish-Scotts with immigrants and aboriginal populations just under the provincial average.

When assessed in the context of the worst case scenario, Oceanside yielded a grizzly but positive conclusion. In order to assess how the Oceanside region would fare in a nuclear war, Casey carried out an effects-based calculation based on historical wind patterns, number and yield of likely weapons systems to be used against the nuclear targets in the Pacific Northwest, and the resulting impact on the regions inhabitants.

He used a variety of web-based tools, supplemented with a mapping application, which allowed Casey to input a location, weapon type and yield, hit "detonate" and be provided a detailed damage assessment.

He repeated the process for all the targets in the region. After plotting the results on a map it was clear that in a nuclear war the Oceanside community would be exposed to considerable radioactive fallout carried by prevailing winds from the Air Force base at Comox. It would be cut-off to the south by Lantzville and Nanaimo having been destroyed. Further down-island, Victoria and the Navy base at Esquimalt would also be hit. To the East, Greater Vancouver would be struck about a half dozen times. To the south, a large number of military and civilian targets in north-west Washington State would be struck.

All of this was, in a grim way, actually positive for Oceanside in terms of site selection. Other than radioactive fallout coming down from Comox, which depended on the winds, *Oceanside itself would be intact*. The effects of radioactive fallout could be mitigated. Oceanside's remoteness from Greater Vancouver meant that there would not be large numbers of desperate victims flowing in. Oceanside would be surrounded by utter devastation and therefore sheltered by it.

The only area that would be in a better position would be the central Vancouver Island community of Port Alberni. Casey also assessed Port Alberni, even though it was not on the Sunshine Coast. However, he quickly eliminated it for being too isolated, with too little local food production, and with a variety of unfavorable characteristics revealed in the census data. Port Alberni residents would be well ahead in the first days after a war, true enough, but they would not have what they would need for the long haul. In that sense, Port Alberni was non-viable.

After confirming that the Oceanside community scored highest, Casey began to mitigate the risks of radioactive fallout. He studied the different types of radiation created in a nuclear blast and how to protect oneself from radioactive fallout. The key was to ensure that a safe area had a significant mass of material, such as a thick concrete wall and a few meters of earth, to shield people from radiation. Casey learned that the gamma radiation from fallout would fade within two weeks or so and that the protection afforded by materials of various thicknesses was expressed in terms of "halving thicknesses". Casey determined that safe areas in the HOTH must provide as many as ten such halving thicknesses.

An air filtration system was essential, to filter out radioactive dust particles. Clean water, sanitation, food, lighting, first aid supplies, security and some scientific instrumentation would also be required.

The more Casey looked into details, the more he realized just how large and complex the task of being prepared for a nuclear war would become. An air filtration system would require a stable source of electrical power, and in the event of failure, a back-up power source had to be in place. A good supply of food and water would be essential during the first few weeks while the gamma radiation dissipated. Follow-on attacks could extend this danger considerably, so an infinite supply of water would be best.

After water, food (or "grub" as Casey called it) would become the most critical issue. The entire food distribution and transportation system would cease to operate. This was also true of other disasters, including the economic collapse and the Juan de Fuca earthquake scenarios. The recent tsunami and nuclear catastrophe in Fukushima, Japan, provided Casey with an excellent case study.

Casey had looked into the disaster plans for the long overdue earthquake and associated tsunami and found that Greater Vancouver and Victoria would be devastated; however, Oceanside would be relatively untouched due to favorable geographic factors. Therefore, Casey made the *assumption critical for planning* that the nuclear war scenario really was the worst case and, therefore, would be the reference scenario.

Providing for grub would be the central task in Casey's plans, while addressing water supply and sanitation, radiation, communications and security were just "Supporting Plans".

Casey had learned that the longer-lived radiation would be largely confined to the immediate vicinity of the target areas. In his research, Casey had found that the world's arsenal of ICBMs and other nuclear devices were of smaller yield than those of the cold war, while their accuracy and reliability had greatly improved. With the arms reductions from the various SALT, SALTII, and the Obama-Medvedev START treaty of 2011, the global arsenal of atomic weapons had seemed to be getting smaller and smaller up until about the end of 2011. After that, however, the US, Russia, and other nuclear powers began rebuilding their nuclear arsenals. In the US as well as Russia, decades long progress on disarmament so alarmed conservative elements and military contractors in both countries that they took steps to overturn this downward trend. Older systems were modernized and upgraded while newer warheads and delivery systems were also being introduced. The total stockpile of Russian and American warheads stood at over 12,000 operationally ready warheads and a further 14,200 warheads in various stages of mothballing, available as a strategic reserve.

All other nuclear powers from Great Britain to China further 1,700 warheads, which was steadily climbing.

The total warhead count was therefore on the order of 28,000. This was way down from the cold war totals approaching 100,000 which made the public complacent and believe that nuclear war was a thing of the past. Yet the world was still capable of destroying itself five times over.

On the American side there were 6,154 operationally deployed warheads including 1,050 Minuteman II ICBMs; 1,980 W-86 warheads rigged as bombs for B-52, B-1B and B2 bombers; 2,024 SLBMs carried on Ohio Class nuclear submarines; and over 1,100 warheads yielding 150 kilotons carried on Tomahawk cruise missiles deployable on ships at sea and custom-rigged aircraft as SLCMs and as ALCMs. A further 4,437 moth-balled warheads provided a strategic reserve, making a grand total of over 10,500 American warheads. The US also had enormous stockpiles of fissionable materials and the industrial sophistication to quickly bring new warheads into production at any time.

On the Russian side, there were 5,864 operationally ready warheads and 9,800 warheads in tactical reserve. This includes 1,788 warheads carried on the SS18, SS19 and SS-27 missiles of the land-based Strategic Rocket Forces. There were 1,152 warheads deliverable as SS-25 "Sickle" sea-based missiles which could be launched from Delta III and Delta IV submarines. There were also over 1,700 ALCMs in the 150 kiloton range and 1,224 older contact-fused fission bombs in the one to five megaton range, deliverable by long range bombers. A variety of small tactical nuclear devices with sub-ten-kiloton yields could be delivered by artillery or other battlefield means.

The official count included Russia's new R-30 Bulava missile, NATO designation SS-NX-30 "Mace". These had recently been fielded as the standard armament for the eight hulls of the new "Borei" class of ballistic missile submarines, with 16 missiles carried on each of the SSBNs. Bulava missiles were also convertible to mobile launchers. In full production by 2010, the Bulava had been replacing the Topol-M missiles in conjunction with an upgrade to the computers and software used for command, control and launch security. Even with a much smaller payload than the Topol-M, the Bulava was a superior weapon because it was shielded to survive electromagnetic pulse effects. In addition to the EMP protection, it had other countermeasures which made it a much harder missile to destroy or to defend against. Some analysis that Casey had read speculated that, in an emergency, Russia could ramp up production of a number of variants of the Bulava, using fissionable material conserved from the scrapping of decommissioned missiles.

While Russia's stockpile of 1,224 older aircraft-delivered bombs were in the multiple megaton range, the newer missile-delivered warheads were less powerful due to the packaging of multiple re-entry vehicles into missile busses carrying six to ten re-entry vehicles in the 550 to the 750 kiloton range for the SS18s and SS19s, and 150 kilotons of the Bulava SLBMs.

Casey encountered some speculation that Russia and the United States each held on to a few hundred of the massive 10 to 25 megaton warheads from the cold war. These were apparently installed on newer, more accurate and reliable launch vehicles.

With all of this in mind, Casey calculated that the actual Net Explosive Quantity of only 10,000 or so high readiness weapons was about *three billion tons* of NEQ yield. When compared to the more commonly discussed official estimate of 4,000 warheads and under one billion tons, the difference was considerable to Casey.

Casey read an analysis of a possible limited nuclear war between India and Pakistan, with only 200 of the combatants' 400 warheads being detonated. This would put enough dust and debris into the stratosphere to increase the reflective albedo of the earth, reducing solar insolation by over 10% and lowering global temperatures by one degree C. The atmosphere would be cleared of these materials within four to five years, but global food production and weather patterns would be badly disrupted.

When Casey looked into the effects of a much larger war, he found there were many uncertainties. Things could be initially warmer due to energy released in the detonations. Night-time radiation of heat into space could be blocked by the hundreds of millions of tons of dust blanketing the atmosphere. The heat of the oceans could also be trapped by the thick overcast layer.

These initial effects could add a few degrees to the average temperatures in the lower levels of the atmosphere in the northern hemisphere, changing weather patterns abruptly.

Casey knew from his meteorological studies that the air masses in the northern hemisphere did not mix all that much with those of the southern hemisphere, due to the opposing coriolis forces of the northern and southern air masses working in opposite directions. So in the event of a nuclear war, the effects would be most pronounced over the continental landmasses of the northern hemisphere. With high humidity and a surplus of condensation nuclei, there would be incredibly intense rainfall accompanied by unusually strong winds. Flooding and wind-damage to buildings would add to the misery of the radiation sickness and blast injuries. Homes and power lines would be damaged by the huge numbers of downed trees, and nobody would be out there trying to clear the debris or restore power.

Once the dust and smoke particles worked their way into the upper atmosphere, above fifteen km, the earth's reflectivity would greatly increase. Much of the sun's energy would be reflected away from the earth in the same way ice cover reflects the sun's energy away from the polar ice caps. With a higher albedo over the entire planet there would be a long period of global cooling, with the continental areas in the northern hemisphere being the most severely affected.

This cooling would cause a nuclear winter. The length would depend on how long that the atmosphere took to clear itself out. Crop failures would certainly occur. And given that there would be no more than six months of food reserves in the railway cars, warehouses, grain silos and commercial shipping of the world, this would lead to starvation on a global scale.

Casey was quite certain that the dust and debris created by a large scale nuclear war would cause extreme climate change. After all, the earth had previously experienced periods of excessive dust caused by mega-volcanism and large meteor impacts again and again over the Earth's long history.

Water droplets could only clean the lowest twelve km or so of the atmosphere. Any dust above about that would be just above the altitude at which a commercial aircraft flies, would be well above the level in the atmosphere where liquid water plays a role. The time required for the atmosphere to settle out was uncertain, because the mechanism for cleaning out the stratosphere was theoretical at best.

While researching the climactic effects of a nuclear war, Casey realized that it did not matter what the cause of the catastrophe actually was. The planned facility should be designed to deal with strong winds, temperature extremes, extreme precipitation, drought, toxic gasses and radioactive fallout no matter what the disaster – man-made or natural.

His reasoning also took him into the social and economic effects of such disasters. As a result, Casey became more and more focused on three essentials: "guns, gold, and grub". These essentials, along with concepts of security and sustainability, informed his thinking on every aspect of his project.

By the time he had enough money available to him from his investment in TFG, and had completed preliminary work on the design features of the planned facility, Casey had also developed a fairly detailed understanding of what the attributes of the parcel of land should have.

With Qualicum Beach as the selected community, the parcel of land should be within moderate walking distance. The land must be somewhat remote, be serviced by a few good roads, but should not be on a major route. Ideally, the property would be on a paved dead-end road. It should be close to local food production, such as hobby farms and the occasional green-house. Socially, the area should have its own community identity.

The acreage had to be large enough to afford some privacy, such as five to twenty hectares. Other properties in the area should be well constructed, demonstrating that their owners have the economic means to enhance their own disaster preparedness. The property should not be near any high-density housing such as a trailer park or housing development, as those areas would be full of people who would not be well provided for in a crisis, which represented a potential threat.

The land should have a source of water, ideally with a luscious water table or a year-round creek. There should be some supplies of gravel and clay material on the acreage, for construction purposes. Sun exposure for a productive garden and orchard would be absolutely essential. Good forest cover would also be important, and some elevation such as ridges and bluffs associated with the lower slopes of a mountain could be helpful provided that the terrain was not vulnerable to flooding or landslide. Wind exposure was important and a view desirable.

With those and other criteria in mind, and with Tanya's support for his taking two weeks to go on a land-hunting trip, Casey had set out in April to buy acreage. He left Tanya at home in Winnipeg to take care of their children. This would allow Casey to spend a lot of time crawling over the acreages that he and Tanya had identified through the internet. With his Helly Hansen rain gear, digital camera and a GPS set, he was ready for some adventures stomping around in the bush.

For Tanya, it was just one more of Casey's many trips. It really didn't make much difference to her routine. She gave Casey a list of things she wanted him to bring back, just to give him a way to show his appreciation for her efforts at home.

Thanks to Tanya's earlier resistance, Casey now had the money in hand. By the time Casey took his trip in mid April, the stock had already taken out the $4.00 level. He would have had no trouble selling off 200,000 or so shares to generate the money he would need to buy a suitable property. He didn't actually have to sell the shares, however, because TFG had now moved from the Venture Exchange onto the main TSX Exchange, so the shares were now marginable securities.

With the price of gold setting new highs above $3,000 per ounce, Casey wanted to hang on to the TFG shares as long as possible. He was certain that the price of gold would continue to rise. Casey was prepared to use up to $800,000 from his margin account without selling a single share.

The best property turned out to be the first on his list. The eighty acres which Casey had pre-selected was listed for $660,000. The site was just one km from the Island Highway and only four km from Qualicum Beach. It was thirty minutes from Nanaimo, where anything needed was available from big box stores and the city's industrial base.

What Casey really liked about the site was the terrain. There were some folds and undulations that offered lots of great locations for the house. A driveway could loop around to the back without being too steep, and still reach a site on a knoll from which he could have a commanding view from the planned roof-top deck all the way down to the town and the ocean beyond.

The rising terrain had good wind exposure and access to the forest-covered mountains to the rear. Some of the rocky outcrops featured the arbutus trees so distinctive to southern Vancouver Island. There were streams on both sides of the property. With clay and gravel seams in some of the lower areas near the front, the site met all of Casey's criteria.

It would certainly lend itself well to the facility Casey planned to build with catastrophe in mind, but even should nothing go wrong with the world the property would make a wonderful place to raise his family.

After giving the other properties a good look just to be sure he was not missing out on anything better, Casey made an all-cash offer of $550,000. The $610,000 he ultimately agreed on with the vendor was the largest transaction Casey Callaghan had ever made, and was the most satisfying. The property was just ideal.

With the property secured by the fifth day of his two-week trip, Casey set about ordering a topographic survey of the property. He obtained the zoning and other regulations from the Oceanside Regional District Office, and collected a variety of topographic property-boundary maps to begin his "Intelligence Preparation of the Battlefield".

Casey started to get intimate with every little detail of his new property, the adjoining properties, and the community at large. Now that he had chosen the site, it was time to begin to set his plan in motion. Now all that he needed was time. Time to get out of the military, time to build the house, and time to move the family before all hell broke loose with the world.

What Casey Callaghan did not realize at the time was just how close he had cut it. Had he delayed even one more year, it would have proven fatal for a great many people.

8

GUN CLUB

28 June: 23 Months Before NEW

H. Lindsay Contracting had been hired for forty hours of excavator time. Harold had promised to send an experienced operator, with a fairly new excavator.

Sure enough, as Casey turned the corner from Grafton Road onto John Wainscott Crescent, he saw the big orange rig that had already been walked-off of its trailer onto a bed of tires laid down to protect the asphalt. The excavator operator, Marc Legrand, was hammering away on a giant steel pin to attach the right size bucket. Casey saw that there were successively smaller buckets nested inside the mammoth 2.5 yard bucket.

"Looks like you're just about ready to go! Hi, I'm Casey Callaghan, but everybody calls me 'Boss'." Casey introduced himself as he took Marc's hand in a firm handshake.

"Hi, Boss! I'm Marc! Harold said you've got a long list of jobs for me, and that you wanted our biggest machine for at least a week. So here we are!" Marc said as he looked up at the beautiful new machine with pride. "While I let her warm up for another five minutes, why not tell me about the job?"

"Sure! Let's start with the big picture. I have the

geotechnical and contour data in the Suburban," Casey said, as he walked Marc over to the well-used 1995 GMC Suburban.

"Well, what do I have here?" Casey asked, mockingly, as he opened the door and brought out a 4-pack of Tim Horton's coffee. A paper bag filled with creams, sugars, and stir-sticks was jammed between the cups.

Over years of dealing with subcontractors Casey had learned that taking time to talk with machine operators and lead-hands was always worthwhile. Marc appreciated this and quickly found that Harold had been right when he described the new customer as a former builder with a good understanding of heavy equipment. Marc liked this "Boss Callaghan" immediately.

"The property itself is eighty-acres. It starts about three hundred meters down Wainscott, over there," Casey pointed, "and goes back almost one km or so from there, past the right side of that hilltop you can just see there, through the trees. From back there, it cuts across to a gulley down the left side of that hill, and then forward here to the road by that survey stake next to that stump over there."

Marc could see a fresh survey stake and orange ribbons near a cedar stump about a hundred meters to the left.

Casey then led Marc back to the Suburban and rolled out a large thick plastic case holding the geotechnical products. On one side was the topographic survey, at 1-meter intervals. Additional details had been hand-marked in different colors.

"You see this brown line?" Casey asked. "It's the rough shape I want for the road. I want to keep the first thirty meters of trees here, along Wainscott, as a green belt."

Marc Nodded, easily following Casey's orientation.

"You see that big cedar there? I want the road to curve around it to where that small alder is, then sweep along parallel to the frontage, and then hook back to the right, there, after that thick holly tree," Casey explained.

"How wide?" Marc asked, while visualizing how he would walk the excavator through the trees on his initial cut, then pull the logs back into that open area beyond the little holly. Marc was always thinking of the most efficient way to manage a job and not work himself into a corner.

"Four meters, plus a ditch on both sides," Casey replied.

"What about Hydro? Do you want me to cut-in from that pole with the transformer on it?" Marc pointed down the road.

"No, it's going underground. I'll mark out a chevron trench for you later. The idea is to have no ugly power lines anywhere on the property and to keep a solid green-space along the road. You see this circle? You can use that as a stump-dump for now. I'll get the permit for the burn. Pile all the large logs and poles in this area." Casey indicated the same spot by a holly tree that Marc had already considered. "I'll buck'em up so you can pluck the stumps out." Marc nodded in agreement.

Casey turned the chart over. The reverse of the case showed the geotechnical data and soil survey. "You should be able to pull a lot of material out here, to build up the driveway as it ascends that left slope up toward that first knoll. Do you see there?" Casey pointed near the center of the chart. "This first knoll is the building site for the HOTH!"

"HOTH?" Marc asked.

"*House - On - The - Hill*!" Casey explained, with a smile. "But it's not really a house. It's more like a combination of house and a commercial facility that will be mostly vacant space at first. One day it will be a large bed and breakfast," Casey lied. "Or a small hotel, as well as living quarters."

"How large will it be?"

"The floor plan is basically an octagon with the middle portion elongated on one axis. The rough excavation will be thirty meters by forty meters, to give me room to work. There is also this barn with a similar footprint, going from the right side of the HOTH excavation and extending to the west." Casey indicated the excavation areas marked off on the chart.

"This four-acre area, here, between the HOTH and the green-space along the frontage will ultimately be a field and lawn. But it'll also house a large septic distribution field.

There will also be a closed loop-geothermal circuit about five meters under the distro field. You can see from the legend that this area has a lot of packing pit-run so you should find it easy material to work. You'll hit glacial pan here and here, but we'll just use that as the maximum depth for the geothermal lines once you've exposed the trench."

"But that's only about four meters deep," Marc observed, reading the depth indications from the chart.

"Good pick-up, Marc!" Casey smiled, genuinely happy that Marc knew how to read a geotechnical chart. "So we'll have to move a lot of overburden from the HOTH excavation and from this esker, here." Casey pointed out a ridge-like feature descending from the barn site all the way down to Wainscott Crescent.

"Even so, that's a lot of material to move. We'll need a couple of tandem-axels here when we get into that; and for all the road-building snaking through the trees," said Marc.

"Already on order with Harold! But that's several days away. I've also ordered ten loads of Three-Quarter-Minus to top-dress the road. But for now, I want you to get started with brush-clearing, piling up the burn pile, and exposing the pit-run and clay seams. Don't bother working the fill just yet; I have some other details I need to work out first."

With that briefing completed, Casey left Marc to start opening up the forested property, confident that Marc understood what to do and how to read the maps that Casey had given him.

Over the next three days, Casey spent hour after hour at the property. Marc proved to be very skilful with the huge machine. He moved the excavator's powerful bucket like an extension of his own arm and the jaws as deftly as his own fingers gripping logs, stumps and rocks and tossing them about.

Marc quickly transformed the dense forest into a beautiful clearing and house site nestled neatly into the rising terrain. The details provided in the geotechnical charts were helpful to

Marc, allowing him to see the property as a whole and to manage the on-site materials efficiently.

The charts also helped Casey plan the special features he wanted to imbed in the site before any construction workers arrived on scene, as these features must remain secret.

While Marc worked, Casey would wander around the periphery of the clearing and often just sit on a rock and watch Marc work the material. At times, Casey would bring Marc some fresh coffee and have him take a break while Casey explained some particular detail about the site preparation. Boss Callaghan knew what he wanted to have done, and clearly trusted Marc's ability to do his job without constant direction.

During this time, there was just one task which Casey engaged in off-site. For approximately two hours each day, Casey would visit the Oceanside Gun Club in Parksville.

Casey was not a gun enthusiast even though he had renewed his qualification on the C-7, the Canadian version of the M-16 assault rifle, and Browning 9mm pistol every year during his years of military service. Casey had maintained fairly good groupings and overall weapon handling skills, but he was not a gun lover. Casey thought of guns as excessively powerful.

During his military service, Casey had been required to refresh his basic military skills with weapons training as well as annual Chemical-Biological-Radiological-Nuclear training. Because the Air Force had always provided Casey with the weapons, ammunition, chemical warfare suit and other essentials, Casey did not have any weapons or CBRN equipment of his own when he retired. In Winnipeg, Casey bought a very expensive hunting rifle and began accumulating ammunition and some very unusual accessories. That way, when he moved to British Columbia and continued buying arms, it would not be immediately obvious that he was building up a small arsenal.

Unlike the US, where gun ownership is a constitutional

right, it was more of an exception in Canada. The stringent weapons-safety and storage regulations in Canada suited Casey just fine, however, as he was not a big fan of private ownership of guns. Casey believed that guns were for killing and that having one in the home was more likely to result in the death of a loved one than the successful defense of one's home. But given the way that Casey expected the future to unfold, and with the added danger of cougars and other wild animals in the forests behind his somewhat remote property, Casey felt it prudent to have some firearms available.

When Casey began signing up for every Weapons Safety Course and Firearms Seminar on offer at the Oceanside Fish & Game Association, however, his goal was not to learn what he already knew very well. Rather, it was to build up his files on the "Gun Club". Casey wanted to get to know the local gun lovers.

Knowing the names, addresses, faces and personalities of the region's more active gun lovers was an essential part of Casey's *Intelligence Preparation of the Battlefield*. Unlike the physical site preparation that Marc was taking care of with the big excavator, Casey had to use his eyes and ears as his tool for this task. To get to know these people, he had to engage with them, participate in their social activities and listen to what they talked about.

Casey was a people-oriented person, so fitting into the network of a hundred or so gun lovers in the region was actually quite enjoyable. He felt that he could become friends with many of these people, but that a few of them were hot-heads and probably not all that trustworthy.

Casey didn't like hot-heads. It didn't take him long to identify the dozen or so quick-tempered loudmouths who liked to take over any conversations they joined into, and shut down any views that contradicted their own. One of these bozos was an RCMP officer from one of the Oceanside detachments. Casey didn't like Constable William Walker, in particular because Bill seemed to think being a RCMP officer gave him authority over virtually anything going on around him.

It wasn't hard to build up a good set of notes on the Gun Club members. The more aggressive types would talk at length about other people's business as long as they had an audience.

Other than a very few jerks, Casey found that there were a great many reasonable, intelligent and thoughtful people in the gun-loving community. Most of them were like him, to one degree or another, survivalists. Many would not use the term to describe themselves, however, as it had such a negative social connotation. The word "survivalist" brought to mind the image of a gun-crazed loner with a huge stockpile of food, weapons, and ammunition – enough to stand up to those evil and conspiring Federal Government types who wanted to interfere with their freedom and God-loving ways!

Casey was not among those who loudly advocated "God, Gold and Guns". Rather, Casey believed that membership in a small community and in a variety of different activities and social groups is the essential element in survival.

Acceptance in the Oceanside Gun Club was easily granted. Casey contributed many hours of volunteer effort in support of the group's little projects and activities. He rather enjoyed this, as he felt more human when he was engaged with people. He hung around watching others firing at the indoor handgun range on Ruffels Rd and helped to police up the shotgun cartridges and shell casings hiding in the grass of the 200 yard range out at the Dorman Road Range at least once a week.

While he seldom spoke about his own interest in weapons, he usually participated in the bi-monthly "shoot-off" events that were the cornerstone of the Gun Club's social life. What Casey enjoyed most of all was having a few beers and some barbequed steaks at the Eaglecrest Golf Clubhouse out on Bennett Road, where the gun club held most of its social events.

In the course of his Gun Club activities, Casey had met Wayne Palomar. "Pal" was the owner of the "On-The-Fly Gun & Tackle Shop", which sponsored the indoor range on Ruffels

Road and provided a small office for the Gun Club. Pal was a very friendly and well loved member of the Oceanside community. His business was essentially just a side-show to his addiction to the social life of the Gun Club. It was a small shop, with just Pal and his eager young helper, Peter Wright, keeping the shop open from ten to five, Tuesday through Saturday. The limited hours of Pal's business made it clear that it was more of a hobby than a money making enterprise.

Sales appeared to be modest, sustained mostly by the forty or so core members of the Gun Club with little in the way of actual growth. One thing Casey learned about Pal, however, was that he was a bit of a renegade. Even though some of his best customers were police officers, and Pal was an honest and upright member of the community, he also had his secrets. One of them was a collection of non-registered weapons.

One day, Pal invited Casey to his home, just around the corner from his gun shop. There, over a couple of beers and a few laughs on the heavily timbered cedar deck overlooking the Strait of Georgia, Pal surprised Casey.

"I know what you're doing, Callaghan!" Pal smiled.

Casey remained silent, and became very tense.

"You're building up a small arsenal!" laughed Pal. "Peter noticed it first, and then I started watching for it. You spend most of your time talking with the others while they shoot off their rounds, but you don't actually shoot that many of your own. Then you typically disappear for a few minutes. What are you doing, going out to your car and back?" Pal asked, rhetorically. "I think you dump off those extra rounds in your car, don't you?" Pal concluded, very satisfied with himself.

There was a long silence. Casey was not sure what to say, because Pal was right. Casey had been slipping rounds into his sports bag, as part of what he thought had been well disguised slight of hand. He had accumulated nearly a thousand 30-06 and 9mm rounds in the last two months to add to the eighteen hundred he had stockpiled in Winnipeg, for his stainless steel 9mm SIG Sauer P226 semi-automatic pistol and 30-06

Remington 700 hunting rifle, not to mention the shells he had accumulated for his Remington 870 pump-action shotgun.

"Relax, Casey, I'm not going to turn you in! We all do it. None of us wants the Feds to take away our guns and ammo!" Pal said with enthusiasm. "We're not like Americans, with their First Amendment rights, but WE love our freedom too!" he went on. "I bet every member of the Gun Club, or at least the active members you've met in the last two months, all have at least 5,000 rounds to go with their guns. And most of them have one or two non-registered guns," he added.

"Really?" Casey said, starting to relax a bit. "So I'm not the only one with off-the-books guns?"

"Yup. And I've got some beauties." Pal volunteered this with a strange look in his eye. Pal was weighing something in his mind. "Wanna see 'em?" he asked, to which Casey nodded.

After leading Casey to his basement rec room, Pal left Casey sitting at a card table with a freshly opened can of imported beer.

"Just wait here, Casey. I'll be right back".

Casey listened to some strange sounds coming from another room, somewhere in the back of the basement where Pal had disappeared to. It sounded like things were being moved aside, then suddenly Pal re-appeared in the rec room.

"You keep my secret, and I keep yours!" he said, as he placed three long, heavy boxes on the table. They were reinforced plastic cases. Once opened, Casey could see that they had padded sides and covers to protect the contents.

"These are my beauties! I've only shown them to a few people from the Gun Club," Pal said. "They're mostly jabber-mouths and gossip-hounds. But you, Mr. 'Ex-Military-Captain-Boss-Callaghan', you I can trust to keep a secret!" he said, as he handed Casey the first weapon.

Casey felt its heavy, fifteen kilogram weight. As Pal explained, it was an Armalite AR-50, 0.50 caliber, bolt-action sniper rifle. Casey could see that it had seen some use, by the scratches and discolorations on the rifle stock, but it appeared well maintained and otherwise in perfect condition. When Pal handed him one of the six-inch long bullets, Casey felt that he was holding a small missile. He knew that the 0.50 caliber round could blow right through a brick wall or take out the engine block of a car, but wondered how it would do against the 8-inch concrete walls of the HOTH. As he was thinking about the firepower of this obviously prohibited weapon, Casey looked up as Pal took the next rifle out of its case.

"I only have a few dozen rounds for the Armalite, but this Accuracy International AWSM uses 0.300 Winchester Magnum, so ammunition is no problem."

"Where did you get it?" Casey asked, as he raised this rifle to his shoulder, surprised by its light weight.

"Its called the 'Arctic Warfare Super-Magnum'. The British and other NATO Special Forces found great success with the it in Afghanistan's snowy mountains. It weighs just over six kilos." Pal explained as he put the AWSM carefully back into its case.

The third rifle he took out was very familiar to Casey from his service in the Canadian Forces. The Diemaco C7 was widely known as the M16 assault rifle, with 5.56 mm caliber rounds in 20 and 30 round blued-steel magazines. Pal told Casey that even though this was a Restricted Fire-Arm he had special permission to own one due to his participation in the National Service Rifle Target Shooting Association of Canada, and was grandfathered under a sporting exception. What the RCMP did not know, Pal informed Casey, was that while he had registered his C7 and complied with all storage, transport and inspection requirements under Canada's strict gun-control laws, he actually had two such weapons. This un-registered one he stored at home along with the sniper rifles. The other one was kept at the gun club, available for RCMP inspection at any time. Constable Walker and other cops had checked him out a few times, and never found anything out of order.

The visit to Pal's house had started a close personal bond between Pal and Casey. It also marked the end of his collecting activities at the Gun Club. He had learned what he needed about the members and had found a better way to continue his stockpiling activities. After that date, Casey would visit the Gun Club only once every month or two, but still participated in some of the social activities.

With the discrete assistance of the Gun Club owner Casey was able to buy ammunition off-the-books with cash. Pal recorded the ammo as expended in Gun Club shooting activities. It was less risky for Casey, and completely illegal.

Pal also helped Casey acquire two AWSM sniper rifles with laser range-finding sights, an M-16 with a day-night scope, and two 9mm SIG Sauer pistols identical to the one Casey owned legally. The deal was always for cash. This suited Casey, who insisted on using a dead-drop at a remote spot on a disused logging road so that there would be no in-person exchanges of the goods. When Casey went to the dead drop to collect the first of the weapons and leave the plastic bag containing the cash, Casey half-expected to be confronted with bright lights, sirens, and the RCMP. But it had not been a set-up, and the secret exchange was repeated several times after that.

Casey ordered other accessories through Pal, including a silencer for one of the AWSMs and two for the pistols, along with 24,000 rounds in various calibers. Casey would never come to know how Pal actually acquired the goods, but he did know that Pal drove down and took the Victoria Clipper to Seattle to visit his elderly mother at least once a month.

Until the HOTH was completed, Casey hid the ammunition and the illicit weapons in carefully prepared plastic containers which he buried in remote locations in the Crown Land forest behind the HOTH property. Casey didn't want to bring any of the ammunition and weapons acquired from Pal onto the property until the time came when their overt use was necessary.

Back on the property, Marc was enjoying his work so much that he was actually a bit sad when, after two full weeks on the job-site, it was time to once again to lay out the bed of scarred-up old tires and walk his big machine back onto the low-bed for the move to the next job-site.

The forested HOTH property had been transformed, and a lot of less visible work had been completed. Casey and Marc had installed three separate 100 meter circuits of the distinctive green two-inch polyethylene piping for the closed-loop ground source heat pump, GSHP, system. The first two loops were for two separate four-tonne geothermal units. The units would be installed in such a way that Casey could adjust the fittings and valves to connect each of the units to heat one or both of the two boilers associated with the hydronic heating system.

Two GSHP units were capable of providing a total of 160,000 BTU's of heating for the HOTH. The third circuit was for a single four-tonne GSHP unit to provide 80,000 BTUs to heat the concrete floor of the barn / greenhouse complex, and the recreation area in the south-facing sub-level below the greenhouse. Another GSHP unit had been retained in its original packing as a spare, along with a box of critical components which could fail within ten years. Casey stored these along with a small pump-and-bucket rig he put together for the annual task of flushing the GSHP units with diluted muriatic acid to clean out any scaling or debris that accumulated.

One of the most fun days for Casey and Marc had been when they installed the two septic tanks. Getting his hands dirty and doing some hard physical work brought Casey back to his youth as a construction worker. He and Marc shared a few laughs when Casey accidentally wiped his face with his pitch-strewn hands – a really 'rookie' mistake. The tanks themselves were assembled from clamshell halves and each had several hundred of feet of perforated four-inch white PVC piping laid in one-foot deep beds of drain rock, forming a distribution field. Normally, of course, there would only be one such tank, however Casey had designed the waste-water plumbing of the HOTH to have both solid waste system and grey water systems. This would allow all of the chemical-containing waste water to flow through one tank, while the other tank would receive the solid waste from the toilets only. The bacteria in the second tank could then break down the solids much more effectively, promoting a healthy, long-lived, sewage system.

In his Factors and Deductions Analysis during the planning of the HOTH, and using the "What if?" process, Casey uncovered the *operational risk* that it would become impossible to get a honey-truck to do the normal five-year clean-out of the septic tank. The "So what?" of it was that septic tanks would eventually become clogged and unusable.

It was essential to design a robust system which could last for decades with essentially no maintenance other than to pour some beer or yogurt into the toilets to promote bacteria in the solid waste septic tank.

Casey also installed connections between each of the tanks and between the D-boxes of the distribution fields, a few inches above the normal high water levels. That way, if one system became plugged the second one would take over automatically.

One thing that Marc had found strange was the massive quantity of overburden material that Casey had him lay on top of the distribution field. It made sense to him that the GSHP lines were installed under the distribution field, so that the heating system could recover some heat from the waste water in addition to the prevailing twelve degrees C of the surrounding ground at that depth. But to put two yards of clay on top of the distro field seemed excessive.

When Casey had been less than eager to answer his questions about it, Marc had stopped asking. But when he saw how Casey had taken care to install six inches of insulated Styrofoam sheeting around the two clamshell septic tanks and around the sewer piping from the foundation excavation to the tanks and D-Boxes, Marc realized that the system was designed to function in extreme cold, perhaps down to minus

40 C!

By the end of the job, when Casey had Marc perform some unusual tasks with the excavator, Marc had stopped asking Boss Callaghan too many questions. He simply shaped the trenches, berms, and gullies according to the directions Casey gave him.

Marc could guess that at least a few of them were intended to have some wires or pipes installed because Casey had Marc pile the excess material alongside the trenches for later filling them back in with. Perhaps they were for decorative lights, sprinkler systems and that sort of thing, Marc had thought.

Marc did not consider that they could also be for security cameras, intercom, and power supply for a range of outbuildings and other aspects of an integrated security system.

9

WOOD PATROL

22 July: 14 Months After NEW

After reading the LED display mounted on the wall opposite the main floor office space, Jason Jenkins knew that today would be a perfect day for a Wood Patrol. The anemometer providing data to the electronic weather station was actually mounted on a pole on top of the HOTH. It provided wind speed, direction, relative humidity and barometric pressure. Zlata posted her twelve-hour forecast and the long-term trend on the bulletin board, right next to Old Mr. Skinner's radiation charts.

By now there were no more changes in radiation. All the gamma radiation had burned itself out and HOTH had not received any of the heavy radiation that had made the area within 20 kilometers down-wind of Comox uninhabitable for decades. Thankfully, the plutonium, strontium and other heavy particles from the blasts at Canadian Forces Base Comox were either carried down the Strait of Georgia, just missing Oceanside,or had been deposited close to the base.

The smaller particles which spread more extensively, blanketing the Oceanside community, predominantly carried radioactive isotopes of iodine and other short-lived hazards.

Even so, the radiation levels had been intense for the first two weeks after the blasts, ultimately fatal to those exposed for any length of time.

Even though he knew that radiation levels had long since fallen to relatively safe levels, JJ still kept a close eye on them.

He also reviewed the Outside Read File, "ORF", for any advisories or maintenance tasks that needed to be taken care of by anybody going outside on a task or mission. It was also a handy way to inform others, who may be on opposite sleeping cycles, about recent activity or other security related issues.

The weather data was added to Zlata's climate database during the overnight shift, as one of the many administrative tasks that the adults of the HOTH took care of during their duties. But JJ did not need to see Zlata's weekly power-point presentation to understand what the high pressure, warm temperature and light south-westerly winds meant.

From the gradual increase in the rate that the barometer was falling, the counter-clockwise trend in wind direction, and the gradual increase in the relative humidity JJ knew that there was a cold front approaching Vancouver Island from the west.

This would bring yet another dump of snow within a day or so, he figured. But it also meant that he would have one good day with the balmy plus two C temperature that they had been enjoying for the last few days. There was no chance that this would melt much of the eight feet of accumulated snow, but the above zero temperatures had cleared the trees of snow and made a good hard surface crust that made travel easier.

The sky would be as gloomy as always, with the dust shroud showing no signs of abating. But even that dim light would feel glorious in comparison to the endless hours of artificial light in the HOTH. JJ loved to work outside, and looked forward to every rotation into firewood patrol duty. Being experienced with skidoos, chain saws and fire-arms, JJ was one of the designated leaders for this type of task. On this patrol he would have five other adults and four teenage boys along to help him.

"Boys – Jack! Adam! Rory! Let's get-a-move-on!" he shouted downstairs to the rec room.

"It's not my turn, it's Decklan's turn!" replied Rory.

"I'm in the Garage, JJ!" shouted Rory's brother. The eldest son of Francis Callaghan, Decklan behaved like an adult, well in advance of his eighteen years.

When JJ stuck his head into the garage, he saw that Decklan had prepared the skidoos. Without being told to, Decklan had moved the stealthier skidoo to the front of the garage, and had the larger gas-powered skidoo with its train of two tub-like cargo sleds lined up to the right side of the other, "Whisper" sled. The garage door itself had been closed for months, and a lumber wall had been erected to reinforce it against the snow-load from the ever-increasing accumulation of snow outside. But the four-foot wide roll-up door adjacent to the main garage door was always kept clear for the skidoos.

By the left side of the garage, Decklan had laid out eight sets of lightweight, mini snowshoes for the Team. In front of the rollup door he had laid out the man-portable plastic sled with two chain saws, two Swede saws, two axes, an adze, a splitting wedge and a couple of small rucksacks containing the fist aid kit, water, lunches and hand-held radios that JJ and the Vogel boys had prepared the night before. Everything other than the fire-arms, which JJ had with him, had been organized exactly as per Standard Operating Procedures, SOPs.

As he zipped up his own one-piece parka, JJ saw that the other adults were entering the garage.

"Amy, you can't be serious!" he said when he saw that Amy was carrying a large black box.

"Hey, it's not me! Zlata wants me to set this up by the South-West Rally Point to give it a good shake-out. She thinks she's solved the power supply problem and wants it set out for a two-week test. I think it's a waste of time, unless we convert back to NiCad batteries, but Zlata's adamant that these old lead-acid types can do the job." Amy explained this as she placed the rugged metal box onto a man-portable sled.

Zlata had been working on a remote camera that could be left for two or three weeks without any requirement for maintenance, and had a theoretical transmission range of two km. It transmitted digital imagery using a modified Wireless Internet set-up that had been adjusted for improved range and could be picked up by the base station on the roof of the HOTH. With this, security teams could set up an automated Observation Post, "Auto-OP", at emerging sites of interest. It would be very useful when conducting surveillance of a raider's base, or watching a travel route. A remote camera would reduce manpower requirements and improve security, and provide HOTH Ops with a live feed when taking out bad guys "off campus".

Today it would mean that the team would have one additional heavy sled to pull on the long, uphill hike. JJ was sure that Amy could handle it, and he accepted the need to support other projects - especially security related ones.

Everybody in the HOTH took security very seriously. It was the most important task, particularly with the number of attacks they had fought off in the last year. The first few months had been dicey, with groups of five to ten desperate men trying to storm the HOTH. In those first few months, with the roads still wide open and the HOTH not as well populated as it was now, more than a few battles had nearly gone the wrong way.

As it was, the five truck drivers assigned to live in and operate the Gate House, fighting to protect their loved ones up in the HOTH, had born the brunt of these first attacks.

Casey's strategy of keeping a sizable armed force at the Gate House, using the cameras and associated security features installed by Marc, had outwitted each attacking group and kept the skirmishes to the front portion of the HOTH property. This allowed re-enforcements from the HOTH to move down to flanking positions at the North and North-East OPs, firing directly into the two ambush sites that attackers were repeatedly lured into by the clever landscaping features.

The truck drivers were the only members of the HOTH group who had not come from Casey's extended family, established friends, or existing contacts within the community. These other people had gradually trickled in over the last year, but it had been in the first hours after the war started, when Casey had made his transmission on the Citizen's Band radio, that the truckers had been recruited.

JJ recalled how fast things happened after the Air Force base in Comox was nuked. His plan to drive his semi-trailer load of canned goods to the Superstore in Port Hardy had gone out the window when he rounded the corner at Fanny Bay and saw two mushroom clouds looming over Comox, twenty km ahead. He had immediately pulled his rig over, and hunkered down with his wife, Gwen, awaiting the blast wave. After they figured out that no blast wave was coming, as it had already blown itself out, they heard Casey's unusual broadcast on the Citizen's Band, CB radio:

"Breaker - Breaker, to all truckers between Courtenay and Nanoose on Highway 19. This is *The Boss*. A nuclear war has started. You are cut off by blasts at Nanoose and Nanaimo down-island, and Comox up-island. Radiation is on its way down from Comox. The blast occurred ten minutes ago at 10:20 local time. The fallout is being blown down-island at 15 km per hour. It will give you a fatal dose of radiation if you are not in a safe location. A safe location means the equivalent of two feet of concrete between yourself and the outside, with filtered air. If you can't find a safe location, your best bet is to take Highway 4 towards Port Alberni, and get out of the winds coming from Comox. You will have to stay away from the fallout zone for up to two weeks, during which time your load will likely be confiscated by community officials or armed gangs. If, however, you are looking for an alternative which will allow you a degree of choice in the matter, then pull over just before the Highway 4 exit from Highway 19. A blue-haired girl will pay you a visit within fifteen minutes, giving you some valuable information. Good luck. Boss out."

JJ and Gwen immediately turned their rig around at the Fanny Bay exit and accelerated down-island to the Highway 4 exit. When they reached it, they figured they had over three hours before the radiation arrived, so they decided to watch for the blue-haired girl and see what this "Boss" had to offer.

The blue-haired girl turned out to be Casey's oldest daughter, Hope, wearing a clown's wig to stand out. She was accompanied by Danny and Yuri. The openly armed men made JJ a bit uncomfortable, even though he and Gwen, like so many trucking pairs these days, were also armed. Once Hope explained the offer, and showed JJ some pictures of the fallout shelter in the basement of the HOTH, JJ and Gwen tentatively agreed.

It all seemed surreal to JJ, surrendering his truckload of over 40,000 pounds of canned goods to a man he had never met before, in exchange for a 1% stake in a collection of assets he had no opportunity to evaluate. But when JJ realized that the young girl was only making the offer to those truckers who were hauling valuable supplies of food, materials or fuel, and that she was only giving each trucker a few minutes to ponder the offer, he decided to go with his instinct and followed the pilot car driven by another of Casey's group, leading JJ to the HOTH.

JJ later learned that of the fifteen or so truckers who had been given the offer, only five had taken Hope and Casey up on it. All the others had fled to Port Alberni. Their loads were taken from them by armed gangs within a week. In most cases, this had been over their dead bodies. The truckers and their co-drivers, in many cases their wives or girlfriends, had lived just long enough to regret passing up on Casey's offer.

After seeing what Casey did with the vast majority of the trucker's goods, however, JJ became convinced that he had fallen into good company. After the radiation had fallen to relatively safe levels, about two weeks after the war started, Casey had only kept about 20% of JJ's load of canned goods for the HOTH. He then divvied half of the remainder to the

Ring families around the HOTH. The remainder was dropped off at the Qualicum Community Center to be distributed to the community at large.

Casey applied the same logic to Trent's load of lumber. However he kept all of Andy and Allison's Home Depot truckload and Duncan's truckload of Portland Cement bags. But Casey instructed Roger and his son, Samuel, to offload just 200 gallons of diesel fuel into the few empty 55 gallon drums and other improvised storage vessels around the HOTH, to give some to the Ring Families, and then to deliver the rest to the improvised hospital in town.

With no more food supplies coming, and with more than a third of the area's 50,000 residents suffering from radiation sickness, the first few months after the war was a turbulent period of wanton violence, looting and lawlessness. The HOTH was one of the few safe places to be. And it was a place which JJ and the other truckers, and the rest of the Casey's group, fought to protect.

The looting and pillaging seemed to fall along with the temperature. After the humid, monsoon-like rains of June and July gave way to cooler temperatures in August, more than half of the regions population had already died from the radiation in May. Survivors then turned to scavenging the abandoned houses, pilfering what they found in commercial buildings, and stealing from those unable to defend themselves.

After the temperature plummeted and snow began falling in August things calmed down considerably. When the temperature dropped enough to stop the rain-showers from washing away the snow, heavy snow accumulation made travel extremely difficult for the unprepared. This helped with security because there were basically only two choices: slow moving and silent forms of travel like snow-shoes or cross-country skis, or very noisy snow mobiles. In both cases, travel was so laborious or risky that most people stayed near their homes and only ventured out for urgent business. With sentries at the Guard House and Ops monitoring video feeds from the five OPs on the property, people on foot moved too slowly to surprise the HOTH and you could hear a skidoo coming for miles.

But skidoos were the best way to move heavy loads of lumber. And as far as JJ knew, nobody else in the region had a silent "Whisper" sled. Developed by McGill University in Montreal, the Whisper snowmobile had a very short range but was rechargeable in twelve hours and operated very quietly.

The Whisper was excellent for security patrols. Casey had purchased two Whispers and spare parts from the customized workshop in Lavalle, Quebec, at considerable expense. A short 50 km range was cut to about 15 km when towing a cargo sled with any load and, once the 28 volt battery expended itself, the Whisper died in its tracks. Thus, the routine was for the wood patrols to walk out, pulling their gear on man-portable sleds, to be retrieved later by the noisy gas sleds when the job was done. HOTH Operations always maintained a listening watch on the radios, and a two-man Security Team on a five minute recall with a Whisper and lots of fire power was in place whenever a team was out on a task.

JJ and this team would soon set out on foot to the South-West Rally Point, SWRP. Once there, they would spend ten minutes simply listening and observing, and then carry on to the wood harvest site. Once they left the property, JJ's team of ten people would be on their own, however they had Danny Callaghan on five-minute alert in the garage of the HOTH.

Danny believed as strongly in the SOPs as Casey did. Being involved in HOTH security operations was a big responsibility for Casey's thirty year-old nephew. He took this role very seriously because he had first-hand experience with the criminal element. After having served two years in prison for assault, Danny never let his guard down. He had no qualms about inflicting great pain. It did not weigh on his conscience one bit that he had killed over a dozen men in defense of the HOTH in just this first year after the Nuclear Extinction War.

To keep himself busy while on cargo sled duty, waiting around in the garage until the Wood Patrol called for extraction, Danny liked to have a good workout by cutting and sorting firewood. As he sized up a fresh log on the chopping stump, Danny focused his aim on the log and swung the splitting maul, the log cleaving exactly as intended. Danny felt strong and vigorous in his labor, but more importantly, he felt that he was contributing to the family that stood beside him through some troubled years.

Intensely loyal to his uncle, "cul-Casey" as Danny liked to call him, he felt that it was his job to lay his life on the line to protect the Callaghan family. He felt this way because of guilt over the many disruptions he had caused. His loyalty extended to all the residents of the HOTH, and he had become very close friends with JJ.

After leading his team on the hike up the well-established trail towards the back line of the HOTH property, JJ motioned for sound discipline as they left the safety of the HOTH property and ventured into the forest beyond.

They soon reached the SWRP. Amy set up the Auto-OP camera and then poured everybody some hot chocolate from a thermos. As she drank, she watched young Adam Vogel nervously radioing HOTH Ops on the XPR to confirm that Ops was receiving the video feed.

With some time on her hands, Amy began thinking about the Vogel family. She smiled when she thought about how close she had come to meeting the Vogel family back in Vancouver, two weeks after the War broke out, rather than *after* her day-long ordeal.

After meeting the Vogels and their three sons after arriving in the HOTH and comparing stories with each other in the evening of that same fateful day, Amy Arnott and Jillian Vogel figured out that they had actually made eye contact earlier in the day, back in Vancouver.

Amy remembered seeing the middle-aged blond woman and the young Asian girl she had been talking with when

Amy's bus had driven by, passing the small military detachment on Fourth Avenue.

Amy had felt a little envious of how easy the Vogels journey from Vancouver to the HOTH had been, but was no less happy for their good fortune. She had listened to Jillian Vogel recount the story.

As part of a quid-pro-quo deal between Casey and his friend Hank, the Vogels had to pay for their boat trip by finding and rescuing a member of Hank's family.

Jillian had finally found Hank's daughter-in law, Gloria, in the line-up outside the medical building at the Jericho Garrison. As the Amy and Jillian had eventually pieced together by comparing stories, Amy had passed by on her old diesel bus just as Jillian had been explaining to Gloria that Hank was coming with his tug-boat to rescue Gloria and to transport the five members of the Vogel family to the HOTH for Casey.

To Amy, having made meaningful eye contact in that random way was more than coincidence - it was synchronicity.

It was also ironic to Amy that both her little group and the Vogel party had fled Vancouver from the same old pier at Jericho Beach on the very same day. Too bad for Amy that she had not had the luxury of traveling on Hank's big tug boat. Her day had been an odyssey.

With the coffee break over, Amy was yanked back from her thoughts, when JJ go the team moving again. They soon resumed their travels, setting out for the two km hike from the SWRP to the designated harvest site up the hillside to the south west. There was a "no harvest" policy for the HOTH acreage, as much to preserve the beauty of the site as for security, as any human activity could draw attention. The harvest sites were always a fair distance up into the crown land forest, away from the HOTH.

Once they arrived at the harvest site they left Amy to set up a "Near Side OP", and Francis Callaghan to set up the "Far Side OP" farther to the South. Each had the standard utility bag with a thermos of hot coffee, and some essential equipment, including an XPR radio, first aid kit, signal flares and night vision binoculars. They would spend the next two hours on watch, with a hunting rifle and a camouflage blanket, and their private thoughts to keep themselves busy.

At the Far Side OP, Francis was as well versed as all of the others in the "Actions on Contact" section of the SOPs, and knew the routine very well. He quickly settled into a relaxed vigilance that he considered a form of meditation. He really enjoyed the tranquility of OP duty. Conversely, Frank didn't enjoy the physical labor of the actual wood harvest as much as the other men did. He was one of the more cerebral types, and not all that comfortable with the prospect of shooting anybody. But to protect his wife and three children along with the rest of his extended family and friends in the HOTH, Francis Callaghan was prepared to kill if necessary.

So far, none of the killing had been his to do, as Danny, Casey, Yuri, and the truck drivers had handled all of the lethal situations that had arisen to date. But Francis well understood that with starvation now so widespread in the area, people were becoming increasingly desperate. The HOTH was keeping a low profile and there had not been any unexpected visitors in quite some time, but these wood harvest patrols were considered to be high risk activities. The secluded location of this harvest site, in a low area surrounded by hills and ridges, should ensure that there would be nobody around to hear them.

After looking the harvest site over, JJ selected a Red Cedar and a Douglas Fir. His powerful Husqvarna was ideal for felling and bucking the large trees. With a gentle westerly wind blowing that day he didn't even need to use wedges to ensure that the large trees would fall in the clearing he had selected. Once the trees were down, two of the Vogel boys attacked them with gusto. They walked along the top, de-limbing the trees with smaller Husqvarnas, while their father, Manfred, kept an eye on them as he worked with other members of the team.

Nora, Casey's sister-in law, was busy pulling the largest branches away as the boys cut them off. She had been among the other members of the Callaghan family that were on a ferry from Tsawwassen to Nanaimo, on their way to one of Casey's big family dinners and a weekend visit, when the war started. If it had not been for the sheer dumb luck of a 30 minute delay, the ferry would have been destroyed at the terminal in Nanaimo. As it was, luck had spared the family group. Nora and Casey's brother Miles, Francis and his family of five, Casey's mother, Faith, and Casey's three sisters had all been on the same ferry when the ship was repeatedly illuminated by a series of atomic blasts on both sides of the Strait of Georgia.

Heading away from the devastation, the Captain had diverted the ship up-island and offloaded it at the single-gantry terminal at French Creek, between Parksville and Qualicum Beach. With most of the ship's systems taken out by repeated EMP bursts, the captain had to rely on the mechanical backup systems to maneuver the old ferry boat into the small, nose-on vehicle ramp. He kept the ship's engines running while his crew rigged some heavy lines to hold the ship to the tiny ramp that normally served much smaller vessels. The passengers walked off the ship, dragging suitcases, as none of their vehicles would start. Once the Captain had the crew mechanically shut down the ship's engines, the Queen of Nanaimo was dead. With her electrical systems fried, she would never again ply the waters of the Strait of Georgia.

The Callaghan family members traveling on the Queen of Nanaimo would have been overtaken by the radiation from Comox if Casey had not spotted the ferry from his roof-top, and sent Tanya and Danny down with the van and an SUV to collect the rest of the family. They arrived at the HOTH just minutes before the radioactive fallout began to register on Casey's detectors.

Her last ferry ride from Vancouver to the Island now seemed a distant memory to Nora as she stacked the thirty-inch logs into a pile. Her thoughts moved on to how nicely the logs would burn once dried and cut into the fifteen inch size that fit so well in the wood-stoves in the HOTH.

While JJ sliced large rounds off the fat end of the log, Geoff Neumann supervised his fifteen year old son, Bartholomew, slicing smaller rounds off of opposite end. Geoff was proud of the way Bart confidently wielded his chain saw, but kept a close eye on him anyhow. Geoff and his family of four had come the farthest of any of the HOTH residents, having fled Winnipeg immediately after it was destroyed.

The crew worked efficiently, but not so fast as to take chances. The Vogel boys were younger than Bart, but were also showing that they had a solid understanding of the dangers associated with chain saws. They were also becoming very good with the snow-blowers, table saws and other power tools and equipment used around the HOTH. At first they had known nothing of small machines, but in the first few months after the Vogels arrived at the HOTH, the boys had shown real aptitude with machines. They never complained about being relegated to maintenance tasks and chain-sharpening duty. The work of de-limbing the giant trees was a real treat for the Vogel boys.

Taking a break now and then to drink some water flavored by a sugary fruit crystal mix, the work-party enjoyed their labor in the outdoors and had worked up some heat despite the cool air. During this break, one of the boys made an observation about how funny the trees would look one day when the snow melted. The stumps would end up being a dozen feet above the ground and would look like whiskers on the face of the earth, not like normal tree stumps cut closer to the ground. It made JJ reflect on how many trees they would have to cut down in the course of heating the HOTH for ten or more years. He loved to calculate such things, and worked it out in his mind. Typically harvesting two large trees every three days at five different wood harvest sites would mean each site would lose about four trees per month, or forty-eight trees per year. After ten years, each of the five main sites would have lost about two acres of trees. All these stumps a dozen feet high really would make the forest look like a scruffy unshaven man's face.

Once the logs had been de-limbed and mostly bucked up, it was time to rotate Nora out to replace Amy and Decklan to replace his father, Francis, at the Observation Posts. OP duty was a job which young Decklan was just old enough to be given. He had already shown his calmness under fire.

He had been cut-off from the group on a scavenge patrol when it was attacked by a group of men from town. He had kept his head about him and snuck back to the Far Side OP during the scavenge recce of a pharmacy. He informed JJ at the OP that four men had somehow gotten inside the perimeter and got the drop on the three men and two women of the scavenge party. As Decklan transmitted the coded radio message back to the HOTH, JJ moved in to take up a covering position, and then Decklan had moved up to join him.

Following the SOPs, JJ and Decklan illuminated the two most prominent men in the hostile group with laser target designating beams. This enabled the scavenge-party leader, Manfred Vogel, to play out the SOPs. He informed the leader of the four hostiles that several snipers now had the drop on them and that they would be taken out in a few seconds if they did not immediately drop their weapons. Seeing a red light centered on his chest and that of another of his men, Peter Wayne decided not to risk it, and quickly complied. A tense situation was averted with no loss of life.

The fact that there had in fact been only one high-powered weapon trained on them, JJ's AWSM, and that the other laser beam was in actually a simple pen-light laser illuminator held in the steady hands of young Decklan Callaghan, didn't matter.

That event had actually yielded the HOTH group a powerful ally in Peter Wayne, who was the leader of a group of families on the Parksville end of the Oceanside region.

The Wayne Group had been scavenging for medication for

Mrs. Wayne, who was suffering badly from a very bad ear infection. She needed antibiotics. Manfred immediately offered to share the scavenge with the Wayne group, and helped them find the needed medicine. He also gave Mr. Wayne one of the radio frequencies that the HOTH used to coordinate with other groups in a loose alliance in the region, and promised to follow up with a well-being visit at a later date. That mission was a success in many ways for the HOTH, but it had also demonstrated Decklan's maturity and ability to follow the SOPs as well as any adult. His knowledge of the "Actions on Contact" would be put to the test on this day.

Just ten minutes after taking over from his father, Decklan heard something in the distance. As it grew louder, Decklan quickly recognized the unmistakable sound of a skidoo. He sprang into action. First, he radioed in a coded report to HOTH Ops. If the next report did not come within the allotted time, in this case five minutes, then help would be sent from the HOTH, otherwise they would remain on immediate standby.

In the HOTH, Casey used the PA system to inform everybody that there was a situation underway. Danny quickly went down to Ops from the garage. As Casey finished marking the details with a grease pencil on a laminated topographic map, Danny looked over Casey's shoulder and immediately understood the situation.

"I'll be ready to take a Whisper with Zlata and have Barry standing by on the gas-sled." With a nod from Casey, Danny then explained to Zlata and Barry what the situation was and the three of them quickly donned their winter kit and held standby with the garage door open, ready to depart instantly if needed.

Decklan's next task was to ensure that the work crew was alerted. He had heard the double-click over the XPR net indicating that Nora, at the Near Side OP, had heard his report.

SOPs called for the non-contact OP to make sure that there was no contact on that side, check the exit route, and then inform the work party of the situation and the exit strategy.

Nora swept the exit route and then walked the 100 meters to the work site, raising her arm high over her head to indicate "SILENCE, I have a message to pass." It took a minute for anybody to notice, but once more and more people put down their tools and raised their arm in the air, the rest of the work party quickly caught on and downed tools.

Once everybody was looking at her, Nora crossed her arms with an X, pointed her arm south, in the direction of the far side OP, then extended her arms at shoulder level and made a double-throttle motion to indicate snowmobiles, then showed one finger, then another X, then five fingers. This silently conveyed the message that: *Far Side OP had contact with one snow mobile and was holding position to listen and report in another 5 minutes before calling for the whisper sled.*

After seeing JJ nod, Nora headed back to the near side OP to protect the extraction route while JJ gathered the work party around him. He had them take up a defensive position about half-way between the wood piles and the Near Side OP. His job was to keep the work party silent and invisible, ready to fight or flee or to return to continue work if it became safe to do so. He had to rely on Nora and Decklan, and trust in the SOPs. Were he to go to Decklan's OP to micromanage him, he could compromise its location and put everybody in danger. So he stayed with the work crew as per SOPs. By now everybody could hear the sound of a skidoo not far off to the south-east.

Decklan heard the sound much better than the others as the OP was on top of a ridge looking over a gulley to the south east. Using the head-strap mounted Yukon Viking 1x24 night vision binoculars, he could see a single man on a skidoo coming over a rise just 500 meters away. Between Decklan and the skidoo was a ridiculous sight he had never seen before.

There was a herd of moose jumping awkwardly in the deep snow. It was strange to see moose in a herd as they were normally a solitary animal. But Decklan understood from the weekly ecology discussions lead by Zlata and Nora that animal behavior had changed drastically during the nuclear winter. They were trying to adapt to the unseasonable snow which had begun to persist and then accumulate last September, after the sky darkened permanently.

Using the NVGs, Decklan saw what was happening very clearly in the dim light. He saw that a hunter was harassing a group of moose. Once he was very close, the hunter pulled up and stopped his snowmobile, and took his rifle out of its mount on the back of the skidoo. Decklan saw that the group of six or seven moose were abandoning their unusual herd behavior of moving in a line to conserve effort against the heavy snow, and were now trying to escape the terrifying and noisy hunter by darting off in all directions. As the hunter took aim and waited for his prey to be in the best position, Decklan looked at the largest moose.

It should have been an impressive animal, with its massive rack of antlers, but it now looked bedraggled and scrawny. It was clearly exhausted, with steam coming out of its mouth. The other moose were also exhausted in their effort to plow through the heavy snow on their own. The cracking of the single gunshot was heard a split second after the moose fell. The other moose looked pathetic and weak, as though they also wanted their misery to end.

Decklan reported that the hunter would remain in the vicinity, butchering and loading his kill into a cargo sled, and did not appear to be a threat.

After figuring that they were safely downwind from the hunter, JJ decided to give the work party an early lunch break. They ate their meal quietly, taking their time as Decklan periodically updated everybody on the hunter's progress.

The hunter soon headed away. By the time the work party had completed its task, with Danny making three round-trips to haul the four cords of firewood to dump outside the garage, it was much later than it should have been. Tired as they were, however, they did not skip the important routine of erasing their tracks in the final few hundred meters before approaching the HOTH property boundary.

Using a clever deception routine that Danny himself had come up with, they made a large circle taking their tracks back to rejoin their path in a two kilometer teardrop. Then, hooking up a section of chain-link fence that was stored hanging from spikes driven into a large tree, Danny pulled the improvised snow-grooming tool across the tracks between the teardrop and the HOTH property. If anybody came across the skidoo trail from the wood harvest site, and followed it to its destination, they would wind up back where they started, having made lots of noise in the process.

While Danny put all the equipment away and had a shower, his thoughts turned to his personal life. He realized that he had already missed his chance to say a special good-night to April. He had been thinking about her all day and wanted to see if she still blushed when he talked with her. She was much younger, but Danny was certain that she welcomed his attention. He had to be careful because the HOTH was so crowded it was difficult to keep anything private.

10

CONSTRUCTION

03 July: 22.5 Months Before NEW

The extra large coffee that Casey had purchased at Tim Hortons that morning had not been enough. He was up all night going over the stack of résumés he had received in response to his newspaper ad: "Help Wanted, construction work, must have own hand tools and experience." The ad had been deliberately vague.

With unemployment now at 24% in the region, Casey had expected a large response. But he was surprised by the quality of many of the applications. Not only had they provided their qualifications and work history, but most had included well written cover letters demonstrating their leadership attributes and good character. To Casey, the level of effort they put into finding a short term job meant that they were in distress.

Casey used an unusual set of criteria for the *Applicant List Reduction*. He organized the stack of résumés into three piles. The first pile, *Too Experienced*, would be rejected simply because they knew too much about construction and would ask too many questions. The second pile, *High Risk*, was for those whose work history indicated that they had had exposure to environments conducive to organized crime and drugs.

Applicants were deemed *High Risk* when Casey found an erratic work history, long gaps in the employment record, too great a variety of low-skilled jobs, and any long term exposure to mining or forestry work.

The third pile was for *Good Prospects*. Being a good prospect had nothing to do with their suitability for employment on his project. Rather, a *Good Prospect* was someone who was likely to be trustworthy, indicated by long-term employment with a single employer, a history of community engagement and volunteer activities, and some indication of strong family ties. Home ownership, particularly rural properties, also helped.

Casey's aim was to employ people who were suitable for construction work, to be sure, but he really wanted people who were not likely to become *Security Risks*.

One of the *Good Prospects* was Stuart Greystone, a hobby farmer with ten acres on Grafton Road. Stuart and his wife had three teen-aged children. Another was a welder named Grant, with a large family to support and a small hobby farm near the Errington Market. Another was a young man named Kendal Kelly.

Kendal had worked the past six years for one of the log-home manufacturers in the region but was now unemployed. So here was a man adept with a chain saw and heavy equipment, accustomed to performing hard physical work, yet also a craftsman. Certainly he could be trained to set up the scaffolding, form-rigging, and laying down of dunnage and plywood sheeting involved in suspended slab construction. Kendal would find working with the styrofoam ICF blocks to be child's play and laying rebar was simple, albeit physically demanding. The man's knowledge of wood working could come in handy as well.

Another excellent candidate was a man still holding down a part time job at Pal Palamino's On The Fly Gun & Tackle Shop. Casey had actually interacted with Peter Wright on a few occasions. Peter seemed to be a respectable young man.

His ties to Pal made him a good strategic pick, although Casey had to be careful to assess his character before exposing him to any sensitive information.

One woman making the *Good Prospects* cut was a single mother, Zlata Jones, who had a seven year old son to care for. Her unusual qualifications caught Casey's attention. She had a Master's degree in Climate Science from the University of Victoria, and several years experience in field work. Of note, she had led a research team to a glacier calving area near Narsarsuaq, Greenland. After a quick internet search, Casey found articles on the expedition and read the Executive Summary of the team's Final Report. He was intrigued once he figured out what Zlata had been researching.

The actual collection of the ice-core samples had gone smoothly, however there had been an unexpected finding that proved to be serendipitous. In one layer of ice, which had been carbon-dated as having been laid down at the start of the last ice age, they had successfully collected a missing series of data which had allowed climate scientists the world over to fill in the blanks on an important question in atmospheric science. It had something to do with microorganisms living as high as twenty miles up in the stratosphere. Casey was skeptical, and did not agree with her theory that the origins of the microbes was from the eruption of a super-volcano. Casey thought it more likely that the source was the effects of a moderate sized meteor impact. Regardless, the paper certainly demonstrated that Zlata was a legitimate climate scientist, and *living right here in the Oceanside area.*

Zlata was an impressive young woman. Casey discovered that she had attained a solid reputation in the area of atmospheric modeling. Yet here she was, struggling along as a single mother in the Oceanside area. Certainly she was a *Good Prospect,* but not for construction work. She was someone who could contribute to the long term survival of his family, and his community, in the face of any disaster or climate crisis.

He added Zlata to the "Special Projects Qualifications

Register", or SPQR, along with the annotation "Climate Science". The only other names on the SPQR at this time were Marty Penner, annotated with "Film Festival", and Henry Davidson, annotated with "VHF-FM/Tug". Two more SPQR files still awaiting names were the "Geiger" and "Kodak" projects.

Turning his attention back to Selection List Reduction, Casey found two more good prospects before reaching the bottom of the mountain of applications. He finished updating his three lists for later database entry, and tallied twenty five *Good Prospects*. He later contacted each in turn, informing all twenty five that they had been selected for a job interview.

The interviews were conducted at Casey's office in Qualicum Beach. When he interviewed Dr. Zlata Jones, and later Dr. Lloyd Skinner, he informed each of the PhDs that they did not meet his criteria for the construction job, but that he could offer them alternative employment if they were interested. In Zlata's case, he made her an offer that she had not been expecting to come out of an interview for a laborer's job.

"In addition to the construction project for which you applied, I am also associated with a private research institute for which I serve as a consultant," Casey began, gauging Zlata as he continued. "I actually am a head-hunter and coordinator of sorts. We've been looking for someone qualified to conduct a short study which will be used in support of a position-paper on public policy. We need expert analysis of the scientific aspects of an emergency response and disaster mitigation piece which we need to back up with peer-reviewed science. We can offer you a $30,000 term contract for a 20,000 word submission over which our foundation will have ownership of the intellectual property including distribution rights. It's a six month contract with monthly draws laid out according to requisite Milestones."

Casey could see that Zlata was interested.

"The task is to complete a review of relevant literature in

Climate Sciences regarding two reference scenarios, to compare and contrast each, and to provide advice in support of disaster mitigation efforts at the local and regional levels." Casey noticed that Zlata has sat up attentively to hear more.

"The first scenario is a large-scale nuclear war with two gigatons yield. The second, the effects of an Apophis impact."

Zlata had no questions regarding the first, as she had been exposed to it in graduate school. The second was another story.

"What exactly is an Apophis impact?"

"You can see on page nine of the Scope-of-Work section in the contract before you," Casey said as he passed her a twelve-page document which included specifics on the peer-review standards, confidentiality agreement, termination clause and other legal aspects. It also had eight pages of supporting details to provide the baseline and start conditions for the research. Zlata turned to page nine.

"Astronomically named "99942 Apophis", the Apophis asteroid was in the news back in 2004 when NASA announced that there was a one-in-forty chance that the asteroid could hit the Earth in 2029. With its 300 meter cross-section and twenty-seven billion kilogram mass traveling at 45,000 kph, the kinetic energy associated with an impact of an Apophis-sized meteor would have an equivalent of one point eight gigatons of TNT. With several years of additional data, astronomers are now confident that Apophis will not strike the earth," Casey summarized.

"Oh, yeah, I remember now. At graduate school back in Warsaw, we all laughed at that first prediction that it could hit the earth. And when they made new observations, confirming that it would not hit the earth, we quickly lost interest in it." Zlata said this with a professional tone. "So you are just using it as a baseline of comparable magnitude to a large scale nuclear war? Why don't you use the standards set out in the – Near Earth Object Program?"

"Simply because we don't know of another NEO close-approach asteroid that has ever reached the public consciousness. And it's about the right size to make life very difficult for humans. After all, the purpose here will be to inform public policy makers, who are not scientists. They need real life examples that will help them understand the issues better."

"You can say that again!" Zlata said, reflecting on her own challenges in getting through to bureaucrats.

"As you see on the final page of the contract, you are free to use a different NEO object that provides a suitable baseline for the compare-and-contrast portion of the project."

"How long do I have to think this over?"

"You can take as long as you like, Dr. Jones, however we are going to post this offer on the internet at the end of the month if we have not found a suitable candidate here in the Vancouver region. Our preference is for someone in this region, as we may have some follow-on questions to have researched."

"OK, I can give you my answer now. My answer is "YES", however that is with the understanding that you will give me some lab access. I live in a small apartment with my son, Pavel, so I need a quiet place to work away from our home."

"I appreciate your honesty, Zlata. You could use one of the rooms here in my office, if you like. And I can provide you with one of these new "Pentium-Premium" computers with an internet feed, if that would be sufficient. You're free to bring in any external hard drives or other equipment you need, however that would be at your own expense. Agreed?"

"Agreed, Mr. Callaghan. However, you can do away with the charade that you're a head-hunter for this foundation. I can see that *you are the foundation*, and want this analysis done for your own purpose." Zlata said this with a mischievous smile.

Casey froze. Yet another one of his attempts at secrecy had been easily seen-through by a perceptive person. The first time had been with Rob Mynarski, the architect; the second time with Pal Palamino at the Gun Club.

"If that were true, Zlata, how would you feel about it?"

"Oh, I'm OK with that. After all, science, like art, is often funded by benefactors. If you're interested in how to survive the effects of war or an asteroid, or other climate disaster, that's your business. I wish that the world at large was more concerned about these things, so I guess I am philosophically in line with you. I can do this project for you. It will be my pleasure - and I need the work!" She smiled.

Casey liked Zlata's energy and directness and, from that moment on, had a trusted ally in her. The position paper she ultimately provided had been immensely helpful in completing the design of the HOTH, and in planning various items needed to fully outfit it. As his friendship with Zlata grew, he gave her additional contracts to chase down minor technical issues. Casey was happily surprised to learn that Zlata was something of a tinkerer and inventor, a habit Zlata had picked up in problem solving on her many field expeditions.

The recruitment of the actual construction workers also went well. Casey had his nephew Danny along for the interviews. His other trusted helper, Yuri, would arrive soon from Winnipeg with his young wife in tow. Other than Yuri and Danny, however, the rest of the workers would be locals.

In all, twenty of the applicants signed the employment contract. Casey had considered having them sign non-disclosure agreements, but he realized that this would provoke their curiosity. Far better to treat it as routine construction work, and have none of them present when he, Danny and Yuri took care of the more sensitive little jobs, Casey decided.

The actual construction started in earnest that June, immediately after a water drilling contractor completed the seventy-meter drilled well. Not surprisingly, given the number of crystal clear rivers in the area, the well was a success. Potable water was intercepted at forty meters, with a volume rate of flow of over one hundred liters per minute.

Casey started with just two of the eighteen laborers, until he was far enough ahead on the high-skilled work of laying out footings and grades that unskilled help could be kept busy.

Once there were ICF form walls going up in several areas, and Casey had trained the initial cadre of laborers, he brought in more and more workers. By the end of July, he had six helpers on at any given time, along with Danny and Yuri.

Casey had lots of experience in construction, but not much with suspended slabs. His troubled young nephew, Danny, however, had worked for six months on high-rise projects in Vancouver before he got into serious trouble with the law and spent the next few years in prison. Danny had always had a problem with his explosive temper. All it took was a sideways look and he would run across the street and beat the crap out of the offender. But he sure drove the body hard, Casey noticed. And Danny was family, which meant a great deal to Casey.

The inexperienced crew quickly became an effective team under Casey and Danny's leadership, and the foundation of the HOTH began to take shape. To disguise the true nature of the bunker, Casey and Danny installed window-sized sheets of plywood over parts of the foundation under the garage, simulating window blocking that would presumably be removed at some future time. The deception worked, as nobody asked any questions.

By the time the construction had advanced to the third level, and other sub-contractors appeared on the worksite, the scale and complexity of the HOTH project was getting hard for Casey to manage. So he called in his old mentor from his construction days in Vancouver. At sixty five years old, Barry Toner was now retired from his developer days, but he still knew how to move and shake. The consummate deal maker, Barry was a high-energy person who was genuinely interested in everybody he met. A "super-grinder" when negotiating materials or contracts, Barry came over on weekends to help Casey with project management. Barry was particularly good at forecasting delays and handling the impact that one sub-trade's screw-up could have on another part of the project. Casey appreciated any help and all the advice that Barry gave him.

Barry was also interested in the true purpose of the HOTH, which Casey had shared with him. Barry had his own sanctuary, albeit less over-the-top than Casey's, down at his winter home in Mazatlan. He always had an eye for opportunity and had Casey hire his young son, Gerard, or "GT", as a lead-hand. GT had met a girl in Nanaimo, so he wanted to find work on the Island. He was not all that experienced, but to Casey he was essentially family and completely trustworthy.

As the project advanced, Tanya and Barry were doing their best to help Casey control costs. However, with the economy lurching from one crisis to another, the increasingly unstable price inflation was making it hard to predict how much the local suppliers would ask for the huge quantities of concrete and other materials that were pouring into the construction project.

None of this bothered Casey, however, as the price of gold and his shares in TFG was outpacing inflation. So in a sense, money was no object by this time. On paper, Casey was now worth millions of dollars more than he expected to spend in building and outfitting the HOTH, however Tanya was still applying her Russian shrewdness, and Barry Toner was grinding the suppliers down relentlessly.

As construction got into full swing, more and more subcontractors appeared on the job site. On one particularly beautiful day in early October, Casey counted a dozen pickup trucks and small vans on the site. He took a few minutes to video the beehive of activity of so many subcontractors working simultaneously throughout the HOTH.

In one location, a brick-layer was working on the brick fire-place for the living room, with its two additional flues. The extra flue dedicated to an updated cooking wood-stove for the kitchen annex had already been installed; the other, for the wood stove in the recreation room directly below the kitchen, was still in pieces stacked on the floor. Near each woodstove would be a custom built stainless steel cabinet for lightweight metal boxes with various types and sizes of firewood. Casey had adapted a design first used by his grandfather, to have a handy supply of firewood enclosed in cabinetry to keep it out of view, and fire-safe.

Yuri and two of Casey's laborers were working on the concrete roof over the penthouse, laying steel rebar before the next concrete pour. In front of the building, a crane was setting up to support the over-reach of a concrete pumper crane that would arrive the next morning for the high pour.

On the lowest level, a heating contractor was working on a complex brass "Christmas tree" of fittings that would link together the many lines of Pex tubing that had been incorporated in all the concrete floors of the HOTH for the in-floor radiant heating.

Another contractor was installing the air handling system designed by Casey and Rob, to move fresh air around the HOTH from the higher floors to the lower ones, keeping an even temperature even when wood burning stoves and fireplaces were providing the heat.

Casey could hear someone using a concrete core saw to cut through the exterior wall, probably to install the ventilation exhaust with the heat-exchanger sleeve. Another racket was being made by a laborer installing metal studding somewhere.

On the second level, the window contractor was installing a large window in one of the bedrooms while the plumbers worked in the pair of bathrooms just outside the cluster of bedrooms at the south end of the second floor.

The five bedrooms at that end of the structure were designed to serve a variety of possible uses. The initial plan was that they would provide each of the Callaghan children with their own four hundred square foot bachelor apartments, with plumbing and wiring roughed-in for small kitchenettes if needed in the future.

These were not just bedrooms, of course, but were actually suites large enough to accommodate a small family if necessary. The unusual overall design of the HOTH had resulted in excess space that would be quite nice to live in as a family of seven, but could be re-allocated to accommodate at least fifty people in a long term crisis.

The HOTH design was based on an octagon that had been split and extended in width by adding a sixty foot block in the middle. The octagonal element gave an extra 15% of floor-space for the same quantity of material as a right-angled structure. The large block of space added to the center of the octagon allowed for the vast majority of rooms to be entirely right-angled, while the more complex 135 degree angles only came in to play at the ends of the facility. The large angled corners were used to advantage, opening up bedrooms and common areas and making for some unique architectural spaces in the kitchen and other active areas of the HOTH.

When Casey saw a man installing some exterior fixtures in the wrong locations, he stopped his moment of calm reflection and sprang back into Project Management mode, stopping the worker and going after his boss to sort him out.

At the end of that day, Casey blew three short blasts from a compressed air type of ship's horn, informing everybody that it was time for the weekly barbeque. He loved to fire up the BBQ and serve cold beers and hamburgers to the workers on Fridays. The workers always participated, and it served Casey by ensuring that the subcontractors would call it quits by five pm on Fridays. After all, it was nearly impossible to keep the guys working when free food and beer was available.

After the BBQ, Casey would then go over all of the work done and note any deficiencies for follow-up with Barry, who would then go after the subcontractors for rectification.

After that, he would have Saturday and Sunday to do any of the "Special Projects" that had to be taken care of without anybody watching; such as installing power, phone, and video lines to the five Observation Posts that he and Marc had prepared.

Casey had a lot of special work to do inside as well. Some

of the interior spaces were framed in such a way as to appear to be for one purpose, such as storage rooms and walk-in closets, only to be converted later once the construction was complete into panic rooms and secret passages.

By the end of September, just three months after starting the footings, the HOTH was closed up with all of the suspended slab concrete work completed. Windows and exterior doors had been installed, interior steel-framed walls were in place, plumbing and wiring was roughed in and a few circuits had been activated for use during the remainder of the construction.

The next phase would be largely interior, starting with a good ten centimeters of rigid polyurethane spray foam insulation to be blown in along the inside portion of all the exterior ICF walls, to raise the insulation value of the exterior walls.

During this time, the GSHP units were installed in the mechanical room, along with the potable water pumps and air handling system. The full range of air filtration systems would not be completed until after the heating and air conditioning contractor was finished. The main air filtration system to be added later was a secret subsystem called "The Lung".

It was essential that the local heating contractor would have no knowledge that the air intake and heat exchange ductwork he had so carefully installed would actually be just a "good times" alternate to the more sophisticated "Lung" assembly that Rob and Casey had come up with.

The Lung would be installed in a room accessible from the penthouse level, comprised of a series of filters designed to remove progressively smaller radioactive and other harmful particles. The first stage would do most of the work by simply drawing the intake air through the perforated aluminum louvers of the soffits of the penthouse level. The overhang and gravity would do most of the work, with the heavier particles being deflected away from the soffits.

A large sack of canvas rigged as a plenum inside the

spaces between the trusses of the overhang would provide a degree of filtration, and had inspired the name "Lung" for the air filtration system.

Intake air was drawn from the canvas plenum by circulation fans and their associated filters. The periodic task of changing the standard-sized HEPA and allergy type filters would be familiar to any homeowner.

These filters would remove particles as small as 0.3 microns, which was the smallest-sized radioactive particles that Casey expected. A further ionic filter had been added to remove particles smaller than 0.1 microns, to remove harmful biological organisms or viruses. The ionic system Rob came up with was overkill to Casey; he was not getting ready for biological warfare, but he installed it anyhow.

The actual volume of air that had to be moved throughout the HOTH was far less than a similarly sized conventional facility, as the primary heating system on all levels was a hydronic system of radiant in-floor heat supplied by boilers heated by the GSHP units, so heat radiated upward from the floors rather than from circulated air.

The Achilles' heel in the GSHP boiler system was the electricity required to run the pumps and compressors in the system. Should grid electrical power fail, as Casey considered likely, the only remaining sources of electrical power would be wind, battery, or generator. In the case of low wind power, and if there was insufficient diesel fuel for backup generators, the fall-back would be to heat the facility entirely by wood stoves.

The system also had the capability to bank heat energy in the concrete whenever wind power was available. The HOTH would be warm enough, but *cooling* was another issue. The GSHP and Pex lines could also be used for cooling the structure and this gave the HOTH a great deal of flexibility.

The Deep Freeze Room in the bunker had to be kept cold as one of the highest priorities because it was essential for the ultra long-term food storage. The "DFR" was a four hundred square foot walk-in freezer. With Pex tubes set in the thermally isolated concrete walls and ceiling, the DFR was cooled to a steady minus eight degrees C by a closed loop of glycol which transferred the excess heat back into the GSHP system. Essentially a concrete box surrounded by eight inches of rigid insulation, and cut off from the structural concrete of the HOTH, the DFR was intended to be rarely opened. Casey and Rob had calculated its maximum heat transfer demand at just two thousand BTUs, which could easily be shunted into one of the boilers using one of the GSHP units for just a few minutes each day. This was well within the electrical budget of the HOTH, given a few assumptions about the historical wind patterns and the output of the helical wind power-plants.

With electrical power so essential to the various critical systems of the HOTH, Casey had spent a lot of money on the helical wind power turbines. He and Rob chose the helical type over the traditional three-bladed type for a variety of reasons. Most of all, however, was simplicity of operation. Each helical unit was comprised of a stack of "S" shaped horizontal scoops. With twenty four scoops making the full sixteen foot tower, each scoop was offset by fifteen degrees from the previous one. So regardless of where the wind was coming from, there would always be a few scoops perfectly aligned. Able to withstand wind speeds up to 120 kph, each of the wind power plants could supply the HOTH with up to 4 kWh of electrical power at a wind speed of 16 kph, and could provide the HOTH's minimum power requirement for critical systems with just 5 kph of wind.

The design of the Bunker was based on the well-established survival factors of *Distance, Time, and Shielding*. Casey couldn't do much about *distance*, once the location of the HOTH was chosen in the midst of the many nuclear targets in the Pacific Northwest. Regarding time, Casey focused on ensuring an infinite source of clean water and sanitation, filtered air and sufficient food for a very long time without any need to venture outside. With the assumption that food supplies would disappear, the *time* factor required a great deal of work on ultra long-term food storage. This culminated in the design of the DFR.

Designing effective *shielding* was a simple task of ensuring that there was a large mass between the radioactive source and the survivors. Casey ensured that the Bunker would have at least ten "halving thicknesses", which would reduce radiation to less than a thousandth of the unprotected level.

This was accomplished by placing the expansive bunker in a windowless corner of the deep excavation, under a twelve inch thick garage floor slab. The eight inches of concrete in the ICF walls, and the six inches of concrete flooring on all levels, meant that even the least protected spaces in the HOTH would reduce radiation by 84%. Even with the HOTH's smaller windows, however, Casey had window inserts custom-made as an additional shielding measure. These sandwiches of concrete "sturdy-board" bolted to steel plates were stored in the mechanical spaces around the elevator and could be wheeled over and hefted into the window wells if needed. This, along with the steel roll-down shutters, added nearly three halving thicknesses to the window cavities.

With ample square footage for bed-down space and a modicum of comfort and entertainment, the 1,600 square foot main bunker could accommodate over 40 people. They would be about as cramped as a family of six would be in a recreational vehicle. However, as the radioactive fallout decays logarithmically, radiation levels fall fastest in the first 12 to 48 hours. So the survivors would be able to use most of the HOTH's 8,600 square feet, and the 6,400 square feet of the barn, greenhouse and recreational building attached to the HOTH within a few days. It would be essential to monitor the radiation levels constantly using the array of hand-held and remotely installed sensors, the product of Mr. Skinner's "Roentgen" project.

The large flat roof area was essentially cut into two halves by the 900 square foot Penthouse which spanned the width of the HOTH. The penthouse level housed the wide, switch-back staircase, and the small four-person elevator. Casey wanted the elevator as much for his elderly mother to reach the rooftop level as for his own golden years yet to come.

Projecting a full ten meters above the driveway on the high side of the HOTH, the flat concrete roof on top of the penthouse provided a solid base for the two helical wind power units and base pads and tie downs for communication antennas and cameras.

In the center of the penthouse roof there was yet another level; the sixteen by twelve concrete room which housed a 6,300 liter water tank. The tank was high enough to provide some hydrostatic pressure for cold water supply should electrical power run short at times. This large, tapered water tank was set into its own interior concrete wall and insulated with blown polyurethane foam to seal it off from temperature extremes and radioactive fallout. This water could also be used to cool the structure and douse any embers from a forest fire, with a small back-up pressure-pump providing a fine spray of water from strategically located sprinklers at various locations around the rooftop of the HOTH. This could also be used to wash away any radioactive fallout or toxic dust particles.

The rooftop over the penthouse also provided a viewpoint for security operations, with a solid concrete perimeter wall acting as a railing. A similar but much smaller terrace was on top of the water tank level, with an overhanging roof feature making shaded areas on the penthouse roof level below. These successively smaller levels gave the entire HOTH facility the appearance of a ship, with the water tank level looking like the bridge deck.

A ladder inside the water tank room provided access to the highest point of the HOTH, the "Bird's Nest", a 144 square foot covered observation level. It was capped with a decorative log-framed gable roof. The woodwork was being prepared by Kendal Kelly using elegantly fluted butts of cedar logs that would be joined together in the centre of the small roof. A hand-worked copper roof, evocative of Hotel Vancouver, would be the finishing touch.

Visible from each successive deck, and from the ground surface around the HOTH, the Bird's Nest would add a feeling of craftsmanship to the HOTH, and tie in well with other log-work features that Kendal would install at various entrances of the HOTH and associated buildings. Once the decorative granite stonework and other touches were added, these features would give the massive concrete structure a more human, West Coast, flavor that fit the forested landscape well. They gave the HOTH a less militaristic form, disguising its true function.

The Bird's Nest had a commanding view of the approaches to the HOTH. Even without binoculars one could make out the taller structures in Qualicum Beach, and see ships plying the Strait of Georgia beyond. An excellent position for a sniper, the nest had roll-down blankets to darken the interior, making security personnel impossible to see from the ground. Tables, sand bags, steel panels and concrete blocks would permit a sniper to set up a very well defended position, oriented to any threat axis. The cameras, intercom and electrical power also installed in the nest were an added bonus.

The penthouse itself included the central spine of the main staircase, also made of concrete, which supported the water tank deck above. With a bathroom, a small kitchen and sunshine type of eating area for rooftop meals, the penthouse level provided a multi-purpose space with access to the expansive rooftop of the HOTH. There was also a small mechanical room which provided access to the "Lung" air intake and filtration system, and housed some of the controls, spares and specialized equipment needed to maintain or repair the two helical wind power plants. The batteries themselves were stored in the basement mechanical room, adjacent to the main electrical load centre and other critical systems.

The mechanical room would eventually house a small hidden room which would be incorporated in the vertical spine of the staircase. Similar sized rooms on each floor served as panic rooms, while the vertical integration of these rooms allowed for inhabitants to fight off a home invasion. At this stage, however, these passages did not exist; the extra square footage was still open to the mechanical space surrounding the small elevator adjacent to the staircase. The enclosures would be completed after the subcontractors were gone. This series of chambers and passages would themselves have hidden walls and other tricks so that if one were discovered it would seem like a panic room, not part of an interior defensive network.

One unusual feature which Casey had specified in design of the custom windows for the HOTH was a 15 centimeter tall panel blanking out the top portion of the windows, and the sturdy mounts projecting on both sides of these panels. Asked about this on nearly a daily basis, Casey's explanation was that the mounts were for interior woodwork and small exterior awnings that would be added as decorative features. The mounts were actually designed to accept an off-the-shelf design of steel roll-up shutters for the inside, and adjustable awnings for the exterior. These shutters would roll up into boxes fixed to the panel mounts at the top of the windows and could be drawn down to secure the window opening against all manner of external dangers be it bullets, hail, fire, cold, excess ultra-violet light, heat or intruders.

Coming in at just under three million dollars so far, the HOTH was way over budget. In terms of gold, however, the project was actually under budget. With gold having gone from $3,000 when he bough the property in April to $3,500 by the time construction was in full tilt in July, and now at $4,150, the gold cost of the project was under 1000 ounces.

Casey's gold investment had also shot up, and was now at $18.00 per share. So Casey's sale of another 100,000 shares brought in $1,260,000 after commission and capital gains taxes. After paying labor, materials and subcontractors, Casey headed to Winnipeg debt free with the HOTH nearly complete and $240,000 in the bank. His remaining shares in TFG were worth an astounding $7,560,000. However, a loaf of bread now cost $20.

11

4-H CLUB

30 July: 22 Months Before NEW

The children are going to love this! Casey thought to himself as he climbed back into his rusty old Suburban. He had just finished meeting with Klara Rekert, the local coordinator for the 4-H Farm & Home Safety Committee. Casey had registered his children in the 4-H club for the family's summer visit.

He was excited to discover that there were a half-dozen different programs and a very active pool of leaders in the Oceanside region. Casey's 4 year old son, Donnovan, would start off with the first unit of the "Cloverbud" program and learn about honeybees, horticulture, and sheep. The girls,14 year old Tara and 15 year old Hope, would be in the "Senior Members Program" for 13 to 19 year olds. They would start with the Oddstock Club and learn about beef, poultry and swine. 12 year old Liam and 11 year old Justin would be in the "Junior Members" program, working with horses and sheep.

Casey was sure that his kids would fit in well. After all, his children were very confident individuals and had strong interpersonal skills. What they lacked was any experience with animals. He wanted to give them as many activities as he could, and the 4-H club was consistent with his philosophy of community engagement with the side benefit of acquiring practical skills. The family would need these skills in the years ahead.

The 4-H club, comprised of "Head, Heart, Hands & Health", was well suited for the Callaghan family. It would keep the children active while learning about animals, farming, small machines, and personal development. Casey had almost no animal or farmyard skills himself. He had never hunted and did not like to fish. So Casey saw the family involvement in the 4-H program as an opportunity to learn along with the children. It would help the family adjust to the rural lifestyle, and to have some fun in the process.

He also wanted to capture as much intelligence as he could about the people involved in the area's many small farms and agricultural enterprises. When Casey began to type up his notes from his discussion with Klara, he made a clear distinction between which notes were for the family activity planner and which were for the tactical database. The entries included a few pictures of the facility or property, relevant infrastructure or equipment present, the site's coordinates on the map, and a summary of the personalities involved. He captured names, phone numbers, vehicle types, license plates, farm equipment and other details. His observations were always in relation to what a particular personality or facility could offer in a crisis, and the role they played in the community at large.

The intelligence collection had started back when he chose the Parksville-Qualicum area, but the lion's share of the work was done during the construction phase. In support of this, and to allow him to maintain a few layers of secrecy for a variety of projects, Casey leased a commercial building in Qualicum Beach soon after buying the acreage out on John Wainscott Crescent.

The building was a two-level structure which had two small apartments on the second level; a one bedroom to the front and a two bedroom to the rear. The building was at the end of a cul-de-sac just behind the Qualicum Beach Civic Center and the Ravensong Pool. It backed on to undeveloped forest land on the west side of town. The ground level was a small brick and glass storefront unit, typical of small town strip malls. It had reception and office space to the front, a few offices and a bathroom in the middle, and a small shipping-receiving area to the rear. A staircase on one side provided access to the apartments on the second floor.

Casey outfitted the office with a phone line and some basic office equipment. Later, these facilities would prove extremely useful, but at present they were simply used as a base of operations and a place to receive shipments and mail.

Casey furnished one of the apartments with basic furniture, to stay in while building the HOTH. He kept most of his tools in the Suburban, which he parked inside the loading bay at night. He set up the second bedroom as his research office.

He also outfitted the lower, office level. On a wall in this main floor office, Casey pinned various pages of blue-prints, materials lists, and project management charts he was using for the construction of the HOTH. For his Project Management Planner, he customized a four-by-eight whiteboard with glue-on stripes to separate rows and columns into: *Tasks, Deliverables, Personnel Involved, Deadlines, Costs* and *Current Status*. Using a variety of colors, the entire project was displayed and updated in the blocky printing style Casey had learned in his Damage Control Centre training in the Air Force. It helped Casey manage the many dimensions of his project without becoming lost in the details. All of his secret information and sensitive materials were developed in the second floor office, for compartmentalization.

In the second floor office, Casey set up large maps and charts. On the largest wall there was a floor-to ceiling map of the Pacific Northwest. On the adjacent wall was the Parksville-Qualicum Regional District Property Boundary Chart. This was where Casey marked zone boundaries, highlighted infrastructure details such as water and power facilities, wrote comments directly on the chart and affixed innumerable yellow stickies with additional information on specific sites of interest. Some of the stickies had question marks to highlight the need for pictures or other information.

The Regional District chart served as the master reference which helped Casey to build up his *Intelligence Preparation of the Battlefield*. This preparation included recording as much detail as he could collect, inputting the data into computerized files keyed to the grid system and cross-referenced by searchable key words. Gradually, by color-coding and shading various areas on the chart, and by placing pins and notes to identify or amplify key locations, Casey gained a comprehensive understanding of the entire region.

His day-time activities focused on the building of the HOTH, rising early so that he could review the plan for the day and be on-site before the first workers arrived. Once things were moving along he would take a late morning nap in the camper he had Danny living in for security at the site. This made up for the lost sleep caused by his evening research.

At times, when he took a break from the nightly computer work, he would head out for a long walk. Sometimes he would walk for an hour or two in a particular direction and take in the sights and sounds of the community. This allowed him to listen, to smell and to feel the area. Then he would return to the Qualicum office and update his Regional District chart and make database entries on what he had collected.

The population base of the Oceanside region of Parksville and Qualicum Beach was about 50,000 people. The task of organizing the mountain of data was made simple by classifying the varied areas into four groups.

The first group in his classification system was "Two-Person Retirement Homes". The TPRH grouping included very comfortable retirement homes and multiple dwelling units that were tailored to financially secure retired people. Casey had poured over the Census data and confirmed his suspicion that the proportion of retired empty-nesters in this region was very high. With the mildest climate in Canada, Oceanside had grown at a hectic 6% rate over the last ten years. The Census tallied more than 14,000 persons over 65 years of age. To Casey, this meant that 25% of the local population would have great difficulty caring for themselves, would suffer greatly, and be among the first casualties in any long-term disaster.

However, a few of these retirees had considerable skills to offer, and Casey made notes about some of them. Many had retired with the intention of not working again, only to be forced back into the workforce due to having lost much of their retirement savings in the unending financial crisis.

Casey gathered information on retired dentists, doctors, biologists, academics, engineers, mechanics, electricians, chemists, lab technicians, farmers, veterinarians, and skilled tradesmen who seemed to have considerable life experience and accomplishments which could be helpful as an untapped resource.

One old fellow that came to Casey's attention had once been a technician at the Atomic Energy Council of Canada's Whiteshell laboratories. The AECL was once the largest nuclear research facility in Western Canada, but was closed down in 1990. When old Mr. Skinner was given his retirement payout he moved away from the frigid Manitoba winters for the much milder weather in Parksville. His pension was insufficient for his retirement, so at the age of 72 years with a PhD in Atomic Physics, he had replied to one of Casey's surreptitious employment ads for a Laboratory Technician. Casey had already interviewed five candidates for a short term project he had in mind, but hired old Mr. Skinner in spite of his advanced age and obvious difficulties with arthritis, rather than the younger applicants.

This was not charity; Mr. Skinner more clearly fit the bill. Lloyd Skinner had no attachments and no obligations. He could be added to Casey's pool of contacts without greatly expanding the support demands that would surely come with those relationships. Mr. Skinner would also not require as many calories as the younger people. His list of accomplishments revealed an interesting history, such as 15 years as a cell-phone tower technical/installer back in the early 1980's, and his current membership in the Radio Amateurs of Canada – RAC.

With his amateur radio call-sign: VA7TLB, Lloyd continued to be active as Vice President for the Parksville-Qualicum Amateur Radio Club. He was also the technical advisor for the Official Bulletin Services and the Amateur Radio Emergency Services Program of the Pacific Region of RAC. This was largely a communications exercise, with a monthly roll-call of ARES and OBS certified RAC members confirming connectivity to the grid, practicing activation and reporting procedures. Should an emergency occur, the participants in these emergency networks might constitute the only functioning communications grid.

Casey wanted to develop a relationship with someone in the RAC network, both to assist in preserving a communications link for the community and to have a window to the world should things go badly. Mr. Skinner could provide that link and not require all that much in return. His technical expertise from the AEC laboratory certainly qualified Lloyd Skinner for the special research project. The project itself was to equip the HOTH with the antennas and radio systems used by ARES and the OBS, and to train and certify Casey under RAC. Once Casey signed Old Mr. Skinner on, he also gave him a research project aimed at outfitting the HOTH with radiological sensors and the procedures necessary to track and interpret the data.

The second group after the TPRH was the Commercial & Public Sector, CPS. While it didn't account for much of the population base, the CPS was well defined. Casey assigned codes for the few warehouses, grocery stores, drug stores, hardware stores, lumber yards and other sites of interest. These he marked with pins on the maps and stickies detailing the more significant factors. With most of the food distribution coming out of Nanaimo, the relatively larger city of 80,000 people just 37 kilometers from Parksville, there was very little in terms of warehousing of food in the Oceanside area. That was a major cause of concern for Casey. It meant that when the trucks stopped coming, food would run out very quickly.

Civic buildings, ranging from the Town Hall, recreation facilities, police, fire and ambulance stations, as well as the medical clinics in both towns had been evaluated as well. There was no hospital in the region; this was yet another concern for Casey. While the Nanaimo Regional General Hospital was a very capable facility, its downtown location was a liability as it would probably be unavailable to Oceanside residents in any major disaster scenario.

Partly due to the lack of hospitals in the Oceanside areas, Casey spent extra time in plotting the location and details of the extended-care facilities, medical & dental clinics, and pharmacies. He also gathered photographs of the buildings and a summary of the key personnel associated with each.

He had gleaned much of this information from the internet, but Casey followed up by making personal visits to each site. He wanted to ensure that he had a solid grasp of the lay of the land and the smallest of details at each location. As Casey had seen in the US invasion of Iraq in 2003, and in the Hurricane Katrina disaster of 2005, medical facilities and infrastructure of all kinds are quickly in danger of looting and other problems when society breaks down in a crisis.

In that regard, Casey developed a considerable file on the Oceanside Community Police organization. This included the two branch offices of the RCMP's Oceanside detachment and the District 69 "Citizens on Patrol" volunteer group. Gathering data on the "D69COPS" had been a lot of fun. Casey, being a newly retired military officer, had been welcomed into their ranks as they always needed more volunteers with actual law enforcement or military experience. He already knew many of them from the Gun Club, and fit right in.

The D69COPS was a non-profit volunteer organization that provided the RCMP with extra eyes and ears to help keep the community safe. Many of the members were retired police officers and others who wanted to keep their retirement haven safe, quiet and calm. In joining the D69COPS, Casey made new friends and got to know some wonderful people. Casey shared their values, so his participation in their efforts was sincere as much as it was purposeful.

The third group, after TPRH and CPS, was the "Agriculture and Light Industry", ALI, category. Casey had remembered many of these businesses from past trips over the years. Be it the log-home builders in Lantzville, the cedar products yard just off Hwy 19 in Parksville, the concrete mixing plants out on Fardowne Road, or the quarry out near Spider Lake, Casey already had a sense of the capabilities in the region. After he completed a methodical survey, he was even more impressed with the range and depth of local enterprises.

Certainly much of this early research was done in conjunction with the construction of the HOTH; however the work was far from complete. There were innumerable "FOQ" stickies, detailing Follow-On-Questions Casey wanted answered.

Other than supporting the HOTH construction project, the larger objective of the ALI survey was to have a solid grasp of food storage, local food production, livestock, butchering and feedstock inputs to the ALI sector. These supplies would be cut off in a disaster and local food production would fall off precipitously. In his assessment of Moonstruck Dairy Farm, for example, he concluded that the dairy herd would have to be cut from eighty cows to about twenty at the outset of a crisis and down to ten or so within a few years due to lack of feed.

During their summer visit, Casey took the family along with him to Moonstruck Farm. His plan was to learn more about the daily routines at the dairy farm and observe the Palaty family that ran the farm and co-located Cheese Works.

Much to the delight of the Callaghan family, the farm and Cheese Factory complex was an agro-tourism operation that gave them a fabulous day of activities while satisfying Casey's thirst for data. The children participated in cheese-wedge go-cart races, swam in the swimming hole, and milked a dairy cow. Little Donnovan even got to chase some chicks.

The Callaghans found out that there was a "Buy a Cow" program, where for $2,500 they could buy a dairy cow which would remain with the Moonstruck herd. The owners were then entitled to $300 in cheese and dairy products from the Cheese Works each month. The investors could sell the cow back to the farm at any time, and their cow would be replaced by another cow should it die. It was a secure way to become farmers without the big commitment. Casey immediately signed on to the program and asked about the feed requirements and other details. This information was then fed into the computer and even featured into the design of the barn and green-house that Casey was incorporating into the HOTH project, along with the planned stockpiling of long-term feed supplies that would be needed.

Certainly now was not the time to consider purchasing a dairy cow for the HOTH itself. But getting the right design features into the barn, feed storage and other requirements needed a lot of hands-on learning. The entire family looked forward to each visit to Moonstruck Farm to see Angelina, their new cow. And with every outing Casey was becoming more and more comfortable with his overall comprehension of the dairy farming construct, even if he still could not grasp how to milk by hand.

A few other ALI properties had been given an initial assessment, but a great many remained un-assessed. If Casey was right, that there were maybe two or three years left before things got really dangerous, then he still had time. So as the complexity of Casey's research seemed to be getting out of hand he decided to slow down, and keep his attention on building the HOTH. The research would continue; he would keep at it steadily like eating an elephant – one piece at a time. For the time being, completing the initial survey on the most prominent Agricultural and Light Industry sites would suffice.

The fourth classification was the most trouble. "Medium-size Residential Homes", MRH, which Casey thought of as "Mr. Hungry". Mr. Hungry was a problem because that was where families lived. Children. The precious future. It was one thing for Casey to imagine how difficult survival would be for elderly people when the supply chain fails, but it was another thing altogether to think about suffering children. At least the elderly would succumb quickly to starvation, radiation sickness, pre-existing health problems, stress, and in many cases, simply giving up. The death of large numbers of elderly people was something that Casey could philosophically come to terms with. But families, with small children, that hit much closer to home. After all, the motivation behind Casey's entire project was the survival and well-being of his own children.

Regarding local food production, his overall assessment was bleak. He considered how quickly the stockpile of locally produced and stored food would be exhausted. The Oceanside region would run out of food supplies within ten weeks of a major crisis. Numerous men, desperate to feed their starving children, represented a serious operational risk that had to be mitigated.

He had to find a subtle way to encourage people to squirrel away emergency food. He would also have to put some attention to developing contingency plans that would help the community conserve and extend the local food supplies once the crisis occurred. He needed to call Marty and Katy.

12

HABIB

When Habib underwent his mission training in a small town one hour's drive from Amman, the beat up old A6 he was provided did not have a working stereo, but at least the air conditioning worked. Habib Al Hassan had spent the past six months driving the Audi. It was better than his old job as a taxi driver. At this point, it was still a game. He knew that the men playing the roles of Israeli police, border agents, and the other security personnel were actually part of a team sent to Amman by VEVAK, *Vazarat-e Ettela'at va Amniyat-e Keshvar*, the Intelligence Agency of the Islamic Republic of Iran.

They recruited Habib not long after he was diagnosed with colon cancer, and found him to be an easy convert. He was a devout Muslim, adhering to the *Shia* sect predominating Iran, in contrast to the ninety percent *Sunni* Muslim of his home country.

Life was very simple for Habib. He obediently followed any guidance or Fatwa his Imam told him, so he was eager to serve the cause when he was introduced to two impeccably dressed men from Tehran. Having four children to support and knowing that his cancer would kill him soon enough, he quickly agreed to the death benefit of $100,000 in Gulf Dinaris for his family upon the completion of his mission. He also believed that he would be given additional rewards in paradise for any small services provided to the Holy Jihad, as he reflected on his favorite quote from the Qur'an: 3:185,

Everyone shall taste death. And only on the Day of Resurrection shall you be paid your wages in full. And whoever is removed away from the Fire and admitted to Paradise, he indeed is successful. The life of this world is only the enjoyment of deception.

The actual mission was a bit unclear. At first he was trained in the art of driving according to the erratic rules that applied to Muslims driving inside Israel. He had to appear relaxed, polite, and servile. The objective was to become seen as a friendly, professional driver and a "good" Arab.

Once he mastered the responses and body language, Habib's training expanded into actually crossing the Jordanian – Israeli border.

Establishing his identity as a driver for the British Embassy in Amman had been the most dangerous part of his training. He had been added to the pool of drivers by an Iranian plant within the British Embassy. The British embassy had a fleet of new Audi A8 sedans which were similar to the A6 he had been training, only his A6 did not have the new-car smell, luxurious leather interior, and gleaming white exterior of the Embassy fleet. Along with a new suit of clothes which the Embassy gave him to wear when driving, Habib and the other drivers were also issued multiple-entry visas by Israel as a favor to the British government.

Habib's medical condition had at first been suppressed, and then disclosed by Habib when he had been instructed to do so by his handlers. The British, humanitarian to a flaw, decided to keep him employed as long as his medical condition would permit.

The first crossing had been quite difficult. He set off a radiation detector and security personnel swarmed out of the bunkers at the border crossing. After a major search of the British Embassy's A8, and a full body-cavity search of Habib revealed nothing, the security personnel turned to the documents in his possession. His documentation as a driver for the British was verified, along with his personal identity documents. Eventually they found the medical documentation he was required to carry on his person, both by the Jordanian Medical authorities and further insisted upon by his Iranian handlers. These showed that Habib was undergoing chemotherapy at a cancer clinic in Amman. There would be low levels of radiation in his urine as his body removed the Strontium-89 and other doses applied to kill the cancer cells in his colon.

The High-Pure-Geranium Detectors widely used by the Israeli security personnel to detect Gamma radiation could not distinguish between Sr-89 in the medical isotopes used for chemotherapy and the Highly Enriched Uranium, HEU, such as that produced at the enrichment facility at Natanz, Iran. As a result, the more the border guards responded to the alarms raised by Habib's low level of radioactivity, the more complacent they became. Each time Israelis dealt with Habib, with his friendly demeanor and respectful submission to their security protocols, the more humanely they began to treat him, even asking after his health on occasion - especially when he carried British diplomats.

Habib crossed into Israel with a simple implosion type of nuclear weapon installed in the heavily modified Audi A-8 that had been swapped for the identical A8 he normally drove.

The radiological alarms had gone off as usual, and the security forces carried out a cursory search before allowing Habib to continue on with his British passenger. The diplomat had ridden with Habib many times and did not notice that the sedan was eight hundred pounds heavier. Nor did he feel the 2,200 roentgens per hour that his body was being exposed to from the radiation leaking past the minimal lead shielding surrounding the device installed in the car.

It would take the diplomat nine days to die from the radioactivity he was exposed to on his two-hour drive from Amman to Jericho. Habib was equally unaware of the contents of his vehicle, however he suspected that there could be a bomb as it felt heavier and rode lower than the other A8s. If this was to be his day of martyrdom, he reasoned, then so be it. His only regret was that he not had undergone the purification rituals that he would have liked. Shaving off his chest and facial hair would have cleansed him for the uplifting to paradise.

After dropping the diplomat off at the International Hotel Jericho, Habib continued on to Tel Aviv. During the drive Habib tuned the Audi's radio to BBC World News. He turned the volume up a bit and listened to the broadcaster: ...*at least 900 dead in the blast. Local officials in Jinan City are calling for people to go to local hospitals to donate blood, which is badly needed to help the hundreds of badly injured students. The cause of the explosion at Shandon University is unknown at this point. Officials are investigating reports of a natural gas leak in the Climate Sciences building, where the students had been sitting examinations when the Great Hall....* Tragic, Habib thought to himself, while turning the radio to another channel. He was happy to find one of his favorite songs, "Al Mu'allim", The Teacher, by Sami Yusuf, was playing.

He remained vigilant for security personnel throughout the drive to Tel Aviv. It was a beautiful day. The trees looked greener than ever to Habib, on this, the last day of his life. He was feeling great pride and joy in carrying out his task, and relished each passing second as his last on earth. His sensory pleasure was intensified by his anticipation of the joys he was going to experience once he reached paradise.

Passing Ben Gurion Airport, he watched a large passenger jet making its approach to land. Then Habib merged to the Ayalon North freeway before taking the LaGuardia Interchange onto Ha-Tsfira road. He was careful to be in the right lane in time for the obscure exit from Yehuda Halevi onto the very short Shadal Road. Arriving fifteen minutes before the planned time, Habib calmly stopped the A8, blocking one of three lanes of the busy street. A beautiful new Audi double-parked near the Israeli Stock Exchange did not draw any attention.

Within a few moments, another olive skinned man noticed the A8 and swung into action. His assignment had been to park a vehicle along the right side of Shadal, and pull out to liberate the parking spot for a white, Audi A8. When he saw Habib stop and wait for a spot, he quickly pulled his delivery truck out into the traffic and drove off. His mission was complete. His orders were to then carry on driving his normal delivery route, stopping to toss out bundles of newspapers, as usual.

After parking the Audi, Habib left the air conditioning on to keep the vehicle comfortable. He picked up the cell phone which he had never used. A pre-programmed phone number was set in the phone's memory. Habib's final act would be to select the number and hit "send". Twelve minutes before the scheduled 4pm timing, Habib took out his well worn copy of the Qur'an and read verses to pass the time before making his ascent to paradise.

It was nearly 10:00pm in Jinan when General Bing was interrupted by Colonel Hua. Colonel Hua had been given strict orders to ensure that the General was awake in time to receive Major Yip's report from Amman. General Bing had adjusted his sleep cycle so that he would be awake during the night hours in China and catch the working hours in London and Washington.

He was comfortable with delegating authority over the more routine aspects of his plan which were playing out within China while he slept, and wanted to be awake at night to keep a close eye on the counter-intelligence operations going on around the world. Knowing what was about to happen in Israel he had been far too excited to get any real sleep, and just lay awake all day long.

"Honorable General, Sir, are you awake?"

"Yes, Simon. What is it?"

"Sir, Major Yip's wire has arrived. We have the report from Amman." Colonel Hua held the single page message.

"You read it to me, Simon; I don't have my glasses on."

"Message reads: *Package delivered, will be opened on time.*"

"Excellent!" General Bing was now wide awake. He had gone to bed worried that the Israelis would intercept the Iranian bomb as it crossed the border. Chinese agents had learned of the plan by virtue of some highly paid double-agents within VEVAK. He was still unsure if the Iranians had planted the tip as a test of Chinese support for their attack on Israel or if the intelligence was a genuine penetration of VEVAK.

Regardless, after having confirmed the plot was indeed real, General Bing allowed the Iranian operation to go ahead without Chinese interference. In fact, Chinese agents had been mobilized to terminate a traitor within the Iranian diplomatic corps when General Bing's Internet Security Division picked up on contact made between an Iranian diplomat and MI6 in London.

That was a risky operation, but essential for protecting the Iranians from discovery. On General Bing's order, Chinese agents had taken out the Iranian diplomat before the traitor was able to pass his information on to his MI6 handler.

Seeing he had a few minutes, General Bing asked for an update on the students killed at Shandon University that day. When he had gone to quarters for rest, his men had triggered the explosion but they had not confirmed that all of Dr. Sun Tingting's students had been successfully terminated.

"There were 14 survivors, however most of them had not yet regained consciousness before we got to them in the hospitals," Colonel Hua reported, with a little too much excitement for General Bing's taste. "All 340 have been accounted for. The follow-on seizure of their home computers and analysis of any extra-campus contact is now underway. Any lateral leakage will be promptly taken care of, Sir!" Colonel Hua concluded.

"Very good, Simon. I'll be in the Ops Centre in five minutes to watch the show. Make sure everybody is in place ready for Phase Two to begin."

Colonel Hua was already backing his way out of the General's quarters, just twenty meters from the Ops Centre in the bunker deep under Jinan Military Region Headquarters, China.

A few minutes later as Habib closed his Qur'an and held it to his chest, taking in his last few breaths before pressing "SEND" on his cell-phone, General Bing was striding into his Ops Center. The General made brief eye contact with the influential men he had selected for the honor of watching the Iranian pawn poke its finger into the Israeli eye.

General Bing was pleased to see that ops had managed to arrange real-time satellite imagery over Israel, with both a wide image view of the entire Middle East, as far as Tehran, and another image zoomed down to a smaller scale, focused on Tel Aviv. He saw the countdown timer passing the two minute mark.

Another screen divided into four squares showed the live feed from CNN, Al Jazeera, RT, BBC International and some German channel he did not recognize, showing routine broadcasts of weather, political talking heads, and daily stock-market images. The stage was set for the big show.

In another operations center, eight hours behind Jinan time, a discussion was taking place.

"Sir, we're picking up another unusual spike in Chinese activity," announced Squadron Leader Albert Jones , gaining the attention of Richard Jessup, the senior analyst with whom he shared the overnight watch at the Chinese Desk.

"What is it, Albert?"

"Well, the level of internet activity out of that region has just peaked. Coincidentally, a great deal of their space bandwidth is now dedicated to transferring data from their *Sunrise-One* satellite. It looks like they're watching something along its track."

MI6 had found a way to monitor the energy being directed through Chinese military satellites, using cryptological algorithms obtained from the French in a *quid pro quo*. It couldn't provide the actual data being transmitted, but it was able to pick up on the magnitude of transmissions and, by Doppler analysis, the source and destination of transmissions. This was one of the few windows into Chinese internet and space-based military communications, and one area in which MI6 had an advantage over their American colleagues.

"Where is *Sun-One*?" asked Jessup.

"Coming up over the Middle East, tracking very slowly. It appears that they've expended a great deal of fuel and moved *Sun-One* into a much higher orbit. It'll have perhaps ninety minutes coverage over the Middle East. It'll close the gap!"

"What gap?"

"There was a thirty-minute gap between *Sun-One* and *Sun-Seven*, which had been in serial orbits with *Seven* following *One* by ninety minutes. Even at widest aperture they would lose coverage over any area of interest for at least thirty minutes. But now, with *Sun One* in a higher orbit, it'll have more hang-time over the Middle East before moving on to the European AOR. *Sun Seven* will then give them another hour or so of coverage before the next gap in their satellite coverage happens, in just under three hours."

"But isn't it highly irregular for them to do that? Doesn't that use up their fuel too quickly?"

"Yes, Sir, but *Sun One* was due for replacement later this year anyhow, so they must have a bit of fuel to spare. Or else..." he paused, then spoke more slowly, "whatever they're doing now is that important to them. I think we better give the Americans and Israelis a heads up that the Chinese are watching something in the Middle East."

Squadron Leader Jones had only just picked up the phone to call the message centre when he froze, looking at one of the TV monitors in MI6's International Divisions Operations Center. "Richard, tell me that's not Tel Aviv!"

13

SQUIRREL'S DEN

09 November: 18 Months Before NEW

When Marty Penner first heard about the idea, he almost choked on his popcorn. He and Katy had been settled in for a quiet evening of movie watching. Their two small children, Grover and Charlotte, were sleeping over at their grandparents on the other side of town. Casey Callaghan had interrupted their rare night off by calling to ask Marty to drop what he was doing and fly down from Whitehorse to Vancouver for a three month project. And Casey wanted an answer right away.

"Hang on, Casey; I've got to talk this over with Katy. I'll call you back in a few minutes. What's your number?"

Waiting for Marty's call, Casey tried to think of someone else he could trust with such a sensitive task. He came up dry.

He knew nobody else who had the artistic, technical and planning skills to pull this off. He was so worked-up waiting for Marty to call back that he couldn't focus on any of the other "Open Tasks". So when the phone rang about twenty minutes later, Casey grabbed it before the first ring ended.

"Casey, this is Katy. Marty told me what you want him to do, and I want to go over it again with you myself."

Casey immediately recognized her distinctive Australian accent. He recalled her face from the last time he saw her, when he flew into Whitehorse with the Twin Otter during the Canada Winter Games. That was the last time they had spoken.

Casey wasn't sure how Marty and Katy felt about him now, several years later. Casey had put Marty onto the TFG gold mine in Yellowknife, and after that the share price had gone down considerably during the early stages of the economic crisis. Casey was worried that Marty and Katy may have lost money on his advice, and had not hung on long enough to reap the rewards of the gold mine now going into full production.

"Well, Katy, what I want is for Marty to go on a big shopping trip in Vancouver, and ship a variety of goods to an office I have set up here in Qualicum Beach. Once here in Qualicum, he is to set up a small business using the items he sourced in Vancouver, and then run that business for a few months." As Casey paused, and listened for Katy's next comment, he actually held his breath. He knew full well that if Katy did not agree, then Marty would never be allowed to come down to the coast. He also knew how shrewd and intelligent Katy was. He knew better than to interrupt her or to push too hard.

"So that's like when he set up that business for Garth, back in 2007?" Katy asked, referring to when Marty had helped his buddy Garth set up an educational toy store in Richmond.

Marty was not particularly well-schooled in business, but he had a sharp mind and was a great problem solver. He knew how to relate to people and had world class networking skills. Marty generally performed best when doing things to help others. As a result, Casey had always considered Marty to be untapped human potential still looking for some challenge that would be meaningful enough to consume his prodigious energies.

"Yes, Katy, just like 'Monkey Mart' only with far fewer items to source and no long-term business plan to worry about. I just need his help buying the initial supplies, establishing a few routines, and training some staff."

"And what about the film bit? Tell me more about that".

"It's like what Marty and I did back at UBC with the Philosophy Association. I want him to put on a film festival."

"And for this, you are willing to pay all of Marty's travel expenses, food, lodging, and $15,000 for his time?"

"Yes, that's my starting position." Casey replied. With that, he knew he had her. She would capitalize on this opening, and throw the door all the way open.

"OK, Casey, I'll bite. Not because you gave us a good tip on Trophy Fish Gold. *That* roller coaster almost cost us our marriage! But we're broke, and Marty can't find a job. So here's our offer. You add another $15,000 for *MY* services, and we'll both come down, *WITH* our kids. You pay *ALL* our travel costs *BOTH WAYS*, provide us a minivan with car seats, and you agree that our names will appear prominently on the program!"

Katy paused, catching her breath after shouting the last part. Whatever deeper meaning that had was lost on Casey.

"Well, Katy, that's more than I had expected to pay. Are you sure you want to bring your children with you?"

"Yes, I'm not going without'em, and Marty is not going

without me. Besides, you know Marty and I work well together".

"OK, but the apartment is a bit tight for the four of you. It'll be a bit like camping out."

"Don't you worry about that, Casey, Marty and I will fix it up to suit our needs," Katy said, with a bit of energy and excitement that Casey was glad to hear.

"Give me your email address, and I'll transfer $10,000 right now for the tickets. How soon can you leave?"

"We can leave in two days. There's a Lufthansa charter flight taking German tourists back to Vancouver, and I'm sure there's still lots of seats available."

"Oh, that's right; you're working at the terminal, right?"

"Yes, I am. They cut my hours in half! I can't feed us on that! I'll enjoy calling in my resignation tomorrow!"

After copying down their e-mail address and reading it back correctly, Casey asked: "Don't you and Marty want to know the subject matter of the film festival?"

"No need, Marty figured it out already. It's about surviving a nuclear war, isn't it?"

"How did Marty figure it out?" Casey was surprised.

"Marty followed your postings on that investor forum, up until you stopped posting on it last spring. We wondered when you were going to call, to brag about how well you did with Trophy Fish. By the way, we sold too early, and missed out on lots of profits, but it really helped anyhow. Marty kept reading your posts and telling me your ideas about how much more dangerous the world was going to become as the economic crisis deepens. He told me you had this crazy idea that a war could escalate into a global nuclear war. I guess you were right, at least if what happened in Tel Aviv last month is any indication", she said. "So I take it that the business you want us to set up has something to do with survivalism? But what I don't get, Casey, is *what's your angle?*"

"What do you mean, Katy?"

"I mean, Casey Callaghan, we all know you don't get into

things without a reason. You didn't get into that gold mine, and all those on-line investor forums promoting Trophy Fish just for the fun of it. You did that to make a shit-load of money. So now you're rich. Well done, really, but what could you possibly hope to make from a little survivalism store?"

After hearing nothing from Casey, she continued. "OK. Putting on a survivalism film festival and getting everybody all worked up about a nuclear war may be good for the business, but how much money do you really expect to make in a sleepy little town like Qualicum Beach?" She asked.

"We can talk about it later," Casey said, uncomfortably.

"Wait a minute. WAIT JUST A DAMNED MINUTE!" Katy said, with a different tone in her voice. "You're *serious* about this! *You actually think there really is going to be a war.* You're gonna be living in that area, and you want other people there to be ready to survive a war. It's not enough to save yourself, your family, your kids; you want to save what, the entire town?"

"You are getting closer. But you're not on target. How long do you think a family, even well armed and very secretive, could hold out against several thousand starving loggers?"

Silence. Casey waited. Then, Katy replied. "OH. MY. GOD! You're right. It's that old debate you and Marty had at the university, about "Community versus Survivalism". Marty told me about that a dozen times! You argued that the survivalists have it all wrong, in their "Guns, Gold and God" mentality. You argued that the solo survivalist really needs to be engaged in the wider community in order to have any hope of surviving in a disaster," she recounted. "Marty told me a hundred times that he won the debate, by arguing that human nature is such that the vast majority of people in the community will not have anything put away for a rainy day and will just come and take it from you, so you had better be ready to defend yourself. You can't save the entire community. So what's the plan, Casey? Get them prepared to save themselves so that you don't have to be the only island in the storm?" she asked rhetorically, but then changed her tone yet again.

"Oh, I get it now! If they get *themselves* better prepared then there will be many small islands in the storm and the community will have a chance to stay civilized; you won't need to hide in a little fortress. But to get that many people to sort themselves out and get prepared, that's the problem, isn't it? And Marty and I are the solution?" Katy's grasp of the issues was impressive. "OK, we're in," she decided. "Now tell me what's on the shopping list."

14

STOCKING UP - SOFT

21 May: 1 Year Before NEW

Casey was surprised to see that he only had $41,380 Cdn left in the bank. So he placed an order to sell 20,000 shares in TFG, now trading at a whopping $19. The $294,880 after commissions and capital gains taxes would probably last about another month at the rate he was spending money getting the house ready for the move of the family in July. He also planned to spend another $120,000 on food supplies and fuel. Even that would not be the end of his spending plans for the summer; he also planned to buy some new vehicles and small machines.

Casey had started stocking operations soon after the HOTH reached lock-up in November, but those early operations were focused on "Last - Chance" caches with the ultra long-lived stores which could be sealed away and forgotten about for years.

The food was prepared by Marty and Katy in the *Squirrel's Den*. After some research and experimenting, they found nitrogen gas was easier than dry-ice for flooding oxygen out of the bulk foods. They had perfected their methods and could process three 55-gallon bulk food bins into forty-two rectangular 4-gallon pails each day. Each of the sturdy little food-grade pails was first lined with a mylar plastic bag then oxygen absorbers were opened and placed in the bottom of the bags to absorb any residual oxygen over time. By holding a burning match over the small opening of the plastic bag, Katy would confirm that there was not enough oxygen coming out of the bucket to support a flame then Marty would remove the nitrogen wand and heat-seal the Mylar bag closed. They would then seal the pail using the integral gasket and affix a dated label.

They had decided to go with various sizes of food-grade rectangular HDPE plastic pails because they were about 40% more efficient than traditional round pails. The snap-closed, gasket-fitted lids are converted to hinge-style flap-up lids when the tear-off strip is removed, so they are perfectly suited for long-term storage and eventual day-to-day use of the bulk foods.

The best size turned out to be two gallon rectangular pails because you could fit six of them into one of the ubiquitous Rubbermaid Roughneck 31 gallon storage bins and still have the top four inches for canned goods and other items. This extra space worked well because you could mix and match a variety of basic food items into the smaller pails and fill the rest of the Roughneck with comfort food items, canned foods, preserves and other supplies until the Roughneck was filled to the top. This way the bins were densely packed and stackable. You could also pack large numbers of serving-sized mylar bags into a rectangular bucket and mix-and-match the rest of the Roughneck to suit.

To get Marty and Katy up to speed on the Squirrel's Den operation, Casey had them prepare 100 such bins for him. These would never appear on any inventory. For Casey's first order, Marty and Katy put together a range of different "loads" which were designed for ultra-long-term storage. These focused on basic foods such as sugar, salt, rice, pasta, beans, oats, wheat and a wide variety of long-life canned and other flavorful and nutritious items to accompany the bland foods. Each bin also contained a few small items such as whisky, tobacco, hard candies, candles, matches, vitamins, tea and instant coffee. These were added in the gaps between the two gallon pails until the Roughneck was stuffed full. Each of the Roughneck bins held an estimated 400,000 calories, or 182 person-days at 2,200 Calories per day - enough to sustain a family of six for one month.

Every tenth bin had a large red cross which indicated that it contained First Aid and medical supplies in addition to a reduced quantity of food items. These contained a substantial First Aid kit, some additional gauze and dressing materials, a small box with a range of ointments, disinfectants, burn creams, sunscreen, insect repellants, aspirin and three medium-sized vials each containing 120 doses of low-dose Amoxicillin, Ciprofloxacin and Cefaclor. A small guide accompanied these basic antibiotic medicines, explaining their use along with graphs predicting the expected reduction in efficacy over time. It would be necessary to increase the number of the low-dose pills taken in order to achieve the desired strength due to the loss of potency over time.

After taking delivery of the bins, Casey cemented twenty into each of five "Last Chance" caches in and around the HOTH.

After that, Casey began to stockpile more conventional food supplies, with life-spans in the three to five year range. He had these delivered from a commercial food distributor in Nanaimo to the garage of the HOTH. He had considered an elaborate and secretive staging process, whereby food deliveries would be made to another location to disguise the destination of the food, but he rejected this as overly paranoid. The driver would have little interest in the end use of whatever he delivered. Besides, in the worst case scenario, any delivery records would long since be lost in the destruction of Nanaimo.

The truckload had five thousand pounds of canned goods

and twelve 55 gallon plastic-lined cardboard drums of bulk dry goods. It was unloaded in the garage at the nearly finished HOTH on May 21st. It took Casey, Danny and Yuri just six hours to dolly the cases and drums to the small elevator, send them down to the lower level, and transfer them to the main bunker under the garage. Marty, Katy and Casey broke down and processed all twelve barrels of bulk foods into one hundred and ten 6.5 gallon pails on the second day. Things went very fast with the larger pails, particularly since Casey didn't have to further process them into Roughnecks bins. He simply piled the cases of canned food in the cool storage corner of the bunker and stacked the bulk-food pails into the DFR where they would be remain at a constant minus eight degrees Centigrade.

That Sunday night, Casey was very tired as he inputted the data. Each of the 180 kilogram bulk food drums had cost almost $2,000, which was by far the most cost-effective source of calories and protein even when adding the cost of the mylar bags and rectangular pails and other materials used to break the load into smaller sized units. As for the caned goods, the variety of vegetables, fruits, meat products and other foods were more expensive, but they provided essential vitamins and nutrients.

The delivery cost over $40,000 CDN, which Casey had paid in advance when he originally placed his order.

Much of this first shipment of food, with sufficient calories and nutrition to feed his family of seven for three years, was not intended to be held on a long-term basis. Rather, it was the first practice run of a multi-year plan.

Despite the devastation in the Middle East, Casey did not believe that a large scale nuclear war was imminent, nor was any other disaster on the horizon. It was still possible that the world would find a way out of the financial crisis and use the horrors of the recent Middle East Nuclear Exchange, MENE, War as a motivation for real progress on arms reduction and peace.

Casey was not optimistic that they would, so having a three year supply of food seemed prudent. More importantly, it allowed him to trial the food preparation and loading operations which he would eventually have to do on a much more ambitions scale.

Six months after that first round of stocking up, with the family having settled into their wonderful home, Casey was being lulled into a false sense of security. The family had moved in early in July, after school was out for the summer. The drive across the country from Winnipeg had been a wonderful week-long holiday that reminded them of past road trips. Using their military move entitlement, the family had little to do other than show the movers around the old house, get themselves to Vancouver Island, and show the un-loaders around the new house.

The large rooms looked empty even after their old furniture had been unpacked. Once Tanya realized that Casey wouldn't complain, she had Yuri and Danny throw most of the junky old furniture into a bonfire pile. After that, the family went on a spending spree in Vancouver and Nanaimo. With new furniture and an obscene amount of storage space, Tanya set about organizing the family's permanent home while Casey and the children were busy with the 4-H programs and other summer-time activities.

As the months flew by, the HOTH began to feel like a home. One night in January, as Tanya and Casey reflected on how well things had turned out, Casey realized that he had become complacent. He spent the next few evenings tearing through his favorite economics and geopolitical websites, re-caging his gyros.

While the Callaghans had enjoyed their own boom time, the economy was starting to degenerate again. The international community was still arguing about what to do about the Israeli-Iranian problem, as the once eager United Nations Mission of Aid and Iranian Disarmament, or UNMAID, had become bogged down in logistical, security and cultural issues that threatened to tear the international coalition apart. Casey thought that a major international crisis was increasingly likely. It was time to move his preparations into high gear.

More than a year before he had planned to, Casey began his Food-Bank ConPlan. The original concept was to rotate the medium-term food items out and donate them to food banks just before the published expiry dates. The 5,000 pounds of canned goods had been purchased just twelve months ago and had been selected for their three year official expiry dates. That left over two years to nominal expiry. The same items sitting in a store wouldn't be as fresh, Casey knew, but he decided to rotate them out early, resetting the clock. So in the first weeks of the new year Casey placed the same 5,000 pound order and received the canned goods and barrels of bulk dry goods by the end of January. He repeated the operation with Danny and Yuri helping with the physical task of moving the old cases of cans back up to the garage, and the new ones down to the bunker. However, he did not remove any of the bulk food pails from the DFR. Rather, he accumulated them and added 110 new pails to the DFR. Taken together, in the past 14 months the stockpiles in the DFR had reached about 20% of capacity.

Rather than having Marty and Katy help with the nitrogen-flooding, heat-sealing and other steps in preparing the ultra-long-term food supplies, he borrowed the equipment and did the work with Tanya. She caught on quickly, and showed real interest in the process. Despite the fact that it kept them up until late in the evenings for a week, Tanya insisted that they take the time to prepare smaller half-gallon sized mylar bags rather than the one large six gallon Mylar bag, to allow for flexibility when ultimately consuming the supplies.

Casey drove the older canned food to food banks in

Nanaimo where they were gratefully received. The families of the unemployed loggers and miners, who received larger than normal food hampers that month, would never know who to thank.

While in Nanaimo on the half-dozen such trips Casey took that February, he made innumerable visits to various big-box stores to buy fittings, accessories, shelving units, hardware and other items needed to outfit and customize the main bunker, the hidden passageways, and the panic rooms. The living areas of the HOTH were long since finished by the subcontractors who had taken the interior of the HOTH from lock-up to completion, as though it were a normal house. The secret spaces, hidden doors, false walls, as well as all the specialty electrical work for security systems had to be installed by Casey himself; it couldn't be trusted to contractors. With all of this work to do, Casey had fallen behind and many items sat on his "To Do" list for up to a year. But with the increase in global tensions, Casey's motivation to complete these tasks was renewed.

With the rotation of the canned food completed, and having doubled-up the bulk food in the DFR, Casey calculated that the family had perhaps four years of food on hand. He decided that it would be better to make the remaining purchases on a monthly basis so that he could balance the workload and have a simpler routine for rotating-out older cans on a re-occurring basis.

But, first he had to know the desired end-state. If he kept purchasing the same sized order each month for a year, he figured, at the end of two years he would have accumulated 345 Person-Years, PYs, of food. This would be enough for his family of seven to live for 49 years. *So it would not be enough.* It wouldn't be enough for the burn rate Casey anticipated.

But Casey had never completed his analysis of consumption versus internal food production. He had no baseline information on the presumed egg, poultry, and swine production that his group would be capable of, nor how long it could be sustained. He also had no idea how successful the hydroponics garden would be, nor how much food could be obtained through trading or bartering locally.

As Casey did not want to create a future problem by buying too much food all at once, he decided to apply the basic rule of operational planning. First, make a list of all the *assumptions* which are critical to support further planning, and list the key questions that needed to be answered. Then, convert the assumptions to *facts* through further evaluation, and find the answers to the key questions through research.

With this guidance in mind, Casey made a few reasonable assumptions about the people who would join the Callaghan family. In considering this, he took care of one open task, "Invitation Letters", and scheduled a family gathering for the next month to take care of another open task, "Family Briefing". Having the entire family and his friend Manfred Vogel over to see the newly completed HOTH gave Casey an opportunity to reveal the true purpose of the facility. This would ensure that they knew where to go in a crisis. The "invitation letters" would add a few more people and, combined with an estimate for Casey's local connections, would result in a number that could now be estimated. The average number of people to support over a ten-year worst case scenario turned out to be 50. Casey could now convert this to a *fact* and continue with plan development based on 500 PYs.

The result was that Casey adjusted the previous food order to include a larger quantity of bulk foods for the next three months to quickly build up the ultra long-term food supplies down in the DFR. Even this fell short of the total requirement of *four hundred million calories*. However, assumptions regarding animal and garden production in the HOTH, a small input from trading and bartering, and a modest assumption of last-minute stocking operations meant that he would only be about two hundred million calories short by June. After that, he simply had to take delivery of just over eight million calories per month for two years and then begin a three-year cycle of rotating out $1/36^{th}$ of the food supplies to food banks on a monthly basis.

Simple enough mathematically, Casey thought, but it was going to get very expensive. Some items were becoming scare, and the price was rising rapidly. This only spurred Casey on.

Once the challenge of fully stocking the HOTH had been revealed by the math, Casey set about dealing with the bulk food side of it first, not thinking about the monthly routine for a while. This helped him focus on other important issues.

One of these issues was to wrap-up the procurement of the medical supplies. He had not completed his stockpiling of Potassium Iodide and the three best long-term antibiotics. And even with cold storage the antibiotics would continuously lose their efficacy. So they also needed some basic lab equipment to process natural medicines produced by fungus and medicinal plants. Casey ordered a supply 0.22 micron syringe-mounted filters and the other supplies that Dr. Pizarski had listed for the infirmary, to purify natural-sourced medicines.

Casey also hadn't finished buying the many small machines, quads, dirt-bikes, bicycles, wagons, trailers, vehicles and other equipment that he wanted to have stowed away in the facility. The family still had not started actually raising any farm animals and Casey had not stockpiled the feed and other hobby farmer's resources that he would need.

He had so much to do, and it appeared that he would have less time in which to do it.

Gene Skellig

15

FIRST TANK ON ME

20 March: 10 Weeks Before NEW

"Was there any mail today, Gina?" Major Geoff Neumann asked his wife as he hung his car keys on the hook below the mirror in the entryway to his excessively large 3200 sq ft house. The house had always been a source of annoyance for him. It was much larger than they could afford, but Gina wanted a big house. He had long accepted that it was easier just to give in.

"There's something from Casey Callaghan," she said.

Major Neumann had been Captain Callaghan's boss for just two years, and they hadn't developed any particular friendship. Callaghan had turned down every opportunity to socialize with his boss, so Geoff stopped inviting him. But he had come to know Casey as a very serious and resourceful officer, although not really suited to military life. Major Neumann had been concerned when his subordinate decided to take such an enormous risk by leaving the military in the middle of the economic crisis. Why would a man with five children quit a high paying government job? Just to move to the West Coast?

Geoff sat down with the package in hand. He could feel an

odd imbalance in its weight. He used a letter opener, and slid the contents out onto his desk. There was a sheet of paper wrapped around a plastic bag containing a folded map, five small yellow packets labeled "ThyroLock", and one small item he instantly recognized.

Shining magnificently in the band of sunlight that cut across Geoff's desk was a $1/25^{th}$ oz Maple-Leaf gold coin from the Royal Canadian Mint. The yellow radiance emanating from the coin triggered a bit of gold madness in Geoff. As he reached for it, he whispered: "Come to me, my Precioussss!"

The coin was issued just before Canada suspended the sale of gold coins. The mint was shuttered temporarily in response to American pressure to cut off the supply of gold and silver *coins of the realm* during the US attempt at gold confiscation. Canada did not take things quite as far as the US.

Without notice, the US Government had declared the three weeks from January 7 to January 28 as a bank holiday. The sale of gold bullion, gold coins, gold certificates and any other form of physical gold other than jewelry was made illegal in both the United Kingdom and the United States. Citizens were given 30 days to turn in any and all gold and silver money, from any country, in exchange for new US or United Kingdom paper currencies. Citizens were "permitted" to retain up to two ounces of gold coins. It was part of a coordinated US – UK effort to introduce the new US dollar and new Pound Sterling, which were to be *partially* backed by gold - for the settlement of international trade but not for domestic transactions.

The US Treasury, Federal Reserve, and the White House had tried to save the US dollar by re-issuing it as yet another fiat currency with only a tenuous link to physical gold.

After the President issued Executive Order 4138 on January 7, the Senate and Congress swiftly passed enabling legislation. Citizens were ordered to exchange their gold coins for new US Federal Reserve Notes, at $4,000 New USD per ounce of gold. The objective was to swell the gold reserves of the US Treasury, as operated by the Federal Reserve banking cartel, to make it impossible for citizens to use gold and silver coins as money, and to force the acceptance of the new paper currency.

The confiscation of gold and the float of the new currency was an unmitigated disaster. American citizens had been through that before when President Roosevelt confiscated all privately held gold in the United States, under the *Trading With the Enemy Act* of 1917 amended March, 1933. This made it *treasonous* to hold gold coins or to use them as money on pain of a fine of up to $10,000 or up to ten years imprisonment, or both.

Partly because of the trust that Americans had in their government back in 1933, and partly for fear of consequences, the gold confiscation worked in 1933. It enabled a return to the gold standard and the stabilization of the economy for almost four decades of stability and prosperity. But in 1971 France began exchanging their massive pile of US Federal Reserve Notes for physical gold. President Nixon was forced to close the gold window to preserve the ever diminishing reserves of gold. From that point on, 1971 until the present day, the US dollar was a fiat paper currency - an IOU which was not actually backed by anything at all. It was, as are all fiat currencies, a giant Ponzi scheme doomed to failure.

This time around people refused to trust Uncle Sam. They saw the re-issued currency as a fraud and they hoarded their gold and silver coins that much more vigorously. The black market in gold and silver coins thrived. The new US currency never gained mainstream acceptance. Those hapless few who obeyed the law soon learned that they had been fleeced.

Economists had warned that confiscation would not work a second time because there simply was not enough gold and silver in circulation available for confiscation. In contrast, there had been a great deal of gold and silver coinage in circulation in 1933 which, once confiscated, gave the US Treasury sufficient gold to back-up the new currency.

The citizenry of 1933 learned a hard lesson about the dishonesty of Government when Roosevelt later revalued the currency, changing the valuation from some $20.67 per ounce to $35.00 per ounce, once the gold had been exchanged for fiat currency. This betrayal taught the citizens a valuable lesson about how the Government's true goal was the actual confiscation of their savings. It was a lesson that the citizenry of the United State never forgot.

With the failed launch of the new currency, the financial emergency brought about by high inflation and currency weakness soon became run-away hyperinflation and a currency collapse.

In Canada, reflected Major Neumann, the Government had been more cautious. While Canada agreed to temporarily halt the sale of precious metals they did not attempt confiscation. With the Canadian dollar backed by Canada's oil wealth and more conservative banking system, inflation in Canada was not as extreme as in the US. Also, the wage and price controls attempted in the United States were not attempted in Canada. Ironically, Canada remained a free-market economy with Government subsidies only for the most vulnerable while the United States had somehow become a command economy that only favored the most privileged elites and had become dysfunctional.

So Casey's gift of a gold coin, even just $1/25^{th}$ of an ounce, caught Geoff Neumann's attention. The price of gold was now at $3,200 Canadian dollars per ounce, $45,000 New US Dollars, or "Nudies", but nobody considered Nudies to be worth anything at all. The little coin had real value.

Geoff knew that what makes gold coins valuable is their purity, such as the international standard of "four nines", or 99.99% purity. They also have to be "coins of the realm", such as the Chinese Panda, the Canadian Maple Leaf, the Australian Kangaroo, and the American "liberty" series. These coins were now illegal in the United States. Their purity, however, made them just as valuable for trade as any other gold coins. Gold coins can always be melted down and therefore they retain their value. Simply making them illegal would not make them less desirable.

In the context of the international currency crisis, now raging across the world, the use of gold for international transactions was becoming standard. Everybody seemed to have realized the world's fiat currencies had no actual value. The only sound money was gold. Those countries, such as Canada and the United Kingdom, who foolishly followed the advice of the United States and sold most of their gold reserves in the 1980's and 90's, were now faced with the urgent requirement to rebuild their gold reserves at record high gold prices.

Major Neumann, as a serving member of the Canadian Air Force, was largely protected by the runaway inflation as his pay and pension entitlements were continually being adjusted to keep pace with the rampant inflation. However, his pay check still purchased less in terms of actual goods like food, energy and consumer goods every month, no matter how often the pay office applied "economic adjustments" to his monthly pay. His pay had nominally increased from $7,500 CDN per month about a year ago, to $17,000 per month now. And yet the cost of groceries had increased from around $1,300 per month for his family of four to over $5,000 per month now. A can of pop now costs $3.50; four litres of milk $18.00; and a loaf of bread costs $15.00. Geoff wished he was paid in gold. As he thought about it, he realized that that's what the package was all about. After all, Casey was a gold bug. He had even introduced his boss to that gold mine up in Yellowknife.

I should have listened to my gut and bought a few hundred thousand shares when it was going for ten cents. But oh no, *she* wouldn't go for it! Neumann thought to himself bitterly. His wife had allowed him to buy just 40,000 shares at $0.15, which she promptly had him sell when the share price went through $1.00 a few years ago. He had made a handy profit, but where would he be today if he had held on longer, or had accumulated more shares? With that thought, he clicked on his web browser and checked the stock price of the now producing gold mine. "Yup, there it is, available for just $42.00 Cdn per share. Man I wish I had some now!" he muttered.

Now, with the price of gold so high, any producing gold mine was quite literally pulling money out of the ground. He did a quick calculation, knowing that Casey had at least 600,000 shares when he left the military. If Casey sold even half of his shares on their way up, Callaghan still had at least $12 million or so in gains. "WOW! I guess he'll get over not having the pension, then," Geoff commented to himself.

Geoff then turned his attention to the second item from the package. It was a map of Western Canada with a couple of routes marked out in different colors. Being a trained Navigator, Neumann could read a map. He quickly noticed that the routes bypassed the cities of Regina, Saskatoon, Calgary and Edmonton, and went nowhere near the Canadian military bases at Moose Jaw, Cold Lake, or any others. All three routes started at Winnipeg.

He noticed a circle around Winnipeg. Then he realized that it was a blast radius centered on the Canadian NORAD Region Headquarters, where he worked. The 11 Km radius around the air base at the Winnipeg International airport was marked off as "Probable Mass Fires - 750 Kiloton". This circle matched fairly well with the foot-print of the perimeter highway around the city. So 750 Kilotons would basically destroy the city, he noted. He understood that most structures other than concrete or steel within that radius would be destroyed and set afire.

There was also a 6 Km radius circle representing the "Certain Mass Fires" where everything that could burn would be destroyed. The majority of casualties in this zone, Geoff well knew, would be from the effects of radiation and from the blast injuries produced by flying glass fragments and debris of anything weaker than reinforced concrete. Only a modest number of people in this zone would survive. Those who survived the effects of the initial blast would then be in dire need of medical attention. It gave Geoff a cold chill to visualize his city experiencing such horrors.

The most likely weapon would be a 750 kiloton MIRV from Topol-M missile, or perhaps the more common R-36 Missile with warheads anywhere from 550 kilotons to 3 Megatons, depending on the variant. So, if anything, Casey's map could be understating the yield. However, Geoff Neumann did not believe that Winnipeg rated one of the heavy warheads that some analysts believed Russia had been reconditioning, with bunker-busting yields up to 20 to 25 megatons. If Russia had any of these monsters, they would surely be used on more important targets in the US.

The blood ran from his face when he saw the route highlighted in yellow which ran directly from his home in St Andrews to the Yellowhead Highway. The hairs on his neck began to tingle as he began to intuit the true meaning of the map.

Geoff then focused his attention on a circle to the west of Winnipeg. There was a distance indication of 17 Km showing the closest path of approach to a Military Base west of Winnipeg, at Portage La Prairie right on the Trans Canada Highway. He noted that other east-west routes south of the Base were all crossed off with X's across their path, and some annotations.

Then he played a hunch, and turned the map over. Yes, there it was on the back, and quite cleverly done. If the map were folded accordion-style to focus on a particular segment, flipping up the bottom third revealed comments and notes which corresponded to that segment of the map.

There was a short explanation to accompany each numbered entry, such as: "G42: Likely closed due to flooding after power failure eliminates flood control at Southport", and

"B37: Insufficient supplies of fuel on this route." This comment appeared in many places.

The chill down his back had not gone away. "This is an evacuation map," he said audibly to himself. Geoff thought about it, letting the reality sink in. A lot of effort went into researching this, all to take him from his home to where? He looked quickly through the three alternate routes, following them through the Rockies at the BC / Alberta border. Yes! he thought excitedly, the south route is through Fernie, the middle route is through Rocky Mountain House, and the north route is through Grande Cache. All three are in the boonies and avoid major traffic arteries. That makes sense!

All three routes converged on Vancouver Island. However, the southern route had lots of warnings and question marks once it entered the Fraser Valley. It appeared to peter out, with simply a dotted line from Hope to where? Parksville? No, Qualicum Beach, Geoff realized. The northern route clearly required taking a boat of some kind from Prince Rupert all the way to Port Hardy, then by road to Kelsey Bay, then several comments he could read later, then by sea the final leg to Bowser. From there Geoff knew the way.

He knew the terrain because he had spent the best four years of his life at the Base in Comox. He saw that there was a blast circle around Comox and that the sea leg of the red route went right through the blast circle, with a few comments.

Sure, Geoff reasoned, the Air Force base at 19 Wing Comox would be hit hard. The radioactive fallout would be blown down the Strait of Georgia, right along the red path on the map. He certainly wouldn't want to be exposed to radioactive fallout. Even a few weeks after an attack, exposure to radiation would have serious long-term health consequences.

Suddenly Geoff put the map down and picked up one of the small yellow packets. The label read: *"ThyroLock TM Thyroid blocking for radiation emergencies. 20 Tablets/65 mg each."*

He flipped the packet over and read the warnings and dosage information on the back: *"ThyroLock TM should be taken as soon as possible after an alert from medical officials."* As Geoff read on, it became clear that taking one dose every day for up to ten days was meant to flood the thyroid gland with Potassium Iodide, KI, thereby blocking the uptake of radioactive iodide produced in an atomic blast and carried in the fallout.

By saturating the thyroid gland during the critical days of radioactive fallout, the risks of thyroid cancer and a range of other illnesses would be greatly reduced. The pamphlet included with the tablets also explained how it would be impractical to saturate the thyroid gland with potassium iodide from table salt, as it would require the unsafe ingestion of several cups of table salt per day to achieve the same level of saturation.

He then opened up a densely packed item that the papers had been wrapped around, and found that it contained ten 3M 8233 N100 HEPA Masks, with the label *"Protects against harmful and irritating fumes. Protects against radioactive materials such as uranium and plutonium."*

Geoff now understood that the entire package amounted to an evacuation plan for him and his family, in the event of a nuclear war. He turned his attention back to the map.

The route past 19 Wing could be viable, if winds were favorable and he and his family avoided the period of heavy fallout. The KI tablets and HEPA masks would help prevent harm caused by the ingestion of radioactive particles.

After a few minutes of analysis, the central route across the country looked best to Geoff. It seemed to cover less ground than the other two and had only one short sea leg, from the marina at Lions Bay to a place called French Creek, on the shoreline between Qualicum Beach and Parksville. Once on the Island, there was a short route marked off from French Creek to some location not too far from Coombs, he figured.

The one problem with the central route, Geoff knew from

camping in the region years before, was that the mountainous stretch of secondary roads from Kamloops to Pemberton could be treacherous. Just as he began to fold up the map, he spotted a pattern in a list of data laminated on the back of the map.

The format of the list appeared to be like licenses plates, such as "VA6CJN" and "VE6ADL". There were hundreds of such locations painstakingly plotted along the three routes. Some of them were in green, and some red. Geoff read one of the entries: "Neil Herbert, 240 Hahn Crescent, Dinsmore. (780) 224-4198." Then he read a box at the top of the list: "Ask to be connected with VA7TLB in Qualicum Beach. For any of the radio operators highlighted in green, also mention 'Boss C,'" it read. Then Geoff realized the meaning of the numerical format.

It seemed that the idea was to use amateur radio operators along the way to update his progress or to get assistance from, regardless of which route he used. Even some of the radio operators who lived off the three main routes were plotted. It clearly implied that the way had been paved with some of these stations, increasingly as you approached Vancouver Island.

With a great many questions now in his mind, Major Neumann turned his attention to the single sheaf of paper. Just as he started to read it, his wife barged in and started nagging at him. She was saying something about helping her set the table for dinner. For the first time in a long while, Major Neumann did not drop whatever he was doing, to help with the family chores.

"I'll be there in about 20 minutes, dear, I'm busy now."

He turned his attention back to the letter without looking up. The letter was very short. It was a letter from Casey Callaghan, all right:

Dear Geoff. I haven't written to you before, and this will be my only letter to you. I consider you to be a friend, even though I couldn't open up to you while you were my boss. From our many philosophical discussions at work, you know something about my values, my concerns about the future, and why I left the Forces. Now I can tell you how things turned out. TFG turned out very well, as you must know by now. With that, I purchased acreage on Vancouver Island and built a very large house near Qualicum Beach. Do you remember that book I gave you to read, that the 'SS Colonel' could not finish? Well, some of that was in mind when I built the house. So if you find yourself in a similar situation as the father in that book, you now have a destination. You and your family are welcome to visit for as long as you like. The first tank of gas is on me!

In fact, why not go out today and fill up every jerry can you can get your hands on from the Wing Fuel Point? Why not sign out a few boxes of IMPs and pack up some camping gear into that rugged Tahoe of yours. Keep your tank full. You will know when it's time to take a holiday. SARNEG:MONKEYSPIT Duress Code:PRAY.

Sincerely, your friend,

Casey Callaghan.

That was a coded invitation to a survival bunker, Major Geoff Neumann was certain. Geoff knew that "SARNEG" was a military brevity code word used in Combat Search and

Rescue. "Search and Rescue Numerical Encryption Grid" is a ten-letter isogram which, if known to the sender and the receiver of a message, can be used to encrypt numbers within a message subject to interception. The codeword MONKEYSPIT transposes as 0,1,2,3,4,5,6,7,8,9, so M means Zero and N means 2, and so on. The duress code of "PRAY" was ironic but suitable, as both Casey and Geoff were not religious men. So if he was transmitting from one of those amateur radio stations on the route across Western Canada, but under some form of duress, he would use the word "pray" to tip off Casey that he was in difficulty.

The personal references Casey made in the letter were things only Geoff, Casey and their boss, the "SS Colonel", would understand. Casey had shocked everybody at work when he referred to their boss, Colonel Cameron, as a member of the Gestapo *to his face*, until the Colonel himself acknowledged how much he resembled the Academy Award winning actor who played the very intelligent SS Colonel in an action movie playing in theaters back then.

The reference to that book, about a man trying to lead his family to safety in a disaster, was the final clue. Casey must actually believe that a nuclear war is imminent, thought Major Neumann. And Geoff knew that it was. With his soul, and with his military mind, he knew that it was becoming increasingly likely that a full-scale nuclear war could actually happen.

The War between Israel and Iran had been the first hostile use of nuclear weapons since Monday, August 6, 1945 when the US had dropped 'Little Boy' on the city of Hiroshima, Japan. 140,000 civilians had been vaporized that day, or died soon after due to the effects of the flash, blast, trauma and radiation sickness. That had been about 13 kilotons. Fat Man had been dropped 3 days later on August 9, killing another 80,000 in Nagasaki. Taken together, it had been a shock to the world, but also the only time such weapons had been used in war.

The Middle East Nuclear Exchange war, MENE War, also

called The Second Yom Kippur War, had started when the Iranian device had detonated on 08 October, almost two years ago, on the Israeli Day of Atonement. This was the second Yom Kippur war, after the Arab-Israeli war that lasted only 20 days, 6 to 26 October, 1973. That time, the state of Israel was nearly destroyed. Were it not for a perfectly executed pre-emptive air attack by the Israeli Air Force, obliterating the Egyptian Air Force in the span of less than an hour, the balance would never have tipped the Israeli way. In fact, recalled Major Neumann from his military studies, if not for a series of blunders by the Egyptian Army, Israel could have been overrun by the Egyptian and Syrian armies.

That war had ended better for Israel than the MENE War. This time it would be just a ten day affair, culminating in the massive intervention of the international community and the cease-fire agreed upon by both Israel and Iran, ten days after the biggest car bomb in history.

The device, stored in the trunk of a brand new Audi A8 sedan, was an Iranian variant of the Russian suitcase-sized "W54" 6 kiloton bomb. The Iranian device was an improvement on the former GRU suitcase bomb as the Iranian atomic weapons program had made such strides in the concentration of U-232 that their bomb had an actual yield of almost 9 kilotons. When it was set off, most likely by a cell phone trigger, it immediately vaporized the core of the most important city in Israel.

The expensive Audi A8 did not look out of place parked by a tree on Sderot Rothschild, about fifty meters from the Tel Aviv Stock Exchange. In an instant, the economy of an entire country no longer existed. The blast consumed everything within a half km radius. The subsequent firestorm destroyed everything within a one kilometer radius. Every man, woman and child died in a few terrible seconds.

Major Neumann remembered the horror that he and the rest of the Battle Staff in the Canadian NORAD Region Operations Centre felt as they watched the images unfolding live on TV.

The international media had been alerted to the threat of a bomb in Tel Aviv just minutes before the detonation, so the blast was transmitted live on camera. People were transfixed the world over, staring at the repeated replay of the first use of atomic weapons in the twenty-first century. The image of that tall mushroom cloud rising out of the centre of the city had been burned into Major Neumann's memory.

The terror was brought to an even higher level when a second device was detonated just 44 minutes later in Haifa, to the north, with similar devastation also broadcast live on television. The war between Iran and Israel quickly escalated until Israel's taste for retribution was assuaged and Iran's meager stockpile of devices was spent. In the end, all 11 of Iran's nuclear facilities and underground bunkers had been obliterated, along with nine cities. The death toll in Iran was staggering, well over nine million killed in the attacks and another six million dead within a month from the after-effects.

Things were nearly as bad in Israel, as ten of Iran's nineteen Shahab-5 Kosar *Eternal Life in Paradise* missiles struck their targets in Israel. Five others were rendered inoperative by a defensive EMP burst put up by the Israelis. Iranian warheads struck Jerusalem, Ashdod, Beersheba, Ramat-Gan, Bat-Yam, Askelon, and Lod. When added to the bombs at Tel Aviv and Haifa, the Iranian attack had dealt a crippling blow to Israel, killing close to two million people in the attacks and weeks of suffering that followed.

The four remaining Shahab-5s and all six of the longer ranged Shahib-6s inexplicably struck major non-Israeli cities within the region. It didn't do the Iranians any good to protest that they had not ordered their missiles to attack Cairo, Athens, Istanbul, Bahrain, Dubai, Musqat, Khartoum, Addis Ababa, and Djibouti. American and Russian satellites confirmed that the missiles had been launched from Iran, and confirmed that the missiles were North Korean Taepo Dong-2 boosters upgraded with RD-216 *Enorgomash* rocket engines provided to Iran by Russia back in 1999. Testimony by various experts on the Iranian nuclear program also pointed to China as the source of sophisticated missile electronics, telemetry, and monitoring equipment.

The MENE War had ended swiftly with the cessation of hostilities between Iran and Israel and an aggressive UN Mandate for a European and American force authorized to strip Iran of all nuclear and missile technology. An unprecedented humanitarian effort was organized to bring aid from Europe, Russia, India and the United States.

A year later, while still unclear why Iran had attacked the non-Israeli cities, the Middle East region was a humanitarian disaster, economic failure and a military powder-keg.

With Israel brought to its knees, Islamo-Fascists fanned the flames and filled the void left in many of the surrounding countries which had lost their capital cities to the Iranian missiles. Many in the west were suspicious that Islamo-Fascists had infiltrated the Iranian regime and deliberately targeted the uninvolved cities. Meanwhile, investigators could find no evidence that Iran had any war plans to launch the full force of their nuclear arsenal. In fact, there was mounting evidence that Iran's plan was to destroy only Tel Aviv and Haifa, and to have the blame lay on Jordan, from which the bombs had been smuggled into Israel in the first place.

With the war in Afghanistan having become mired in the cross-border battles reaching deeper and deeper into a failing Pakistan, and with what's left of Israel paranoid that a war of annihilation was being planned by enemies on all sides, the ferocity and power of nuclear warfare was a palpable danger.

Reflecting on the MENE war, and the increasingly unstable global situation, Major Neumann knew that the possibility of a larger conflict escalating into a global nuclear war had become a real possibility. Events were moving in a direction that nobody seemed to want to talk about. It was as if ignoring it or highlighting the few positive developments would somehow make the problems just go away. That kind of head-in-the-sand thinking had started with the economic collapse of 2008 and, despite all the "green shoots", "signs of a moderate recovery", and years of stimulus spending, the US was now in a severe depression. So maybe Casey was right and a full scale nuclear war was on the horizon, even in Canada; Even in Winnipeg.

Geoff knew that as the alternate command and control site to US Continental NORAD region, CONR, the Canadian NORAD Region, CANR, would be among the first targets that would be taken out. The Air Division in Winnipeg was a target of the highest priority. Geoff's office was at the center of the crosshairs.

With a heavy weight on his shoulders, Geoff leaned back in his chair and closed his eyes in concentration. After a few minutes, he calmly sat up and burned the letter, to destroy the secret information. Moreover, the SARNEG and Duress Code must not be left with the map. "Shit!" he said to himself, "he's really laid it all out, hasn't he?"

During dinner with his wife and their two young children, Geoff was unusually silent. He had not told his wife about the contents of the package and would not ask for her permission to do what he had decided to do. After dinner, he told her that he was going out for a few hours and would be home in time to tuck the children in. He then spent the next twenty minutes banging around in the garage before leaving, with no explanation of what he was doing. Gina was too afraid to even ask.

For the first time in a very long time, Gina was excited and terrified by the decisive way that Geoff was behaving. Hopefully he would tell her what he was doing. Whatever it was, Gina knew it was extremely important that she should not interfere.

16

O.P.E.

Robert Beck took down last year's calendar and replaced it with a fresh new year. He reflected on how the world had changed in that year. The fear and insecurity that the previous year had started with, in the aftermath of the terrible MENE War some fifteen months ago, had been a true gift for his candidate.

Rather than throw away the heavily marked up and somewhat tattered planner, Robert carefully rolled it up and inserted it into a paper tube, attached a label, and placed the cylinder into a large box marked: "Parker Transition Team – Robert Beck".

A lifetime student of political history, Robert felt a deep reverence for important historical documents. He knew that this document was important, with its many comments written in his own hand documenting Susan Parker's successful presidential run. Being the man behind the election of the first female president in America was an achievement that Robert accepted as being his contribution to history.

Robert had been campaign director for the former Governor of Montana. Now he was the head of her Transition

Team. With just fifteen days before Inauguration Day, Robert had turned his full attention to the transition. Of course he knew that he would be the President's Chief of Staff, and they had long since selected most of the Cabinet. Now they faced the daunting task of sorting out as many as 750 key appointments and directorships which would ensure that the Parker agenda would be effectively carried out.

President-Elect Parker had an agenda. Her vision was to change the path of the United States and to restore the prominence of the Constitution as the cornerstone document of American identity. She saw herself as a champion of the founding fathers vision for America, and her campaign had been centered on this theme.

Under the former President, the United States had attempted what she considered to be a socialist transformation into a command economy with an obscenely expanded government role. Government interference in the free market was a particular problem, as it was not limited to the wage and price controls that the former administration had resorted to, but also the increasingly frequent interventions and down right manipulations of the marketplace to such an extreme that the capitalist system itself had begun to collapse. The currency crisis, and hyper-inflation that went with a collapsing dollar, was the direct result of this insane explosion of government interference in the life of the nation, she knew. And her task, on *day one* after all the pomp and ceremony of the Inauguration, was to restore confidence in the United States of America, in the US dollar and in Democracy.

She had to admit that it was not all the fault of the last administration, as the actions of the US Treasury and the Federal Reserve system were at the core of the problem. The profligacy and short-sightedness of Congress should have been constrained by responsible monetary policy rather than being fueled by an unstoppable printing press that was churning out trillions of paper dollars to throw at the economic crisis. The abuse of the world's reserve currency was the root problem.

The history of the US dollar as a world reserve currency would soon end in failure, Susan Parker knew from the data presented to her by the highly secret briefing she was given by The Secretary of the Treasury. The Federal Reserve had tried everything they could to hide the massive monetary inflation, including making further changes to the definition of *inflation*. The dishonesty of it reminded her of another president's famous testimony: "It depends on what the meaning of the word 'is' is."

After quietly removing energy and food costs, and by allowing substitutions of one good for another, the basket of items used to define core inflation had become a basket of goods that had no relation to the items which people actually consumed on a daily basis. Similar chicanery in employment statistics allowed the government to claim that unemployment was only 12%, when it was actually over 30%, if one used the more honest definitions that had once given government statistics real validity. Now the numbers were no longer taken seriously.

All of this sophistry would become a thing of the past once her administration officially took the reins. In order to restore the integrity and servitude of the government *for the people,* the first order of the day was to restore the *Constitution of the United States* by returning to sound currency. Among the next highest priorities would be to delouse the US government by making it illegal to earn a living from lobbying for government influence. This, she knew, would be a tall order as the entire machinery of the US Senate, US Congress, and the Executive Branch had become a juggernaut powered entirely by influence peddling. This return to the revolutionary principles that the United States was founded upon would amount to a *second* American Revolution.

In the days before Inauguration day, however, President Parker was having her eyes opened. She and her Transition Team were briefed-in on every major file that the outgoing administration had been contending with. They were also given advice on key decisions that had yet to be made, in the interest of continuity and stability during the transition.

President Parker and her team soon learned that they would be facing a currency collapse and imminent social collapse within the United States, increased international tensions due to the knock-on effects of the MENE War, *and the requirement for direct US involvement in a pre-emptive war with Pakistan.*

Susan Parker, along with Joseph Alderman and Jones Webber, her choices for Secretaries of Defense and State, had been given a ninety-minute briefing on the unfolding crisis in Pakistan by their outgoing counterparts. They were told that an Islamo-fascist regime was taking over Pakistan's nuclear arsenal, comprised of over 180 viable Highly Enriched Uranium, HEU-based warheads. The warheads were stored in component form, with the fissile materials stored separately from the explosives packages, and also from the delivery platforms. But the new regime was consolidating control over the arsenal and would be in a position to begin to assemble the weapons systems within weeks. A war between Pakistan and India was imminent.

The briefing then went into the details. India and Pakistan had a long history of conflict which stemmed from the poorly executed division of British India into India, Pakistan and Bangladesh. The root of the problem was, as with many other crises in the region, with religious divisions left simmering from previous wars. India had shown great restraint after a series of high profile terrorist attacks from groups based in Pakistan.

After it had become clear that the Pakistani Intelligence Directorate had been incompetent if not complicit in the 2008 terrorist attack at Mumbai, India became increasingly distrustful of Pakistan. These events exacerbated the cycle of espionage and subterfuge on both sides, increasing the tension between the two long-time adversaries.

The situation became urgent ten days ago, with a

successful coup orchestrated by radicalized Islamic factions within the Pakistani Army. After infiltrating key positions within Pakistan's Directorate for Inter-Services Intelligence as far back as 1998, radicalized Islamists loyal to Mualana Abdul Aziz had built up their organization in a patient and methodical manner. They bided their time waiting for the NATO adventure in Afghanistan to come to its inevitable demise. Their goal of staging a coup and converting Pakistan into a true Islamic state under Sharia Law was now being achieved.

On 8 January, the anniversary of the assassination of Benazir Bhutto, Abdula Aziz's men swung into action. They took control of the organs of government, radio and television stations, and the vast majority of Pakistani military bases. The nascent *True Islamic State* immediately began transforming Pakistan's 180 million people into Shia Muslims, with harsh new laws and Fatwa published on a daily basis in the days following the coup. The speed at which the situation was evolving in Pakistan was alarming, and could not have happened at a worse time for the United States.

Islamic fundamentalists now had over 180 nuclear weapons, averaging 30 kilotons apiece. With the successful fielding of the Shaheen-1 and Ghazvani missiles, the radicalized Pakistani military had a new generation of more accurate missiles that could reach 650 and 300 km respectively. The twenty or so Shaheen-II missiles, moreover, had an extended range of 2,500km, albeit with a smaller 10 Kiloton warhead.

In a highly classified document entitled "Pakistan – Strike Options", a range of scenarios and corresponding military options was laid out. For a breakdown of the Pakistani state with the emergence of a radicalized Shia regime, there were no easy choices. The plans had been updated in recent years in recognition that NATO forces would lose the war in Afghanistan and be forced to make a strategic withdrawal from the region.

It was a worst case scenario, but one that the United States was required to address. As the MENE War had shown, leaving nuclear weapons in the hands of Islamo-fascists was simply far too dangerous a situation to leave unaddressed.

It would be the Parker administration that would have to complete *Operation Peregrine Eagle*, or *"OPE"*. Susan Parker was half way through bursting out in laughter at the obvious nod to Stanley Kubrik's "Dr. Strangelove", but choked it back when she realized the full implications of *OPE*.

"This is madness!" she said, looking at her two closest advisors for support. "We'll be starting a major war, with a nuclear armed enemy motivated by the Islamo-fascism that has just defeated us in Afghanistan!"

"I know, it's ludicrous, but unless you come up with a better option, and fast, this is our only option," the outgoing Secretary of State explained. "The Joint Chiefs have not come up with anything else."

"It'll be a well-coordinated strike using bunker-buster and other custom-selected munitions," an Air Force general began explaining. "We will hit all 24 sites simultaneously. This will *disrupt* their ability to coordinate an attack and *deny* them the initiative. Follow-on cruise missiles will further *dislocate* their forces, which will then be *destroyed* by our Indian allies. The Indians will put 120,000 troops over the border and into all key objectives within 72 hours, and a further 250,000 general-duty troops will seize control of the entire nation within a further 7 days," he explained.

"We do not need a lecture on basic military doctrine, General Adams," the incoming Secretary of Defense, Joseph Alderman, objected to the general's tone. *He* was going to determine the strategic objectives of any war conducted by the Parker Administration, and not be pushed around by the military.

Without missing a beat, the outgoing Secretary of State jumped in to support the General. "Unlike Afghanistan and Iraq, and Libya, this won't be *our* war to get bogged down in. It'll be an Indian operation. Our military liaisons have worked out the details and the Singh administration has not only signed on to the plan, but has repeatedly implored us to help with the opening moves."

"This really has to happen?"

"Yes, Madame President Elect," General Adams said, with a more respectful tone. "Our role will be to take out the primary and retaliatory weapons and to hit their *Decisive Points* to constrain their military capabilities. The Indian military, with the billion plus population to back it up, has the weapons, the proximity, and the political will to defeat these Islamo-fascists once and for all. But they need our support, as they don't have the deep-penetrating munitions that are essential to this plan," he concluded. Seeing resignation and acceptance on President-Elect Parker's face, he went into the details.

"As you can see with the OPE summary, the negotiation and coordination between our military and India has been completed. *Phase One*, the preparation and pre-positioning of our air strike force, as well as naval units into the Indian Ocean, will be complete by the end of your first week in office. The schedule calls for you to give the Executive Order: "Mandrake", to begin the stealth bomber and cruise missile attacks. Simultaneously, the Indian invasion begins. They will provide their own air and missile support. They do request that we take out the Pakistani naval forces, which consist of less than a dozen major surface ships and only four functioning SSK diesel subs."

"What will be the likely Pakistani response to the Indian mobilization over the next two weeks?" Alderman asked.

"While the Pak army is aware of some of the Indian movements, we project that they will be confused and disordered by the initial attacks. The leading units of the Indian thrust will gradually move to their starting off points, disguised in part by a deceptive media story about military assistance to floods in the Jodhpur region. So hopefully India will have the advantage of surprise on their part. The

Pakistanis will certainly be reeling from our air strikes," General Adams said.

"But what about it escalating into a larger-scale war?" asked President-Elect Parker.

"Couldn't Iran come into it? – and what about China? Don't they lease a naval base in Pakistan?" interjected Parker's choice for Sec-Def, Jones Webber. "Aren't China and Pakistan allies?"

"They *were* allies," replied the Secretary of State. "That was until the coup. China is having its own problems with Muslim extremism, so we don't expect any problems from the Chinese on this one. We have not contacted the Chinese, the Russians, nor any other Security Council members on this issue, other than to schedule a conference on the implications of the emerging new regime in Pakistan for early March in Vienna – a conference we won't be attending, to say the least," referring to a deception plan meant to convince the enemy that an attack would not occur until some time after the conference.

"By that time, the war will be over and we'll be dealing with the fallout from our participation in India's invasion of Pakistan. That will be your problem, Madame President, but our advice is to make no apologies for the United States standing behind its age-old promise to never allow nuclear weapons to fall into the hands of terrorists."

After the meeting, once President-Elect Parker had discussed the new information with her trusted advisors, she accepted that there really were no other options.

Three weeks later, as President Parker prepared to address to the nation from the Oval Office, the Indo-Pak War had been all but wrapped up. It had not gone as well as hoped. Even though the Islamist regime in Pakistan had been fooled by the deception plan, and had been under the misguided notion that once again America would take many months seeking United

Nations resolutions and assembling a large coalition of international support, the attack had not succeeded in destroying all the nuclear weapons.

The majority of the coup leaders were killed in the first wave of cruise missile attacks, aimed at decapitating the enemy. Those who survived, however, were surprisingly effective at communicating with their forces, who launched a major strike against India and the American naval fleet.

While 40% of the Pakistani nuclear force was taken out in the initial attacks, thirty of the sixty-four Pakistani nuclear missiles which had been prepared for launch-on-warning had made it out of their silos without being destroyed. Of these, one destroyed an entire Carrier Battle Group in the Gulf of Oman, and twenty-two reached their targets in India. The rest were taken out by American and Indian antimissile defenses.

The Indian retaliation had been harsh, with the cities of Karachi, Hyderabad, Multan, Quetta, Islamabad and Peshawar being completely obliterated by a barrage of twenty-six Indian missiles. There was no follow-on strike from Pakistan.

While many of the Pakistani military bases had been utterly destroyed, a large number of air and land bases were left intact for Indian forces to seize. The bases had been set aside to support India's occupation of the devastated nation that had lost 24 million people in a matter of hours, and was now faced with 30 to 50 million people in desperate straits.

The suffering and death in Pakistan and India, with a combined death toll of over 50 million and rising in the aftermath of the Indo-Pak War, had matched the death-toll of the Second World War - yet the world didn't care.

Indian military units were not on a humanitarian mission, and there was no talk of an international humanitarian operation to help Pakistan. An emergency resolution by the UN Security Council, calling for India to cease hostilities and to withdraw from Pakistan *once it had achieved its military objective of disarming Pakistan* had passed unanimously. Russia and China had not used their veto powers. It was clear that the superpowers were united in their opposition to the Islamo-fascist ideology that had led to two regional nuclear wars in as many years.

This gave India a free hand to root out the Islamist leaders and provide aid only to the more moderately inclined political and tribal groups. The plan was to remake Pakistan into a secular democracy mimicking the Indian model, after a ten to twelve year occupation. India planned to spend those years restoring democracy, weeding out Islamo-Fascism and stripping Pakistan of all manner of nuclear capability.

The reconstruction and humanitarian resources of India were focused on dealing with the devastation that was caused by the Pakistani missiles. With an entire continent to disperse its military resources, and having chosen the hour of the conflict, India had preserved its military forces and had evacuated key military and political personnel to safe locations before the war. Even so, India had lost over 25 million souls and would lose a further 20 to the effects of the war. However at less than four percent of its population, these losses were considered modest by military standards.

The knock-on effects of the Indo-Pak war began to ripple across the globe. In China, there was a growing sense of fear and unease as the loss of one of the pawns on the chess board, with Pakistan being taken out of play, left China more exposed to a newly empowered India. Now that Pakistan was no longer a constant threat to India, the gargantuan might of the Indian subcontinent could more readily focus on their competition with China for regional ascendancy. This caused the Chinese premier some consternation; but it suited General Bing.

In the United States and the Russian Federation, the concern was that the two regional nuclear wars had pricked a big hole in nuclear deterrence. Nuclear weapons were now being used to settle long-simmering scores. There was a growing sense that a new era of warfare had begun. The world may not have recognized the significance of the revolution in military affairs represented by the MENE and Indo-Pak wars, but the Russians and Americans had. Contingency Plans to raise the readiness of nuclear forces, reactivate stockpiled weapons, and to pour money into nuclear and civil defense supplies were being activated.

Russian President Ivan Valeriovich Dvorkin feared that the direct American involvement in the Indo-Pak war had ushered in a new era of American interventionism.

Dvorkin, the one-time Air Force General who had seized the reigns of power left by the disintegration of the Putin – Medvedev regime, had begun to restore order over the chaos and social unrest that had boiled over in Russia. By ruthlessly using the fist of the Russian military against its own people, he had crushed any opposition to his vision for a renewal of the Russian Empire. But with America throwing its weight around, Dvorkin felt as though Russia now had a target on its back, and began preparations for defending Mother Russia.

With the nuclear warfare genie out of the bottle, Dvorkin accelerated plans to upgrade Russia's Strategic Rocket Forces. He signed a variety of orders which would begin the process of reconditioning, refueling, re-assembling and otherwise raising the readiness and lethality of Russia's missiles.

One urgent set of orders he signed was to bring another 2,000 older missiles back to strategic readiness, out of the stockpiles that the world believed to have been 'destroyed' under START II. The next series of orders, codenamed "OPUSTOSHENIYE", or *DEVASTATION*, would see that a stockpile of over four hundred 25-megaton warheads would be reassembled. These most powerful of warheads had been decommissioned under the 1991 START I treaty, but the fissionable materials and explosives packages were still available. Their destruction had been delayed for decades by incompetence, cost and technical difficulties. Once re-constituted, the warheads were to be installed on reconditioned R36 missiles converted from the unreliable rail launchers of the '80s onto older, though reliable, road-mobile launchers based in the Perm region.

These monsters were designed for only one use: to destroy and render uninhabitable enemy population centers in a retaliatory strike. While they could be used against hardened military targets; however, they could not be produced in large enough quantities to make a meaningful dent in America's widely dispersed weapons silos and were therefore best used for all-out extermination of the enemy population. This was the cornerstone of the MAD doctrine.

The reactivation of these massive fission-fusion-fission devices was the embodiment of Dvorkin's belief that through superior numbers and the ferocity of their attack, Russia could actually win a nuclear war. Whoever took on the Russian people, Dvorkin thought with satisfaction as he placed the OPUSTOSHENIYE files in the out-box on his enormous antique desk, would be in for a surprise or two; or four hundred.

In the first months of her administration, while the world began to recover from the dual shocks of the MENE and Indo-Pak wars, President Parker had taken office and taken the reigns of power. With the Indo-Pak war behind her by the end of February, she turned her attention to the economy. By the end of March, she had kept her campaign promise to restore the US Currency.

President Parker signed *Executive Order* 13971 and 13972 on 21 March, which created a bank holiday from 22 to 28 March. The week was intended to allow the US Treasury, US Post Office, US Military services and the various levels of government to execute the two ground-shaking Executive Orders.

The first Order was entitled "Abolition of the Federal Reserve Cartel", which effectively seized all assets of the cartel of private banks which had operated the Federal Reserve System and supplied Federal Reserve Notes used as currency in the United States ever since 1913. The Order also transferred all assets and instruments of the Federal Reserve back to the US Treasury, ending 100 years of organized fraud.

The second Order was entitled "United States Treasury - Dollar Restoration". In the preamble to the Order, President Parker reaffirmed the Constitution of the United States as the fundamental law of the land; stressing that under the constitution, only silver and gold could be used as money. Therefore, issuance of fiat money, constituting *a promise to pay* and fundamentally a fraudulent scheme, was *illegal*. The Federal Reserve Notes *had never been legitimate legal tender in the United States,* and were immediately outlawed. A newly minted *US Treasury Dollar - Gold*, "Dollar-G", or "$G" currency would be issued, backed by the gold held in the vaults of the Treasury of the United States. Effective 30 April, the $G would be exchangeable for gold bullion or certified US Gold coins of the realm.

This time, importantly, there would be no attempt to confiscate gold. The $G notes would be printed and distributed in proportion to the actual reserves of gold held in the vaults.

The first independent audit of gold in over fifty years had been conducted in the first eight weeks of the Parker administration, under the watchful eye of the new Secretary of the Treasury, Mark Rogers. The audit revealed that the Federal Reserve had been using the gold reserves of the United States to manipulate the price of gold. The effort to support the value of Federal Reserve Notes had been a disaster as the Fed had "permanently leased" and "swapped" increasing quantities of gold over the last decade, eroding the reserves by over 2,000 tons in the process. So the US actually had 6,116 tons of gold rather than the 8,133 tons that had been reported for decades.

With 6,116 tons of gold at 32,152 Troy ounces per ton, the US treasury's only real money was the 196,641,632 ounces of gold. That was less than two thirds of an ounce per citizen. There were $79 trillion dollars of unfunded liabilities, entitlement commitments, Federal Reserve notes in circulation, and Treasury Bills. This meant that for the United States to make good on its obligations, each ounce of gold would have to be worth $ 289,867.40 in Federal Reserve Notes. So the Federal Reserve currency was essentially worthless. It had lost its intrinsic value in 1971, when President Nixon closed the gold window, and abandoned any pretence of a gold standard. This conversion of the US dollar into a fiat currency would take forty years to reach its forgone conclusion. With the US dollar entrenched as the world's reserve currency, and the dollar finally becoming recognized as worthless, the economic engine of the world was sputtering and about to quit. President Parker's elegant solution was to *pull out the spark plug*.

Rather than issue the $G at an exchange rate of $290,000 per ounce gold, President Parker and her team had come up with a revolutionary concept: Let it happen - *let the banks fail.* Let the businesses and large corporations evolve or die, let the government spending programs come to an end, and let the US default on its debt obligations, but don't let the American people suffer a corrupt banking system or the tyranny of credit and debt for one day longer.

The $G was issued through the Post Office, not the banks. Every American resident was given a US Postal Money Order valued at $G 5,950. It was exchangeable for gold at the permanently fixed exchange rate of $G 10,000 per ounce, and silver at $G 500 per ounce. The newly minted gold and silver coins ranged from one ounce down to 1/100 ounce. The coins contained alloys to make them durable, making their weights slightly heavier.

Alternatively, the money order could be exchanged for $G 5,950 in paper US Treasury Dollar – Gold banknotes that had been secretly printed in the weeks prior to the announcement. The new paper money had an unusual appearance, a plastic feel, complex anti-forgery features and the guarantee: "Backed by the gold of the United States Treasury". The various denominations sported nostalgic images of the founding fathers on one side, and iconic American imagery on the other. Each banknote bore the signature of the Secretary of the Treasury, Mark Rogers.

All that inhabitants of the United States had to do in order to claim their share of the US Treasury was to present themselves to the Postal Official; swear the Oath of Allegiance to the Constitution of the United States; fill out a card with their legal name, place and country of birth, marital status, and list their immediate family. Then, with the firm and helpful assistance of the many soldiers and police personnel augmenting the Postal officials, affix all ten finger prints onto the back of the form as a record of their having taken the Oath, and then receive two items. The first was a permanent, deep scar and tattoo on the right index finger, a visible sign of their having been welcomed back into the United States. The second was the Postal Money Order which the "renewed citizen" of the USA was entitled to spend in any manner they saw fit.

The 100 million or so landed immigrants and other visitors were now just as entitled to swear their allegiance to the Constitution and flag, and become American citizens, as were the original 237 million citizens of the United States before the *Second American Revolution.*.

President Parker's team knew that this process would create mayhem. The entire banking and economic system was built on debt and credit; it was not geared to putting *real* money into the hands of the people. The public and service sectors, moreover, suddenly had no guarantee that their services would be needed the next day. With no credit cards, bank loans and other instruments having any validity, all banks were at risk of failing as they suddenly had no claim on the real property that had once been collateralized.

So the coming days and weeks were expected to be very chaotic, as those banks and other institutions that could rapidly adapt to the restoration of a sound money economy would create new products and enticements to get people to deposit some of their $G or physical gold into their vaults. Others, who could not convince citizens that their money would be secure, or who did not have the ingenuity or creativity to offer the newly empowered citizens anything of real value, were doomed to fail.

Local, State and Federal Governments, and the myriad Government agencies, were suddenly without the deep pockets of the deficit spending - dollar printing machine of the past. The new order would be *Government of the People, for the People, and by the People*. This, along with the financial emancipation of the population from the tyranny of credit and debt, meant that citizen engagement in decision making was going to become intense. Without popular support, the vast majority of public programs, entitlements and basic political pork would become extinct.

While these events would play out over the coming months, all the Parker Administration could do was call out large numbers of Militia, National Guard, and Military to protect public infrastructure and to assist the police in keeping the streets safe as the citizens remade their country into a Constitutional Democracy, as it had been from 1776 until 1913.

These months, from Inauguration in January through to the restoration of the US Treasury Dollar-Gold standard in April, had been truly revolutionary. Now, heading into the second week of May, Robert Beck and the rest of the Parker Administration were seeing the world come around to the wisdom and efficiency of a true gold standard. Austrian economic thought had replaced the Keynesian economics of the Welfare State. The economic system of the world now had a single world reserve currency that was redeemable anywhere, was not a liability to anyone, was immune to inflation, and would permit the worldwide economy to begin to function once again. The world had gold.

From this perspective, it was essential to the Parker Administration that US Citizens, and the rest of the world, believed that the new US "$G" would be convertible to gold from the outset and that the US would be constrained by the gold standard. There could be no deficit spending. All Government spending programs would have to be funded entirely by Government income, from flat rate income tax and from the Government share in the bounties that a healthy economy and the riches of the American territory could generate. Not one $G more.

And President Parker knew that in defaulting on its international debts, and cutting out a large number of powerful people in Washington, she had created a great many enemies.

17

LETTERS

15 March: 9 Weeks Before NEW

Casey had been prepared to act quickly if a game-changing event occurred. When the new President had thrown American support behind the Indian invasion of Pakistan in February, Casey thought that such a moment may have arrived. While he was assessing the impact of the pre-emptive strike against the new Pakistani regime, and watching the consequence of the Indian invasion of the failed state, he prepared to act. But when the American president initiated yet another sudden and unexpected move in mid-March, by essentially admitting that the United States was bankrupt and would default on its debts,

Casey was certain that the long dreaded moment had come.

Philosophically, Casey agreed that the Federal Reserve system was an illegal cartel and he certainly welcomed the idea of an international gold standard being initiated by the United States, however he also knew that such a dramatic change in world affairs would not come without major upheavals and violence. Whether it would be reprisals from those who had lost billions in the default of the massive US Debts, or simply as a consequence of the death of the old order, the world was going to fly apart at the seams. So it was time, Casey decided, to pull the trigger and send out the invitations.

It took five days for them to reach their destinations. Casey had mailed them out individually as each personalized package was completed. Some were sent to friends and associates whom Casey Callaghan sincerely hoped would eventually make their way to the HOTH, if disaster should come. Others were sent to men Casey had no particular bond with but who had skills and knowledge that could be useful in a disaster context.

A few would come from the Canadian Air Force. Casey was optimistic that at least a few of the guys like Ken, Dave, Bruce, Geoff, Pat, and Coops would find their way to the HOTH. He sent the more personalized letters to these military men. On something of a whim, however, Casey sent letters to some military men who were not his friends at all.

Major Stradins opened his own Callaghan letter after he had taken off his uniform and settled into his favorite chair. Rodney Stradins had no particular fondness for Callaghan. Casey had worked with him at Wing Operations and on more than one occasion they had respectfully agreed to disagree. They had nothing in common, moreover, as Stradins's one and only hobby was bow hunting, while Callaghan was into what, construction? Stradins remembered how Callaghan had always been involved in some kind of renovation or new house project.

The letter from Callaghan was very short, simply saying hello and letting Stradins know that he had built his retirement house in Qualicum Beach, with "all the features from his past houses, and more!" Casey had also included some crazy kind of map, with blast radius circles around some cities and all the bases in Western Canada, with symbols and a legend explaining the location of various amateur radio operators. Rod put it down to Casey being like some of those guys at the Wing who thought that the wars in Iran and Pakistan meant that the world was headed towards a big war.

The letter concluded with an open invitation.

Why would I ever want to visit Casey? thought Rod . He attributed it to some kind of mid-life crisis and tossed the package onto a shelf above his desk. Rod intended to throw it out, but decided to give it a few days. Something strange was going on with that man, to be sure, but he also had a begrudging respect for Casey.

He recalled how Casey had been given a difficult task, to organize an exercise to validate the "OPERATION ABICUS" contingency plans for 17 Wing, in preparation for the expected disruptions associated with the Y2K event.

Casey had only been with the unit for a few weeks, but he came up with an intensive, four day long exercise. Every conceivable contingency was exercised, ranging from a hostage taking at the Wing Comptroller's office to failures of the phone lines, power lines, sewer system and water lines. On top of these breakdowns, a variety of very complex military missions were also thrown at the Wing. There had even been a simulation of extreme cold temperatures making operations much more difficult. The Wing had to react to simulated water line failures, mechanical breakdowns, aircraft servicing difficulties and exposure injuries in the simulated -40 C weather. The exercise had been the largest multi-agency exercise ever held in Manitoba, with participation from police, fire, ambulance as well as provincial and federal emergency response organizations.

The exercise was a success and had proven to be a much harder workout than the actual Y2K non-event had later proven to be. The one thing he had taken away from observing how Casey Callaghan had performed during that time was that he was an extraordinarily careful contingency planner. Rod thought of Casey as having some undiagnosed form of Obsessive Compulsive Disorder, OCD, because of the level of detail Casey put into his planning assignments. He challenged the troops by throwing difficult problems at them, and the Wing's personnel rose to the occasion. Casey always said: "The troops never fail! It's we officers in the chain of command who are always the weakest link." And that was how it had gone. The troops demonstrated their readiness to do their jobs; the cluster-fucks were in Ops.

When he thought about the carefully prepared map that Casey had sent him, Major Rod Stradins began to think that maybe there was a good reason for it. Only weeks later did he fully understand what the package had represented; he regretted his lack of insight for the remainder of his life.

18

STOCKING UP - HARD

30 April: 3 Weeks Before NEW

Tanya was the first one up. She looked forward to the last day of the month. It was when she and Casey usually went over their finances and really discussed their many projects.

There had been a flurry of expenditures after they had first moved in, with a big up-tick when the economy got really haywire. At that time, Casey took advantage of the latest economic crisis and bought a fleet of cars and a variety of small machines.

Casey had explained that if the supply chains fail, labor saving machines, vehicles, spare parts and gasoline would become very scarce.

Diesel, on the other hand, could be produced from a variety of sources during a crisis, as the Germans had proven in the Second World War. On a modest scale, Bio-diesel can be made from vegetable oil, a variety of household waste products, algae and even fungus collected in the forest.

Casey had hired a student at British Columbia Institute of Technology to determine the most idiot-proof method to make bio-diesel from resources widely available on Vancouver Island. Algal bio-fuel turned out to be the best option.

Casey had the student negotiate a price for a complete small-scale bio-fuel operation. Then he purchased two complete systems and all the spare parts and other hard-to find items so he would have the capability to fuel his next purchase. The Ford dealership in Nanaimo could not believe their luck when Casey snapped up five vehicles, all Fords and all diesels.

In the end they bought two new Super Duty F-250 Long Box King Cabs, a G-Series full sized van outfitted to carry up to 12 passengers, and two identical Ford Invaders – the biggest SUV on the market. As part of the deal, the excited dealer threw together a crate of spare parts, including some essential electronic components. Casey explained that the fleet would be used at a remote logging camp so he wanted everything his mechanic might need to keep the vehicles going for years without interruption. The dealer's lead mechanic kept throwing in more and more spares as the salesman tried to keep up with the tab.

When the tally came, Tanya had a go at the dealers and ground him down on the price of the vehicles first, then got into the details of the spares list. When the dealer caved, the deal was done.

With the fleet of new vehicles nicely parked in the paved area on the high side of the HOTH, Casey did the entire thing again at another dealership, this time buying four small electrical vehicles. He wanted some electric cars which were easy to maintain, and ran on an infinitely renewable power source.

With the helical wind power as a backup at the HOTH, electricity would be a reliable energy source even if things went very badly with the world. ZENN "Runabouts" were very handy for short trips, with a 200km range between charges and speeds up to 100 km/h. They were also extremely easy to maintain. The spares package for the ZENNs amounted to a few replacement brushes, some accelerator-generator assemblies, and some odd little electrical components

The nine new vehicles had not made all that much of a dent in the family finances. The Callaghan's were flush, because Canada had joined with the US in their second attempt to restore their currency, this time going all the way to the Gold Standard. The US and Canada pegged their currencies to gold, at $G 10,000 per ounce. So the world's producing gold mines were literally pulling real money out of the ground.

Casey's gold mine, TFG, had ramped up annual production to 220,000 ounces. This made TFG a great investment, particularly when considering the wave of state seizures of gold mines and other strategic assets in many of the more volatile regions of the world. Even with the new Gold Tax in Canada and increased costs for fuel, the stock was now $G 65 a share. Even after Casey's profligate spending to build and equip the HOTH, the Callaghan's 140,000 remaining shares were now valued at $G 9,625,000.

As Casey tried to explain it to Tanya during their morning coffee that day, the reasons for their gold investment having gone ballistic should not be a source of comfort.

"I don't understand. We're rich now, so why not relax and enjoy it a bit? Why don't we take a trip when the kids get out of school in June?" Tanya asked, as she added an extra spoon of sugar to the latte she was preparing for Casey on her newest kitchen appliance.

"Because even if the gold standard works fine for us, and appears to be restoring confidence in international markets, the vast majority of people in the States are going to have problems with it. Most of them were dependent on an income stream that has now suddenly been cut off. Their pensions are gone. It will take months for the government to re-calibrate all those benefit programs. They might cut off all those entitlements altogether."

"Why?"

"Because the US can't just print money any more."

"What do you mean? They are issuing those pretty new Treasury Gold Dollars and gold coins now, aren't they?"

"Yes, but every dollar they print now has to be backed up by physical gold. They can't spend more than they have. If they do, their currency will become a fiat currency again and not a gold standard, so the entire system would collapse again."

"I understand a lot of people will lose their government benefits, and will really suffer. But how does that affect us up here in Canada?"

"It's not just the unfortunate people who will be hurt by these changes, it's the instability that all of this is creating. The Chinese, Russians, Japanese and other creditor nations are angry at the Americans for defaulting on their debt. A large proportion of American citizens are not happy about the revolutionary changes taking place in their country, and a lot of powerful people in the States have just lost control of the system that they had bought and paid for, through lobbying and influence peddling," Casey explained, getting a bit worked up.

"So?"

"So, it's like a room full of kerosene right now, all it would take is one match, and KABOOM!" Casey said.

"Come on, it's not that bad, is it?"

"President Parker has done a remarkable thing in attempting to restore the US Gold Standard. It could work, and put the US back on top. The rest of the world seems to have recognized pure gold itself as the world's reserve currency. But by killing the spending power offered by a fiat currency system, and all the political influence that the spending power offered, she has made a great many enemies. And with so many enemies, and with such chaos in the world after those two nuclear wars, anything can happen." Casey slowed down as he recognized the look on his wife's face. She wasn't big on economics and geopolitics, but she knew what it meant when powerful people were threatened. That theme had played out enough times in Russian history.

"OK. I understand now. You're saying that she did the

right thing, and it *could* work, but it's made things more dangerous for everybody in the meantime, right?"

"Right. And we won't know how it worked out for a year or two, if we have that long."

"What do you mean?"

"I mean, it could all come apart in an instant. Do you remember when Benazir Bhutto flew back to Pakistan?"

"You mean that brave woman who knew she would be assassinated?" Tanya replied, starting to get the point.

"Yeah. Remember watching on TV, when she got off that plane? We talked about how brave she was, and that she might not make it through the week. Well, now we are watching another brave woman, President Parker, taking an equally brave step."

"You think they will kill her?"

"That's one of the possibilities. Or a civil war in the US. Or a World War. Or the annexation of Canada by the United States. Or peace and love breaks out all over the world, and nature somehow cleans up the mess we're making of her planet."

"What if things don't work out well? What if President Parker is assassinated, or there really is a war?"

"I want to sell most of our shares in TFG, and convert the proceeds to gold and silver coins. We can hang on to about 40,000 shares, but I want to liquidate the rest, and complete outfitting the HOTH to be ready for what I think's coming."

"Why the big rush? Won't we have time to assess how things are going in the world? Do you really think it's not going to work itself out?"

"I just can't stop thinking about how many people President Parker has pissed off. The political and social elite will hijack her agenda, or kill it altogether. Once that happens, this moment of sunshine that her gold standard has ushered in will be snuffed out," Casey said, somberly. "And then all bets are off. I don't think the system can take a third currency collapse in as many years. I don't know how this will play out, but the economic system will fail in a matter of months unless the Parker Administration can hold it all together. This is the moment of truth. If the globalized system truly fails, we'll be turning the clock back by a hundred years or more. We'll have to learn to live with what we can grow, make, or recycle. There won't be any more trucks coming," Casey concluded.

"OK. Until things get better, we'll assume the worst. We'll stock up and stay close to home." Tanya sounded unconvinced.

"You've seen it already, Tanya, when you came back from the fabric store with nothing to show for it," Casey reminded her.

"Yeah, but that's just because it's getting dangerous to shop in town, you can still buy stuff. It's just not worth taking the risk of being mugged or carjacked when we already have everything we need here," Tanya countered.

"But if things are about to get really bad, then it's time we make a big push and stock up HARD, to be ready to lock down."

"OK, OK. We'll get started on it. What can I do?"

They got into the major stocking up over the next two weeks. For Tanya, it was exciting to see how fast things moved when they had money to absolutely burn. Casey was like a general in a war, taking decisive action.

The level of activity at the HOTH was significant. There was a constant parade of "truck-and-pups" delivering as much as possible in the shortest time, ranging from soil and split firewood to deliveries of bulk food. Casey and Yuri assembled rugged shelving racks to store the chain saws, generators, pumps and other small machines that made the workshop side of the garage look more like a tool rental business. With so much firewood and equipment being packed into the massive garage there was no room for the many new vehicles. Two sea-containers were delivered to the HOTH, and Marc prepared a flat area behind the woodshed for them with his big '450. He left an eight foot gap between them, which Yuri and Danny covered with wooden beams, plywood, and a thin layer of earth. This made enough space to provide secure long-term covered parking for all nine vehicles. It also meant that most of the vehicles would be protected from an EMP burst by virtue of being in their own Faraday cages.

They lined the perimeter of the barn with three solid rows of densely packed hay bales, and then assembled a scaffold onto which they stacked two layers of the heavy round bales, making the inside of the barn something of a tomb. They also squirreled away specialized feed supplies and a variety of food additives. They had already stored the tools, rigging, harnesses, tack and other items they would need.

Casey and Tanya gave the task of arranging the initial stock of farm animals to their children. The girls took the lead, but gave Liam and Justin important tasks. In total, they chose two pregnant Canadian mares, a pregnant sow, a dairy cow, a rooster and a dozen laying hens. Little Donnie got a black lab puppy, Abbey. After that, the HOTH was also a farm.

Casey wanted lots of fuel. He stockpiled 3,300 gallons of fuel: two thirds diesel, one third regular unleaded gasoline. The fuel was pre-mixed with antioxidants and other treatments to extend the life of the fuel for as much as ten to fifteen years, only requiring simple annual additives. He had the equipment to fabricate diesel if push came to shove.

When they took stock of all the food stored in the many caches and bunkers in and around the HOTH, Tanya and Casey figured there was enough food to feed a group of fifty people for ten years. But would that be enough for what was coming?

19

KUGLUKTUK

20 May: Day of NEW

It was not until the early morning of 20 May that the weather finally broke. Ken had expected to see an improving trend in the 1800Z forecast, based on the outlook that he had read before going to bed the night before. By the time Ken's copilot showed up in the small restaurant in the ramshackle hotel they had been confined to for nearly a week, Captain Ken Thompson had already filed the flight plan and printed off the weather for their flight to Resolute Bay.

"How's it look, Skipper?" Kevin asked the pilot in command of "Vampire Five", a small Canadian military transport aircraft, a military variant of the ubiquitous DHC-6 Twin Otter.

"Weather looks good. Strong southwesterly winds. We should be able to make it to Resolute tonight."

"Too bad your computer's fried, so Combat Quest is not an option. What are we going to do there tonight? The place sucks!"

"Maybe Ozzie will lend us one of his laptops. I've still got the disk. If worse comes to worst, I'll have to work on your Performance Evaluation."

"Very funny, Boss. Hey, did you hear about what happened in Russia two weeks ago?" Ken simply shook his head. "Those stupid Russians, they can't organize a piss-up in a whorehouse! They put their strategic nuclear forces on high alert, as part of some cluster-fuck of an exercise."

"What was screwed up about it?" Ken asked.

"Turns out there wasn't supposed to be an exercise, but some computer error ordered 57 batteries of Topol-M's onto high alert status. Those are those new SS27 'Sicle-B's' with 550 Kiloton warheads, with up to 6 MIRVs and 2 or 3 dummies apiece," Kevin explained, demonstrating that he had completed another block of the Air Force Officer Development Program.

"Anyhow, there was some confusion as you would expect with the Russians. The BBC reported that there was *no order from Moscow*. Apparently there's some problem with command and control in the Russian Federation. They're not supposed to increase their readiness postures without a confirmed order from Moscow. So then the Russians went through a series of computer exercises last week. They rotated each mobile battery, all the ground-based silos, and all 14 of the at-sea SSBNs through launch preparation drills. NATO sent some observers because of concerns about the readiness of perhaps 6,000 warheads being exercised in such a compressed timeframe without the normal degree of bilateral coordination. Both Russia and the US are saying that there is no increase in tension, but the BBC is reporting that the Europeans are concerned. Everybody's getting nervous because of what happened in Pakistan and Israel." Kevin explained this, as though Ken had not been following the ongoing crises closely himself.

"Yeah, that sounds about right. It's about what Casey Callaghan has been saying," started Ken.

"That freak?" Kevin jumped in. "I've heard about that guy. I heard he went crazy, saying there's going to be a war!" Kevin laughed. "I heard from some guys in Winnipeg that he quit the military and moved his family to BC, just two years away from a full pension! What a fool. They say he wanted to get as far as he could from Ground Zero at CANR HQ!"

"Yeah, Kevin, that's about right. And Casey is a friend of mine, so watch what you say about him."

"Hey, wait a minute, isn't he the guy who talked you and other guys into buying shares in that gold mine?" Kevin went on, only to stop himself when he realized where that was going.

"That's right, Kevin, he did. And I did very well on that investment, thank you very much." Ken smiled, enjoying a rare moment of silence from Kevin.

"OK, so he's not stupid, but he is nuts! There isn't going to be a war. The real threat is climate change. Have you seen how much snow they've been getting in Washington DC and other places in the States? The world's climate is fucked up, and getting more out of control all the time." Kevin finally stopped talking, and fixed himself a coffee at the grimy little coffee set-up in the hotel dining room.

"Yeah, Kevin, that's what I think too. But you know what? Casey's built a house designed to stand up to climactic extremes. He told me all about it. It's built of concrete, so it can stand up to drought and forest fire. And it's also well insulated for extremely cold conditions. It even has its own drilled well so he'll have clean water no matter what."

"Where is it?"

"Qualicum Beach."

"It'd be great to check it out if we get another Comox mission. I'd love to have a house completely off-the-grid like that," Kevin concluded, having inverted his opinion about Casey.

Three hours later, Ken pushed the two power levers suspended from the ceiling of the Twin Otter to full-forward, accelerating the aircraft smoothly down the runway for a nicely executed cross-wind take-off five minutes before their 1700Z flight planned departure time.

20

AMY

20 May: Day of NEW – Vancouver B.C.

Amy didn't mind standing, even if a real gentleman would give up his seat on the Skytrain for a woman with her child. She enjoyed traveling on the Skytrain, especially the "Canada Line" built for the 2010 Winter Olympics. Amy always took the front car so she could watch the serpentine path the tunnel followed under the downtown core.

This tunnel would have been impossible fifty years ago. The tunnel was built in two different ways. Under the downtown core, a tunnel-boring machine resulted in a circular cross-section. But for the stretch from Olympic Village to Marine Drive, a simple "Cut and Cover" excavation was used. By simply tearing up Cambie Street to install the line and then repaving the road, the city saved a great deal of money. The rectangular cross-section of the Cambie Street portion was just 20 meters underground, obediently following the surface street's path. While less sophisticated than the bored section downtown, it was an effective engineering solution.

Entertained by yet another journey on her favorite Skytrain line, Amy pushed the stroller carrying her fifteen month old daughter, Janie-Lee, off the Skytrain and headed for the elevator to the surface above.

Ten minutes later Amy arrived at the reception desk at

MacQuarrie - Hobkirk Engineering, at 777 Hornby Street. There, greeted with a smile from the lady seated at reception, Amy took an application form and filled it out in her precise engineer's lettering. After attaching her résumé, she handed the clip-board back to the lady.

"So how are things going here?" Amy asked.

"Not too bad. We may be hiring soon, if we get stimulus funding for the Spanish Banks Wind Project," Triona Hobkirk answered as she smiled at Janie-Lee. "Why don't you and your little sweetie come back to the lunch room? Have a cup of tea. We've got some crayons and paper. I'll try to get one of the boys to meet you while you're here. They're in a meeting now but should be done in a few minutes," Triona said encouragingly.

"Sure, thanks! A cup of tea and some crayons would be great," Amy agreed, gratefully embracing the offer. She wheeled Janie-Lee to the staffroom, following Mrs. Hobkirk. After setting Janie-Lee up with crayons and paper, Mrs. Hobkirk turned on the news channel and showed Amy where the kettle and teabags were. After that, she returned to her desk, started reading the resume, and watched for her husband to come out of the meeting.

Mrs. Hobkirk liked the young engineer immediately. Amy had a solid, self-confident nature that Triona respected. The young engineer clearly had a good balance of Computer-Aided Design skills to accompany her solid background in large-scale wind energy projects. If the firm got the contract to build the controversial Spanish Banks project they would need a dozen engineers like Amy, but a personal introduction would also help.

Suddenly Amy rushed past the reception desk and threw the door open, pushing the stroller with one hand as she fled the office as though it was on fire.

"What's the matter, dear?"

"There's a war! You've got to get out of here!"

"What do you mean?" called Triona Hobkirk as the door

closed. Amy was already inside the elevator jamming her finger on "M" when Triona poked her head out the heavy oak door just in time to see the elevator door closing. She went back to the TV in the lunch room. In disbelief, she stared at the image of a mushroom cloud looming ominously over a city in the prairies.

Down in the lobby, Amy rushed past the security guard, and then ran down Hornby Street towards Georgia Street as little Janie-Lee erupted in howls and tears of protest.

I've got to get underground! Amy thought urgently as she pushed Janie-Lee along. *I've got to get away from downtown. That was Winnipeg! If Winnipeg has been hit, Vancouver will be next. I have NO TIME!*

One of the front wheels couldn't stand up to the forces as Amy careened around a lamp-post. One of the paired wheels on the right side shattered. As the pieces flew in all directions, nearby pedestrians stared at Amy's frantic progress down the sidewalk. They gave her a wide berth.

Amy wasn't surprised to see that terrible image on the TV. There had already been a nuclear war in the Middle East and a much larger one between India and Pakistan and it hit her like lightning.

The war that was clearly underway would be going global. That meant only one thing: the probable extinction of the human race. But it was not going to be *her* extinction, Amy thought to herself. Right now, that meant getting underground. When she reached the Skytrain Station at Pacific Centre, Amy took one last look back at the skyline of the city she loved. As she looked up at the tops of the gleaming skyscrapers she realized that she was looking towards the very office where she had been only minutes before. The high hopes of finding a job and returning her life to a sense of normalcy were now utterly destroyed. Looking up at the corner office, in her mind's eye she sensed Mrs. Hobkirk looking down at her.

She turned her attention to fighting the stroller down the escalator to the Canada Line.

Amy grew up in Richmond, adjacent to Vancouver, until she left home to study Engineering at the University of Calgary. After completing her degree, she spent ten years working on wind-farms in southwestern Alberta. Her promising career came to a screeching halt when she became a victim of down-sizing. Pregnant and unemployed, Amy moved back to Richmond to have Janie-Lee.

Amy became unemployed the same day she told her boss she was pregnant, and that it was *his*. She didn't want him; he had been only a means to an end. Amy had lied when she told him that she was on the pill that night when they were forced to weather a storm in a small maintenance trailer on a wind-farm site. The sex had been unimportant to Amy. What she had really wanted was a baby. Her engineering career had kept her from finding the man of her dreams but she would not let a small detail like that deny her the chance to be a mother. Now, in her early thirties, she had her Janie-Lee.

Amy tried to quickly make her way down the escalator but the stroller wasn't cooperating. It kept pulling to the right and getting hung up on the jagged steel teeth. She had to wait until the escalator reached the bottom. At any moment she expected to see the intense light and feel the heat of an atomic blast. But it had not come. She made it down to the platform. There was at least twenty meters of solid clay and concrete over her head. *Is that enough?* she thought.

She boarded the Skytrain to Richmond. The doors closed, and the Skytrain accelerated down the tunnel towards Yaletown Station. Amy felt her heart racing and finally looked down at Jannie-Lee. Looking up at her mom in a way that was almost disturbing, Janie-Lee wasn't crying or even talking. She just stared up at Amy as though she knew that something important was happening. This was no time for tears.

Amy crouched down and held Janie-Lee's face close to her own. "Everything's going to be OK, sweet-cakes, Mommy's here. We have to go on a trip now, and we have to hurry." Satisfied with that, the toddler smiled at her mommy and turned her attention to her stuffed dog, Finnegan, pinned to her shoulder strap.

As the Skytrain approached Yaletown Station, Amy saw a few men rushing down the stairs to the platform and then waiting impatiently for the doors to open.

"Winnipeg's been nuked!" a well dressed but disheveled looking man shouted. "Don't go up there! We're going to get hit too!" he pleaded to passengers getting off the Skytrain as he pushed his way on. One or two passengers paused, looking at the man, but then continued off the train.

As the doors closed and the Skytrain began to leave, several more people came running down the stairs and escalators, all with the same fear spurring them on, only to watch in despair as the Skytrain departed. People in Amy's car were now shouting about what they were reading on their cell phones, blackberries, I-Pods and Net-Scrolls. News of nuclear attacks at Anchorage, Inuvik, Winnipeg and other places had gone viral.

It had taken twenty minutes for the panic to really get underway after the first report of the nuclear detonation in Alaska. It had been described as a terrible accident. But when Winnipeg was hit, and there were reports of other detonations in the Arctic, the news services started to speculate about the possibility that a nuclear war had started. Fifteen minutes later, when reports of American missiles having been launched and more reports of nuclear detonations in Canada had come in, it was clear that a nuclear war was underway. *Time to panic.*

At the next station, there were more frantic people trying to flee the city. They rushed in when the Skytrain's doors opened at the Olympic Village station. This time nobody got off and the train was getting crowded. Many passengers tried desperately to call loved ones, to coordinate where to go and what to do. Amy's Skytrain was getting so full that some people couldn't push their way on before the doors closed.

At the same time, a Russian R-36M2 SS-18 missile passed a calculated point in time and space. The navigation computer sent a signal to the sequencer, which sent other signals to various timing and enabling circuits. As the bulky missile passed through 172,000 feet over the Rocky Mountains, explosive bolts blew off twenty-four cover panels and exposed ten *Upravlyaemaya Golovnaya Chast* Multiple Independent Re-entry Vehicles, MIRVs, to the light of day. Each assigned a different target in the Pacific Northwest, the re-entry vehicles began to separate from the R-36 missile. Once clear of the missile bus, their navigation computers updated their positions and began to course-correct their trajectories.

The pre-programmed target data from the Strategic Target Database had been downloaded into the missile's central computer during the Launch Warning Phase just before this particular R-36 was launched. Designed for a counter-strike, the Russian MIRV's were assigned widely dispersed targets. With up to forty decoys carried on the massive R36 missile bus, the resulting array of targets would easily overwhelm any antimissile defenses.

This particular R-36M2 had stood up well over the 30 years since it was first assembled at the Dnipropetrovsk assembly plant in what was now Ukraine. It had been reconditioned in a renewal program in 2009, demonstrating Russia's commitment to restore the reliability and serviceability of their strategic weapons. And now it was in the terminal phase of its journey to the Pacific Northwest of North America.

As a result of the upgrades, fully 80% of the 1520 warheads installed on R-36 missiles found their targets. The targets assigned to this particular R-36 included a hydro-electric dam over the Columbia River at Revelstoke, a coal terminal in Prince Rupert, an oil refinery in Bellingham, the Naval Air Station at Whidbey Island, the industrial park on the south banks of the Frazer River at Surrey, the sprawling McChord Air Force Base at Tacoma, the Canadian Air Force

Base at Comox, the Trident submarine base at Bangor, the Canadian Forces Underwater Naval Test Range at Nanoose Bay on Vancouver Island, and a carefully calculated target site over Vancouver. The target coordinates corresponded to the center of Water Street in "Gastown".

The ten warheads carried on the R36 were not identical. Six were 750-kiloton warheads, each fifty times the explosive power of the atomic bomb used at Hiroshima. The larger, two-megaton, warheads were allocated to the Canadian Air Force base, the Trident Ballistic Missile Submarine base, and McChord Air Force Base. Programmed for surface bust, these more powerful weapons were meant to destroy hardened military facilities up to thirty meters under ground. .

The lowest yielding weapon was the one nickel-chromium encased neutron device, which was assigned to a strategic target at Prince Rupert, which was meant to be preserved for later re-occupation.

The flexibility inherent in the various types of warheads allotted to each R-36 missile was an example of the advanced state of nuclear weaponry that the Russians had achieved over the Cold War years and beyond.

It took just an instant for the detonation signal to set off the shaped charge of high explosives compressing the sub-critical sphere of lithium-deuteride into a supercritical implosion. The energy from the primary *fission* stage caused a secondary *fusion* reaction of the second-stage tritium material, and a far more intense final fission of the depleted uranium casing. This *fission-fusion-fission* detonation liberated an awesome quantity of energy in the form of visible light, Alpha, Gamma, Beta, Neutron and other forms of radiation along with a range of highly unstable isotopes of heavy elements directly over Vancouver's Gastown district.

Amy's Skytrain had just completed the final S-turn as it followed under the path of Cambie Street, winding its way around the Little Mountain hilltop at Queen Elizabeth Park, when the warhead detonated. When the intense burst of nuclear plasma encountered the solid matter of buildings, vehicles, trees and people within 1,000 meters of ground zero two things happened. First, the surface material was vaporized, adding its matter and energy to the expanding ball of plasma. Second, some energy was converted into a massively powerful electromagnetic pulse.

The EMP expanded at the speed of light until it was exhausted some twenty kilometers from the thermonuclear blast. It increased the voltage of any live circuits it encountered by thousands of volts. The sudden increase in electrical potential burned-out delicate components and connections. This rendered useless all manner of energized devices from computers and telephones to automobiles, and from the electrical systems of aircraft to common household electrical panels. Even wires buried twenty meters underground were affected. The linear-induction engine of the Skytrain whirred down to an eerie silence. Amy's Skytrain came to a sudden stop. The mass of passengers surged forward, crushing a number of people. The lights went out. After a few seconds, the cries of pain and screams of panic began. Just as quickly, the noise subsided into whimpers and moans as the emergency lights came on.

Amy remained calm. She bent over and wrapped her arms around her daughter to shelter her from the coming blast wave. She feared that this would be their last moment of life.

At Ground Zero in Gastown, a one km wide ball of plasma was created when the intense energy was released. A searing fireball expanded outward from Ground Zero, following behind the EMP and initial shock wave that had stopped Amy's Skytrain. The fireball torched its way into every vacant space within two km of Ground Zero.

People standing at the Olympic Village Station were incinerated in an instant as the fireball surged through the ventilation grills and access tunnels, sending a massive dynamic overpressure shock-wave further up the Skytrain line.

The Skytrain three minutes behind Amy's, with 589

terrified passengers crammed into it, was pulling out of City Hall Station when it was also torched by the fireball.

The heat and energy began to dissipate by the time it reached the next station. There was merely enough heat left to severely burn the lungs and exposed flesh of the 220 people waiting at King Edward Station. Their dying bodies were tossed about and propelled further along the tunnel like leave propelled along by a leaf-blower. A wave of debris continued along the tunnel for another two km before it reached the chicane at Queen Elizabeth Park.

In the confined space of the subway tunnel there was enough force to overcome the resistance of the electrical motors and propel Amy's Skytrain down the tunnel with a terrible screeching. The lurching acceleration and sudden stop 250 meters further along the tunnel threw the passengers about for the second time in as many minutes.

Crouched between two rows of seats Amy held on tightly, protecting her daughter as they were bounced around violently. She didn't feel the blows as she was battered by the surfaces and passengers around her. All she could feel was the precious life of the child in her arms, and the instinct to protect her.

As the Skytrain screeched to its final resting place, just short of the dimly lit platform at 41st Avenue Station, Amy started to breathe again. Passengers began picking themselves up in the dim illumination provided by emergency lights that had been unaffected by the EMP. Amy saw that Janie-Lee was unharmed but weeping, staring wide-eyed up at her. Amy felt as though she had been severely beaten as injuries made themselves known.

Over the next few minutes while some of the men worked to open the door and others tried to kick out the large front window of the lead car, Amy took stock of their situation. She felt the air change direction as though it was being sucked back down the line towards the city.

Outside, over the cauldron that had been a beautiful city, hundreds of thousands of tons of radioactive particles began to rise skyward. The mushroom cloud could be seen for over thirty kilometers as it rose to an altitude of 60,000 feet over Vancouver.

They had gotten away from Ground Zero just in time. Amy realized that the lurching of the subway car was the blow-gun effect of a column of air shoved ahead of the blast, pushing her Skytrain like a cork. What blew past was air and dust from the floor of the tunnel, not the lethal radioactive materials which would soon be carried by fallout. They had not been exposed to any radiation yet. That meant that she had to get upwind, *fast,* or hunker down in some kind of shelter.

Amy knew what to do. Just last year, while visiting her parents in Qualicum Beach, she had gone to the impromptu movie theatre that had been set up in the Community Centre. There was a disaster film festival on, featuring the ten most significant war and disaster survival movies of all time. During the nine day festival, all ten films were shown at least twice and in some cases many times.

The films were on survival themes and ranged from the 1983 film about surviving the effects of a nuclear war, Jason Robards' "The Day After" and the similarly themed 1984 BBC documentary "Threads", to the 1936 film that eerily predicted the devastation of a global war in HG Wells' "Things to Come".

With her parents spending some rare time with Janie-Lee, Amy watched all ten movies and became hooked on the genre. After repeatedly going to the screening rooms, Amy got to know some of the regulars that came out for every film. On some nights, as many as sixty people turned up. It was a friendly atmosphere, with people hanging around to talk about the films and enjoy the free coffee and snacks provided by the organizers.

People's interest seemed to be motivated by the recent wars in the Middle East and Pakistan. Films on nuclear war drew the largest crowds. From the way that people surreptitiously took more than one copy of the handout, Amy could tell that people were very interested in the core subject of the film festival.

The "Survival Squirrel's Film Festival" handout contained a few things that were interesting to Amy. First, there was a list of thirty movie recommendations, including the ten selected for the festival. This gave Amy a "hit list" of films she would later track down and watch in her apartment back in Richmond. There were also a few TV series recommended, including a short-lived miniseries about a town coping with a nuclear attack on the United States. Internet links were provided for the books that the movies were based on.

There was also a list of recommended books on survivalism topics such as radiation shelters, long term food storage, food scavenging, edible mushrooms, hobby farming, hydroponic growing, small-scale wind power, canning, and nutrition. There were also books on financial and social collapse. Amy bought many of the books to read during her quiet, lonely evenings. With no social life to speak of, Amy had lots of reading time on her hands.

Another interesting part of the pamphlet, to Amy, was the coupon offered by the event organizers. When Amy read the details on the tear-off coupon, she understood the motivation for the film festival. Marty and Katy had organized the entire film festival as a promotional event for their survival food and accessories business. The coupon entitled a customer to a 25% discount on any one of three main products offered at "The Squirrel's Den".

The first product was a 31-gallon Roughneck storage bin packed with sufficient calories, essential vitamins, nutrients and a few simple pleasures to sustain two adults for 90 days on a 2,200 calorie-per-day diet. A range of basic food items were nitrogen-packed along with food-safe oxygen absorbers and sealed inside heavy-duty mylar plastic bags. The beans, rice, sugar, grains, dehydrated fruits, freeze-dried meals and other basic foods could last well over ten years. The mylar bags were themselves sealed in two-gallon rectangular EZ-Store pails, made of some type of food-safe plastic.

The second product was the same Roughneck bin filled with: candles, lighters, matches, two sizes of alcohol-fueled cooking stoves, alcohol fuel bottles, water purification tablets, a hand operated reverse-osmosis water purification pump, three hand-powered rechargeable flash lights, a hand-powered "EMP sealed" hand-rechargeable radio, assorted hand tools, knives, an extensive first aid kit, assorted mosquito and bug lotions, burn creams, wet-wipes, and wide range of non-prescription medicines and an impressive first aid kit.

It also contained a "CBRN Kit" for Chemical, Biological, Radiological and Nuclear. It included some multi-purpose items: six pairs of rubber gloves, two rolls of duct-tape, three N95 Particulate Respirator Masks, six cheap plastic rain ponchos, three pairs of cheap plastic goggles and a small tube of baby shampoo. There were also some zip-lock bags containing specialized CBRN items: military-grade RSDL - Reactive Skin Decontamination Lotion, hand sanitizers, disposable Bio/Chem Warfare Agent Detection Strips, one-time dosimeter strips, and six ten-packs of 65 mg potassium iodide pills with instructions. For an extra fee the "Essentials/CBRN/Medical" bin came with an EMP-packaged "Gamma Scout" radiation-detector with audio-alarm and ticker, measuring immediate and accumulated exposure.

The third, "Tasty Treats" Roughneck, contained a large number of quality freeze-dried meals, long-life canned goods, tobacco, hard candies, flavored drink crystals, tea, sugar, artificial cream, and instant coffee in individual packets.

Amy figured that the three main products would allow a person to save time and energy by buying one of each, and then add more of the first and third type as needed. There was also a long list of individual items available which could be thrown together to customize other Roughnecks or accompany one of the three core bins.

What Amy was more interested in, however, was finding out what motivated Marty and Katy to put so much energy into providing such a service to what must be a very small number of customers in the Oceanside area. The business must be operating at a loss, as the contents must cost more than the bins were selling for. No matter how she approached the question, Amy couldn't glean anything from Marty and Katy about why they were doing it. She noticed that they were stockpiling a large number of these bins in the warehouse at the back of their office.

After the festival, Amy returned to her apartment in Richmond and busied herself with working through the rest of the films and doing some fact-checking on some of the more interesting survival strategies she had become aware of.

Amy found the films to be deeply depressing. They made her worry about the future she was bringing Janie-Lee into. Something about the genre was very intriguing to her, however, and kept her interested in learning more. She was drawn to the intellectual challenge of surviving some of those worst-case scenarios. As an engineer, she noticed a great many logical and scientific errors in the films but she also recognized a few things that the film-makers had gotten right. She was particularly interested in the nuclear war scenarios.

Her web-searching confirmed that gamma radiation levels diminished quickly. Every hour that you could stay in a well protected location would greatly increase your chances of survival. She found that the more than 1,500 Roentgens per hour that an unprotected person could be exposed to in the first hour of fallout would be fatal. However, this would be cut to $1/10^{th}$ as much radiation within just seven hours, and $1/100^{th}$ as much two days later. By staying sheltered for two weeks after the heavy fallout, this improves to $1/1000^{th}$. So the immediate danger from radioactive fallout could easily be mitigated, as long as one does not ingest radioactive particles.

On another level, Amy found the film genre to be deeply challenging. She worried about the inherent conflict between her own moral standards, her determination to improve the situation for her daughter, and the larger context of a world which could no longer support the demands being placed on it by over seven billion people. Fairness and the idea of equitable distribution of scarce resources now seemed to be an unsupportable ethical fantasy.

Now, faced with the horrifying reality that all of those disaster movies had suddenly become sickeningly real, and that she and her daughter were in peril, Amy no longer had any qualms about what she should do to survive. She would do *anything* necessary to survive and to assure the safety of her child.

Janie-Lee was surprisingly well behaved, or at least very quiet and attentive to everything her mother said. After making their way out of the Skytrain and into the tunnel, Amy found that there was just enough space along the raised concrete path running alongside the tracks for Amy to push Janie-Lee's stroller. Most of the other passengers made their way along the concrete between the rails, moving faster than Amy could.

The emergency lighting grew stronger as they neared 41st Avenue Station and ascended the first flight of stairs towards the surface. Amy took Janie-Lee out of the nearly useless stroller and carried her in her arms as she climbed up the immobilized escalator. At the middle level, Amy notice an "Orange Julius" kiosk and considered stopping to scavenge some food and drink, but then realized where she was and had a much better idea.

Remembering that this Skytrain station would come out in the plaza in front of the Oakridge Center, Amy immediately knew where to go for shelter. For a moment, as she stared up at the beautiful sky in disbelief, Amy hoped that the blast had been some other kind of accident, and not a nuclear strike. But when she turned and looked to the north and saw a huge vertical cloud dwarfing the mountains beyond, reality came crashing back.

Not knowing where else to turn, most of the other passengers headed towards the shopping mall. A few, probably locals, headed in other directions.

The lower levels of the buildings and houses nearby were intact, however north-facing windows on the upper floors of the few five and six story buildings were heavily damaged. Amy figured that the Oakridge neighborhood must have been partly sheltered from the blast by the rise at Little Mountain, just one km north of Oakridge Centre.

Amy calculated her distance from downtown Vancouver as she hurried across 41st Avenue to a small four-storey concrete building on the northwest corner. Just as she came up with the answer, *six km*, she put Janie-Lee down for a minute and looked up at the partly flattened top of the tall black cloud that loomed over the city. It was being blown northeast. So she was safe from fallout, Amy reasoned, because she was southwest from ground zero, basically in line with the airport.

She suddenly turned 180 degrees to look towards the airport. What she saw next made her turn and run. She saw a flag blowing in the gentle south-westerly breeze.

Amy tried to work out the geometry in her head as she ran along the east side of the commercial building, passing a few small businesses before reaching the far end of the building. She turned left at the corner and rushed for the concrete half-wall surrounding a steep concrete staircase that went straight down to the Bus Driver's Club. She held tightly to the railing as she carried Janie-Lee carefully down the steep stairs as fast as she could. *The airport is five kilometers from here, upwind*! she kept thinking to herself. She knew that the terrain between Vancouver International Airport and Oakridge was gently sloping with no hilltop like Little Mountain to shelter them.

Amy tried the door-knob and found it open. She carried Janie-Lee inside and quickly closed the steel fire-door behind her. Suddenly blind in the near darkness, Amy held Janie-Lee close to her and tried to catch her breath. In the dim light, she could see that nobody appeared to be in the Bus Driver's Club or BDC as she knew it. As her eyes started to adjust to the darkness, she could see that at least one of those wall-mounted emergency lights was on, at the far end of the large room. It cast a dim glow throughout the large open space of the BDC.

"Who's there?" asked a man's voice from behind the bar.

"I'm Amy Arnott," Amy said, moving closer. She was surprised to see a pair of very hairy legs and the distinctive blue uniform shorts that bus drivers in Vancouver wore on warm days like today. When he stepped out into the light, Amy saw that his shirt was wrinkled. He smelled like beer and vomit. "Who are you, a bus driver?"

"Yeah. I'm John Simpson. Nice to meet you, Amy. You've just come in from the street, right? What the hell happened out there? I was sleeping it off in the back room there when the building started shaking. I woke up in total darkness."

Amy was now close enough to see the bearded face of a stocky little man no more than five foot four.

"There's a war! Vancouver has just been nuked, and I think the airport will be next."

"Get serious! I felt an earth-quake or maybe a bus drove into the building, but nothing more. You're pulling my leg."

"OK, John, then why's the power out? Check your cell-phone, it'll be dead too," Amy said, looking around the club.

The BDC hadn't changed since she was there with a bus driver from the 41-UBC route. On a late-nite bus ride back to the 41st Ave station to transfer to her Skytrain. The friendly bus driver had invited her to join him for an after-work beer at "his" club. Amy agreed to go, and was introduced to the underworld of bus drivers and heavy mechanics. She was shown something that few non bus drivers would ever know existed, an after-hours speak-easy where bus drivers and mechanics from the "Bus Barn" on 41st Avenue could drink beer in their uniforms.

"I'll go look outside, then."

"I wouldn't advise that."

"Wha-" was all that John could say. He was suddenly bathed in bright light blazing under the fire door. The entire BDC was illuminated like when the lights come on at closing time. Every ugly stain on the carpet was visible. Even the grime on the tables stood out distinctly. He covered his eyes as Amy wrapped her hands around Janie-Lee's eyes and pressed her own face into her wrist to block out the light.

After what felt like minutes, but was more like two or three seconds, the room went black again. The emergency lights failed. All three of them folded to the floor, disoriented by the flash and subsequent blackness. Janie-Lee began to cry.

"Don't be afraid, sweetie Pie, mommy's here."

"What was that?"

"The airport, I think." Before Amy could say more, she was drowned out by the rumbling sounds and vibration from what sounded like a train crashing through the building overhead. She realized that the shock wave must have reached the building above them. Then a much more violent force struck, and the entire building shook like it was being ripped up out of the ground by a giant hand. Nearby, there was a shrill whistling sound, and then a "clunk-kuh-clunk-clunk-BAM!" as something rolled down the concrete stairs and smashed against the fire door, bursting it inward. An orange glow came through the door, and the shrill whistling stopped.

"Samson, get over here!" Amy sprang into action, leaving Janie-Lee crying where she lay on the middle of the floor.

"What? OK. By the way, it's Simpson!" as he hurried behind her to the fire door.

Amy tried to dislodge a heavy four-drawer filing cabinet out from where it had come to rest in the doorway. When Simpson joined her, they stood it up and pushed it back outside, into the debris-filled stairwell. Then they looked up.

"That's a… That's a…" He couldn't finish his sentence as he stared into the hellish conflagration up at street level. They quickly closed the door, and the shrill whistling resumed.

"We have to seal this door. The firestorm is sucking the air out of here."

"There's some duct tape behind the bar." John disappeared into the darkness. Janie-Lee screamed as John stepped on her leg and fell on her in a heap. Amy crawled toward the sound, reaching out with her hands. Then light sprang up from John's cigarette lighter, and Amy rushed to pick up Janie-Lee.

When John found some candles and duct tape, they sealed up the fire door. Amy felt some hot, smoky air moving into the club from the building's air-handling system. After tracking the smell to the mechanical room behind the bar, she found the damper to stop the air coming into the club from the building's mechanical system, and then she sealed off the cold-air return where air had been escaping.

In the hours that followed Amy and John rigged some table cloths over the air vents, hoping to filter out any fallout particles once the firestorm on the surface abated and they could allow some fresh air to circulate.

Amy explained to John that they would have to stay-put in the BDC for up to two weeks as the fallout from the blast at the airport would be coming down directly on them. They were safe, as the club was deep under street level and the thick concrete building above would help. But there would be radiation coming through the thin fire-door, so John stacked all the beer kegs in front of the door and then he pushed a candy-bar machine up against them to stabilize the wobbly wall and add mass to the fire-door. Then they stood the BDC's two pool-tables on their sides to make a small sanctuary in one corner. They stacked food and drinks from the bar into one corner, and brought all the table cloths and linen they could find for bedding. Amy found that the building still had some residual water pressure, so she filled several pails of drinking water, and had filled a few more for sanitation in the club's washrooms before the water pressure died completely.

In the first hours after the nuclear explosions, Amy had secured the critical elements: water, food, and shelter from radiation. Their chances for survival were good, considering that they had been within five or six kilometers of two large detonations. But they were not out of the woods yet.

Then Amy remembered that she had been carrying those four packets of Potassium Iodide pills she had bought from

The Squirrel's Den. She crushed one pill for Janie-Lee, and gave it to her with water as she explained to John what they were for.

Eventually John remembered something about Potassium Iodide being scarce in the weeks after the Japanese nuclear disaster after that Tsunami, but John was still skeptical. He did not really believe that the greatest danger from radioactive fallout came from ingesting radioactive iodide produced in nuclear explosions. The radioactive iodide is taken up by the thyroid gland, leading to all sorts of deleterious health consequences. But he accepted the logic that by flooding the thyroid gland with potassium iodide, the danger was mitigated. Amy tried to share hers with him, but when he found out that she only had enough for her and Janie-Lee for ten days, he refused.

After an uncomfortable first sleep in their sanctuary, they only knew it was the next day by John's the mechanical wristwatch. Without it they would have had no way to keep track of time.

In the days that followed, Amy told John as much as she could remember from the disaster film festival. John became increasingly frustrated with Amy's insistence that they not unseal the door until fourteen days had passed. They had no way of knowing that the gamma radiation had fallen to safe enough levels after just eight days, because most of the fallout had been blown to the east; not much had fallen on their area.

When they emerged from the BDC on June third, it was to an alien landscape. The larger structures were recognizable from their concrete shells but the interiors had been completely removed by the blast and firestorm. The asphalt had been boiled off in most places, leaving only whitened pea-sized aggregate behind. The now gravely roadway was covered with scraps of wire and metal that had been burned to a greyish white, devoid of any color. The fires were out, and pools of ugly black water proved that rain had fallen in recent days.

With as much water, beef-jerky and other bar food as they could carry, the three left the BDC at first light and made their way west on 41st Ave. After one block they reached the burned-out wreckage of the Bus Barn. The destruction seemed to be getting less the closer they got to Oak Street. A small ridge to the southwest must have deflected some of the blast.

Following a hunch, John led them to an old concrete building behind the Bus Barn. Sure enough, the old garage was basically intact thanks to the nearby ridge-line and sturdy 1940's era construction. Inside was an old 1977 GMC "New Look" diesel bus. It was from a disused line, kept as a training aid for apprentice mechanics. John Simpson knew all about it. He had driven the old bus on a test run with some of the apprentices just a few days before the blasts.

The old bus had been powered-off when the nukes hit. Because it had none of the sophisticated computer systems of today's buses, the bus's simple electrical system was not damaged by the EMP. The battery itself had been ruined, but they found a new battery in the workshop, and a Honda generator. The new battery was fast-charged for two hours while John replaced a tire that had been punctured by flying debris. Once the battery was charged enough to make an attempt, the old bus started easily. Before heading out with the bus, John asked Amy to explain the plan again.

"We'll follow the ridgeline cutting across 33rd Ave, then follow Alma down to 4th. That should keep us in areas that were sheltered from the blast at the airport, and still far enough from downtown. If the way is clear enough to drive through with the bus, we should be able to get to Jericho Beach before noon."

"And you expect to find a boat there, in all of this?"

"No, I don't expect to. *We need to*. So we'll go and see what we can see," Amy said with confidence.

In their journey across Point Grey they avoided the devastation of Kitsilano to the northeast and Dunbar to the south, running the gauntlet between the two blast zones. Traffic was non-existent, but they did see some people on foot.

Before reaching Jericho Beach, they passed a Canadian Forces establishment on 4th Avenue. A long line of survivors were waiting outside the hospital building of the small Jericho Beach Detachment of 73rd Communications Regiment. As they drove by, Amy made eye contact with a woman who was talking to a young woman with a long pony tail and an extremely pink jacket.

For Jillian Vogel, standing in the line-up talking with the young woman she and Manfred had been seeking for three days, it had been strange to see a bus operating on 4th Ave. There were few vehicles operating ever since the nuclear blasts had destroyed almost everything electrical in the region. Only a few fire trucks and police vehicles in the more sheltered areas were still working, particularly up at UBC where many of the survivors on the west side of the city hoped to find help.

After passing the Jericho Detachment, John drove past the burned-out ruins that had been the old wooden Youth Hostel near the beach before arriving at the WWII-era concrete building that housed the Jericho Beach Sailing Center.

The fence had been stripped away in the blast, along with all of the sail boats and windsurfing boards that had been in the compound. The building itself had stood up well but its contents were burned and melted into a charred mess. Amy led them around to the west end of the building, farthest from what was left of Vancouver. They paused to look around. The office buildings downtown were gone. Only a few of the apartment buildings in the West End remained. It was as if a giant bite had been taken out of the downtown skyline. Following the shoreline with her eyes, she saw that everything from Kitsilano Beach to Locarno Beach had been completely destroyed.

Amy looked to the west and saw the wreckage of a commuter aircraft stuck in the mud out on Spanish Banks. She felt the wind on her face and estimated that a westerly wind was blowing ten to twelve knots. The air felt as fresh and clean as the last time she had taken Janie-Lee sailing, about a month before. Thinking of that reminded Amy of something.

She led John and Janie-Lee to the garage-door at the northwest end of the building. The massive steel door was intact. John helped her turn a large wheel, rolling the sturdy door aside on its tracks. Inside, there was a large space that served as a repair shop for the Sailing center's membership.

Cut off from the rest of the building by an internal concrete wall, the "Boat Bay" had been protected from the blast.

The messy appearance of masts and hulls lying around in pieces was just as Amy remembered from once hanging around and talking to an old dentist, Ted, as he worked on his cedar-hulled canoe. The canoe was broken into kindling now; a heavy sail-locker had toppled over onto it. But a few other hulls appeared intact.

They chose *Queen of the Sea.* The name made them laugh. The tiny sailboat was just large enough for four people, definitely not suited to the open ocean.

The small boat was clearly in good repair, with her bright green hull looking recently painted. It took them a while, but they soon figured out which of the masts fit the Queen. Once they got her onto a long two-wheeled boat dolly and pulled her outside, they had little difficulty erecting the mast. After finding the kick-up rudder and a sail bag with "Queen of the Sea" stitched on to it, John and Amy threaded the mainsheet up the mast to rig the mainsail, followed by the simple Jib.

After finding some life jackets in a storage locker, and throwing in the sack with the food and bottled water from the BDC, they eased the Queen down the ramp into the water. It was already two o'clock in the afternoon.

After fumbling around a bit trying to get the centerboard to swing down into place once they were afloat, she soon had the

Queen moving along at a brisk fifteen knots. The winds were perfect for a cross-wind tack, cutting across the open waters of the Strait of Georgia. They were very cold six hours later when they reached Qualicum Beach. It had been was a rough ride.

They walked into town just as evening turned to night.The town was intact, and the street lights were on, but there was no road traffic or noise. There was trash blowing around on the streets, and no businesses were open.

John was coughing badly and was very weak by the time they reached the Arnott's condo. Amy and Janie-Lee were also very tired but Amy felt a rush of hope and relief when she saw activity inside her parents' main-floor condo. The hairless, zombie-like ghost of a man who let her inside bore only the slimmest resemblance to her father.

21

1720Z

20 May: Day of NEW - NORAD

Major Rodney Stradins went out of his way to drive past the "Headingly Range" on his way to work, hoping to see some game in the open field near the 300-meter range. Looking north into the property he saw no activity in the firing pits. That was always a good sign at 0730 hours. With no such activity by this time, Rod knew that the Range would be inactive all day.

"Looks GOOOOD!" he said aloud to himself as he drove past the range. Rod was a hunter. His weapon of choice was a compound bow. As he turned towards the Base, he looked forward to returning in the late afternoon to hunt. He would take his time walking a km or so into the expansive property, staying near the tree line and moving quietly. Once far enough from the road he would select a gentle rise and find a patch of trees in which to set up his hide. He could sit for hours, listening to the sounds coming from the small critters in the forest, and watching the little struggles between birds, rodents, bugs and other life all around him. Then, when a rabbit or a mule deer wandered into the thirty yard or so range at which he was lethal with his bow, he would slowly draw back his binary-cam bow until he felt the wall of resistance and then ease back for that peak let-off he had mastered over his years of practice. He always enjoyed the strain in his biceps as he held off. He felt the rhythm of his own breathing and the small changes in the air currents playing out in the prairie grass around him as he waited for the perfect moment. And then WHAM! He would let loose his carbon-graphite arrow, almost feeling the impact his prey would experience as it was struck through the center of mass, becoming impaled as if by a bolt of lightning. Those were the moments he lived for, when he tested his mettle against the struggle for existence in nature.

Still thinking of his planned hunt, Major Stradins pulled into his parking spot on the golf-course side of the entrance to 1 Canadian Air Division Headquarters, which was also the HQ for the Canadian NORAD Region, CANR. After passing through security and entering the Canadian Air Operations Center, or CAOC, he glanced at the Wall of Knowledge. Everything looked routine.

Just two hours into his watch, however, Major Stradins realized that this watch was not going to be routine after all. His eyes were drawn to the flashing alert on one of the screens. Something was definitely going on. Major Stradins jotted down the time automatically, 1015hrs local – 1515 Zulu.

As the Intelligence Officer, or A2, prepared to brief the Battle Staff on the Air Force role in an incident taking place in

Richmond, British Columbia, Major Stradins scanned his screens to ensure that he knew the disposition of CANR Air Assets.

For a moment he was unsure what the Twin Otter, "Vampire Five", was doing up near Kugluktuk, but then recognized that the slowly moving icon was a "Ranger Re-supply" mission. The four-pack of CF135 Joint Strike Fighters and the air-tanker supporting them were still in Comox, on deployment from their home base in Alberta. Everything else was absolutely normal.

He then looked at the fish-tank display of the Canadian NORAD Region. The fish-tank was a three-dimension projection in the centre of the room which gave everybody a "God's-eye view" of the continent. It was fed to CANR directly from Continental NORAD Region, in Colorado, through the newly installed "Strategic Information Management Operations Network". The Americans had installed SIMON in all of their Command and Control facilities as part of a major "Net Centric Warfare" upgrade to all classified networks and command systems.

The Canadians now had SIMON as well, but preferred to rely on their existing equipment for Canadian-only operations.

As the A2 began, a new Icon appeared over Richmond, on the SIMON display, hovering like a dagger.

"There has been an incident in Joint Task Force Pacific's Area of Operational Responsibility," he began.

He was cut off by the Commander, Major-General Charnley, who had just entered the room and interrupted the briefing.

"Thank you, Alphie, I'll give the short version," said the Two-Star General, cutting off the A2. "Ladies and Gentlemen, an integrated RCMP - CF Task Force is being stood up in Vancouver in response to an emerging threat. Last night, an RCMP operation saw the arrest of twenty-seven members of a previously unknown Chinese gang. This uncovered intelligence indicating that hostile actions against Canada's shipping and infrastructure may be imminent. The report, which the A2 will brief you on in more detail, is being investigated by this new Task Force under the code name OPERATION FINGER TRAP. The initial goal of FINGER TRAP is to determine if China is indeed involved. Admiral White has the Regional Command over at JTF Pacific. Full command stays with Canada Command and the Strategic Joint Staff at Star Top.

I think it needs to be stressed here and now that this is potentially *an act of war*. My intent is that we shall over-respond until we know otherwise." The general went on to explain what he and Commander Continental Region NORAD, CONR, had agreed to in terms of NORAD assets and which Canadian air assets he would deploy. As both the Commander 1 Canadian Air Division and Commander CANR, General Charnley had all of Canada's air assets potentially available to him.

In addition to sending four new CF135 Joint Strike Fighters to the area, he ordered follow-on fighters and A400M tankers along with maritime patrol aircraft from Canadian Forces Base Comox. He then ordered an increase in security at Canadian Air Force bases, and cancelled all leave. Major Stradins watched to see that all the squadrons had received and acknowledged their new orders via SIMON, and watched until their icons changed to "Unit Tasked". While waiting, he noticed an unusual character momentarily appearing on one of the data pages hovering along the periphery of the SIMON display in the Fish Tank. He only saw it for an instant, but it looked like a "t" with a smaller "t" beside it. He did not recognize that it was the Chinese symbol for "Dragon".

The NORAD Command Center at Peterson Air Force Base in Colorado Springs was also abuzz with the intelligence report from Richmond, but the four-star general in command of NORAD and US NORTHCOM, General Adams, knew that the Canadian commander in Winnipeg would prosecute their incident exactly as any other NORAD Battle Commander would. General Adams had learned over the years that while the Canadian military did not have vast stockpiles of military armaments and was relatively puny in terms of available platforms and personnel, they made up for it by their excellent coordination, professionalism, and attention to detail. Nevertheless, Continental NORAD Region was also spun up to a higher readiness posture and an incident summary was being prepared for the Joint Chiefs and the White House. It would take some time for the report to work its way to the Executive Branch.

By 1625Z, additional information from JTF-P confirmed that Chinese involvement was probable. The RCMP had arrested two more Chinese nationals in the expanding network of OPERATION FINGER TRAP. The arrested men appeared to be members of the People's Liberation Army "on leave" in Canada. The Task Force reported that the arrested Chinese personnel were refusing to talk. They would not even explain why they were in Canada, nor why each of them had large sums of cash and gold coins. The prisoners each had a cyanide-tooth which the RCMP had not discovered until one of the men activated his capsule and died.

The Estimated Time of Departure of the CP-140 maritime patrol aircraft which had been assigned to support FINGER TRAP was for a 1650Z launch from 19 Wing Comox, with an on-station time of 2030Z in the North Pacific. The CP140 was armed with four torpedoes, a full load of sonobuoys and twelve hours endurance. The mission was to sweep a large area of the North Pacific, recording all ships within the Canadian sector, with an emphasis on Chinese flagged vessels. Just as Major Stradins noticed the change of status of the DEMON 54 maritime patrol aircraft, indicating that it had launched on time. Then the entire Battle Staff was shocked into silence.

"SIMON Tech, confirm that this is a live feed!" General Charnley demanded with a sense of urgency and a higher pitch in his voice than Major Stradins had ever heard before.

"Yes, Sir! This is real."

"What the hell?" Major Stradins remarked, as he looked at the lines appearing along the perimeter of the fish-bowl projection provided by SIMON. "These are inbound missile tracks?" he asked, knowing the answer would be yes.

"There are 247 inbound tracks, all in excess of air-breathing speeds. Point-of-origin analysis confirms launches from Russian ICBM sites. Hold-on! Now it's 495 tracks, and counting. These are confirmed missiles, Sir!"

"We're getting the impact projections now, Sir." The SIMON Tech reported, as everybody looked to see the dotted lines from the numerous missile icons that were approaching from three sides. A massive number of inbound missile tracks could be seen converging on targets throughout North America.

General Charnley was in a heated telephone conversation with his counterpart in Colorado Springs and the noise level in the CAOC was rising quickly when someone turned up the audio feed from US STRATCOM, at Offutt AFB, Nebraska.

"Attack Profiler indicates First Strike! They're going after our eyes and ears with the first 440 tracks... 560 tracks in a second wave are targeting our ICBM sites, C4IR, and military bases... Another 310 tracks in a third wave will strike population centers and critical infrastructure... Each of these tracks contains up to three MIRVs... Sir, this is consistent with the Russian First Strike Strategic Target List," the Weapons-Effect technician in Nebraska reported.

For a good five seconds there was total silence in the CAOC. A *First Strike* nuclear attack from the Russian Federation was simply impossible to believe, but the SIMON system had several redundant algorithms which ensured that a computer error or war game could not result in a false alarm going undetected.

"Russia? Not the Chinese?" Stradins broke the silence.

"The indications of Chinese activity could have been some kind of deception operation meant to dislocate and confuse us," advised the A2.

At the NORAD / US NORTHCOM Command Center, General Adams had exhausted any possibility that the inbound tracks were in error. He was forced to accept the reality of the situation when one of his Battle Staff interrupted him.

"Sir, we have a Video Teleconference link coming up with General Crossman at USSTRATCOM. The VTL will include all of the Joint Chiefs and the Executive Branch, and all ten Unified Commands. You need to be in the CP right now, Sir."

"On my way, Colonel. General Peters, you have control," General Adams said as he and some key staff left for the small Command Post adjacent to the Command Center at Peterson AFB.

Seconds later, General Adams was in his CP. He saw most of his peers from the other Commands on the screens and noticed that the President had not yet arrived in the Situation Room. Most of the Joint Chiefs had already assembled in a secure VTC briefing room in the Pentagon.

"Where is SHARPSHOOTER?" asked General Crossman from his Command Center deep under Offutt AFB, in Nebraska.

"Sharpshooter" was the name the White House Communications Agency has assigned to President Parker. "Sharpshooter" had been selected because the president was a gun enthusiast. She had been very popular as the Governor of Montana, and had often been seen on TV with a rifle or shotgun in her hands. The President loved the monicker. She believed it reinforced the fact that she was Commander–in–Chief. The nickname was widely known and used publicly, which bolstered her image as a Second Amendment loving, gun-toting pioneer.

"She's being brought in to the conference, but it may be a few minutes, Sir. She's having tea with the Australian PM.

President Parker smiled at the young USMC Captain who normally sat arrow-straight with just a telephone and notepad on his small, 18th Century French desk in the corridor outside the Oval Office. The impeccably dressed Marine bent his neck down so that his mouth was a few inches from her ear.

"Madame President, SHOELACE."   Her expression dropped. By discretely speaking that brevity code-word into her ear, the Marine Captain had told her that she should drop whatever she was doing and move *immediately* to the Situation Room.

Sharpshooter had selected the code-word herself. It was meaningful and therefore memorable to her. As a child, she had often been annoyed when her mother would make such a big deal about her running around the ranch with her shoelaces untied. So it was easy to remember that "shoelace" meant that she had to get over to the Situation Room and be told what the big deal was. Usually it was just another intelligence briefing on some new risk that would never actually happen, but she understood the requirement to respond immediately to critical situations, as long as the procedure was not abused.

One minute later, as an aide explained to the Australian PM that the President had been called away on urgent business, Sharpshooter settled into her chair at the head of the table in the Situation Room. The military officers assembled in the room were subject-matter experts and stand-ins for the Commanders. The actual Joint Chiefs were usually ensconced in their offices at the Pentagon. By the number of officers that had been thrown together to assist her, Sharpshooter immediately understood that there actually was a *big deal* to deal with.

The military men were all looking nervously at the plasma screens arrayed along the side walls. As she looked at the screens herself, she understood why. "Is this an exercise?" she demanded, before the Air Force Colonel could even start the briefing. "Uhh, no Ma'am!" he stammered, then started the brief.

"Madame President, we have the Secretary of Defense and the Commanders or Deputies of all ten Combatant Commands on the various screens on the left wall," he gestured un-necessarily. "As you can see, the right wall has the strategic plot and our global forces disposition, as per normal setup. On the central screen, General Crossman at US Strategic Command will take it from here."

Turning her face to the camera that she knew was in the center of the far wall, President Parker looked into the camera lens, thereby looking each of the Combatant Commanders in the eye on the screens in their various briefing rooms.

"Proceed, General Crossman."

Commander USSTRATCOM wore a lot of hats. He commanded US Army Forces Strategic Command, at Redstone Armory, Alabama; Fleet Forces Command, at Norfolk, Virginia; Marine Corp Forces US Strategic Command, at Quantico Virginia; and Air Force Space Command, at Vandenberg AFB, California. This gave General Crossman unified command over all forms of Ground-Based Midcourse Defense, Global Missile Defense, Navy Tomahawk Cruise Missiles, Marine Corps Strategic Capabilities, Space and ICBM Forces, Ballistic Missile Warning, Global Positioning System, Defense Satellite Communications Systems, Space Shuttle Range Support, Satellite Tracking, Solar Flare Warnings, Defense Meteorological Support, and all Atlas II, Delta II, Titan II & IV launch vehicles. General Crossman spoke with authority.

"Ma'am, we have over 1300 inbound missiles from various launch sites within the Russian Federation. This amounts to over three thousand warheads. The first will strike Alaska NORAD Region Headquarters, at Elmendorf Air Force Base in Anchorage in less than...three minutes. We have confirmed our data. Confidence is HIGH. This attack profile requires that you authorize the 'Launch on Warning' counter-strike immediately, Madame President."

"Are you serious? This can't be! What happened to the

thirty minutes warning I was told we would have from your space-based sensors?"

"We're still trying to piece that together, Madame President. But early indications are that an ion flux from yesterday's solar flare was just passing over the Russian Federation and may have disrupted our launch monitoring satellites," he explained with embarrassment and anger.

"All I was told about the Russians at this morning's Early-Bird brief was that they were continuing a validation of their Missile Command and Control systems, *and that we had people on site in their command centers!"* the President exclaimed to the anxious looking men in the Situation Room, and the strained faces she saw over the video teleconference.

"Ma'am, we had no warning. But our data has been confirmed by space and ground-based sensors. We need you to give the order and then relocate yourself at least to the PREOC immediately. There are already seven tracks inbound to Washington, with the first to strike in eighteen minutes."

"I need to give the order now? We don't have time for more confirmation? Wait a minute; DID YOU SAY THE FIRST TARGET WOULD BE HIT IN THREE MINUTES?"

"Seconds, Now, Madame President."

As she began to comprehend, she noticed that the military men were looking at the strategic plot on one of the screens. She followed their eyes and saw missile tracks converting to flashing red dots, which she knew meant strikes. At the same instant, the video feed labeled "AASOC/NORAD ANR Elmendorf" went dead. Soon after, a new image was pushed into the same screen. Live streaming data from an aircraft showed a distinctive mushroom cloud rising from a forested valley framed by a small coastal city and a long range of impressive mountains.

"Madame President, that was Elmendorf AFB and most of Anchorage. We just lost NORAD Alaska Region Headquarters. You are now looking at live video from an F-15 Eagle. Madam President, you *must* give the order NOW, before it's too late."

She gave the order, authorizing the "Well Done" retaliatory option recommended by Commander USSTRATCOM: an all-out retaliatory strike of ICBMs, SLBMs, SLCMs and ALCMs. The Secretary of Defense confirmed the order.

"I am now evacuating to the PREOC and then to Mount Weather. You all know what to do. I hope that you're safe wherever you are, or can get to safety. We'll re-establish this conference when I'm safe. How long do I have?"

"Fourteen minutes."

Sharpshooter had only gone into the Presidential Emergency Operations Centre once in the four months since Inauguration Day, but she remembered that it would take a few minutes to get through the twists and turns of those corridors and that first elevator. Then there would be that terrifying free-fall as the elevator seemingly fell the entire 500 feet to the deeper level. From there, she could stay in the small bunker. That would keep her close to the White House but safe from most dangers, or she could take the very small and fast-moving underground shuttle to the staging bunker under the Pentagon; or all the way to the Deep Underground Military Base at Mount Weather.

Ten minutes later, President Parker was moving at a hair-raising 95 miles per hour on her subterranean journey from the PREOC under the White House to the Mount Weather DUMB.

In the Canadian CAOC, General Charnley heard from General Adams that an American counter-strike had been ordered and that all NORAD units should issue immediate evacuation and dispersal orders. At the same time, he learned that CANR's counterpart in Anchorage, ANR, had been nuked. This matched the strategic plot that he and his Battle Staff had been watching in stunned disbelief on SIMON. With no antimissile forces under his command and probably only minutes to live, General Charnley focused on passing what he knew through secure VTC to Canada Command and the

Strategic Joint Staff the in Ottawa. Canada Command was keeping the Government of Canada and all Canadian military commands in the loop, but it would take time to send dispersal and evacuation orders to all of Canada's military bases and to activate regional emergency response organizations. But the news that Canada was under imminent nuclear attack had already gone out over the airways, as the media was far more efficient.

Meanwhile, clearly under attack by the Russian Federation, subordinate commands under USSTRATCOM activated America's antimissile defenses. Others warmed up the 2436 highest readiness of the 5,913 currently operational warheads, now that formal Launch Authorization had been given. National Military Communications Center would send the Emergency Action Messages to the various Commands, Control Centers, Ships' Captains and Battlefield Commanders to carry-out selected strike options against pre-assigned targets.

They understood that they had to work fast, as they had lost at least twenty minutes of response time due to the failure to detect the Russian missiles when they were first launched. Having seen what happened to ANR in Elmendorf, they did not take the time to thoroughly examine the theory that this lapse was due to the solar flare activity. Russia had actually been in solar shadow when the relatively minor solar flare had surged past the Earth.

Other personnel, working at a slightly less frantic pace, were reviewing procedures to bring the remaining 4270 warheads of the "Responsible Reserve Force" back to active status, to replenish the soon to be depleted number of ICBMs, SLBMs, B61 bombs, Tomahawk cruise missiles and smaller yield battlefield nuclear artillery devices.

While disarmament over the last few decades had reduced the American stockpile considerably, they retained the fissionable material in the form of Plutonium, U232 and other highly enriched materials and had the technical might to quickly ramp up the assembly of delivery systems, provided these were not all knocked out in the Russian first strike.

The highest readiness American missiles were the Trident-II's and Minuteman-III's. The 450 LGM-G Minutemen-III missiles distributed in missile silos spread across Wyoming, Montana and North Dakota could each carry up to three Multiple Independent Re-entry Vehicles. Each MIRV was armed with a variant of the W87 warhead, outfitted with defensive shielding and capable of dispensing decoys and chaff. Reaching the target at Mach 23 to detonate in air-burst mode or as bunker-busters at the surface, the W87 warheads would be delivered precisely on target with yields ranging from 300 to 475 kilotons.

The missile fields of the Midwest were a "use-it-or-lose-it" resource. Their fixed locations made them the first targets to be attacked by the Russians. As a result, few of the Minutemen-III missiles were held in reserve. 410 of the 450 missiles, comprising 1230 warheads out of the full compliment of 1350, were launched in the primary retaliatory strike. This left 120 warheads on 40 Minutemen-III missiles in reserve and subject to losses in the Russian first strike.

The Trident-IIs, on the other hand, as standard armament for the eighteen Ohio Class submarines of the US Navy, would be more difficult for the Russians to take out. When the Launch Orders were received through VLF-VHF communications, there were twelve fully-armed and war-ready Ohios on station throughout the world. Nine of the Ohios were outfitted as SLBM subs, each carrying twenty-four Trident missiles with MIRVs up to five W88 475 kiloton missiles. The other three Ohios were rigged as SLCM subs with 154 Tomahawk cruise missiles each, with "dial-able" variable yields up to 150 kilotons. The Ohio's at sea were available to strike up to 1542 individual targets. But only 800 of these warheads were given targets in the initial attack. This allowed a few subs to be completely depleted right away, to redeploy for reloading and replenishment. This apportionment left a few

Ohios with full or near-full wartime loads after the first strike, ready for follow-up and re-target strikes.

There were an additional 250 nuclear-armed Tomahawks available from various surface combatant vessels of the US Navy. Two thirds of these were held in reserve, particularly for the eleven Carrier Strike Groups, of which seven were at sea and the remaining four were in various stages of refit rotations.

The final 240 missiles in the counter strike would come from a small but useful stockpile of 500 nuclear-armed Tomahawks deployable as Air Launched Cruise Missiles.

The balance of the American nuclear arsenal was comprised of the reliable B-61 bombs which could be delivered by B-52, B-1B and B2 aircraft, and a variety of artillery-delivered tactical nuclear weapons with yields in the tens of kilotons. These were considered follow-on weapons because they could be brought to bear only through air and land attack.

That left 1190 warheads on the highest readiness missiles as an immediate reserve, ready to be re-programmed with new targets once the Battlefield Damage Assessment results of the first wave were analyzed and follow-on targeting was computed.

In Winnipeg, Major Stradins saw that American missile tracks were now being displayed. As the blue tracks began to multiply, one particular red track closed in on CANR HQ. The Battle Staff became silent. There was nothing more to do but wait for the end. Without sufficient time to get out of harms way, and with the bunker at 17 Wing having been decommissioned years ago, there was no way to survive. Their fate was sealed.

As Major Stradins waited for the painless death by instantaneous vaporization, he thought of the letter from Casey Callaghan. He now understood that it could have been a lifeline. It certainly would have been useful if he had been off-duty and out there at the Headingly Range, hunting with his bow, when the blast occurred. But it was not to be, so Major

Stradins spent the last fifteen seconds thinking of his favorite past-time. He felt the warm breeze in the trees and smelled the musty aroma of the grassland as he imagined it. He was at peace with the universe.

"Time to impact: 5, 4, 3, 2, 1," he read from the display.

Strangely, the counter continued: "0, -1, -2, -3, -4,"

That's not possible, Major Stradins thought to himself. He looked at Fish Tank and saw that the Headquarters of the Canadian NORAD Region was now showing as having been destroyed.

"-5, -6, -7,"

Major Stradins was just opening his mouth to speak when the timer on the nuclear device completed its own countdown to zero and detonated. The device had been assembled by personnel of the Academy of Engineering Physics at the Mianyang facility in Sichuan, China. Custom-built for the job, it was identical to the ones which had just detonated in Honolulu, Fairbanks, Anchorage, Inuvik, Yellowknife, Frobisher Bay and other places.

It had been designed to mimic the effects of a Russian 550 kiloton warhead delivered by SS25/RT2PM Topol ICBM for ground-burst. The bombs had been shipped in specially rigged Evergreen sea-containers which had arrived at pre-arranged sites before the commencement of Phase IV of General Bing's operation. This particular bomb had been sitting in the fenced-off parking-lot of a small rented warehouse, less than a kilometer from CANR HQ.

To the SIMON technicians at USSTRATCOM in Omaha, and to the Battle Staff in Colorado Springs, the 7-second discrepancy between the Detonation Alert on SIMON and the actual time of the detonation in Winnipeg went un-noticed. They were experiencing information overload as the complexity of Russian attack rose faster than human beings could process. Nobody wondered why the Strategic Information Management Operations Network had *confirmed* that Winnipeg had been destroyed by a 550 kiloton ground burst of a Russian SS25/RT2PM Topol ICBM *a full seven seconds before the Chinese bomb had detonated* in the Evergreen container. And why would they? SIMON was never wrong.

The busy technicians simply announced the destruction of two bases in Alaska, one in Hawaii, and three in Canada as each detonation alert was displayed on SIMON. Their main focus was to provide updates on the progress of the launch of American missiles from their silos and sea-based platforms.

Russian missile tracks closed in on key command and control sites. When the Commanders of those sites were satisfied that the bulk of the American counter-attack had been launched in time, many ordered their staffs to evacuate to any bunker or shelter they could reach in the few minutes they had left. They wanted to give their personnel a fighting chance.

At military bases throughout North America, the emphasis was on "Survive to Operate", with aircraft and personnel ordered to disperse from their bases or to get personnel into bunkers and shelters. Aircrew scrambled into their aircraft and took off without Air Traffic Control clearances, desperate to get beyond the range of the detonation they expected at any second. Personnel on the ground jumped into any vehicle they could and drove as fast as they could away from their bases. Those with loved ones attempted to contact them and give them what warning they could.

In Russia, there was confusion. The Americans had suddenly launched a massive wave of missiles without provocation. This initiated a chain of events at the headquarters of the Strategic Rocket Forces, and at the Russian equivalent of the War Room. President Dvorkin made only one attempt to contact President Parker by Red Phone. Learning that all communications with Washington were cut off, and seeing that missiles fired from American submarines in the

North Atlantic would strike Russian targets within minutes, he ordered a full retaliatory strike.

Once he had given the order, he began his own evacuation. He knew that dispersal of military forces would be automatic, and that the civil defense apparatus would provide what warning they could to the civilian population. Russians had long experience with civil defense drills, during the Cold War. More recently, nuclear defense had returned to the public consciousness in the crisis of the previous week, when Russia almost launched an attack based upon a computer error.

With robust fallout shelters in most cities, and with hundreds of km of subway lines buried deep under Moscow and Saint Petersburg, Russia had sufficient fallout shelters for nearly six million citizens for up to four weeks, and military shelters to preserve over a million personnel for up to six months. However, the food, batteries, stored fuel and other supplies were now over thirty years old, and completely useless.

President Dvorkin and his staff traveled by underground train to the primary bunker in Solnechnogorsk, forty km outside of Moscow. This was the best location for top government and military leaders to relocate to because it was also the headquarters of Lt General Sergey Ivanovich Maatsal, Commander Third Space and Missile Defense Army, responsible for early warning and detection. The facilities in the underground complex at Solnechnogorsk were first rate, employing the latest computer technologies stolen from American and Western industry and adapted to Russian needs.

The progress of the American missiles tracked by a network of Series 2400 Cosmos geo-stationary satellites and "ORTU" early-detection radar sites was displayed on the impressive wall of plasma screens. By the time President Dvorkin arrived in the Command Center, the first American missiles had struck in Saint Petersburg, Murmansk and Petropavlovsk. The detonations had been confirmed by adjacent military units. Other missiles would be striking their targets within minutes.

Meanwhile, the Russian counter-attack was just getting underway. The Russian missiles were launching with a surprisingly good 62% success rate. President Dvorkin had been prepared to live with an overall 55% success rate. Even at 55%, Russia would be able to put over 2300 warheads in the first wave of the Russian counter-strike, and up to 1400 in the follow-on strikes that would be launched after the results of the American attack and Russian counter-attack were known.

That would leave 4400 mission-ready warheads of over 25 different types and delivery systems that could be deployed for subsequent strikes, after a few weeks of concerted effort to bring them into operational status.

Much depended on what was left after the American first strike. He knew that cruise missiles would be first to strike, as their flight time from the patrol areas of the American Ohio submarines was on the order of ten to twelve minutes, while the larger yielding ICBMs from the American Midwest would take thirty minutes to reach their targets.

There were unconfirmed reports of American missiles failing to detonate, or having been shot down by the antimissile defenses of the Third Army's A-135 missile defenses protecting Moscow and other key sites. While the accuracy of the 51T6 "Gorgon" long range and 53T6 "Gazelle" short range interceptor was less than perfect, they did give the Muscovites and others a fighting chance. If they were indeed taking out some of the American missiles this was a good sign, but Dvorkin would wait for a full assessment.

Another series of reports got his attention. Early reports of American missiles striking targets in Great Britain, France and Germany had been received and were being confirmed. If this is true, President Dvorkin thought, then the Americans are launching an all-out global attack. This made no sense at all. The Americans had no reason to attack their allies. Sure, they were suffering the consequences of decades of overspending, debt, and the erosion of their manufacturing base while China and Europe continued to be net exporters, but to attack Europe? That made no sense at all.

His attention was drawn to the plasma screens, indicating that Russian missiles were obliterating targets in North America. Targets in Europe were also being hit by Russian missiles, as part of the Global Counter-Strike Order he had given back in Moscow some 35 minutes before. According to the *Prikaz Silniy Udar*, "Hard Strike Order", all key NATO bases in Europe were being hit, along with the same range of critical infrastructure, manufacturing and communications capabilities that were being targeted in North America.

He was initially pleased to hear that, of 2720 warheads in the first wave, only 10% had failed to detonate or were defeated by NATO antimissile defenses. He was perturbed by reports that some missiles had gone rogue. The new targeting computers confirmed that the missiles had hit their assigned targets; however telemetry reports from 3rd Space and Missile Defense Army, using some of the older generation of computers and intelligence sources, were reporting that some of the SS27s had hit targets in the Persian Gulf, Africa, and Australia.

These reports would have to be checked, he thought. The SS27-C's, designed in 2007 by the Moscow Institute of Thermal Technology, were special warheads mounted on Topol M's. Rather than MIRVs with ten warheads, as in the standard R-36MTs, these R-36 Mod-D and Mod-E missiles could only carry 3 warheads. The warheads were allocated on a 2:1 basis, with one massive 25-megaton bunker-buster Mod D paired with two 1-megaton neutron bomb Mod-Es. These special warheads were meant to be held in reserve and not used in a first strike unless specifically added to the strike package. If any of these special Topol M's had been launched, he had to find out how this had happened.

Another report indicated that missiles fired by France had hit American naval units in the Atlantic Ocean, and targeted some American bases in Germany. This was presumably in response to American cruise missile strikes against major population centers in France. As many as thirty American missiles had struck France. Paris itself was hit by at least three American cruise missiles. Strangely, the United Kingdom had not used any of their Trident Missiles and the locations of their six Vanguard ballistic missile submarines were unknown. England had been hit by as many as forty American missiles and seventy-five Russian missiles. He could only imagine the devastation that the tiny island nation was experiencing.

His initial satisfaction of having hit the Americans hard in the first counter-strike was wiped-away by the next message he was handed by the white-faced Colonel who had quickly scanned the incoming report. The report was a decoded intercept of some communications between the Canadian Navy, in Victoria, and a subordinate command of the American Northern Command, US Naval Task Force 51, in Washington State. The intercept amounted to a Canadian assessment that China was attempting to hijack a large number of bulk-cargo ships from port facilities on the West Coast of Canada. The report intercepted at 1140Z, occurred *six hours before the American attack was launched* at 1755Z.

As he digested the meaning of the report, he was handed another. It was an assessment of American warheads that had struck Hong Kong, Taiwan, and as many as sixty other Chinese cities. The targets had been struck with *enhanced radiation neutron bombs.* Neutron bombs had also been used to strike industrial targets in Korea, Japan and other Asian centers. Why would the Americans use Neutron Bombs in Asia? Hadn't China once threatened to attack Taiwan with Neutron bombs? And how had Russian neutron bombs been launched without approval against targets in Australia, Africa and the Persian Gulf?

When he began to put the pieces together, he had a moment of cool, clear, and completely terrifying understanding. Neutron bombs were designed with nickel and chromium casings rather than uranium or lead, he thought to himself. This allowed the neutrons generated in the atomic detonation to escape rather than being reflected back into the reaction. The resulting intense pulse of ionizing radiation would be effective at penetrating structures and vehicles, but would also result in lower yields.

The neutrons would be quickly absorbed by air particles after having done their killing work. The effects of neutron bombs would be much less persistent than a conventional nuclear detonation. They would kill the population without destroying the equipment, buildings and infrastructure. While personnel may not die immediately from the massive dose of radiation of the neutron flux, they would die from the effects of radiation within weeks.

These weapons could depopulate a city without rendering it uninhabitable. There would, of course, be the requirement to dispose of the rotting corpses before they spread diseases and ruined the water table. He imagined vast Asian cities standing intact, filled with corpses. President Dvorkin almost vomited when he fully comprehended the situation.

The Chinese themselves are behind the attacks. It was the only explanation that fit. They had somehow tricked the Americans into attacking Russia and Europe, and we had no choice but to launch our counter-strike. By ensuring that their own cities were hit with neutron bombs, the Chinese would come out of this heavily depopulated, but intact, infrastructure while Europe and North America would be devastated wastelands. That fits with the intelligence report about China seizing cargo ships, he realized. After this war, crops wouldn't grow for years so food would become a strategic weapon.

His analysis was confirmed by a report that the American attack had been a reprisal for the Russian first strike. *But there had been no Russian first strike;* the data the Americans had acted on didn't match reality. Some of the first targets destroyed in North America were destroyed by surface bursts, yet they should have been targeted by airbursts. Also, the timing was strange. Some targets were destroyed several seconds after the timing presented in the missile-tracking data. This meant that the data was contrived somehow, and the dozen or so initial blasts had been delivered some other way. They may have even been pre-positioned.

He thought about the loss of communications between the Russian and American Presidents in the minutes before the Americans first noticed the apparently Russian missiles. The communication systems were vulnerable to computer network attack, and the physical land-line backups could easily have been sabotaged, making direct communications impossible at just the right time, he reasoned.

"*Konyets Attack!*" he shouted, halting the Russian attacks. While General Matsaal began issuing direction to his staff to cancel any remaining launches and to abort the few remaining missiles in flight, President Dvorkin continued giving orders.

"We need to order a full strike against China. Military and civilian targets. Do this immediately, before our remaining missiles are destroyed. Pay special attention to their bunkers and other prepared locations. Task our navy to locate and destroy all of Chinas naval forces, and to seize any Chinese flagged commercial shipping worldwide. Isolate and shut down the newer computers - they have been compromised by the Chinese. Use backup computers and secure land-line voice commands only. Have the Missile Control Centers program the targeting computers manually," he ordered, demonstrating that he had not lost touch with the details of Russia's Strategic Rocket Forces. He had spent years as Commanding General of Third Artillery Regiment before he seized power from President Putin.   While the battle staff quickly responded to the orders, President Dvorkin continued speaking to the room.

"We have all been fooled. We have gone to war with the Americans for no reason. They were tricked by the Chinese, and we in turn were provoked by the American attack. The Chinese are behind this, and are attempting to destroy the world in order to emerge supreme afterwards. They intend to seize the world's food supplies and to move in and take control of Australia, India, the Persian Gulf and who knows where else after annihilating their populations with neutron bombs from our very own arsenals!" he shouted, enraged by the success of the Chinese deception.

"Read these reports!" he said, looking at the Defense Minister and senior generals around the planning table. "I want all hostilities against American and NATO forces to cease immediately and for our field commanders to be told that the war with America was a terrible mistake. The real enemy is China! This has become a global war for survival, and we're not going to let China come out of this on top!" he concluded.

After a few minutes of frantic activity, President Dvorkin regained his composure and spoke quietly to General Matsaal.

"Get your Staff together and prepare an update on our casualties, the American casualties, and the global situation. What countries were hardest hit? Which were left alone? What's going on in China? Where are Chinese military units deployed? And get me Sergey Illyich. I want a briefing on the status of civil defense efforts. How badly have we been hit?" he ordered, suddenly appearing exhausted and defeated as the immensity of the disaster took hold of his soul.

22

SUN TINGTING

14 September: 44 Months Before NEW

Dr. Sun Tingting was nervous. He was summoned to give a briefing to the most powerful man in Jinan Military Region. Lieutenant-General Chen Bing was likely the next Chief of General Staff of the People's Liberation Army. If confirmed into office by the Chairman of the Communist Party of China, General Bing would be one of the most powerful men in the world. After all, with the United States in an economic collapse while China owned the majority of America's debt, Sun believed that Chinese ascendancy was taking place in his lifetime. However, the science, contained in the laptop tucked under his arm as he was ushered into the briefing room, created a problem - and it was his job to lay it all out for General Bing.

It would not be like the academic presentations that he gave every day to the post-graduate students whose grasp of climate science was his responsibility to hone.

Dr. Tingting was chair of the Climate Science Department at Shandon University, Jinan City. Three uniformed PLA Officers had interrupted his preparation time at his small office at the Qianfoshan Campus. They had the Director of the Earth Sciences Division looking terrified at their heels, and simply informed Sun that it was *time*. He had dreaded this day ever since the PLA began funding his climate-modeling project five years before.

He knew that this day would come, and had prepared the materials and rehearsed the presentation over and over again. He hoped it would never actually be required. His fear of the military was strong, but what he feared most was *being believed*.

He was nervous and sweaty as he set up his laptop in the modest briefing room inside the Jinan Region Headquarters. He felt his heart racing as he tried to make himself invisible behind the small podium. He had never met a *Shangjiang* level General before, but he knew the meaning of the shoulder wreath and three large stars on the man's shoulders. It was crucial to know one's place in the order of things. So when the powerful man made eye contact with him, Sun understood who was sizing him up. General Bing was the master of his fate.

Sun had no misconceptions that this presentation would open any doors or be in any way helpful to his academic career. Regardless of how successful his modeling software had proven to be, in this case the messenger would most likely be killed. All that was left was to deliver the presentation with the pride and dedication which Dr. Sun Tingting had lived his life.

"Honorable Generals, esteemed Officers of the People's Liberation Army," he began to the small group of Generals and Colonels seated around the far end of the table. "My name is Dr. Sun Tingting. I am project chair for Climatology Modeling at Qianfoshan Campus. I am humbled and grateful for your kind invitation to provide you with this briefing on the Chiang-Lee-Tingting Model," he started, feeling himself relaxing into the rhythm of the presentation he knew so well.

After providing an overview of the theoretical foundation of the model, he drilled into the data itself. Four of the six independent variables required considerable explanation, which he covered at essentially the second-year university level. Surprised to see that he had not lost the interest of his audience, he watched their faces as he advanced through the power-point slides. One key slide told the whole story.

"As you will quickly see from this seven-dimensional scatter-plot, the first three variables of Population, Time, and Aggregate Consumption are provided in a conventional manner. Then, as you go into this three-dimensional block, the points themselves are depicted in a variety of emoticons, shapes, colors and vectors indicating the Quality of Life Index, Ecological Viability Index, Biosphere Viability Index and Incipient Trend respectively." Dr. Tingting let that sink in for a minute, before pressing the slide advance key on his wand.

"To make it easier to see the outcomes, we can shade the Blue, Green, Red and Black categories." He clicked each band on and off to show the differences.

The military men had by this time figured out that an Orange band of the Biosphere Viability Index meant that the cumulative effects of human activity were degrading the biosphere in a harmful manner, but could be mitigated by reducing some of the contributing factors. A Red BVI band indicated human activity was having a severe long-term impact which could not be restored in a human lifetime.

The Black Zone in the BVI was a theoretical point at which the ecosphere could no longer provide the minimum of essential inputs such the regeneration of oxygen and water in the atmosphere, the screening out of dangerous levels of ultraviolet radiation, and habitable temperatures in at least the milder latitudes. Simply put, a Black BVI meant extinction for the vast majority of animal species, including mankind. The Red zone meant extinction was certain, but would take time as the Incipience Vector progressed from Red to Black due to the momentum characteristics of the associated trends. A Green BVI meant that human consumption was being accommodated within the biosphere with no long-term consequence. Orange meant that things could go either way.

The low end of the Quality of Life index, represented by "Yuck-Faced" QOL emoticons, corresponded to what philosophers termed the "repugnant conclusion" whereby an infinite number of human beings consumed the most efficient form of food production possible, essentially plain rice with algal paste and protein-rich worms to eat and water to wash it down. All resources would be devoted to basic sustenance for the largest possible number of human beings, without much biodiversity. The high end of the QOL index, of course, was characterized by humans free to enjoy a wide variety of consumptive inputs with robust biodiversity.

None of the Time plots intersected the green BVI zone since the eighteenth century, however the Happy-Faced emoticons of the QOL index continued through the orange zone, right up to the present time. About half of these were already entering the Red zone, and all of them were in the Red *within ten years.*

"Even if we scroll through the Ecological Foot-Print from the low end to the high end, it's basically the same outcome." Before Dr. Tingting could go on, General Bing interrupted him.

"Total extinction of human life, along with much of the biosphere. Take us through this region-by-region," he ordered.

As Sun took them through the same presentation region-by-region, it was the same story. The only difference was that the emoticons were already in the Glum and Grim range for the Indian subcontinent, Africa, and much of Asia. They remained Happy and in the low end in North America, Australia and Europe, and were just starting to be Neutral to Glum in South America.

Sun noticed the concentration on General Bing's face. What he saw in the General's dark eyes surprised him. He recognized the look, which he had seen in his students on occasion. It was the look of *comprehension*. It hadn't taken General Bing long to get his mind around the relationships between the variables.

"The data is inescapable," Sun began to explain, "we will see continued over-extension of consumption with concomitant extremes in the leveraging of natural resources, reaching the limits of agricultural technologies as we move through the Orange Zone into the Red Zone. Within twenty years, only Canada, The United States, Russia and Europe will be in the Orange Zone. The rest of the world will be in the high end of the Red Zone. The planetary average will go Red within the next eight years," he continued, to a silent room.

"Global temperatures will rise by two degrees; however the water-holding capacity of the atmosphere will rise four-fold. This will result in increased droughts and an increased rate of snow-cap losses in the Himalaya and other ranges. The resultant loss of fresh water supplies will exacerbate an already precarious fresh water distribution system, leading to increased desertification, plant and animal diseases, and steadily decreasing regional food production. The changes are already occurring faster than the biosphere can adapt, resulting in the catastrophic Incipience Vectors you can see here.

Food production, access to fresh water, and crop viability will be the nails in the coffin. With a population increasing from 7.2 billion today to 11 billion by 2040, the pressure on the natural resources becomes extreme. Increased mortality rates in developing countries will be offset in part by longer life expectancy elsewhere. However, we will reach this point," Sun indicated with his pointer, "where in all cases the planet faces the exhaustion of biodiversity and a catastrophic die-off of all inter-dependent species," he paused before concluding. "Without biodiversity, as we are seeing in the trouble with bees and other helpful insects, food production becomes non-viable."

"So it will be just as people attribute to Einstein as having said?" interjected General Bing. "If the bumble-bee disappears then man will only have four years of life left. No more bees, no more pollination, no more plants, no more animals, no more man," General Bing explained to his colleagues, some of whom were still coming to grips with the information.

"Yes, General, quite astute. However, we will have this die-off *regardless of the fate of bees*. It's a mathematical certainty."

For the next two minutes General Bing was silent, thinking. Sun didn't say a word, expecting to be ordered to recalculate, to find some other outcome than the extinction of the human race. And then the General changed his tone completely, with an inquisitive look on his face.

"So what is that Happy Grey emoticon down at the bottom right, in the lower Green band, with a horizontal vector to the right?" he asked.

This caught Sun Tingting off guard. "Oh, I'm most embarrassed; please excuse my sloppiness, General. That's from the baseline model used to contain the uncertainty field."

"A what?"

"It's a mathematical model which is used in the calculations, sort of a mathematical starting condition onto which our data was infused statistically, but the baseline should have been suppressed from this depiction," he replied.

"But what model does it come from?"

"Well, it was originally taken from an old database from the 1989 study that Director Lee did on the Nuclear Winter Scenario," Sun explained. "Dr. Lee's mathematical model provided the core formulae for our calculations. His approach continues to be the most dynamic and expandable basis for climate science to this day. I should have suppressed it from the presentation.

In any case, his nuclear winter model demonstrates what happens when a global thermonuclear war of sufficient magnitude lofts a large enough volume of dust particles into the stratosphere to raise the albedo of the planet by 45%. Solar insolation would be further reduced by the perpetual cloud layer below, resulting in daytime surface illumination being reduced by 75% to 85% of normal," Sun warmed to the topic, encouraged by the query.

"I have a quote here somewhere from a study in which Dr. Lee makes reference to in his work. Let me see if I can find it in my laptop." Sun began to sweat as he furiously searched his files.

"Here it is. Taken from the Turko, Toon and Sagan study of Nuclear Winter, 1983: *"Significant hemispherical attenuation of the solar radiation flux and subfreezing land temperatures may be caused by fine dust raised in high-yield nuclear surface bursts and by smoke from city and forest fires ignited by airbursts of all yields,"* Sun quoted form his laptop, and then continued.

"There would be an initial spike of global temperatures and a rapid rise in humidity and rainfall as the heat of the earth is trapped in a heavily particulated mesosphere, vastly expanding the supply of condensation nuclei to start raindrops. The increased snow and ice melt, as well as the increased evaporation with the initial warmer temperatures will result in a several weeks of extremely intense storms and heavy rainfall globally. Then, as the residual heat is ablated and less and less insolation gets through the stratospheric dust to replace it, there is an accelerating drop of global temperatures. Continental areas will drop by twenty to thirty degrees C." Sun paused, noticing that the generals were still with him and that General Bing was looking strangely satisfied.

"In his original study, Dr. Lee calculated that widespread crop failures, poisoned water supplies, immediate and long-term effects of the blasts, complete loss of food production, certain breakdown in social order and likelihood of years if not decades of inhospitable climate would result in the mass starvation of the human population and most animal species. Some life in the seas and temperate coastlines would continue, however a nuclear war of sufficient magnitude, on the order of five gigatons, would lead to the extinction of the human race," Sun explained.

"So why does Dr. Lee's model show a later *recovery* in the baseline population?" General Bing asked, not missing a beat.

"Dr. Lee updated the baseline to reflect the much smaller arsenal of weapons, after the arms reduction of the START I and START II treaties. His baseline was calculated for one thousand megatons. We can tweak this model to reflect any number of megatons you like," Sun explained.

During the silence that followed, Sun's brief feeling of relief due to General Bing not getting angry at the conclusions he presented was suddenly replaced by a new kind of fear.

Sun saw in General Bing's calm and somehow contented face that that was precisely what General Bing was thinking. As he typed commands into the laptop, to adjust the Lee calculations to reflect 500 megatons, and hit "enter" to update the model, Sun felt a large rock in the pit of his stomach.

"Here is the outcome based on a medium-sized nuclear war, such as one thousand of the 500 kiloton weapons in the modernized American and Russian arsenals, resulting in 0.5 gigatons Net Explosive Quantity," Sun explained. The graph had a sudden die-off starting at "T-0" of the theoretical event then remained flat for five years or so, and then recovered quickly to resume the exponential population growth that has been normal since the end of the industrial revolution. It soon reached into the Orange and Red bands, then into the Black band followed by a vertical drop off to zero, at about "T + 40" years.

"Am I reading this correctly? A medium sized war with 1000 warheads would cause a large die-off but in the end population growth would result in the predicted extinction being put off by only, what, forty years?" General Bing observed.

"That's right, General. Not enough of the population is killed-off to forestall the deleterious effects of human consumption on the ecosystem. The environment is unable to cope with the impact of the renewed population growth. If I adjust the data again," Sun adjusted the data to two gigatons. "Here a war of about 4,000 warheads, or two gigatons NEQ, results in a 90% to 95% die-off of the human population. The surviving population growth is held low due to the harsh climatic conditions in the nuclear winter, which would last far longer than in the earlier example. Even after the climate normalizes, the aggregate human consumption continues at a much lower rate because mankind has been thrown back by several centuries. The new climate is also marginal for food production, so the population also faces higher mortality rates and has to devote more effort to food production, less on economic growth. The Neutral emoticon here indicates that life is challenging but viable, and that our impact on the biosphere is greatly reduced.

As you can see from the way the line barely moves upward at all, the resulting level of human population, on the order of 350 to 600 million, is sustainable for centuries. Biodiversity goes up faster, but levels off in the Green band," Sun concluded.

"So what you are advising, or more accurately, what Mr. Lee's model advises, is that mankind should be culled by over 90% so that the resulting population would then be sustainable?"

Stammering and terrified to be put on the spot, Sun Tingting could only reply: "Honorable General, I am a fly on the back of a cow. I can not make such immense decisions. All I can do is present you with the mathematical model, and turn my efforts to the next assignment I am given."

"Relax, young man, I am only thinking out loud." General Bing sounded happy, as though he had been given good news.

"Thank you Dr. Tingting. That will be all. Colonel Hua will accompany you to your office, where you will retrieve all of your data and any reference materials. You will then collect what personal items you require from your apartment, and then you will be taken to your new billet here at Jinan District Headquarters. You are no longer a professor, and are now under my exclusive authority. That means you will talk to nobody about your work. Thank you for your competent presentation." General Bing turned his attention to his colleagues while Sun and Colonel Hua silently removed themselves from the briefing room.

General Bing gave his carefully selected colleagues the broad strokes of his vision, the *Higher Commander's Intent*. In this case, the intent would be to bring about a nuclear war of sufficient magnitude to kill off over 90% of the human population, resulting in a sustainable level of human activity over which Chinese military forces would have dominance. This plan would be developed in secret, even from the Party.

The plan would use the enemy's *Center of Gravity* – their superior technological and military power - against them. For General Bing, the Chinese C of G was a toss-up between their successful infiltration of Occidental computer networks and China's ability to mobilize human resources on a massive scale in secrecy, without their movements appearing on CNN.

The *Strategic Plan* was to convince the superpowers that they were each under attack from the other, so they would expend their high-readiness nuclear forces. The enemy's *Operational C of G* was their ability to communicate with each other. There must be no last-minute peace initiative by red-phone. So the plan had to address the flow of information to the decision-makers during the critical timeframe.

In order to ensure that the war was devastating to all other western military powers, General Bing's staff would make subtle and unobserved changes to the Joint Integrated Priority Target Lists of the Strategic Nuclear Forces of the United States and the Russian Federation. In effect, changes made by Chinese effects-based planners would have the enemies attacking their own friends around the world.

Supporting Plans would be drawn up to infiltrate Chinese agents throughout the world to support follow-on forces which would seize strategic sites, critical infrastructure, lines of communication, and more than a few small countries. Other Plans would ensure that a sufficient proportion of China's citizens would also perish. However, essential civilian and military resources would be removed from harms way in advance.

After three weeks of concerted effort, General Bing's staff was ready to provide the General with an Information Briefing, in which they told the general what was understood to be the intent of the operation, any constraints and restraints, assumptions necessary for planning, and the strategic aim. General Bing approved the Concept of Operations and strategy for initial plan development as briefed, and *OPERATION WINTER SNAKE* began to take form. The staff had come up with the name "Winter Snake" because General Bing was born in the Year of the Snake, 1965, and the Snakehead wanted a nuclear winter.

To keep his operations secret for the ensuing years of preparation, training, and the manipulation of the myriad international players whom he saw as mere chess pieces, General Bing relied on a core of military personnel from his own Jinan Military District. This helped him keep WINTER SNAKE from the eyes and ears of even the nosiest of Party Members. However, when anybody turned an unwanted eye in the wrong direction, General Bing either brought the offending party on board the operation, or discouraged them in a more permanent manner.

One aspect of his plan that helped keep a lid on things was that most of the tactical operations could be developed on paper, with orders and movement tables prepared in advanced, and issued only in the hours before the *Execution Phase*. The rigidity and effectiveness of the Chinese state organs and military apparatus lent themselves to rapid, unquestioning mobilization. What General Bing had to do was plan the operations well in advance and have key people that he could trust ready to step forward with him when the time came. By this time, General Bing had reasoned, the world would be in such a state of panic and confusion that nobody would be looking that closely at what the Chinese military units were doing.

What's more, General Bing thought with satisfaction, the Chairman of the Communist Party will have confirmed him as the Chief of the General Staff of the People's Liberation Army. For now, however, General Bing did not want to be given that title. The incumbent Chief, General Wang, could be used as a tool for deception. Wang was an incompetent old fool. His meaningless operations would continue to support the enemy's bigoted belief that China was incapable of operations on a strategic scale.

General Bing was inspired by Sun Tsu:

Engage people with what they expect; it is what they are able to discern and confirms their projections. It settles them into predictable patterns of response, occupying their minds while you wait for the extraordinary moment – that which they cannot anticipate.

23

LITTLE DRAGONS

15 May: 5 Days Before NEW

The copilot was annoyed, but Ken felt relaxed. He knew from experience that the load of provisions and ammunition for the Rangers at Grise Fjord would arrive in time for their 0700 departure. The plan was to fly to Kugluktuk, normally 2.5 hours flying time from Yellowknife, and then to refuel and press on to Cambridge Bay. But Ken also knew that the weather wasn't looking very good. With such limited range their DHC6 Twin Otter was not the ideal aircraft for this type of mission.

The mission was to transport a standard "Ranger Re-supply": 50 cases of Individual Meal Packs and a dozen steel ammo-boxes with one thousand rounds of 0.303 caliber rounds each, for the Ranger's preferred hunting rifle, the venerable Lee-Enfield No.4 Mark-1. The rifles were over 100 years old, but perfectly suited to the harsh operating conditions in the Canadian Arctic.

"This is the third time this week you guys have been late!" Kevin, the copilot, shouted at the Ranger Quarter-Master.

"Don't get your panties in a bunch, Sir!" replied the cranky old Warrant Officer. "We had to wait for the ammo."

"Well, you guys are supposed to have your load here one hour prior to launch!" Kevin said firmly. "And when you're late like this it affects other people. The Flight Engineer still has to load the aircraft, strap down the load, and do his weight and balance! So now we'll be at least half an hour late departing. We may not even make it to Cambridge Bay tonight!" Kevin ranted.

Kevin had gotten quite a reputation as a "berserker" at the Squadron. He tended to explode at people at the slightest provocation and never seemed to understand how to sit still and relax. But he was an excellent hands-and-feet pilot, and Ken was certain that once he settled down and learned how to deal with people he would make a fine Aircraft Commander.

Ken gave Kevin the left seat for the leg to Kugluktuk. He was pleased with how carefully Kevin correctly followed all the procedures. It was interesting how Kevin behaved more calmly when he was behind the controls of the aircraft, Ken thought.

The flight to Kugluktuk went well, and even the weather

seemed to be holding. After an uneventful landing, Ken, Kevin and Rick the Flight Engineer put the aircraft to bed. The wind had picked up and was blowing in from the open ice of the Inside Passage with a wind-chill value of minus 30 C. The crew took extra care to make sure that the electrical oil-pan heaters were working. Without electric heat, the oil in the engine would be too cold to start again in the extremely low temperature.

It was five days before the crew could depart Kugluktuk. A persistent low pressure system had brought blizzard conditions to the tiny arctic hamlet. The crew, accustomed to such delays in the arctic, simply settled into a daily routine of checking the weather throughout the day and making the occasional trip to the airport to check on the aircraft. They also watched a lot of TV.

Ken had brought along his laptop computer and was hooked into the hotel's Wi-Fi connection. With nothing better to do, he thought about the letter Casey Callaghan had sent him a few months before. He Googled "nuclear winter, climate change, extinction, war" to see what would come up. The first item that matched his search criterion read: "...*plans to start a nuclear war. The resulting nuclear winter will cause global devastation, severe climate change, and mass extinction...*"

It was uncanny how fast the internet search engine came up with strange documents and phrases that matched whatever was put in the search window. Ken clicked on the link. He was not aware that the instant he did so, alarm bells would sound at General Bing's headquarters in Jinan province, China, and then later in a computer lab at an MI6 facility in east London.

"General Bing, we have another one." Colonel Hua alerted the General that another one of the traitor Sun Tingting's files had been discovered. Colonel Hua himself had put the bullet into the back of the climate scientist's head when it was discovered that Sun had been trying to warn the world about OPERATION WINTER SNAKE. Sun tried to get documents past the firewalls and search-and-destroy viruses that the Chinese military were using to snuff out any communications regarding the WINTER SNAKE. So far, they had been successful in shutting down Dr. Tingting's many attempts to spread the word.

The first step had been blowing up a lecture hall at the university, where Dr. Tingting's students had been called in for a 'surprise quiz'. The entire group had been killed or taken care of soon after in the region's hospitals, with only moderate collateral damage. It was covered up with an elaborate operation to disguise the blast as a gas leak. Had legitimate forensic investigators spent any time in the blast crater they would have found evidence that the explosion was caused by twenty barrels of Cyclotrimethylenetrinitramine. General Bing's men had placed the Cyclonite under the lecture hall and detonated it once Dr. Tingting's students had begun their exam.

That, along with follow-on investigation of each student's cell phones, home computer and social media contacts had ensured that none of Dr. Tingting's lectures or theories about the ultimate die-off that mankind would face, nor any of his research for General Bing, would get outside of China.

However, Dr. Tingting's colleagues outside of China were another problem. So Colonel Hua had personally taken charge of a small army of PLA's best computer wizards to hunt down any sniff of information from Dr. Tingting, or any of his peers, that could draw attention to any aspect of the operation. They had launched aggressive hunter-seeker viruses that would seek out any references to Dr. Sun Tingting, his students, Dr. Lee's model or any use of specific keywords. This included the very search cues that Ken had Googled with his laptop.

The vast majority of hits were computer-assessed and algorithmically filtered out for being caught by too broad a net. However, this time they hit on a file that had not been identified in the past. It was another of Sun Tingting's attempts to warn the world of General Bing's plan.

By the time Ken clicked on the file, expecting to see some conspiracy theory type of nonsense, the Chinese hunter-seeker virus had searched the linked document in a microsecond and determined that it met the criteria for files that must be destroyed. It then carried out a subroutine embedded in the virus that would flag the computers and internet service providers involved, send a summary to the HQ in Jinan, and then infect the associated computers with an instantly fatal virus.

What Ken saw was a momentary opening of a document, then a sudden flash on his computer screen, followed by blackness. Moments later Ken heard swearing from down the hall where a man playing a web-based computer game reacted to his computer suddenly going black as well. The whole town of Kugluktuk, with over forty computers on-line at the time, was cut-off from the internet when Colonel Hua's virus took down the local network.

Computers at Arizona State University, into which Sun Tingting had implanted one of his warning files, was identified by the Chinese viruses as the source of the file that Ken had uncovered with the search engine. The entire computer network of ASU was taken down. Thousands of computers were immediately rendered useless. Even if the network could be rebooted once the cause of the network failure had been identified, it would only go down again due to malevolent coding that the virus had written into the machine-language core of the university's computer system.

The full arsenal of Chinese military computer network dominance was being deployed to shut down any threat to WINTER SNAKE. With just a few short days to go before the commencement of the next phase, Colonel Hua had removed all stops, employing more aggressive and destructive programs.

One unintended consequence of the attack triggered by Ken's computer was that the increased computing activity between a network based in Jinan, China, and the rest of the world was powerful enough to be detected by both the National Security Agency's supercomputers in Washington and by MI6 International Desk technicians monitoring Chinese computer activity.

In London, they picked up on the intense computing activity between China, the Canadian Arctic, and ASU. There was enough data to consider the events linked. On its own this did not reveal much, but when added to as many as fifty other such bursts of activity, all ending in the destruction of computers and the shutting-down of computer networks with nasty computer viruses, it began to reveal that the Chinese were up to no good.

The MI6 analyst, Squadron Leader Albert Jones informed his supervisor, Mr. Richard Jessup, of the activity.

"Sir, the Chinese have attacked another university, this time in Arizona".

"Another one," said Jessup, blandly. "Do we have any information on what their target was, or did they hit another flea with a bazooka?"

"This time, they took out the entire university computer network, with collateral effects into the city at large," said Jones, slowly, like a detective in a crime novel revealing a crucial piece of evidence.

Jessup's eyebrows rose as he suddenly took more notice. "What triggered this one?" he said.

"Looks like the ASU attack was preceded by 5 microseconds by an attack in the Canadian Arctic, where an internet link in a hamlet of 1,500 or so people was taken out."

"How does this fit your hypothesis?"

"Seems to be consistent with our working theory that the

Chinese are suppressing information and that someone in Canada stumbled upon something the Chinese wanted suppressed. Mind you, one aspect does seem rather odd.. All the other attacks involved academic or other intellectual centers, but – and I hope they won't mind my saying this – I doubt there is anything of value, intellectually speaking, in Kugluktuk."

"Anything else on this?"

"Well, it looks like the Chinese attacks are becoming less frequent, as though they are succeeded in snuffing-out whatever they were going after."

"And that's not good news, is it?" said Jessup, sounding defeated.

"In what way?" said Jones.

"I mean that, in the undeclared internet war we are fighting against the Chinese, they're winning. They've infiltrated our computer systems and the internet with such audacity that it's as though they are no longer afraid of any repercussions."

"Yeah, that's certainly true. They're a few key-strokes ahead of us. They've got an army of technicians actively engaged in every form of computer espionage imaginable."

"And, more importantly," Jessup continued, "they've infiltrated US and European defense contractors. I read a report the other day that concluded that the Chinese had hacked the defense contractor who'd upgraded the Pentagon's computer system and the Command and Control computers used by all of the Functional Commands, US STRAT Command, NORAD and some of the deployed Regional Headquarters abroad."

"Yes, I've seen those reports - but do you really think they have a back-door into SIMON?" asked Jones .

"I fear that it is no longer 'SIMON says', but 'Sino-says!'

The two men laughed, but were left feeling less than happy.

"Who knows what the Chinese intend to do with it. So far, it seems to be more of a long term view, positioning themselves for the future, but not aggressively so," Albert said.

"I'm not so convinced. The fact that little harm has come of it doesn't mean that no harm is intended. Rather, it appears to me that the Chinese intend to do real harm, but at a time of their choosing. These attacks you are tracking may be just the tip of the iceberg. They're coming out of the woodwork and actually taking out entire computer networks now! Why would they reveal themselves in this way, unless it's crucial that they keep something from getting out? We need to find out what they are suppressing. Is there a way to do that?"

"I doubt it," said Jones. "We won't be able to get any data from the networks that have been attacked."

"Well, what about contriving data?" asked Jessup.

"Contrive data? How would we do that?"

"By provoking a Chinese attack."

An excited look of comprehension came over Albert's face. "You mean set up some kind of bait, such as a workstation at a university that searches for key words until it gets noticed by the Chinese." He began to think out loud. "And if we pre-program the search items and have them executed by a timed routine, we could track the time of the attack and identify the search items that provoked the attack!"

"Exactly. It's like sending a foot soldier ahead of the main force to see if he can get a sniper to reveal himself."

"OK, what level of authority will we have? I mean, we'll need some sort of permission to conduct an operation that if successful will harm a university."

"Don't worry about that, I'll bring it to the Minister at the afternoon briefing later today. You get a team together to come up with the details of the plan, and be ready to execute it immediately when we have approval. It shouldn't take more than a day or so. How fast can you write the programs you'll need?" Jessup asked, in a manner that told Albert this was fast evolving into an Op Order.

"If it's our new highest priority, I could have it ready by noon tomorrow. With the processing speeds we've seen from the Chinese, we have the luxury of throwing an enormous amount of data at them, so we can start with single-word searches, then doubles, then triples. That way we'll identify the search words that brought out the Dragon. But there's a risk that a Chinese attack will harm a great many people. We would be culpable."

"We'll deal with the fallout if and when that happens, and we'll have Cabinet level support. What is essential is that when this happens we'll have the data that proves it was a Chinese attack and we can hold them accountable for it."

"So what do we call this operation?"

"For now, call it what it is, *OPERATION PANDA STING.*"

Two days later, Colonel Hua was giving General Bing an update on the revisions they had succeeded in making to the American Joint Integrated Priority Target List, PIPTL, and Russian *Glavnii Strategicheskii Speasic*, GSS, Main Strategic Target List.

"So when Phase Three begins in just over 68 hours, the first wave of American Missiles will hit 530 of the 890 European targets; 45 of the 137 Canadian targets; 156 of the Central and South American targets; 175 African targets; the 317 special Asian and Chinese targets; and the 1170 targets in Russia. The Russians first volley will take care of the remaining European and Canadian targets; clean up what's left to hit in India – the new regime in Pakistan gave us a good start there but we still need 150 or so sites hit in India; take care of the Asian targets including 80 Japanese targets, and hit the 24 Australian and New Zealand targets. We'll have the Russians hit our 280 Asian and Chinese targets. That will leave 2026 Russian warheads to take out the Americans. The last 100 or so of the Russian missiles we can re-target just before apogee, to fine-tune the target list to hit any emerging military targets we missed, such as naval task forces and nuclear submarines." Colonel Hua paused, allowing the General to look over the disposition of nuclear forces and their selected targets depicted on wall-mounted screens.

To General Bing, looking over the details displayed, it was as though he commanded almost all of the world's 12,000 high readiness strategic warheads, even if he could not control all 27,000 warheads that could ultimately be brought to bear. General Bing was the most powerful man in the world, and nobody knew it outside of his organization.

"That will leave our 150 short-range missiles for the Asian AOR, and the 220 long-range missiles for emerging targets. However we expect to lose up to a third of these if we don't use them before the inevitable Russian, American and British response once they realize they have been manipulated."

"So far, there's no indication they're on to us, however they have raised the readiness of their high-readiness strategic forces, and sortied a higher than normal number of ballistic missile submarines. Their reaction to the Indo-Pak war has been exactly as you had planned for when Phase Two began. They are indeed angry bees that don't know who to sting!" Colonel Hua concluded, looking eagerly at General Bing.

In addition to the information-suppression operation that Colonel Hua had reported on, General Bing also received updates on other aspects of OPERATION WINTER SNAKE. By far the longest briefing was given by Colonel Leung, who updated the assembled military and Party officials that had been brought into General Bing's fold. The Secretariat of the Communist Party and the People's Liberation Army at large were still not aware of WINTER SNAKE; however, leadership within the PLA and many governmental agencies had been recruited by the expanding tentacles of General Bing's now rapidly expanding network.

The larger his organization became the more he relied on his co-conspirators. Each had been recruited based upon their span of control, areas of influence, and what they contributed to the plan. But, the most important characteristic held in common was ruthlessness. These carefully chosen people were capable of anything in the pursuit of their own interests. They had demonstrated it in different ways, but it was not difficult for General Bing to select who the leaders of the future Chinese world would be. They had to be willing to hold the fate of the world in their hands, and to crush any opposition. They had to be capable of mass-murder on an unprecedented scale.

Once brought into the WINTER SNAKE fold they threw their weight into making their contribution. Some of them saw to the conversion of underground mines into bomb shelters, outfitted with the equipment, systems and stockpiles that would support human life underground for several years, and storage space for the arms and equipment they would need once it was safe to venture forth to re-occupy the surface.

Others saw to the infiltration of Chinese agents at innumerable locations that would be crucial to the building of the New China that would emerge after the war.

Still others were charged with planning for the tasks that were to be carried out just before and just after the start of Phase Three, the Proxy War part of the operation.

For its part, China would claim to be innocent and blame American aggression. Later, when China's enemies determined that the war had been engineered by China, a massive counter-attack against China would occur. The vast majority of Chinese military bases would be obliterated. The known underground bunkers would be attacked repeatedly, as would major industrial cities and infrastructure.

The flooding from the inevitable destruction of the Three Gorges Dam would likely wipe out the seventy five million Chinese who lived and worked in the largely agricultural region downstream from the enormous dam. This attack on China, which corresponded to Phase IV of General Bing's Plan, would kill upwards of three hundred million people at the outset, and a further three to four hundred million more in the months that followed.

The Chinese people would bear the greatest number of casualties, losing as many as a billion souls as a result of this war. But this was acceptable to General Bing, as long as the rest of the world lost an equal or greater proportion of their population. The resulting world population would be on the order of five hundred to eight hundred million - at least half of them would be Chinese. The Chinese, under General Bing, would be several steps ahead of everybody else in seizing control of the more viable food producing regions and a long list of strategic locations that would give New China a solid grip on the world after the Nuclear Extinction War.

Among the plans that had been communicated to select units prior to the commencement of war were two very special programs for which General Bing himself drafted the Supporting Plans. The first was called OP PLAN LIWU, or "Gift"; the second was OP PLAN XIAOLONG, "Little Dragon".

OP PLAN LIWU was a simple plan that was to be carried out by Major General Yang Lee, Commander Second Artillery, who had overall Command and Control of the PLA's Strategic Rocket Forces. It was not all that expensive, as General Lee could use resources already at his disposal within Second Artillery. His task was simple: build twenty special sea-lift containers with conventional appearance. These containers were to be heavily shielded to hide the nuclear warheads they contained. Eight of the warheads were to mimic those of the Russian land-based SS18 550 kiloton warheads; six were to mimic the 18 kiloton warheads carried on Delta IV ballistic missile submarines; four were to mimic the 205 kiloton warheads of the latest American land-based ICBMs, and the remaining two were to mimic American SLBMs carried on Trident submarines. The devices were to have the American and Russian markings to sow confusion if discovered.

The containers were then shipped by commercial container

vessels, moved by rail and truck, and ultimately delivered to rented warehouses or storage space where they sat for a few weeks, in place before the start of Phase Three.

The progress of the containers was easy to track, using the Automated Information System. The AIS was a commercial system that anybody in the world could access to see the position of almost any commercial ship at sea. Using the AIS to track the gifts of OP PLAN LIWU, General Lee didn't have to install a GPS-based tracking device on the containers. The progress of the twenty containers was illustrated in a few power-point slides, as the gifts made their way to their assigned locations.

The AIS also helped keep track of the 1,330 Chinese and 2,386 chartered bulk cargo carriers and container ships that would bring what would be the last of the pre-war food supplies away from the food producing nations of the world. They also tracked the 1,900 other commercial ships that the Little Dragons were going to seize once they received the Yinglong signal.

General Bing had recruited the highly efficient Admiral Zhen He to coordinate the chartering of the vast majority of Chinese ships and almost one third of the commercial ships of Panama, Korea, Japan and other major shipping nations. It was also his responsibility to infiltrate agents into the ships' crews, to be activated during Phases Three and Four.

Many of these agents had been in place for over a year, establishing reputations as excellent crew members, worthy of training on the most sophisticated systems on their ships. They were trusted with access throughout the ships as they traversed the oceans of the world, month after month.

The AIS was a wonderful tool to see which ships were yet to reach port; which were ready to be loaded with grains, corn, processed foods, meat products, oil, coal and other crucial commodities; and which were already at sea on their voyage to their assigned coordinates. But the real focus was on tracking the twenty containers carrying the gifts to the enemy.

General Bing considered Phase Three to have really begun when the gifts were shipped, as they were impossible to recall or defuse once they left China. However, he decided to go with the actual detonations of the containers as the commencing action of Phase Three, as it would be a more definitive signal.

The other special project was OP PLAN XIAOLONG, "Little Dragon". Disguised as a motivational program to reward the top personnel in the most prestigious units, the best of China's armed services were briefed by their Commanding Officers that they had been selected for a two-week holiday abroad. They would be given all-inclusive travel packages which they would enjoy without the interference of their spouses and children. They were required to stay within 5 km of the designated resort, hotel, bed & breakfast or other location, and were free to enjoy themselves within that area. They were also briefed that they may encounter other Chinese military at their resort, and were encouraged to befriend them but not to openly discuss the program or the instructions they had been given.

They were also given a special gift, a small porcelain statue. Most of the men and women of the PLA and other services who were given the "Reward Program" briefing recognized the meaning of the piece. It was a small statue of the most prominent of ancient Chinese deities, the *Laozi,* seated on his throne. Its deeper meanings were intertwined in the Taoism that underlies Chinese spirituality and harkened back to the greatness of Imperial China.

Very few recognized that the face of Laozi had been crafted with a subtle resemblance to General Bing. Those who did understood the role that General Bing was playing by restoring the Three Jewels of the Tao to mankind: *Compassion, Moderation and Humility.* The Tao was fundamentally a philosophy of harmony through the constant battle between pairs of opposites. Therefore, to bring mankind to the True Path of the Tao, of course, the *Western evils* - Greed, Profligacy and Arrogance - *would have to be defeated.* A great

Chinese empire would emerge from the ashes of an epic battle for harmony in nature.

The small statue embodied the spiritual and philosophical propaganda that General Bing and his allies had come up with as a way to inspire bravery, sacrifice and zealousness in the spies that they were to send abroad prior to the commencement of Phase Three. A great deal of importance was attached to these icons, and the recipients were duly reverent when first reaching out their meek hands to accept their Laozi statuettes.

Then, in the moment of spiritual epiphany, the soldiers were informed that they were being given a special mission. During their holiday, they were instructed to rent the largest, most rugged vehicle they could find, with HMVW or a large SUV being the recommended type. They were to stock this vehicle with water, camping gear, dehydrated, canned and other long-lived food items, and any fire-arms or other weapons they could get their hands on through local Chinese contacts.

They were required to bring rugged rain gear and, regardless of destination, they must bring *winter clothing*.

They were also required to be in their assigned accommodations and to pray before the Laozi at precisely 1720Z, Universal Standard Time, each day. They were to have a television tuned to CNN, BBC News or any other major news channel so that they could be given a sign when their task was to begin. They were even told what form the sign would be.

They would recognize the *Yinglong,* or "Responding Dragon".

In Chinese Mythology, the Yinglong was said to be the god of rain. One of the nine most powerful of Chinese Dragons, the Yinglong was said to create clouds out of his fiery breath. When they received the sign of the Yinglong, all descendants of the Dragon, as the Chinese people referred to themselves, would emerge from their slumber and spread their wings.

The details of their specific mission were hidden in the

Laozi statuettes, so these "Little Dragons" as General Bing liked to refer to the agents sent abroad before the war, were to destroy the statuettes and remove the instructions that they would find in a paper roll hidden inside the porcelain dolls.

The dolls would not be mistaken as cultural relics when passing through airport security, however, as they were obviously mass-produced and marked "Made in China" on the bottom. They were General Bing's clever solution for smuggling secret orders into the various countries where Little Dragons were sent, without greatly risking OPSEC.

After removing the paper from its air-tight chamber in the doll, they would have ninety seconds to wipe both sides of the paper with a lemon wedge to reveal the message invisibly written behind an innocuous prayer, to fix the ink. If, after ninety seconds they had not applied the lemon juice, the invisible ink would evaporate and the message would be lost.

The message in each Laozi provided specific mission orders, unique to each agent. In many cases, it was simply to go to some location and join other agents to form a unit that would then move on to take some simple objective. In other cases, they were assigned to monitor the movement of civil defense and military personnel after Phase Three began and to be prepared to brief follow-on units on the disposition and composition of whatever forces were active in the assigned area.

The orders given to the more talented agents provided more details on their tasks. Some were to destroy power lines, water lines and communications infrastructure. Others were to seize control of specific facilities or entire towns, or cut off a particular transportation corridor.

Agents were sent to destinations all over the world; however, there was a considerable emphasis on locations in Australia, New Zealand, South Africa and other places in the southern hemisphere where the effects of Phase Three were expected to be less severe. Many agents were placed with orders to engage the local Chinese to become influential or at least get close to the more powerful members of those communities. When the time came, the Little Dragons were to recruit "Dragon Flies", using rhetoric, gold, vice or any other means of persuasion. These ad-hoc militias loyal to the Chinese invasion would then take control of strategically important locations.

Code-words were provided which would enable these small units to recognize the authority of follow-on agents or forces which would eventually relieve them and take control. These Little Dragon operations were intended to establish a foothold at critical locations to dislocate, confuse and delay the enemy long enough for follow-on forces to arrive.

While each of the Little Dragons briefed into the program may have thought that they were one of a very select group, over thirty thousand Laozi statues were actually handed out. With each Little Dragon mission costing about $G 40,000, the Little Dragon Supporting Plan had drained the treasury of the Chinese state by $G 1.2 billion. Spending related to other aspects of WINTER SNAKE added another $G 3.5 billion.

This certainly would be noticed within the Treasuries of China and the United States had it not been camouflaged as Chinese participation in the issuance of the New US Dollar-Gold, which came into effect on 01 May.

General Bing and his upper echelon of the future leaders of the great Chinese Bing Dynasty laughed at the foolish Americans for *asking* China to repatriate the $1,900 billion in old US Treasury Notes that President Parker had ordered null and void. In return, China would receive ninety billion in new US Dollar-Gold along with America's promise to apportion nine million ounces of gold to be held in trust in US Treasury vaults. The US wanted China to begin using the new $G US currency to re-start trade with the US. China would be paid for the worthless Federal Reserve Notes; the US would get an economic lifeline.

The movement of such enormous sums of money gave General Bing's men in the Chinese Treasury the means to fund the massive program of stockpiling food supplies, ordering and shipping military equipment to various safe locations called for in the Supporting Plans, paying for the Little Dragon operation, and chartering all available shipping to haul food supplies from the food producing nations of the world to designated locations at sea without any of this spending being recognized for what it was, *mobilization for war – funded entirely by the Americans!*

Had the war not started on time, however, the enormity of the spending and preparations would be recognized and General Bing's strategy would have been revealed. His enemy was already defeated, General Bing was certain, even if it would be a few more moves before the end game was played out.

General Bing could not have anticipated that one impatient Little Dragon would put WINTER SNAKE in jeopardy. But the loss of a few Dragons and Dragon Flies was inconsequential, as General Bing was still many moves ahead.

24

D.U.M.B. ONE

28 February: 9 Months After NEW

The cool air rushed in as the huge door rolled back on steel tracks set in the concrete. Warrant Officer Blakely stood a few hundred meters inside, at the first 90 degree turn. He found himself surrounded by a whisper of fog as the warm, humid air escaping from the tunnel flowed overtop the cooler air coming in from the outside world. He felt re-energized by its freshness, and looked forward to having a smoke outside. Smoking in DUMB One was prohibited everywhere except for the "Smoking Pits", but nobody had said anything about not smoking outside.

His bunker had been nicknamed "DUMB One" because this Deep Underground Military Base was home to President Parker and her cabinet. It was probably the most well outfitted bunker to have been activated since the war started last May. It was officially named the Mount Weather Emergency Operations Center, located in Bluemont, Virginia.

The original facility was built in the 1950s and occupied 600,000 sq ft. Where WO Blakely now stood was quite distant from the old facility; however, both the large new annex and the original site were referred to as the Mount Weather EOC.

The facility was now the permanent home for the US Government, comprised of the military and political leadership, their support staff, facility maintenance engineers, security forces and a variety of top civilian and military experts assembled hastily when the war started. They had been evacuated to Mount Weather because both the original site, and the newer annex, had been designed to survive high-yield nuclear attacks.

The engineers who had built the original facility during the cold war had done their job well. They had built it to withstand repeated hits with 25 megaton ICBMs. So when the Department of Homeland Securities had began the massive upgrade to the Mount Weather and other Deep Underground Military Bases in the first years after the September, 2001 attack on the United States, there was already a robust infrastructure to start with.

The engineers of the 21st century had more sophisticated equipment at their disposal than their 1960's predecessors. They also had an almost unlimited budget funneled through

FEMA and the DHS to the consortium of construction firms involved.

The task had required a great deal of secrecy, which had been guaranteed by the enormous profits to be made. These contractors had also had lucrative maintenance contracts which would provide an income stream in perpetuity. The secretive consortium that had been assembled for the construction and maintenance of the five larger and sixteen smaller DUMBs would never be made public, due to the project's National Security classification.

The fantastic notions of conspiracy theorists were a long way from what actually had been achieved. Rather than a fully integrated set of underground cities, the actual capacity of the 21st century DUMBs was much more modest. The five largest DUMBs each contained upwards of three million square feet, and typically had eight to ten levels. These "Jumbo DUMBs" were equipped with the small "Pressurized Water Marine Reactors", PWMRs, used by the US Navy. This meant that they had been able to 'plug and play' existing, off-the-shelf, naval marine reactor designs. They had simply produced sixteen extra 350-MW PWMRs and five 500-MW reactors and accounted for them as part of the four hundred PWMRs already on inventory with the US Navy.

This had also helped to disguise the procurement of spares and the metal-zirconium alloy fuel rods. Standardization had also made the training of maintenance and operational personnel quite easy. The task had been assigned to the US Navy, which had decades of experience with these reactors and thousands of trained personnel who could be called upon to staff the facilities.

It had been strange at first for some of the inhabitants of these DUMBs to see US Navy uniforms, but once they understood how essential the reactors were they treated the Navy personnel with respect that verged on reverence.

The marine reactors were well suited to installation in the confined space of the underground bases, as they were compact designs for fitment into warships. They provided sufficient, reliable power to operate the DUMBs for up to twenty years. They could sustain the power and cooling needs of 9,200 personnel each in the Jumbo DUMBs and 2,500 personnel in the sixteen smaller regional DUMBs.

Considerable electrical power was required to cool the facilities from the 26 C of the surrounding rock to a more comfortable 20 C for the living and working spaces of the facilities. The next largest electrical demands were for water purification, reverse osmosis of recycled water, air filtration and de-humidification. Also high in electrical demand were the lighting systems for the hydroponic gardens. The computer and communications systems of the government and military Command Posts, laboratories, and the administrative workspaces rounded out the electrical demand.

The five largest facilities were located in key areas of the United States, with the primary, DUMB One, located 70 miles west of Washington DC. The other four Jumbo DUMBs were located in remote areas of Oregon, Colorado, Minnesota, and Tennessee. Each was connected in some way to an existing facility. This had made it possible for contractors to move key equipment and personnel in and out of the known locations without revealing anything about the new annexes. Resources had then been transferred by underground tunnels to the adjacent new site. In this way, the "new" facilities had been hidden in plain sight. Interior spaces of the original facilities had been stripped-out and largely abandoned, other than for necessary maintenance and logistical staging.

Construction activities had been further disguised by mining operations, simulated road construction and the continuous mundane activity of gravel pits. This had allowed the engineers to remove millions of tons of waste material through the long tunnels and simply dump the overburden alongside the tailings of some innocuous mining venture or incorporate the material into the feedstock of gravel crushers at quarries. As part of the overburden management, huge quantities of crushed rock had been set aside at unassuming locations surrounding each installation, for future use in preparing egress portals.

There had been a great deal of waste material to dump. Each DUMB required large volumes of space dedicated to quarters, storage of food supplies, water treatment, marine reactor, cooling systems, air filtration systems, recreational and administrative spaces, living quarters and vast storage areas for machinery. Space was also required for light armored vehicles, helicopters, earth moving equipment, specialized engineering equipment, mobile nuclear laboratories, mobile biological laboratories, mobile command posts and general duty all-terrain vehicles. There was also a fleet of very capable civilian pattern vehicles such as the ubiquitous GMC Suburban and various types of mid-sized SUVs and pickups, along with a considerable amount of spares for all of the above. More space yet was needed for the workshops and maintenance areas for the vehicles.

Large chambers were required for the tank farms containing the fifty million gallons of diesel fuel needed for the operation of the large fleet of vehicles. Vast caverns had been blasted out and prepared for hydroponics and other forms of underground agriculture that were meant to augment the survival rations of the inhabitants. Areas had also been required for the water storage and recycling facilities that were so essential for the facilities to operate without additional inputs.

The final category which had required extensive engineering had been the "back doors". These were necessary because it was likely that DUMBs would be discovered and attacked multiple times with nuclear and bunker-buster weapons. The entrances must be convoluted and hardened enough that even if the overlying mountain of rock were pulverized, the facility would not be breached. Certainly the fact that these facilities were buried as deep as 5,000 feet underground had addressed part of this problem, but the planners had still been left with another one.

If all entrances to the facility were destroyed, then the inhabitants would be entombed. To solve this problem, the engineers had taken their cue from the common prairie groundhog. They had built numerous *incomplete* tunnels in many directions and at various elevations. On a three-dimensional model, the network of tunnels and causeways linking the working and living spaces and leading to the prepared and unprepared entry/exit portals resembled a plate of spaghetti with cubes of some kind of meat interspersed, representing the caverns and chambers excavated for human activity. The reality was quite impressive, as this plateful of spaghetti that had been created by removing millions of cubic yards of hard rock had taken just five years to build.

All of this was old news to WO Blakely, as he enjoyed the fresh air coming in from the outside. He and fifty soldiers, engineers and construction workers had been waiting for the green light to go outside. Some of them contemplated what had happened to their country and seemed somber, and yet excited, about working on a new exit. Having been confined to the underground bunker for nine months, the lack of an exit had weighed on their minds. Ever since the panicked evacuation into the facilities when the war started and all five of the original portals had been destroyed, their sanctuary had been their prison.

Given that they had only had about thirty minutes warning, all of the DUMB facilities had been seriously under-utilized. Of the 85,000 personnel that the 5 Jumbo and 16 regional DUMBs could house, only 24% of this capacity had been used. With so little warning, few of the pre-authorized personnel had been transported into the entrance portals before the attack.

Things were slightly better at the Mount Weather facility, as there was an underground shuttle from the Capitol Building joining a line from the Pentagon to the original Mount Weather facility. This had enabled nearly 1,200 key government and political personnel from the White House and Capitol Hill, and 952 Pentagon personnel to be evacuated to DUMB One in time.

The 250 or so support personnel located within the facility on a 24/7 basis and more than 300 personnel from the Mount Weather's "Area A" surface facility had been evacuated to the annex. Among the last to arrive had been over 500 specialist personnel who had been whisked away by helicopters from a variety of military and government facilities, such as the CBRN experts from Fort Dietrich, medical personnel from Walter Reed Army Medical Center and Bethesda, US Navy marine reactor specialists from Washington Naval Yard, soldiers from the joint US Army and USMC base at Fort Meyer and engineers from Quantico Marine Corp base.

Finally, 347 personnel, including flight crews, maintenance personnel, rapid-reaction companies and advance parties from nearby bases had made it into the facility before it had been sealed off just three minutes before the first missile struck.

Had there been more time, over three thousand additional soldiers, airmen and naval personnel would have reached the facility. However, these service personnel, largely caught in the open in assembly areas or in the traffic jam outside the entry portals around Mount Weather, had perished in the attacks. This was particularly hard for the advance parties from the same units to bear, having reached safety inside the facility just a few minutes ahead of their unit convoys. The same was true at many of the other DUMBs, as there had been so little warning.

All in all, over 3,600 of the designated 9,200 personnel had made it into DUMB One, or at least past enough blast doors, before it had been sealed.

The armed services of the United States had been at Defense Condition Four, with no recognized immediate threat. So, to suddenly jump all the way to DEFCON 1, *Maximum Force Readiness for Imminent War,* had been an unexpected escalation that caught the nation completely by surprise.

At the Mount Weather facility, columns of ground forces had arrived from all directions. Helicopters quickly disgorged their passengers and either lifted off to minimum safe distance or in many cases abandoned their helicopters in favor of the sanctuary of the facility. But when the time came for the large blast doors to close, just three minutes before first impact, the majority of inbound personnel had been trapped outside.

In one tragic mishap, a secondary door had been blocked partly open by a light Armored Vehicle that had been driving desperately through when it became jammed by the closing blast door. This had taken away a valuable layer of defense and had resulted in a breach of as much of one third of the original facility and the needless death of 457 personnel who had felt that they had made it. A second nuclear strike penetrated deep into the old facility. The resulting jet of plasma and radiation included heavy radioactive particles from the "salted" warhead, designed to maximize radioactive fallout. The heat and intense radiation had consumed the entire "C" level of the original facility, incinerating all manner of supplies and equipment that had been staged in the otherwise disused storage and logistics bays.

After having reached safety in the Mount Weather Annex, the inhabitants were as thankful for their new sanctuary as they were grimly aware of its tomblike nature. Eventually, issues of claustrophobia replaced the initial elation of having been saved. This, along with survivor's guilt, contributed to a host of psychological stresses that they increasingly faced the longer they lived underground. Being aware that all of the portals were destroyed in the attack and that they could not open up the prepared *new* portals until the radiation levels reduced to safe levels, made the feeling of being trapped that much more palpable.

Radiation detectors showed how long it took for the radiation to fall to safe operating levels. In the eastern states, the radiation levels had been very high due to the large number of targets and the prevailing winds bringing additional fallout from across the United States and Canada. At sites in the west, some sites remained radiation-free in at least one or two directions, where prevailing winds brought clean air from the north Pacific and scattered the radiation to the east. There were also a few commercial sites deep underground, like the Bethany Falls SubTropolis near Kansas City, which had not been targeted. With 10% of the available 55 million square feet leased out largely for the warehousing of food products, this facility was the largest food cache on the continent. After the war started, the SubTropolis had been quickly federalized by civil defense officials and the contents distributed in less than four months.

The areas east of Mount Weather had received heavy fallout because the attacks on Site A were surface-based detonations aimed at taking out the underground facility. Some of the warheads had even been "salted" with additional linings of gold and other heavy elements to increase the proportion of long-lived fallout. Areas further southwest along the Blue Ridge Mountains, including most of the prepared new portal tunnels, were largely clear of heavy radiation.

What held the authorities back from opening the new portals was the strategic situation. It took time to determine who had been behind the infiltration of SIMON and other computer networks, which had led to the nuclear war between the United States and the Russian Federation. Soon after the commencement of hostilities, however, USSTRATCOM and other commands had begun to piece together data pointing to Chinese involvement.

When it had been confirmed that the Russians had aborted over 200 missiles just minutes before reaching American and European targets, and had ordered their field commanders to cease all hostilities against US and NATO, the picture had become clear.

Russia's subsequent pulverizing of China gave the Americans solid proof of how deeply the Russians objected to having been manipulated into a war of annihilation by the Chinese. But, somehow, China continued to fight.

USSTRATCOM had reported that a previously unknown type of Chinese ICBM, with a surface detonation in the thirty megaton range, had obliterated the very deep and well fortified Russian bunker at Solnechnogorsk. This had destroyed the Headquarters of Third Missile Defense Army and decapitated Russia by taking out President Dvorkin and his top military and civilian advisors.

President Parker had been briefed that in the two weeks after the war had started, President Dvorkin had ordered the deployment of humanitarian assistance to European countries that had been so devastated by Russian and American missiles. He had sent hospital ships, engineering units equipped with water purification equipment, food aid, nuclear de-contamination and battlefield medical services. Russian aid was making a difference.

When the Chinese counter-attacked the Russian command and control sites, it had become clear to President Parker that China still had some surprisingly capable missiles and was intent on using them to thwart any efforts at stabilization. The hot war was not over yet. This made the Parker administration unwilling to come out from under the rocks of the Blue Mountains. So they stayed hidden, and did not open up the prepared exit portals until the military picture became clear.

It had taken eight months before the recursive process of Damage Assessment, Target List Update, Mission Planning, Weapon Selection, Strike, Battle Damage Assessment and so on had been repeated enough times that the Russians and Americans agreed that China no longer posed a missile threat. They had had to hunt down all twelve of China's nuclear submarines and destroy the sixteen known and ultimately six previously unknown facilities of China's Second Artillery Corp. While that had been considered to be an attainable goal, it was also recognized that China had a head start on mobilization and deployment in what was now clearly a global war of national survival. China also had the weight of numbers. This had left the Americans and other allies extra cautious, even defeatist.

In the Mount Weather annex it was not until 15 January that the Base Commander approved the order to start blasting the remaining hundred yards of one of the partly completed tunnels. With each eight yard "round" blasted, the tunneling crew got closer to the outside world. With each progressive round blasted the shock was more pronounced on the hillside. The final blast dislodged several rocks, which rolled down the snow-covered hillside.

The sky overhead was thick with the billions of tons of soot and dust thrown up during the nuclear war. The resulting grey skies were a cloak of darkness which, even in the midday gloom, no spy satellite could penetrate. Even so, the plan was to connect the new portal with the existing road infrastructure as quickly and quietly as possible.

WO Blakely's task was to take a reconnaissance team out on a snow-shoe patrol, establishing a security perimeter for the engineers. Before anything could be done, however, they had to wait while two CBRN techs headed out to ensure that the radiation levels were safe. They took readings on the yellow boxes attached at hip level, the ubiquitous CD V-715 Civil Defense High Range Survey Meter, which could measure rates of up to 500 Roentgen units per hour. Levels in the 0 to 2 R/h level were considered safe for operating in, as long as the workers had been given their Potassium Iodide tablets and were wearing dosimeters to track their total accumulated exposure. If levels were higher, personnel would rotate more frequently.

The CBRN techs were dressed in Level A CBRN suits. To keep warm, they also wore thermal underpants and a fleece layer much like a track suit. This made things surprisingly comfortable in the minus 32 C temperature they were operating in. The suits would not protect them from any hazardous materials and harmful radiation but would protect them from inhaling radioactive or toxic particles. The suits had Self-Contained Breathing Apparatus, SCBA, and were outfitted with a range of particulate detector strips which would alert personnel to any CBRN hazards.

They also had other specialized equipment that could be heard humming away as the little machines drew air into sampling chambers.   After a few minutes of tromping around and looking ridiculous in their awkward slow steps in the deep snow, the CBRN technicians confirmed safe radiation levels.

Blakely's security team swung into action, moving swiftly on their standard military issue magnesium-alloy snow-shoes. Their tracks, leading out of the portal, looked like the tracks of enormous birds. Blakely's team broke into two sections. One detail set up an OP on top of the bluff above the portal while the second squad walked down to the end of the spur road below and to the right of the portal. While treading up and down Edmonds Lane for a few hundred yards in either direction, they set up a few cameras which transmitted a live feedback to a repeater station being set up at the portal.

The men set about their tasks silently, using the microphones strapped to their throats to give short, concise reports to the "Net-Zero" signals operator who had set up his listening post just inside the portal.

The blast had come out of the hillside exactly as planned, three yards higher than the Mathew's Pond spur off Edmonds Lane, east of the once green forests of Sky Meadows State Park. The Major leading the Engineers looked over the area below the portal and identified the snow-covered pile of crushed rock that had been set aside years before.

Thankfully, the snow was no more than six feet deep. It would present only minor difficulties for the heavy equipment. The Major looked out over the surrounding countryside. He wasn't surprised that the nearby roads hadn't been plowed. From where he stood near the tunnel, it appeared that there was no smoke, noise, nor any other sign of human activity. It would take a loader about two hours, he figured, to dress up the ramp leading from the spur road up to the portal using the stockpiled gravel.

Looking back inside the tunnel, he saw a crew drilling blast-holes to remove an overhang just inside. Another crew was assembling a steel footing for a rapid-stand aluminum building that would serve as a gate-house and disguise for the portal.

After WO Blakely's team set up cameras at a number of locations, and settled in as sentries for the remainder of their twelve-hour mission, the WO moved on to his next task.

Standing on a rise close to the highway, Blakely had a good look up and down the valley to get a sense of the level of activity in the area. Having studied the maps and satellite photos before the mission, he knew the terrain. But looking at it live, on a cold wintry day after such a long confinement, he felt he had emerged into a strange and wonderful new world. He could just make out the red metal roof forming the spire of the Methodist church in the nearby hamlet of Paris.

The WO had been briefed that the hamlet used to have sixty people in it, and would be an early gauge of the status of the local population. He could see a few houses on the ridge northeast of the church, and the dimpled impression in the snow piled atop the odd-looking houses told him that their roofs had collapsed under the heavy snow. While it was far less than the snow piling up on the west coast, at least two yards of snow had been deposited across the entire North American landmass.

One of the Intelligence Requirements he was to take care of on this first patrol outside was to collect some digital images from the Edmonds Lane intersection with Highway 17. The main object of interest was Fleetwood Farm, just 400 yards north of where he stood. He could see that the farm was still inhabited. There was smoke coming out of the largest barn and the nearby house. Snow had been cleared from the areas between the house and the complex of farm buildings and grain silos, so it was immediately clear that the farm was operational.

WO Blakely and other soldiers from the Utility Battalion would be paying it a visit. With food supplies running low in DUMB One, and a decade-long nuclear winter ahead of them, they would need to nationalize any viable agricultural operations in the area. After all, the inhabitants of the Mount Weather facility, directly supporting the President of the United States, were far more essential to the survival of the nation than some farmers in rural West Virginia.

It had been a difficult ethical problem for President Parker, but in the end she had left the problem to the military. She had already ordered Marshal Law into effect in the first month after the attack. The military calculated that the 3622 DUMB One personnel had consumed almost three billion calories in the nine months after the facility had been sealed. They would need another thirty-seven billion calories to operate out of DUMB One for the anticipated ten years of the crisis.

This quantity of food would not have been a problem if it had not been for the fact that fully 80% of the facility's carefully prepared long term food supplies had been incinerated in the mishap at the northeast portal of the older part of the facility. The supplies were being rotated out, with the replacement supplies already staged in the logistics bays for rotation in. With the loss of the bulk of their food supplies, and the problems they were having with internal food production, they only had sufficient food supplies for two or three years.

Ops came up with a plan to seize food supplies from the surrounding region, and to ensure that no word of the status of President Parker or the personnel in DUMB One would leak out. Consequently, local citizens posed a *clear and present danger* to a Federal Government in a devastated nation, under

Marshal Law.

The more cooperative farmers would be brought into DUMB One to solve the problems they were having with underground food production. The others would be summarily executed.

It was not only the well armed local population that the Government had to be prepared to fight, but also the actual enemy, the Chinese military that had proven extremely difficult to find, fix and destroy. Despite the pounding that they had received from the Russians, and despite the on-going battles still taking place, the Chinese were still a threat.

The missiles had basically stopped after just a few days, but the conventional war raged on. It truly was the Third World War. And China was winning. They had dispersed and pre-deployed considerable forces worldwide. They had invaded Australia, New Zealand, Taiwan, Korea, Hawaii, several countries in Africa, much of South America, and even parts of the west coast of the United States and Canada.

The Chinese had employed some surprising tactics in their invasions, which completely invalidated the existing assessments of the Order of Battle of the Chinese military forces. The Chinese OrBat did not include a large blue-water navy, or a global-reach Air Force. Their sole strength was their massive numbers of highly disciplined and completely expendable soldiers, but they had no expeditionary capability.

By the time the US Government hiding in DUMB One figured it out, the Chinese had deployed over a million personnel into strategic regions of the world. Whether seizing oilfields, port facilities or agricultural regions all around the globe, Chinese personnel knew exactly where to go.

How they had arrived there was the game changer.

The Chinese had carried out a well-coordinated, three stage set-piece invasion: First, they had infiltrated "Little Dragon" spies into the objective areas to act as a Fifth Column, organizing bands of local Chinese sympathizers, Dragon Flies, to gather tactical data and track civil defense efforts.

Second, commercial aircraft loaded with lightly armed Chinese Special Forces had suddenly appeared at smaller regional airports in the objective areas. Separating into small units, they had commandeered local transportation, linked-up with the Little Dragons for up-to-date intelligence, and then swiftly captured their largely undefended objectives. Most of these had already been at least partly seized by the Dragon Flies.

Third, much larger follow-on forces had been transported on commercial ships that had been hijacked or leased by Chinese forces just prior to the missile attacks of 20 May. Some of the ships were role-on role-off vessels which had been seized fully-loaded with brand new SUVs and pick-ups *manufactured in America.*

After the devastation of the missile attacks and the chaos in the weeks after the war began, any resistance the Chinese forces encountered was poorly coordinated, logistically unsupported, and easily defeated.

Now, nine months later, battles were being fought all around the world by local citizens and small military units acting without effective intelligence, logistical support, or any kind of a plan. But slowly, organized opposition to the Chinese invaders was beginning to build. In many cases, Chinese were fighting Chinese; locals of Chinese extraction fought desperately to defend their homelands and the freedoms they cherished. There were signs of hope, but no major victories.

So it was in this context, of having already lost the opening moves of a global war with China, that President Parker's administration had become desperate for their own survival, and fearful of being taken out by a Chinese missile.

Follow-on attacks had occurred twice already. The first was when FEMA broadcast on the Emergency Alert Service that the 36th Engineer Brigade had successfully evacuated Fort Hood, Texas, before the sprawling base had been destroyed.

FEMA announced that a new base was being established just west of Waco, Texas. While the FEMA comment had been viewed as only a minor breakdown in Operations Security, OPSEC, the Chinese had picked up on it.

They launched a Dong Hai-10 nuclear-tipped cruise missile from a Type-035 Ming diesel submarine that had been lurking 100 miles southwest of Mazatlan. The missile destroyed the new base, along with everybody at the Reconstruction and Aide Center.

At the same time, Chinese ground forces had completed their marine deployment into Mazatlan and seized control of the port, but had run into a surprisingly strong Mexican force of local militia, regular Mexican Army and even some American tourists who figured that this was their chance to fight the Chinese.

When one of US STRATCOM's remaining satellites picked up the launch of the Dong Hai missile, and the technician reported that Fort Hood was the target, there had been resistance to the idea that it came from a Chinese sub. While it was well known that the Chinese version of the Russian Kilo class diesel SSK submarine was suited for littoral operations, nobody had ever heard of a Chinese cruise missile capable of reaching targets over 600 miles away. But it had.

The USS John Paul Jones, DDG53, a multi-purpose guided-missile destroyer capable of antisubmarine warfare, had been tasked to investigate the origin of the missile. Originally based out of San Diego, DDG53 was one of the few remaining assets of the 5th Fleet. Their home base at San Diego had been destroyed, along with 37 of 56 major surface combatants, including both the USS Nimitz and the USS Ronald Regan aircraft carriers and the principle USMC assault ships.

The crew of USS John Paul Jones had been operating out of a small dock at a resort at Santa Catalina Island when they had been given the urgent orders from the Mount Weather EOC. Racing at thirty-two knots, they reached the area west of

La Paz in under thirty hours and quickly picked up the acoustic signature of the Chinese SSK. The Chinese sub was heading due south, hoping to evade detection in the deeper waters off Puerto Vallarta.

DDG53's sonar operators verified the acoustic signature of Chinese Kilo SSK hull number 374. A Tomahawk missile from DDG53 placed a variable-yield W80 warhead just five hundred feet above the surface of the water and nearly on top of the Chinese Kilo. It vaporized the ocean for a radius of 1,200 feet. The 2,300 tons of metal, machinery, weapons and men in the Tomahawk's fully dialed-in 150 kiloton blast radius no longer existed.

The resulting plume of radioactive fallout was blown ashore by the gentle ten knot breeze. It reached the resort hotels of Puerto Vallarta within two hours. 310,000 locals and 113,000 tourists had considered themselves forgotten about in the war and were busy working out how to survive the coming nuclear winter in what had been a tropical paradise. Now they had to contend with a rapidly approaching blizzard of freshly charged gamma radiation from the Tomahawk's warhead and the fissionable material of the 13 unused warheads on the Chinese Kilo. They had not escaped the war after all.

A second follow-on attack had come from a Chinese land-based missile several months later; however, this was not a surprise. General Masterson, the top surviving general, had recommended that President Parker test the waters and see if enemy forces were still actively targeting the government. The plan was to include remarks in the weekly presidential broadcast that would lead the enemy to conclude that the broadcast was coming from the old bunker under the Greenbrier Hotel, in West Virginia. Being a well known bunker, the Greenbrier had been destroyed in the initial attack. But by using the green-screen wall in the Mount Weather facility, the audio-visual technicians could depict whatever they wanted as a backdrop behind the president as she made her address. They overlaid a duplicate of the backdrop from the Greenbrier, a picture of the White House that had been wall-papered on the wall behind the president's speaking platform in the old bunker, and touched up the deception with some artfully crafted props that matched the original furnishings of that now completely destroyed room in the Greenbrier Bunker.

The trick worked. It deceived the Chinese into believing that despite three Russian missiles, Greenbrier was intact. The Chinese didn't want there to be a functioning US Government so quickly after the war, so they dedicated one of their very few upgraded Fengbao-Tempest missiles, with a 13,000 km range.

This particular missile was launched from one of the hardened land-based silos near Wuzhai. It was just sufficient to propel the 3,200 Kg bunker-buster variant of the DF-5A missile. By adapting it with the DF-7K bus rather than the MIRV bus of the DF-5A, they were able to install a 10 Megaton warhead. The blast consumed the radioactive rubble that had once been the Hotel and bunker complex at Greenbrier, and the town of White Sulphur Springs. The 3743 residents of the nearby town of Lewisburg, West Virginia, and the 2,900 refugees that the kindhearted towns-folk had taken in, were also wiped out by this much larger explosion's ten mile radius of total destruction.

The shock waves were felt more then 50 miles away by President Parker and the rest of the inhabitants of DUMB One. It was as though a subway train had rolled over their facility. This left no doubt in their minds that there was still a target on their backs.

From then on, President Parker accepted the need to remain a government largely in hiding. All broadcasts of any agency would be vetted by the military for INFOSEC and OPSEC, and various tricks would be used to make the enemy believe that the broadcasts were coming from different locations each time. The new trick was to make the enemy believe that the government was hiding in remote areas of

Maine. There were no further attacks.

Now, nine months after the war had beguan, the government knew that the war had been extremely severe. 4138 warheads had detonated in Russia and the US alone. There had been a further 1160 strikes in Europe, 475 strikes in China, and 1400 strikes against principle cities in the rest of the world, making a grand total of 7173 detonations, with over four thousand megatons in combined yield.

Each of the 659 cities worldwide with over 500,000 inhabitants had been hit at least once. Key cities had been hit repeatedly, ensuring that the strategic infrastructure, power facilities and other important capabilities had been destroyed.

In addition to the yield produced by the atomic blasts, vast quantities of radioactive material had also been released by the destruction of missile silos, arms production facilities, warhead storage facilities, nuclear power plants and nuclear-powered warships. To make matters worse, more strikes were yet possible even though the stockpile of high readiness missiles and bombs had been expended. Replacement missiles and bombs were being made ready for subsequent nuclear battles, with thousands of warheads being readied for use on all sides.

The resulting shroud of radioactive particles, toxic smoke, ash and debris had caused a full-blown nuclear winter. Average temperatures had dropped by twenty five degrees celsius over continental areas of the northern hemisphere. Vast areas near and immediately down-wind of the many detonations would remain uninhabitable for scores of years.

From 350 million before the war, the population of the United States had fallen to 130 million in just 9 months. It would be below 80 million in another year.

The horrible reality was that the best case scenario achievable in the context of this global catastrophe would be for as few as 50 million American citizens to have survived for the hardest five years of the nuclear winter. Beyond that, it was anybody's guess. The nuclear winter had changed the climate so suddenly that a tipping point may have been reached. The skies might never clear. The continental areas could be stuck in a mini-ice age for centuries. Or things could suddenly improve and allow food production to begin to be restored.

If the nuclear winter lasted more than ten years, as a growing number of scientists believed likely, the forecast was unimaginably grim. Without new inputs of food production, other than what could be grown by hydroponics and other artificially illuminated agricultural systems, the actual sustainable number beyond the ten year timeframe was five to ten million in the US - just one to three percent of the original population. The real unknowns amounted to: how strongly could the American people hang on; how well would individuals fare without well-organized government guidance? How well could people adapt to a prolonged extreme winter with little or no sunlight?

It was in this context of unknowns and fear for their own personal survival that the personnel of the Mount Weather facility were emerging. Secrecy and self-preservation were at the forefront as they began to reconnect with the nation. The subordination of local property and food resources to the needs of the DUMB inhabitants was a necessary evil. The government would continue to function, but could do little to help the nation. The citizens would have to fend for themselves.

By the end of the twelve-hour engineering operation a thirty foot by forty foot garage had been completely assembled. The garage was nestled up against the hillside with a gravel driveway leading to it. It had just a few windows and a man-door to go along with the oversized garage door. Engineers had even blown snow around to cast a layer over the work site, making it look like the Garage had been there for years.

Who would suspect that the utilitarian structure housed the entrance to the bunker from which the President of the United States and the upper echelon of the US Government, FEMA and the Department of Homeland Security were operating.

It would be the responsibility of WO Blakely and others in the Utility Battalion to seek out and capture food and other essentials, and to overcome any opposition. Hopefully the locals would not put up too much of a fight.

Little did Blakely know that *put up a fight* was exactly what the local network of over 2,500 farmers, loggers, miners and combat veterans of Afghanistan and Iraq were preparing to give to the 512 soldiers of the DUMB One Utility Battalion. Their food was not for the taking.

25

VOGEL SHELTER

25 May: 5 Days After NEW

The Vogels were very smelly after five days in the basement. Manfred Vogel's last shower had been on the morning of his last flight. He had just completed the post-takeoff checks on the Air Canada Jazz Dash-8 that he was piloting from Prince George to Vancouver, when he heard from an Air Traffic Controller that Winnipeg had been 'nuked'. He immediately called his wife in Vancouver. He told Jillian to get the boys out of school, and to start moving food and water down to the basement. He would land in Vancouver within the hour, and somehow find his way home and join them in the basement.

Forty minutes later, when the EMP wave from a blast over Vancouver took out the electrical system of his Dash-8 Q400, he and his copilot had been in descent through 12,000 feet over Lions Bay, just about to come visual with the city. Mountains had protected them from the blinding light of the flash from Vancouver to their left and another blast at the Air Base in Comox behind them on their right, but the EMP fried their electrical systems and started fires in their aircraft.

After donning emergency oxygen masks and initiating an emergency descent, they barely managed to force-land the aircraft on a low-tide sandbar at Spanish Banks. They had landed just moments after the blast and shock wave from downtown had died down. Fires could be seen in the wreckage of the Kitsilano neighborhood that lay between Spanish Banks and downtown. It was a horrible sight to behold, as the secondary explosions and whirling firestorm consumed the lives of the people in that area like a hellish monster. Closer to the crash site, the damage was less severe and fires were more scattered. Manfred saw that the far side of the Jericho Beach Sailing Center was on fire, as was the old wooden pier.

After evacuating the passengers from the burning aircraft, Manfred told the passengers that they should follow Marine Drive for two km to the west, to find help at the University of British Columbia. The copilot knew why his aircraft captain would not go with them to UBC, so he led the passengers. They were silent, stunned by the devastation they had witnessed and shaken by the emergency landing on the beach.

Manfred wished his copilot luck, and then ran as fast as he could up Trimble hill to Eighth Avenue. Then he walked for a block to catch his breath before jogging the rest of the way along Discovery Street to his house on West 15th Avenue.

He had just made it to his front door when the skyline on the opposite side of his house was suddenly filled by the intensely bright light of a detonation overhead Vancouver International Airport, five km over the Dunbar ridge from his home. He ducked down and covered his eyes with his forearm in the sheltered alcove of his front porch. This saved him from being blinded by the detonation of the third atomic blast he had experienced in less than an hour.

After the house had been shaken by the shock wave from the airport, Manfred entered the house and headed down to the basement.

On his way, he saw that although his windows had been blown in, his home was basically intact. He figured that was because his street was in the lee of the Dunbar highlands. He was grateful that today's westerly winds would blow the fallout from the airport eastward, and not immediately threaten his family.

He found Jillian and the boys in the basement, terrified but intact. With perhaps four hours before the fallout from the blast at the base in Comox would reach Point Grey, Manfred knew that they didn't have much time. Before he could say much, they all felt a deep rumbling from yet another blast, this one more distant. Manfred wondered if radiation from Victoria or Nanaimo could arrive sooner, but then remembered that the winds were westerly, and would probably take that fallout over Richmond, well south of his home in Point Grey.

Having had the lecture from his long-time buddy, Casey Callaghan, he knew he needed to make a shelter that would put as much mass as possible between them and the soon-to-be radiated exterior of his house. Casey had even given Manfred some diagrams and pamphlets, which Manfred quickly forgot about once they had returned home from their weekend visit with the Callaghans.

He hadn't read the "How to Survive a Nuclear War" pamphlets after all, and hadn't watched any of the disaster films Casey had given him on disks. So Jillian and Manfred now had to rush through the diagrams to make sure they knew what to build.

Fortunately, they had a good starting point. Not only had Manfred been a construction worker before he became an airline pilot, but he also had a very well-built home. Thanks in part to his younger brother's success in the 'dot com' craze, Manfred had built a very large home for his family, just three blocks from where he had grown up, in upscale West Point Grey. The house had a deep basement with a 'nanny suite', rec room, bathroom, and modest-sized utility room.

With the lives of his loved ones at stake, Manfred suddenly took survivalism very seriously. Jillian found the package of reference material that Casey had given them for an improvised basement fallout shelter. Manfred scanned the handout and found a section that listed the "halving thicknesses" of various materials: Concrete, 2.3 inches; Steel, 0.99 inches; Packed Soil, 3.6 inches; Water, 7.2 inches; and Lumber, 11 inches.

He understood the physics involved in maximizing the mass surrounding the shelter. Each halving thickness that he could put over their heads would cut the radiation level by one half. A footnote to the chart said that ten halving thicknesses would reduce radiation to $1/1024^{th}$. He had some materials on hand and, after assessing them for a few minutes, came up with a plan.

Working efficiently in the little time that they had, they first shoved the rec-room furniture away from the deepest corner of the basement. Then they brought the six plastic shelving units from the utility room and set them up in three rows of two, four feet apart, and laid some 2x6's across the top shelves. Then they piled two four-by-eight sheets of plywood on the 2x6s, making a clean, flat roof about five feet high.

Then they covered every inch of this improvised rooftop with empty Roughneck bins and cardboard boxes lined with heavy-duty plastic bags. Ten year old Tyler was given the job of filling the containers with water. Soon they were bulging and pressing up against each other. This made a fairly tightly packed layer of additional mass. The sturdy plastic shelving showed no sign of buckling under the heavy load of water. Just to make sure that the structure would not crash down on them while they slept, Manfred reinforced the shelving units with landscaping ties that he cut to length and strapped to the ends of the shelving units to carry some of the load.

When Jillian and Manfred took a break to assess how much protection their shelter would give them, they realized that the huge quantity of water would be helpful later on, if water pressure failed. Nevertheless, Jillian had the boys fill every water bucket or pot they could find.

Manfred added up the halving thicknesses. He figured a half for the clay-tile roof and associated lumber, two and a half for the total of eight inches of concrete in the main and upper floor's 4 inch thick concrete slabs of the in-floor radiant heating system, plus perhaps another one for the lumber, plywood and drywall upstairs, and one and a half for the ten inches of water in the boxes on top of their shelter. That came to just five and a half halving thicknesses.

"If we don't come up with a way to add a more halving thicknesses, I don't know if this will be enough," he said.

"Can we add another layer of bins of water on top?"

"I don't think that would be safe, Jillian. That's a lot of weight, and we'll be staying under it for over ten days."

"What else can we do?" The adults stared at each other, worried about the effects of only cutting the radiation to $1/50^{th}$ of the unprotected level.

"We need mass? On top of our heads, right?" 11-year old Adam asked, wanting to help his parents. They looked afraid.

"That's right, champ. Any ideas?" Manfred held his son.

"Why don't we pull up the bricks in the patio and lay them on top of the floor right above where this shelter is?" he said.

"HEY! That would work! It would be like adding three inches of concrete to the floor, adding another halving thickness. That would DOUBLE our protection, and not add any danger of collapse. But we've only got about two hours left. You boys get started tearing up the bricks, and Mom will show you where to put them. Jillian, this corner is directly under the area in front of the bay window, in the formal living room. I'll grab Bob's wheel-barrow and help the boys."

"And we can add even more on top of that, come to think of it," Jillian said, excitedly.

"How?"

"THE INFLATABLE POOL! It's not even half full, so we can dump the water out of it, drag it into the living room, and set it up on top of the bricks. We could lay the area rug on top of the bricks to make sure we don't puncture the pool, and then throw the hose into it and fill it all the way up to the rim. It'll take hours to fill, but we can run the hose through down here with one of these "Y" shutoffs, and turn it off when we hear it overfill."

"That's a great idea!" said Manfred. As everybody got busy with the plan, Manfred rushed across the lane to his neighbor Bob's house, and took the wheel-barrow. He calculated that the three inches of bricks and thirty inches of water would add almost five halving thicknesses, taking them to the full ten. That would cut the radiation down to $1/1024^{th}$, which had to be enough.

As Manfred rushed back with the wheel-barrow, something was clattering around at the back of his mind but he couldn't figure it out. Something he had seen at Bob's house.

Soon after, when a small wind-up alarm clock Manfred had set went off, they realized that it was time to get into the shelter. Manfred turned on the Survey Meter and saw no radiation indicated. He wondered if he was using it correctly. Just to make sure, Manfred headed up to the second floor deck by the Master Bedroom and tried an outdoor reading. He could see that the mushroom cloud over the Vancouver International Airport had blown to the east. But at least a fraction of the radioactive particles must have been swirling around at lower levels since the survey meter now registered the occasional burst of about ten Roentgens per hour.

He thought that this was safe for short exposure, but was worried about the radiation headed their way from Comox.

Just before he left the bedroom, however, he remembered to go to the safe hidden in the closet and took out the smaller package that Casey had given them and which he had locked-up and nearly forgotten about. It had to be locked-up and not kept in the basement with the half-dozen Roughneck boxes of survival food and equipment Casey had given them, because it contained some serious items. He had decided the gun, gold coins, and map should be locked in the safe. Manfred had not worried that the boys would do any damage if they got into the survival food, or played with the yellow CF V-715 Civil Defense High-Range Survey meter that he was holding, or the Pen-type dosimeters that were still in the "Special" Roughneck box, so he had stored these boxes in the Utility Room. But he had been very uncomfortable about the gun.

Of course, in the frantic four hours of putting together their shelter, Manfred and Jillian had torn into the "Squirrel's Den" boxes and stacked them on the shelves in their shelter.

They had also broken open the Special Roughneck also marked "Faraday Cage", containing the survey meter and other electronic items. These had been protected from the effects of an EMP by being placed inside a series of cardboard boxes that were lined with simple tin-foil and some other type of wire mesh. With the electrical system having failed when Vancouver was hit, the items in the Faraday Cage might be the only functioning electronics in the neighborhood.

When Manfred rounded the corner on the main floor, on his way to the basement with the package from the safe, he looked to the kitchen to make sure that nobody else was still upstairs. He looked out towards Bob's house across the lane, and saw that Bob had lowered the rugged wind-down awnings, closed broad shutters over his windows and nailed a sheet of plywood over his exterior French Door. As Manfred headed down the stairs, he once again had that strange feeling that something about Bob's house was trying to get through to his mind.

After finding everybody else on a couch next to the shelter, and telling them that he had detected radiation outside, Manfred had everybody take the Iodine pills that Casey had provided. Then he complimented the boys for the clever way that they pushed the washing machine and dryer against one of the side walls and piled heavy books on top of the steel machines, adding three feet of mass to the side wall. The other side wall was now blocked by the billiards table, on top of which the boys had piled boxes of paint cans and books, all the way to the plywood decking above. The extra space under the heavy table would really help.

Jillian left a gap near the top of the pile, to let air escape from the small enclosed space that they would soon be confined to. The entrance between the washing machine and dryer was just wide enough to crawl through, like an Eskimo's igloo, and had Manfred's heavy metal tool box parked just in front. It could be rolled in to block the opening once they were inside.

While they watched the survey meter, Jillian explained the difference between *hourly rate of exposure* and *total cumulative exposure.* The boys understood, and were interested in reading the plasticized table that the Squirrel's Den had provided.

The chart listed various total exposure levels and listed how fast symptoms would begin to appear, what they would be, and what the ultimate disposition would be. They read that that as long as they kept total exposure below about 70 Roentgens, "R", the worst they would experience would be headaches and nausea, but they could expect a full recovery. If they had up to 150 R, they would have trouble healing from any wounds or infections, but should still make a full recovery.

If total exposure got close to 300 R, they would experience fatigue and weakness along with the nausea and vomiting. They would need medical care and there would be up to 10% mortality. If exposure reached 530 R, they would experience diarrhea, fluid loss, infections and hair loss within 14 days and, even with medical care, there would be up to 50% mortality. Approaching 830 R, even with medical care, mortality would be up over 50% within 6 weeks, and ultimately up to 99%. With infections, severe bleeding, fever, gastro-intestinal ulcerations, bloody diarrhea and other terrible symptoms, death would be painful. Beyond 830 R, death would be certain and, mercifully, within a few days.

On the opposite side of the card, there was a depiction of fallout patterns for 200 kiloton, 500 kiloton and 1 megaton blasts. These showed that if Comox was hit by a 1 megaton blast, and the fallout took 4 hours to arrive in West Point Grey, then the exposure rate this far from the blast would be between 0.5 R/hr and 250 R/hr, depending on the winds.

One of the boys took out a calculator from the Faraday Cage and worked out that their shelter would cut even the highest rate of 250 R/hr down to 0.24 R/hr. This would drop quickly to less than 5 R/hr within 48 hours, which meant only 0.0049 R/hr in their shelter. This meant that by cutting the radiation by ten halving thicknesses, their shelter would cut their total accumulated exposure to less than ten Roentgens by the end of the tenth day. But if they were exposed outside, or even upstairs in their house, they would have been exposed to well over 2,000 Roentgens and would be "completely toast".

That put it into perspective for the Vogel family. They spent the next ten days speculating about what had caused the war and what to do once it was safe to go outside. After a few days of this, they became more familiar with what Casey had provided them. They played cards a lot, read books, and talked about family trips and other good memories. Then suddenly, on the fifth day, Manfred remembered out of no-where that something about Bob's house had seemed important. He remembered that the folded map that was in the special package along with the gun and gold coins had labels indicating amateur radio operators. The funny letters and numbers pasted on his map, right next to their house, turned out to be Bob's call-sign. Then it hit him: when he had gone to retrieve Bob's wheel-barrow to move the bricks into the living room, he had noticed the tall antenna mounted to the side of Bob's house. That's what had been gnawing on his mind.

If Bob had been at all prepared to survive the radiation, or if Manfred could get his radio working, they now had a plan.

While the Vogels were busy setting up their shelter, Casey was even busier putting his Contingency Plans into effect. Within fifteen minutes of the first blast in Winnipeg, Casey had broken out his five "Actions On Nuclear War" ConPlans and sent Tanya to collect the children from school. By the time the first blast happened in Vancouver some 35 minutes later, Casey had given everybody their tasks.

The first was to send his seventeen year old daughter, Hope, with Danny and Yuri to the Highway Four exit to offer the 'Shelter Deal' to any truck-drivers who responded to the invitation Casey made on the Citizen's Band radio. This first ConPlan was aimed at quickly gaining manpower to defend the HOTH. He had Tara and Liam on stand-by to direct the rigs to park on the large gravel pad behind the Guard House.

The second was for Casey to call his contact at the local radio station on his private line and remind him about the ten-minute "Civil Defense Briefing" that he and Marty Penner had gone over with him during the disaster film festival. It was soon being pumped-out on the Sunshine Coast Radio Network. It informed people how to calculate the time for the fallout to reach them from any upwind targets hit by a nuclear weapon, how to evacuate across the island towards Port Alberni or other out-of-wind locations, and the essential features of an improvised fallout shelter like the Vogels were assembling in Vancouver. The broadcast also listed which public facilities in Oceanside were amenable to quick conversion to fallout shelters, and used authoritative language which got people moving in the right direction. Marty knew the details and set about organizing the community effort centered on the Oceanside Community Center while Katy managed her own children and those of others in the soon-to-be crowded HOTH.

The next ConPlan was to contact Moonstruck Farms and a few others to offer space in Casey's barn for some of their animals, *for a price*. Many of them knew about Casey's well stocked but under-used barn. Over sixty large animals and more than a few children were delivered to Casey's care for the expected two weeks of danger from radioactive fallout.

The fourth ConPlan was to invite families from the 4-H club and the Ring Families to drop their children off at the HOTH for shelter while the adults roughed it out at home. It was a small burden for Casey, who figured that even crammed full with over 60 people for two weeks, the HOTH would be the best place for his neighbors' children.

The final ConPlan was to implement security measures by activating the cameras and monitoring them in the HOTH. Once Danny was back from the Highway, he had him kit-up with a security uniform for the Guard House as a visible deterrence, and to orient the Truck Drivers as they arrived. JJ, the first truck driver to sign on, immediately began to contribute. Meanwhile, Yuri and Liam went around hanging signs around the property, reading: *"DEFENDED PROPERTY. Approach Guard House along main road unarmed (follow arrows). Use main access road only. Leave weapons at marked Amnesty Box."*

26

INDIA

10 June: 21 Days After NEW

Group Captain Patel had been expecting four IL78Ms at the improvised Air Station he was setting up in the small central Indian city of Itarsi, but only three arrived. One had crashed due to engine failure during takeoff from its dispersal airport at Gungapur. Six of the Indian Air Force's original sixteen IL78M air tankers had been destroyed at their home station in Agra during the nuclear attacks which destroyed most of India's air bases. Of the remaining IL78Ms, two were in Alaska on a joint exercise, two were operating in support of Su-30MK2 fighters patrolling the India-China border, and two were in Pakistan with the Occupation Force.

India had ordered the dispersal of all aircraft, ships and ground personnel immediately after learning of the nuclear attacks in Alaska and Canada. It was a cautious move, but they couldn't afford to take anything for granted. After being hit hard by Pakistan, the Indian armed forces had been on wartime alert status. They had prudently dusted off their contingency plans in case of a wider nuclear conflict and acted promptly.

With nearly a quarter of their four million personnel engaged in the occupation of Pakistan, the Indian military had been under considerable strain. But the non-deployed forces still left India as the fourth largest military in the world.

Now, just three weeks after the devastating attacks, the Indian armed forces numbered less than a million. Dispersal had proven difficult because the roads had become clogged by the military convoys. Even with 30 minutes warning, many of the evacuating soldiers hadn't reached safety in time and had perished.

The dispersal of aircraft had gone better, with 585 of India's 1320 combat-effective aircraft being dispersed to their pre-assigned regional airports. Now, with aircraft and soldiers scattered about the country, the leadership of the Indian forces designated two hundred sites for improvised bases, including the base being thrown together in the sprawling Itarsi lumberyard.

The Indian Army's main effort was to restore combat readiness, to begin large scale mobilization and, ultimately, to bring the fight to the enemy. After the country had been devastated by their second nuclear war in less than six months,

India was enraged. Combat operations against China were being planned even as the casualties were being tallied.

There had been confusion at first, with most of the missiles striking India coming from Russia. But it didn't take long to realize who was really behind the nuclear war. India had considered China to be its true adversary ever since defeat by China in the first Sino-Indian war in 1962. India had a comprehensive set of War Plans for the inevitable Second Sino-Indian war, ready to put into action. It would take time, however, to reconstitute India's military capabilities.

India had been busy in the weeks since the NEW had broken out. Vast areas of India were now devastated wastelands, uninhabitable for decades due to the intensity and permanence of the radioactive fallout from some of the salted Russian warheads. With the 64 largest Indian cities having been destroyed, the Indian forces were grappling with the complexity of reorganizing onto new bases which had, weeks before, been armories or other small military facilities located in the smaller, more remote, cities which had not been attacked.

Having lost over three hundred million people so far, and with hundreds of millions more to die from radiation and starvation, India was facing a war of national survival. They had known that the Chinese were a threat, but had not been prepared for such a decisive opening move.

India knew what China's next move would be, however, and had the means to counter it. The Americans in Alaska had shared a report with Group Captain Singh, leading a group of Indian Su-30's and air tankers on exercise in Alaska. Singh had the Americans transmit the report through to an Indian satellite in geosynchronous orbit over the Indian Ocean, and on to India.

The report had originated from a Canadian patrol aircraft that had been investigating a reported Chinese threat to commercial shipping.

The report gave India a clear picture of China's goals,

confirming Russian and American assessments that China's ambition was to become the dominant power in the post-war world.

The strategic center of gravity of the Chinese plan was the securing of food. With global food production and distribution essentially wiped out, the only food supplies were those already stockpiled and warehoused. China had been stockpiling these commodities with a vengeance in the months prior to the war. They had control of vast quantities of agricultural products at sea in bulk cargo and container ships which would remain out of reach on the high seas during the opening weeks of the war.

Meanwhile the Americans and Russians had expended much of their remaining warheads in a retributive strike against China. While the counter-strike destroyed as many as 240 Chinese cities and a great many military bases, it most likely had come too late. China had already deployed a sizeable number of her forces before the war and had pre-positioned vast stockpiles of armament to depots safely out of harms way.

With the bulk of China's most sophisticated weapons platforms having been destroyed in the pawn-for-pawn battles with American and Russian forces in the first weeks of the war, a new form of warfare was emerging. China was in the process of deploying upwards of a million personnel to seize control of food producing regions. The strategic move was not that much of a surprise; however, the methods used were. Chinese forces had used piracy to build up a massive number of commercial aircraft and ships of all kinds. With these they had already begun moving forces into Australia, South Africa, Asia and South America.

These invasions had come as a complete surprise as the commercial aircraft arrived unannounced, disgorging hundreds of Special Forces. These well-prepared soldiers immediately seized airports and key transportation nodes at numerous smaller cities which had been left intact after the nuclear strikes. Medium-sized port cities were seized by commandoes swarming the docks as they disembarked unexpectedly from commercial ships at wharf-sides, container terminals and other facilities.

By the time the rest of the world realized the scale of the Chinese ambition, China had already seized key footholds in Australia, Chile, Argentina, and Zimbabwe. Operating in the radioactive wastelands of Taiwan and Korea, specially equipped Chinese units seized strategic locations even before the radiation fell to safe operating levels.

The Chinese attempt to seize airfields in British Columbia, however, had been thwarted by CF135 Joint Strike Fighters operating from their improvised base at Port Hardy. The Canadians splashed three commercial aircraft about to land in Abbotsford, and one in descent for Prince Rupert. The 1150 Chinese Special Forces on the four aircraft were eliminated within sight of their objectives.

Intelligence reports from the Americans and Canadians indicated that China had deployed spies to these locations in the weeks before the attacks to gather intelligence on their targets and to seize some of them in advance of Special Forces.

The Canadians had captured some of these Little Dragon agents and their newly recruited Dragon Fly militia forces. They interrogated one prisoner successfully, having removed his suicide tooth. That particular Dragon Fly was supposed to seize a "roll-on roll-off", RoRo, ship loaded with American SUVs and take it to a pre-determined location in the North Pacific. Once there, they would hold their position for a few weeks until given a final destination for the vehicles. This fit the overall picture of China planning to use commercial ships and in many cases the contents of these ships as the logistical armada for their follow-on forces.

India immediately agreed to do its part to counter the Chinese plan. They would do what the tiny Canadian Naval Task Force had done just five days after the nuclear strikes, and begin to take the ships back from the Chinese. Three bulk cargo vessels and two other ships had been brought back to the Canadian west coast, providing food supplies to the coastal communities.

Knowing the Chinese strategy, the Americans and other allies now had all the information they needed to search for the convoys of Chinese controlled commercial shipping, and dispatch warships to seize them. The only problem was that so many allied warships had been destroyed in the initial nuclear strikes, that there simply weren't enough of them to seize the thousands of commercial ships at sea.

What India could contribute to the fight against China was to seize as much of the sea-born food supply as they could and deploy expeditionary forces to halt the enemy advance.

First, they would send an Air Expeditionary Force of Su-30Mk2 air superiority fighters to Western Australia. Group Captain Patel's assignment was to deploy two Squadrons to help the Australians regain air superiority by defeating the swarm of Chinese SU-27s. The first nine-pack of IAF's Su-30s would launch from Itarsi tomorrow. Three more waves of fighters would follow, supported by the IL78M air-to-air refueling tankers.

The second contribution by the Indian Forces would be to bring as many as 180,000 soldiers of the Indian Army, along with their upgraded T-90 Main Battle Tanks and the entire Western Command's elite XII Corps, to assist the beleaguered Australian Defense Force. If all went well, the Indian Army would be operational within two weeks, ready to join the Australian drive to liberate Adelaide from Chinese occupation.

The Naval Task Force accompanying the Indo-Australian Expeditionary Force on its eastward crossing of the Indian Ocean would seize control of all shipping within the Indian Ocean AOR, along with as much of the oil coming out of the Persian Gulf as they could get their hands on.

The American Carrier Battle Groups that were operating in the Persian Gulf and Gulf of Oman had been destroyed in the initial strikes. A third CBG had intercepted a cruise-ship loaded with a reinforced battalion of Chinese soldiers, along with two Ro-Ro ships carrying the force's armor and transport vehicles. Immediately after the American CBG had taken out the Chinese force bound for Zimbabwe, it was destroyed by a nuclear-tipped SLCM from an accompanying Chinese destroyer. This left the Indian Navy, with its two Russian-manufactured aircraft carriers, as the sole naval power in the Indian Ocean.

27

PRIME MINISTER CURROTHERS

16 June: 27 Days After NEW

When he was sworn in as Prime Minister, Christopher Currothers was finally in a position to make a difference. After ten years working on the Afghanistan file, first as "Ambassador Extraordinary and Plenipotentiary" and later as the "Special Representative of the UN Assistance Mission in Afghanistan", Chris knew what a failed nation was. Rather than restoring the floundering Canadian economy as he had set out to do when he was first elected, he was now faced with the utter devastation and hopelessness of a global thermonuclear war.

He had been elected on a solid platform of fiscal reforms designed to greatly reduce the size of government, a plan to re-structure the Canadian economy around domestic production, and a plan to return Canada to the gold standard. The actual re-issue of the Canadian currency as the Canadian Dollar-Gold, CDN $G, had been a difficult task. He had harmonized his launch with President Parker's new US Dollar-Gold standard, pegged at $G 10,000 per ounce. Effectively, the Canadian and US currencies were now simply receipts for the one true international monetary standard – pure gold. But, since Canada had been manipulated into selling off most of her gold reserves by the Federal Reserve during the Greenspan years, Canada had very little gold to work with.

To resolve this, Canada had accelerated the issuing of permits and licenses for gold mines to begin or to increase gold production. Canada went so far as to provide loan guarantees to promote the rapid increase in Canada's gold production. Taxes and loans also had to be paid in gold bullion in order to begin to replenish Canada's meager gold reserves. With twenty percent of all gold production now flowing directly to the Central Bank, Canada had started issuing the new currency in proportion to the gold accumulating in the vaults in Ottawa and Winnipeg. This had forced extreme austerity as the government couldn't pay wages or benefit programs anywhere near the former level. Printing dollar notes in excess of gold reserves had been made *illegal* under *Gold Standard Act*. Simply put, the government now had to live within its modest means.

But the currency became sound and Canada had appeared to be rewarded with a rapid increase in trade, particularly in the many types of commodities which Canada produced. In the first quarter alone, a suddenly resurgent China had placed sufficient orders of agricultural commodities to cause a wave of economic activity that had benefited everybody from the farmers of western Canada to the railway workers in the west, and from the longshoremen at the ports of Vancouver to those in Prince Rupert. It looked as if there could be a real turnaround for the economy.

But it was not to be. Prime Minister Currothers was as guilty as the other world leaders in falling for the allure of Chinese financial clout. He didn't see that Canada was being manipulated as a pawn in a dangerous game of chess.

With fleeting thoughts of how much the world had changed in just a few short weeks, an exhausted Prime Minister took his seat at the table. He organized his notes and prepared to begin the long broadcast. No longer the slick and carefully edited television broadcasts, this would be a voice-only communication sent out live through the Emergency Alert Service. The only live audience would be amateur radio operators who were always prepared to record the EAS broadcast and distribute it to local authorities. They were the backbone of civil defense and the Prime Minister's only effective way to govern the country.

One of the listening posts was in the Ops Centre in the HOTH, where Casey Callaghan was training the newly arrived Major Geoff Neumann in the EAS routines. While Geoff and Casey discussed how the Radio Terminology was a bit different from what they used in the Canadian Air Force, Geoff quickly caught on and was eager to absorb all of the SOPs and other rules and habits that the other survivors in the HOTH had begun to live by. Geoff knew that Tanya Callaghan was settling Gina, Gloria and Bartholomew into the suite that one of Casey's sons had graciously given up in order to give the Neumann family some private space within the HOTH. Their 3200 km journey from Winnipeg had been a real ordeal, especially their close call getting out of Prince Rupert on a jet-boat they stole from a crazy Chinese gang who were pilfering the wreckage of a downed commercial aircraft.

Geoff turned on the digital recorder when the EAS began, right on time at the top of the hour:

"This is a broadcast of Canada's Emergency Alert System for Sunday, 16 June. If you have the means, please record this broadcast and provide it to your local authorities by order of the Government of Canada. This broadcast is coming to you live from the office of the Prime Minister of Canada, the Right Honorable, Christopher Currothers," the preamble concluded.

"Good morning, ladies and gentlemen, People of Canada. This is Christopher Currothers speaking. In my first broadcast two weeks ago, I assured you that the Government of Canada would not fail. I promised that we would organize emergency assistance and that we would provide you with a full account of how this terrible event came to be. Now, with thanks to the hard work of our Canadian Forces, and with information from our allies in the United States and Europe, I am able to explain what has happened to our world," he began.

After explaining the Chinese role in starting the war and how widespread the devastation caused by American and Russian missiles was, his tone changed as he went into the details.

"We stand shoulder to shoulder with the people of the United States in expressing our sorrow to the people of the Russian Federation who were so wrongly attacked and who have suffered so greatly in the destruction of their great nation. It now appears that at least thirty million people of the Russian Federation were killed in that first strike, and as many as forty million more have already died in the aftermath. Faced with a barrage of missiles inbound from the United States, President Dvorkin had no choice but to order a full retaliatory response. All of this, I must stress, was orchestrated by the People's Liberation Army of China.

Russian warheads found their way to targets around the world. Approximately 150 individual targets in Canada were struck. The details will be provided after my address to you. However, I can summarize by saying that the thirty largest cities in Canada have been largely destroyed, along with our military bases. Initial estimates are that four million Canadians have perished. Another five million are severely hurt and likely to die within weeks from blast injuries, burns and the effects of the radioactive fallout. Ten million Canadians are now homeless and in need of medical care, food and water.

With our transportation systems destroyed, our critical infrastructure in ruins, and our ability to organize and provide relief extremely reduced, the Government of Canada is currently unable to provide meaningful assistance at this time." Pausing for a moment to drink some water, the Prime Minister went on.

"In the United States, fifty-five million people were killed in the initial attack. Untold millions more are in need of medical attention, food and water.

The situation is just as bad in Europe, which was hit by missiles from Russia and from the United States. We have learned that Chinese infiltration of the computer systems used by the American military forces allowed the Chinese to re-target American missiles to strike Europe, South and Central America, and other locations throughout the world.

The United Kingdom has been utterly devastated by radiation from the nuclear weapons and by the heavy-radiation released when nuclear power-plants were destroyed in the attacks.

The world owes a debt of gratitude for the fact that when the United Kingdom was faced with missile attacks from her closest ally, the United States, they did not fire back. The people of the United Kingdom are suffering greatly, but did not cause others to suffer in the madness of this war. Prime Minister Arthur Smyth is missing but believed to be alive. The status of the King and the Royal Family is unknown at this time. Our hearts go out to the people of the United Kingdom and to all people of the world who are suffering such terrible loss in this war." Another pause, and a drink of water.

"We know that China was behind this war. The remaining military forces of the world are cooperating in a grand alliance to counter the Chinese global aggression.

Here in Canada, our Air Force has destroyed several Commercial aircraft carrying Chinese Special Forces who intended to link up with pre-positioned spies and armed sympathizers in Abbotsford and in Prince Rupert. The Canadian Navy has seized commercial ships which had been hijacked by Chinese spies, and are presently commencing the distribution of food aid to several communities along the west coast.

As part of a joint military and RCMP operation that started in the hours before the war, Canada was able to uncover valuable intelligence on the Chinese intentions, and we shared this with our American and other allies abroad. This has begun to thwart the Chinese master plan of seizing the world's scarce food supplies and strategic locations around the world.

In short, ladies and gentlemen, the world is at war with China. We are fortunate in Canada that the Chinese incursions have so far failed and we are doing what we can to turn the tide back in our favor but, at present the Chinese forces still have the upper hand. I must stress, however, that even though there are agents of the Chinese state operating in Canada, we are not at war with the Chinese people; we are at war with the Chinese military.

There will be no internment of Chinese Canadians. Hostile acts against Chinese Canadians will be treated as criminal acts. Be on the lookout for suspicious activities and report these to local authorities, but do not take the law into your own hands."

Here the Prime Minister paused, briefly unable to continue. He knew that law and order had broken down right across the country and that looting and robbery were rampant. He could only imagine what would happen to innocent Chinese Canadians after his broadcast. But he felt it best to be honest and to warn the country that enemy agents were in their midst. It was personally difficult for him and his wife, Sue, a second-generation Chinese Canadian whose birth-name was Xue.

"We are in a state of Martial Law under the *War Measures Act*, as I ordered in my first radio broadcast. Civil authorities, police forces and all military personnel are empowered with the use of deadly force in the maintenance of law and order and in the protection of critical infrastructure, food and water. This leads me to the good news. Canada is intact. We remain a viable nation. We are successfully defending our sovereignty. We are reconstituting the Government of Canada, which will now be centered in the small historic town of Smith Falls. We are building our new Capitol City here, just seventy km southwest of where Ottawa once stood. It will take time, but we hope that as we rebuild our country anew, you will find hope and inspiration." Christopher Currothers could feel a surge of adrenalin as he came to the last part of his speech.

"Your local authorities will coordinate relief and reconstruction efforts in your area. In many areas this will focus on disaster mitigation to relieve the suffering of people who have been injured and displaced by the destruction of our cities.

I ask all Canadians to open their homes and take in individuals or families who are in need of assistance, as you would hope to be taken in if you were in need. In the coming months, we must prepare for uncertain times. This will require your assistance. The war has destroyed the road, rail and shipping routes which once brought food and supplies to your community. It is therefore my order, under both the *Emergency Measures Act*, and the *War Measures Act* that all wholesale food storage, all commodities and any large stockpiles of consumer goods at any commercial facility in Canada or in our territorial waters are now the property of the Government of Canada and are liable to seizure and re-distribution as coordinated by civil authorities on a local and regional level." Prime Minister Currothers took another pause, dreading what came next.

"The war has had an effect on our climate," he began again, somberly. He then spent a few minutes explaining nuclear winter. There would be almost no food production. At this point in his public address, the Prime Minister felt his resolve waver. He knew that he was lying to Canada about how desperate the situation really was. His advisors had calculated that even if all the food supplies, including rail cars full of grain and all the warehoused food were to be distributed – a monumental task on its own – it would not be sufficient for more than two to three years. The outlook for the remaining Canadians was starvation, depravity, suffering and death.

He continued with in a stern tone. "Effective immediately, the Government of Canada orders that the distribution of required materials will be managed by public officials. The hoarding or looting of materials needed for survival is a criminal act. Home-owners are protected by law in the use of lethal force to preserve their lives and property. Your survival depends upon cooperation since any help you will receive from the community resources will likely be very limited." Having given as much information as his advisors had assembled, Prime Minister Currothers could only close his broadcast with the truth.

"People of Canada, we have only a month or so before the onset of an extremely long winter. Some will be evacuated to areas where the prospects for survival are better but, with so much of our country devastated and in a world that is suffering as much or more than we are, our prospects are extremely poor. I pray that we will find the way to survive and I commit to working as hard as possible to coordinate the national effort. Canada will survive, God willing."

After the Prime Minister's address concluded, an official representing Public Safety Emergency Preparedness Canada, PSEPC, read off a seemingly unending list of cities which had been attacked. Listening in Ops, Casey and Geoff both knew the government had underestimated the magnitude of the coming winter, and was giving contradicting orders. Facing several years without food supplies, how could hoarding be illegal?

Casey brought this up with Ken, who had established

himself at the Qualicum airport along with his crew. They had made it all the way down from the Arctic by stopping at Forest Services airstrips, thanks to a set of maps Casey had prepared for him. They had camped out at one airstrip for two weeks, partly to de-bog their aircraft from the soft mud it had become stuck in and partly to take stock of their situation. The Crew of Vampire Five got through to Casey on the satellite phone, and figured that the Oceanside area was their best option.

Casey had viewed the video-footage Vampire Five had taken with the flight engineer's video camera. They had over-flown the bases at Comox and Esquimalt, and also taken footage of the devastation in Vancouver, Richmond and Nanaimo. It was clear that the region had been hit multiple times. Firestorms had destroyed most of the residential areas adjacent to the urban targets, leaving the lower mainland a wasteland. It sickened Casey and caused everybody to accept that no real help would be coming to the Oceanside area. They were on their own.

Ken had made contact with the Canadian Navy and had begun to coordinate military assistance along the coast. Inspired by the tactics of Somali pirates, they had used fast Rigid Hull Inflatable Boats, concealed on the deck of a Ro-Ro liberated from Chinese agents, to seize control of the commercial vessels.

Now, with just a small coastal defense vessel and the Twin Otter, what was left of the Canadian military struggled to ensure the fair distribution of food supplies from the grain ships that the navy had moored at the French Creek marina and other sites along the coast. Without effective national command, military personnel across the continent threw themselves into local and regional efforts, providing crucial organizational and leadership skill sets. In many cases the repsence of men and women in military uniforms gave added credibility to the local efforts.

Along the west coast, the food assistance coordinated by the military was a life-line to so many communities up and down the coast. Any efforts to nationalize local resources, however, was met with open hostility. It was one thing for the feds to help with coordination but it was another thing altogether to give up prescious resources, no matter who claimed to be in charge.

Unlike the catastrophies playing out in the United States, with federal authoriteis engaing in armed conflict with citizens, community groups, survivalist militias, Canadian authorities never crossed that line. The Canadian military would never seize food *from* civilians. That would be un-Canadian.

28

NEW NORMAL

A loose external shutter was rattling in the strong winds outside as extra chairs for the weekly briefing were being set out in the large living room. Today the focus was on climate change, with Zlata getting ready to give a Power-Point presentation on the latest data.

Everybody was interested, since the last few months had seen some very strange weather. When snow began falling in August, it was the first such summer snowfall in local history.

Danny had been worried about Uncle Casey, who had not returned from his visit to the old Fire Chief down in Qualicum Beach. The forest had been bleaker than ever that day, with a dark grey sky made that much more dismal by the falling wet snow. Danny was careful not to cross the highway; the SOPs were very clear about unauthorized travel outside of the Callaghan area of influence. After checking the roadways and other more commonly used paths from the HOTH to town, Danny had checked the deer tracks along the south side of the highway.

When he found strange drag-marks along one trail, Danny realized that someone was dragging themselves along or perhaps crawling on hands and knees. When he found Casey laying face down in a puddle, Danny radioed in his coordinates and requested assistance. While he waited, Danny applied what little First Aid he knew, talking out-loud to remind himself of the procedures.

"A. B. C. Airways. Breathing. Circulation. Casey, are you breathing?" Danny said, as he leaned down to listen. He put one hand on Casey's cold, clammy forehead and used the other to lift Casey's jaw, tilting the head back to open the airway. Then he used a finger to gently pry open Casey's mouth. It was full of pine needles and mud. Danny scooped out what he could, and decided that Casey was not breathing.

"Fuck it!" Danny exclaimed, after failing to find a pulse, and went right to CPR, which Casey had taught everybody in the First Aid lectures in the first weeks after the war started.

After a few minutes of cycling between chest compressions and artificial respiration Danny was rewarded by Casey coughing profusely and starting to breathe on his own. Danny checked again and could feel that his uncle had a pulse. Danny grabbed Casey's left arm and knee, and pulled the large man over onto his side, into the recovery position. Then he took off his own jacket and laid it over Casey for warmth.

Danny then got out a pen-flare from his packsack and radioed that he was sending up a candle. He fired the pen-flare through a small gap in the forest cover. A few hundred meters away, Manfred Vogel was leading a group of rescuers along the same deer path that Danny had used. Miles Callaghan had been watching for the flare and saw the bright burst of red light through the dense forest. The rescue party soon found them.

Once they got Casey back to the infirmary in the HOTH, they stripped off his cold, wet clothes and warmed him gently. JJ and Manfred headed out to retrieve Dr. Pizarski from the medical station that had been set up in the Community Centre. Dr. Pizarski treated Casey's four cracked ribs resulting from Danny's exuberant chest compressions.

Casey had imagined that he heard someone calling his

name only moments before graying-out and falling on his face. His last memory was the taste of mud as he choked in the puddle. Danny had most certainly saved Casey's life.

Casey's mother was constantly at his side during his convalescence, as much as to be there when Dr. Pizarski came to check on Casey, as to watch over her son. As Casey began to recover he recognized the look in his mother's eyes; something was going on between Grandma Callaghan and old Dr. Pizarski.

Now, almost four weeks after Casey's brush with death, the wet snow had changed to persistent dry snow. The daytime highs were no warmer than minus five C, with overnight lows down to minus fifteen. Zlata could not explain the extremely rapid cooling on the West Coast. She had expected the temperature to fall more gradually after the war. She needed more data.

What little they could learn from the broadcasts that Geoff and Manfred were monitoring on the radio nets did not give a clear overall picture. Zlata had taken the initiative and told Geoff and Manfred to ask other stations to report temperatures, humidity, wind direction and speed on a daily basis. She plotted this information on print-outs of weather charts. Zlata was not a meteorologist but she was a climate scientist and had the help of Geoff Neumann's Air Force training in meteorology. Now Zlata was ready to report her findings.

"Today we're going to focus on the climate changes we are seeing and what this means for our future. Once we're done, we'll break into four planning groups. Casey will lead group A, Amy will lead group B, Geoff will lead group C, and JJ will lead group D. I'm telling you this now so that you can take notes or ask questions during the briefing and be ready to start on the planning right away.

The main theme for all planning groups is the impact of the changed climate on the assigned subject areas," Zlata explained. Geoff got up from his seat near the laptop and projector that were situated on a card table. The Power Point presentation was viewed on a large white wall of the Great Room. Geoff moved to an easel off to one side and flipped the first large sheet of paper to reveal a list of names assigned to each planning group.

Zlata continued, "Casey's group A, with Nora as assistant leader, will focus on the likely impact on surrounding neighbours including the Ring Families, Parksville and Qualicum Beach, and the Sunshine Coast in general. Don't get lost in the details. Just come up with general conditions and any advice that needs to get passed around." Zlata paused, as people looked to the easel where the names under Group A were listed. The Mission Statement was presented in Geoff's clear, military printing.

"Amy's Group B, with Jillian as assistant Leader, will look at HOTH systems as they relate to the colder weather. Focus on the impact of heavy snow, increased energy consumption, hydroponic operations, maintenance of the helical wind power and diesel generators, and other integral HOTH systems.

Geoff's Group C, with Tanya as assistant Leader, will focus on the HOTH Battle Rhythm of personnel rotations, chores, rest cycles and "Assigned Tasks". The intent here is to adjust the work allocation and degree of effort assigned to everybody.

Finally, JJ's group D, with Danny as assistant Leader, will focus on security routines," she said.

Up until now, Danny had been an "also ran", participating in group discussions but had never been given much of a role in decision making. It was JJ who had suggested that Danny be given increased responsibility. The men relied upon for security had taken well to Danny's role as shift-manager down in the Gate House. That he was a Callaghan family insider was not counted against him as he had a toughness and demeanor that the truckers respected.

"If there are no questions, I'll get started on the Climate briefing," said Zlata.

"What about Roger, Duncan and Andy?" Blaine asked,

referring to truck drivers whose names were not on the lists.

"Roger asked to be left on Sentry. He doesn't like doing planning discussions. JJ, Andy and you, Blaine, will have to rotate coverage at the Gate House in order to participate," Geoff replied, beating Zlata to the punch. "And Duncan will stay camped out up at the South OP for the rest of his 3-day stint," Geoff went on, referring to the big Scotsman who preferred to spend a few days camped out in the OP that overlooked the HOTH from above. He amused himself by reminiscing about his days with the British Army or his boyhood in the Scottish highlands.

Duncan was particularly moody, ever since the loss of his best friend in the raid on the Walker Gang. JJ, Danny, Duncan and two others had gone after Constable Walker and the other men who had tried to capture Casey. Duncan had piped up about the lack of planning, but had been over-ruled by JJ and Danny who were very angry about Constable Walker's attempt to capture Casey. While they had surprised the Walker gang, the ensuing gunfight was a draw. One or two of Walker's men were hit, while Duncan's buddy Rory was fatally wounded in the skirmish.

The group had barely made it back to Callaghan territory after they had tried to sneak up on the Lodge occupied by Walker and his thugs. Rory died painfully and, from Duncan's point of view, for no good reason. It was a harsh reminder that Casey's SOPs existed for a reason and should be followed.

JJ was severely reprimanded when Casey learned of the fiasco, but his role as Security Lead was not diminished. It was clear to Casey and even to Duncan that JJ took his failure to heart. He would follow the SOPs in the future and listen to Duncan, Geoff and others with military experience.

Seeing no other questions, Zlata started her presentation while Geoff ran the slide show. "The long term climate forecast we received from the Emergency Alert Service was mostly accurate. We did see the increased humidity and temperatures in the first six to eight weeks after the war, and the heavy rains and flooding they had forecast. Then the cooling started in August with that first wet snowfall when Casey got hurt," Zlata said, looking at Casey with the concern she still felt for his health. "And then it got *really* cold, when the rain showers became heavy snow in the last two weeks." Zlata completed the background summary, nodding to Geoff to advance the slide.

"Here is the current weather pattern. For those of you who don't know all the symbols, I'll walk you through it. This is the 850-millibar weather chart. Normally it would apply to weather at 1,500 meters, or 5,000 feet. But, with the increased atmospheric pressure caused by the billions of tons of dust and smoke added to the atmosphere, the 850 millibar level is now more like 1,200 meters, or 4,000 feet. It's still a good altitude to see the major trends, however.

As you can see, the upper winds are coming to us off the Coast Mountains, northeast of here, basically from Whistler Mountain. This is the new normal, with winds being more than 60 degrees clockwise off from the traditional northwesterly wind patterns. The reason for this is mostly due to changes in the location of the strong upper wind known as the Jet Stream, which used to spend most of its time over Canada. Now, with the changes to the atmosphere as it cools into nuclear winter, this powerful west-to-east jet of air, which essentially drives the weather, now lies across the mid-latitudes of the United States."

Zlata highlighted the strong wind barbs of the jet stream on a 250-millibar chart before returning to the 850. "This makes sense, when you think about it. It's as if we are in the middle of an extremely cold January, with the Jet Stream over, say, Kansas, rather than Winnipeg," she explained.

"And while we deal with heavy snow accumulations and cold temps here in the Pacific Northwest, they're dealing with persistent heavy rain in California and northern Mexico. They're getting Pacific typhoons there and heavy snowfall in Arizona and New Mexico," Zlata went on, paging through slides showing the frontal activity from Portland to San Diego.

"How long will the snow accumulations go on and how much snow are we talking about?" asked Nora, clearly worried about the weight of snow piling on rooftops in town, her assigned task for the planning session to come.

"From what we're seeing in the sea-temperature data being reported from Tofino and Astoria, the sea temp has dropped by a full degree from normal," Zlata said, as she directed Geoff to jump ahead a few slides. "This slide shows global sea temps. You can see that we live in the green, temperate zone where normal sea temps would be around ten to twelve degrees. They have dropped a full degree in just the last six months.

According to the best climate-change models I have in my database and my own hunch, the lack of solar insolation and the subsequent loss of heat will be at its maximum rate for the first six months, which we have seen. Then it will gradually slow down as the nuclear winter unfolds, say, over the next five years." Zlata explained this while Geoff clicked ahead a few more slides to a depiction of colder temperatures in North America and the surrounding oceans.

"So these are the temps we'll be living with?" JJ asked.

"Yes, I'm afraid so," Zlata replied, as everybody took in the details projected on the wall. "The Arctic Ocean will be permanently frozen-over for years to come, and there will be surface ice in the inlets from Seattle all the way to Anchorage. But we won't be able to walk across from Vancouver Island to the mainland, because strong tidal currents along the Inside Passage will prevent total freeze-up."

"And what about snow accumulations?" Nora asked again, this time knowing what the answer was going to be.

"It's going to be like the last two weeks have been and it will keep going for another six months before it tapers off. To make matters worse, from time to time that persistent Low centered on Portland will break down and we'll get heavy rains on top of the snow. Then the Low will re-establish itself and bring colder temps back. So we'll alternate between heavy snow and rain."

"So we'll have what, a hundred feet of snow in five years?"

"Well, no, Manfred. It'll compress as it accumulates. The occasional rain will make hard ice layers, adding weight. So, we'll probably see a snow pack of five meters by this time next year."

"What else have you got to cheer us up?" asked Tanya.

"Well, we think that the higher air pressure we're experiencing will have a modest effect on chemical reactions. Water will boil at a higher than normal temperature and internal-combustion engines will have denser air to work with, as though they were supercharged. We don't know how this will affect us, but we should watch for things behaving a bit outside of normal parameters. The one thing we have absolutely no idea about is what is happening up above. The nuclear explosions threw huge amounts of dust and soot as high as 150,000 feet into the stratosphere. It's so far above the level where water is present, say 40,000 feet, that there's no mechanism to wash the dust out of the atmosphere. So it could linger there for decades, leaving us in a new ice age, only worse."

"How could this be worse?" someone asked.

"A normal Ice Age affects North America and Eurasia, but the rest of the world still gets sunshine. In this nuclear winter there will be Ice Ages happening in all the continents, and no sunshine *anywhere*. There's no place to go to escape the cold, and nowhere to grow food. We really are facing extinction unless something happens in the stratosphere, that we don't know about, to clear out all the material that's cut off the sun."

29

MOONSTRUCK

Manfred was saved by the SOPs. He had been leading a three-man run to Moonstruck Farm, with his son Jack riding with him on the whisper sled. Duncan followed with a gas-powered sled a thousand meters behind, towing a heavy cargo. They were going to trade a barrel of diesel and some food supplies for an active bee-colony. Nora had convinced the others that the HOTH needed a beehive in the Barn/Garden complex to increase food production and eliminate the work required for hand-pollination.

The SOPs called for approaching Moonstruck Farm from the forest rather than following smoother paths on former roads now buried by eight feet of snow. As Manfred and Jack quietly came to the end of the last stand of trees they stopped; the electric sled became instantly silent.

Having been to Moonstruck many times by now, Manfred immediately recognized that something was wrong. There was no smoke coming out of the barn's chimney. This meant that Clayton Palaty had let the fire burn out, something he would never do in this minus-twenty weather.

Concerned that something may be seriously wrong,

Manfred clicked several times on his XPR radio, hoping that Duncan was wearing his ear-piece. Sure enough, Manfred heard the distant clattering sound of Duncan's sled abruptly stop, bringing absolute silence to the wintry landscape.

"Two, this is one, over."

"Go ahead one."

"MODERN ART", Manfred gave the code-word for *something looks wrong*.

"Roger, out."

Jack took up a defensive position, watching the path they had made with the whisper sled, while his father scanned the scene with his binoculars. At first Manfred couldn't see anything wrong, but then he noticed the two dogs at the snow-covered entrance to the main farmhouse. They were Shepherd – Rottweiler crosses. Manfred recognized Zeus and Adolph from the surveillance pictures in the Ops Center. These were Walker Gang dogs. That meant that at the very least their handler, Big Joe, would be near. They certainly wouldn't be welcome at the Palaty farm, given the many atrocities that the Walker gang had carried out. All of the Ring Families and most other survivors would shoot Walker and the more brutal of his henchmen on sight.

A rumor had spread that a few of Walker's men didn't agree with his methods. His habit of terrorizing those that he ambushed, taking everything from them, had made him an outlaw in the Oceanside region. Other gangs, even some of the bad ones, didn't go quite as far over the line as Walker's men. However, it was also well known that the former maintenance engineer, Frank, and sometimes Big Joe, had intervened and talked Walker out of some of his crueler ideas. Some lives had been spared.

Before jumping to any conclusions, Manfred needed more information. According to SOPs, this had to be called-in before any further actions could be taken.

"Zero, this is One, Over."

"One, this is Zero, Send, Over."

"MODERN ART confirmed. Subjects Delta-one and Delta-two present. No British in the meadow." This made it clear to Geoff, manning Ops, that there were no British Thermal Units - heat - at the place where the animals should be - the barn.

Casey wrote the script for Geoff to broadcast on the frequency used for communications between the HOTH and Moonstruck Farm. JJ, Danny, Casey, and GT armed themselves, taking extra pistols and clips, and headed out on two gas sleds.

"Moonstruck, this is HOTH. Over," Geoff transmitted.

After several attempts, an awkward reply finally came. "HOTH, this is Moonstruck Farm. Everything is normal here. What do you want?" This was so far away from standard radio-telephony that Geoff knew that a stranger was operating the radio. So Casey's plan could work.

"Roger, Moonstruck. Sorry that our delivery is a bit behind schedule, but Casey had some mechanical troubles on the way. He just reported that he's mobile again, and should be arriving at your place within ten minutes."

"What does he... Just a minute." Moonstruck came back on the air after a short silence. "Roger, HOTH, we'll have some coffee on for him." They had taken the bait.

Switching to the private channel that the HOTH XPRs were preset to on Channel 2, Geoff told Duncan and Manfred to wait for Casey, out of sight near Moonstruck Farm, for an assault briefing. When Casey linked-up with Duncan and Manfred, there were a few other men present. He and JJ killed their engines, while Danny took up a defensive position looking to the rear. Manfred came over to brief Casey.

"Walker plus eight hostiles are in Clayton's house. The two dogs are tied up at the entrance. The heat has gone out in the barn, so I think it's deserted. These are some of Clayton's people," he indicated, of the six men and five women.

"Hello, Peyton! Where are the rest of your people?" Casey asked Clayton Palaty's eldest son.

"Most of our people got out. They're 200 meters that way, in one of our defensive positions. Walker's men got in by overtaking our grain-run and forcing their way inside. Those of us who got out the back tunnel were not observed, so Walker may not have found the hidden entrance. He has Mom, Dad, my sisters and five of our men. Everybody else is OK. I think he's hurting my Dad, so I want to get in there quickly. Will you help us?" Peyton asked, clearly upset and worried.

"How many of your people here are armed?"

"Just two of the ten men. We had no time to get our guns when Dad ordered us out the tunnel." Peyton seemed ashamed.

"OK, we've got six extra pistols for you," Casey said, nodding to JJ who began handing them out. "Walker's expecting to see just me, arriving in a few minutes, to be ambushed. I'll fake another breakdown of my sled and radio them that I'm going into their barn to grab some tools to re-seat my tread. By that time, JJ, you, Duncan, GT and Danny have to have gotten to the barn, and entered from the side farthest from the farmhouse. Hit Walker's men when they enter. You choose the moment to open fire, and I'll dive for cover when the shooting starts." As Casey concluded, GT and Danny were already climbing into the whisper's cargo sled. JJ gave Casey a meaningful look as he and Danny mounted the whisper itself, ready to go.

"What do you want me and Jack to do?" asked Manfred.

"You stay out of sight here, and keep Ops informed. Be ready to come in with a sled to medevac me or any other casualties back to the HOTH. Take my Super-Magnum and snipe any of Walker's men who exit the farmhouse once the shooting starts. As for you, Peyton," Peyton nodded that he was listening, "wave a white towel or something to indicate all clear once you've cleared the farmhouse, and Manfred here won't shoot at you."

"So I take my guys in through the tunnel and liberate the

house while you guys draw some of them into an ambush in the barn?" asked Peyton, clearly eager to rescue his family.

"You got it. How much time do you need to be in position?"

"About ten minutes. Can you stall that long?"

"Sure. Will they be able to see as far as the main gate from your second-floor sentry post?"

"Yeah, but not much farther. Too much snow's piled up."

"Perfect. Everybody get moving. I've got an appointment with an old friend!" Casey said, starting up his sled. He drove noisily, snaking his way through the forest to waste twelve minutes. Then he took a more direct route to the farm.

Once he was in sight of the second-floor sentry post, some 500 meters from the main gate, Casey faked his sled getting bogged down, stopping roughly abeam the end of the main barn. Then he transmitted on the channel set for the Moonstruck farm.

"Moonstruck, this is Casey. Over."

"Go ahead Casey; is that you there by our gate?"

"Yeah. I've thrown my belt off its rollers again. I need to get a shovel to wedge it back into place. I'll just go over to your barn and get one, it won't take long." Casey turned off his radio, making it impossible for Walker's radio man to reply.

He walked towards the back end of the snow-covered barn. Everything hinged on Walker deciding that the barn was the best place for an ambush, and one of his own men provided the reason. Walker told his men that they should kill Casey when he entered the house. Frank objected, just as he had about the beating that Walker gave Mr. Palaty.

"Boss, we don't have to kill him. We could trade him for food. Killing him gets us nothing; why make so many enemies?"

"You are such a wimp, Frank! That's probably why you lost Casey the first time. We finish him once and for all. After that, his HOTH people will be easier to cut down. They won't have their great leader. But I'll tell you what, we'll do our business out in the barn, rather than in here, so we don't offend you and the other women, you WHIMPSHIT!"

Walker and three men rushed to the barn. It was dead quiet. Once inside, Walker waited for his eyes to adjust to the darkness. The only light was from a single lantern, hanging from a beam further back in the humid, putrid-smelling barn.

Suddenly there were muzzle-flashes from four directions. Walker raced head-down out of the barn. The wood along the wall beside him was splintered by an intense volley of bullets.

He started for the farmhouse but then realized that there was shooting going on inside. He saw a sudden puff of pink mist spraying from the head of one of his men on the second-floor lookout. He had been shot from somewhere inside the house.

Walker ran to his right, into the forest. He made good time thanks to the snow being trampled by the Palaty family's constant trips into the forest for firewood.

From his vantage point several hundred yards to the left, Manfred saw which way Walker had gone, but the few shots he was able to get off didn't find the target. So he kept his eye on the main entrance, and occasionally swept it back to the barn.

"All stations, this is HOTH Actual. Send Sitreps. Over" requested Casey as he held his breath.

"Actual, this is One. One hostile has fled south-east into the forest. White flag visible at Farmhouse. Over."

"Actual, this is Two. Three hostiles Black, one escaped."

"Actual, Zero, Peyton reported in on Moonstruck channel that he is in control there now. Three hostiles Black, two Green, no friendlies hurt. Over."

"Zero, this is Actual. We are green here, will advise. Out to you."

"Actual, Zero. Good copy. Out."

Casey drove his sled to the barn and went in to see who had died. The fatalities were three of Walker's worst goons, high on the "with prejudice" list in Ops. JJ thought that the fourth had been Walker, but JJ and his men had only just made it into the barn by busting through the ventilation shaft. They had barely been in position when Walker's men had entered the barn.

Peyton had surprised the five remaining Walker men inside the farmhouse. They didn't have a reason to shoot Frank or Joe. The two prisoners were laying face-up on the floor when Casey addressed them.

"Joe, do you want a chance to redeem yourself, right here and now?" Casey asked upon his arrival at the farmhouse, holding the sweat-soaked fur hat that he had found in the snow, which Walker had obviously lost.

"Yes. What do you want me to do?"

"Give your dogs this scent." Casey handed Joe the hat. "Order them to kill."

30

LODGE DEAL

06 October: 20 Weeks After NEW

JJ and Danny were with Casey when he returned to the Lodge. They brought the bodies of Walker's men and the badly mauled corpse of Constable Walker himself with them.

Friends and family were granted permission to pay their respects. They carried out a solemn funeral pyre.

Casey explained to Frank and Joe how things would go from then on. There would be general amnesty for the rest of Walker's group. But first the Lodge would be given back to the elderly couple from whom Walker had seized it when the war began. But the owners didn't want to kick the gang out. They wanted to help as many people survive as possible, and they cared deeply about the women and children they had come to know so well.

The HOTH security team had a good look throughout the facility and confirmed that cannibalism had not been practiced, and there were no persons being held there against their will. They identified a number of items that other groups had reported stolen, such as generators, skidoos, and a few farm animals.

When they inspected the weapons locker at the Lodge, Casey recognized the AWSM and AR50 sniper rifles from Pal's personal collection. Finding Pal's possessions in the Walker lair confirmed Casey's suspicion that it had been Walker who murdered his friend. Casey took the Super-Magnum, the Armalite, an M16, several handguns, three hunting rifles and two shotguns for the HOTH. He also took about half of the ammunition, including 36 missile-like 0.50 caliber rounds for the AR50. He sent most of the other guns to Staff Sergeant Wright, who had succeeded against all odds at keeping the Oceanside RCMP office secure.

With Frank and Big Joe now in charge of the "Lodge Family", Casey thought that they could be brought back into the community fold. He offered them a deal they couldn't refuse.

Casey's people installed a wind power-plant and provided some basic lighting equipment and chemicals to get the Lodge Family started on a small indoor garden to go with the chicken operation they already had. He also gave them a young sow and a few immature male pigs. In return, Casey required them to formally disavow hostile operations against other people, and to promise to serve what was left of the Oceanside community. Then he offered them a food-for-service contract.

The deal involved mutual self-interest. They would keep the skidoos they had stolen from others, but would be required to use them for weekly transport runs. The first would be to supply and transport three cords of fire-wood to the Qualicum Community Centre, where Marty Penner would distribute the firewood to needy groups in town. The next run would be to pick up a load of grain from the supply ship in French Creek and transport the grain back to Marty in the Community Center. They then were to do another grain run out to Parksville where the Wayne family was running a soup kitchen and trading post. Their final weekly run would be to take a grain shipment to the Errington market to support the survivors in the rural acreages. This would also give them a chance to trade for needed supplies, using the grain as money. After completing the tasks they could swing by the HOTH for some gasoline - just enough to replenish what was used in the required supply runs. They would also receive a food hamper and be invited to a meeting in the HOTH, where they could report on the condition of survivors in their area.

Frank agreed, promising to make the travel routes in the vicinity of the Lodge safe for travel. This would make it possible for townspeople to resume trading at the Errington Market without interference. In this way, a gang of marauders became a lifeline.

31

PROBE

"Zero, Actual. I'm in position now, searching for targets," Casey said over his headset as he settled on the sniper's platform in the Bird's Nest. He and Hope had been enjoying some father-daughter time during their shift in the Bird's Nest when Miles Callaghan interrupted their quiet time. Ops had multiple contacts on perimeter video cameras.

With the heavy snowfall in recent months, there had been fewer and fewer incursions of men attempting to case the HOTH. Word had gotten around that trespassers would be met with a lethal response and that the "Defended Property" signs were truly a final warning.

"Roger, Actual. You should be able to make out the leader, just approaching Sign 14," said Miles.

"It's been a while since we've been probed," said Casey.

"Yeah, I think the word is getting out."

"How long before Amy and JJ are in position?"

"They should be on-net shortly. Will advise."

Watching through his Yukon NVGs from the Guard House, Duncan saw movement and focused in on a gap between the trees as Danny and Yuri scanned in other directions.

"Zero, this is Gulf, I have three X-Rays stationary at the Alpha Bravo," transmitted Duncan.

"Zero copies. We have them on video now. One male, two females. Interrogative: What's that on the leader's back?"

At that moment, Rob Mynarski paused to read a sign: AMNESTY BOX – LEAVE WEAPONS HERE BEFORE APPROACHING GUARD HOUSE.

"Jessica, you and April stay here. Don't make any sudden moves, I'll go and talk to them." As Rob said this, he noticed a tiny red dot on Jessica's chest. Realizing that it must be a target designator he looked to see if he was also being lased. He was, and so was April. Not having any weapons to deposit in the Amnesty Box, Rob thought it a good idea to remove the extra ski-pole from his backpack and drop it on the snow.

In the Eagle's Nest, Casey saw that the leader of the group was taking something off his back.

"Zero, Actual. I see a weapon. Hostile intent confirmed!"

"Actual, this is Oscar Papa, we are illuminating the other two. They are armed and taking defensive positions. We are losing our sight lines. Over," said JJ from the OP.

"Roger, they are inside the perimeter, armed and leader is pointing a weapon with scope. Taking him out now," said Casey.

Seconds later the man in Casey's cross-hairs slumped as his head exploded in a spray of blood and brains. Casey's AWSM was equipped with silencer, so there was no sound in the forest. The sudden fan-shaped arc of blood in the snow told his companions to run. Laser-designator dots bounced on their backs as they struggled through the heavy snow.

"Zero, Oscar Papa. We'll take out one more and leave the other alive for deterrence value. Confirm?" said JJ, as he lased his target with his rifle.

"Oscar Papa, Zero, affirmative. Take one, leave one."

The target fell to the ground before the report of JJ's un-silenced rifle was heard by the final intruder, who dove to the ground and disappeared from sight.

April Mynarski lay face down in the snow, expecting death at any second.

"Mom! Dad! Are you hit?" she whimpered, terrified.

"It's OK, sweetie, I'm OK. Daddy's OK, too. That gunshot was not aimed at us," said Jessica Mynarski, from her own depression in the snow.

"Stay down until I call you," said Rob. He got up slowly, with his hands raised. He noticed that there were now two laser-beams on his chest, so he stood still.

"Zero, Gulf. Two are prone, appear to be unarmed. Leader is standing with arms raised, unarmed. Actual can you confirm?"

Switching his aim point from the kill zone by Sign 14 to the three people near the Amnesty Box, Casey chimed in: "Gulf, this is Actual. Confirmed. Leader has only ski-poles. The two groups may be unrelated. Break. Oscar Papa, I'll cover your assessment of the two Black from group One at Sign 14 while Gulf handles the second party at Alpha Bravo. Over."

"Roger, Actual. Moving in to process. Over," said Duncan.

After being replaced in the Bird's Nest and hearing from JJ that the first two intruders were dead and that a third had fled to the west, Casey went to the Guard House. He was surprised to find Rob Mynarski. After Rob introduced his wife, Jessica and seventeen year-old daughter, April, Casey just had to ask.

"So, Rob, how did you find me?"

"I ran into Jim at a trade show. He was showing pictures of a recent installation and I recognized the mounts I designed for you. Does that put me in the dog house?" Rob's question brought a mischievous smile to Casey's face.

"So, Jessica, how was your trip?" asked Casey.

"We paid the last of our silver coins and gold jewelry for a boat-ride from Delta to Duke Point, then skied along the power-lines. It took us three days, and we were very cold at night," replied Jessica, clearly holding something back. When she couldn't take it any longer, she let it out.

"I have to know right now. You know what Rob can do, and I am an ER nurse. And April is a very hard working girl. Do you have space for us here? Will you help us?" she asked, exasperated by the tension she felt, so close to the sanctuary that had kept them going for the last three days.

"I'm sorry I didn't make that immediately clear. You must be exhausted. Danny! Take the ladies up. I'll be along shortly. Rob and I have some catching up to do."

Looking at the man that had helped design the HOTH brought humanity to the tough exterior of Boss Callaghan. With genuine affection, Casey asked Rob a playful question. "By the way, Rob, can you guess where I'm going to billet you?" Rob simply looked at Casey, not understanding. "You three will be living in what you once called an 'excessively large storage room' by the side entrance. Remember? You thought it would make a nice dog's room.- So you'll be in the doghouse!" Casey and Rob simultaneously broke out laughing; Casey at his own joke, and Rob at the prospect of experiencing the sanctuary of his own creation.

32

CHERRIES

03 November: 24 Weeks After NEW

After the tea-break following the off-site operations portion of the weekly briefing, Patti took the floor.

"Nora and I have analyzed the nutrition and caloric value

of our food supplies, and while there are many positives to report there is also a major problem."

Her opening statement caused the thirty or so adults to listen intently. It took a few minutes for the older children to pick up on the vibe, and pay close attention. As Patti paused for effect, the only noise heard in the HOTH was the muted noise of the younger children in the play room down in the basement, oblivious to the serious discussions upstairs.

Patti and Nora gave a detailed report on the inventory of long-term food supplies, hydroponic food production, and the contribution of eggs, poultry, swine and milk products from the barn facility. They then detailed the losses due to cans that would ultimately fail the botulism and other tests, factored in a gradual decline in food production as hydroponic equipment eventually wore out, and applied a factor to account for caloric-degradation of long term food supplies over time.

"So as you see on this graph, as of today, here, seven months into the nuclear winter with seventy mouths to feed," said Patti as she pointed on the bar chart projected on the wall, "and this level of food production from the indoor farming operation, we only have enough calories for another three years."

"But last month, you showed how we have enough food for eight years!" interrupted Danny. "What's changed?"

"Last month we hadn't done a detailed inventory, and went with Casey's receipts for the bulk orders he had put away, not what we could actually inspect and count in the DFR and cool storage areas. But now that we've done the inventory, we've had to deduct ninety million calories for the discrepancy. We've also expanded our obligations in terms of support of the Ring families, have seventy members of the HOTH now, compared to just fifty last month, and we also have to project food used in support of trading at the Errington Market. We also deducted fifty million calories for the livestock, as last month we all agreed to plan to keep them alive to build up livestock after the winter ends, although technically they are available as a contingency reserve. So that's the hundred and forty million missing calories. - Not to mention this assumes stable food production and that there will be no losses from our food stores," Nora added with emphasis.

"OK, I see now," Danny said. "So where's that leave us?"

"We have to cut down food commitments somehow. Or we have to find a way to increase food production, particularly for vegetables or other sources of vitamins. Hopefully those honeybees we got last month will help, but it's too soon to say. By the way, have you all read about what to do when the 10 new queens swarm out to start new hives? Better get ready, the swarm will happen some time next week. It'll take us a few days to settle them down after that, before we sell off most of the new hives. We've got sting medications and EpiPens ready in the infirmary, but if we follow the instructions, there won't be a problem.

Anyhow, back to the problem. We have to deal with the nutrition problem, as that's what's screwing up our burn rates."

"Let's table the discussion on caloric calculations for the moment and focus on the nutrition problem," Casey suggested. The HOTH operated by consensus as much as possible, but when Casey spoke, people listened. He usually kept his mouth shut while others ran the meetings, and only got involved when it was necessary. With the 46% stake he had in what was once his own facility, Casey was the majority shareholder in a joint venture with the other residents, and essentially *Chairman of the Board.*

All the other inhabitants of the HOTH had each been given either 0.5% or 1% ownership stake in what had evolved from private property into a collectively owned enterprise. Casey had done this for strategic reasons. He believed that each new member, adding expertise and potential, improved the odds for survival for his loved ones. It didn't hurt that another 7.5% was now held by his extended family members, and another 8% was held by long-time personal friends. Having a stake in the facility provided the HOTH members with a very real sense of ownership, and ensured their loyalty to the organization.

"OK", continued Nora, "because of the un-forecast obligation to supply essential vitamins and nutrition to the Ring program, rather than just bulk calories, we are going through the canned fruits and vegetables too fast. This will get even worse in future years as the nutritional value of the canned goods decays, resulting in even faster consumption rates.

The top level of our "nutrition pyramid" will disappear faster then the lower, more basic levels. This is a problem because while we may not starve to death, we'll have long-term problems like malnutrition and increased susceptibility to illnesses."

Casey could see where this was going, and exchanged a knowing look with Tanya. Seeing the calm, confident expression on Casey's face, Tanya also relaxed. She was one of the only people who knew where the missing calories had gone. She also knew about the caches of Roughnecks that Casey had cemented under the floors of the HOTH.

Tanya had stuck her head into the DFR and had seen Casey and Danny transferring hundreds of those rectangular EZ-Store bins into the large hidden chamber at the back end of the DFR about a month before the war. She saw lots of boxes with the orange labels that told her that the boxes contained Mason jars. She saw other boxes that must have held canned goods. She suspected that the Mason jars were from Casey's visits to that berry farm in Coombs. Tanya understood that the secret supply would be enough to cover the shortfall in calories, but would it also cover the shortfall in vitamins? She wondered.

Casey hadn't known that supporting the Ring families was depleting the essential nutritional sources so much faster than planned for. He would have to give that some thought. For now he'd keep silent and let the group work through the issues.

"Can't we increase internal food production?"

"Not that much, Adam, but it's a good idea. We're limited by the energy budget as it is. Geoff, what do you think?" JJ asked Geoff, the leader of the "green thumb" group.

"That's right. We're maxed out in terms of lighting, but the current levels of production are sustainable. Unless we can get our hands on another wind power system and create some more growing spaces, we can't expand the growing operation."

"What about fish?" asked Gwen, JJ's daughter. "Couldn't we start a fish farm? Or go fishing at the lakes?"

"We could try that, but I don't know if it would be worth the effort," replied Patti, and then followed that line of thinking. "Fish *would* add valuable nutrition to our diets, including omega-oils, and make for a bit more variety in the meals. What do you think, guys, would fishing be possible?"

"We don't have any fishing gear. And wouldn't they be full of toxins from the fallout?" asked Danny.

"The lakes up towards Mt. Arrowsmith wouldn't have gotten any fallout from Comox. So they should be relatively clean, the fish should be fit for human consumption," Said Zlata.

"And we could add fishing gear to the Wish List for the scavenging and trading parties. Come to think of it, I think there was fishing gear all over the floor at the Canadian Tire store when we looked it over," said Danny.

"We could send a team back to Canadian Tire when we do our trade-run to the Community Center next week," said JJ.

"And we can research the dietary contribution of the fish in more detail, and come up with tests for toxins," added Nora.

"Can we plan a fishing tasking into the rotation?" asked Manfred. "I'd love to take my boys out fishing."

"OK, JJ, how about you and Manfred plan a fishing trip to the upper lakes for next week, using whatever we can salvage in the mean time? We should also plan to swing by that trout farm out on Highway 4; it would be on the way. Besides, it's on the Intelligence Request List anyhow. It could be worth looking over, now that we're looking at starting a fishing program."

"What about increasing our trading activities to supplement our food stores?" asked JJ, continuing with the food supply topic. "Can't we start spending gold now?"

"No. It's far too soon to use the gold, other than where absolutely necessary. We have to stick to bartering and trading the scavenged goods. It's absolutely essential not to give anybody reason to think that we represent a treasure trove for the taking," Danny interjected, beating Casey to the punch.

After a few minor domestic items, the weekly meeting concluded with Mr. Skinner and Zlata's updates.

Exterior Radiation had fallen to one roentgen per hour. Radiation levels in the HOTH were $1/32^{nd}$ as much due to the five or more halving thicknesses. This meant that the danger posed by radiation was negligible, as long as cumulative exposure was limited.

The weather continued to be dominated by the more southerly jet-stream. The extremely cold northerly winds would keep the temperature around minus twenty for the foreseeable future, but also keep the helical wind power-plants working at full power.

The meeting broke up with excitement over the upcoming fishing trip that Manfred and JJ were organizing. But Casey was thinking to himself of a way to reduce the number of animals without reducing the viability of the herds. Perhaps they could make some deals with some of the Ring families to build up their own indoor farms now that the radiation levels were much lower.

Because of the stockpiling drive just before the war, when Casey had piled up all those hay bales to provide radiation protection for farm animals, he was able to save many of the local farmer's best animals from the fallout from Comox. Casey had contacted Moonstruck Farm and others in the area, and offered to shelter as many of their animals as they could drive up to the HOTH, until radiation levels fell to safe levels. In return, he had accepted 10% of the dairy cows, pigs, cattle and horses for his services. The farmers had balked at first, but then quickly agreed once they realized that giving a few animals to Casey while saving many more was far better than losing them all to radiation. Most of the lucky animals to be saved were pregnant females. They were the most valuable, and also the most vulnerable. Casey took his share of the calves, foals, and piglets that were popping out of the livestock during their confinement, as it was nearing the end of the birthing season.

The dairy cows, young bulls, stallions, mares, and pigs that Casey picked up in the deals were added to the horse and cow inventory from the Callaghan's first tentative move into hobby farming. Even after the farmers retrieved their livestock, the rate of consumption was too high. The dozen large animals Casey was left with ate two round hay bales per day out of a stockpile of just 1900. However, if he *loaned* some of them out to Ring Families to help them build up their own small indoor herds he could reduce their dependency on the HOTH. Otherwise he would have to look at having a few animals butchered at the Errington Market, to right-size his little herd.

Another Callaghan left the meeting with his mind ablaze with secret plans. Fourteen year-old Justin, Casey's second youngest child, had been listening intently and had finally found a way to contribute just like an adult. Justin's idea related to his daily play time outside with the other kids. They made snow forts along the hillside between the HOTH and the area where the orchard had been planted before the war.

From tonight's briefing, Justin understood that fruit was important to the adults for vitamins or nutrition or whatever. So on the next day's outside play time, he took a plastic bag with him and made his own little snow fort on top of where he thought the orchard was buried beneath the snow. While the other kids had their snowball fights and played hide-and seek in the trees on the high side of the HOTH, Justin secretly dug into the snow. He was sure that the snow would be strong enough to be safe. Snow can be very strong if it's compressed, Justin knew, so he just kept on digging, making a descending ramp that was not quite as steep as a staircase.

After digging down about six feet, Justin found the first branch. It was bent over dramatically by the snow, but it still held bunches of cherries. The trees were five years old when planted and had grown-in for another two years before the war.

Justin filled the bag with frozen cherries, then stuffed his pockets. By this time he was soaking wet and cold from the snow that had worked its way down his neck. Suddenly tired after so much digging in the snow he was also becoming increasingly afraid of the tunnel collapsing. The more he looked up the chute, the more claustrophobic he became.

After climbing out of the tunnel he hid the bag under his parka and headed back to the warmth of the HOTH. He was just in time to hear Granny-G call everybody in for lunch.

Once inside, Justin hid the cherries under his blankets in his bunk, changed out of his wet clothes and went down for lunch. Granny-G and Grandma Callaghan usually managed the children during lunch hour, getting them into the right frame of mind for the afternoon of schooling. Justin enjoyed school, but couldn't stop thinking about the big surprise he had in store for everybody. But he was tired and had a runny nose, so it was quite an effort to hang on until the school day ended. He just had to wait a few more hours until the evening meal, when everybody would be together and he could impress them all.

After school, Justin snuck upstairs with a plastic bowl from the kitchen. He took the cherries to the bathroom to wash, carefully picking out the few spoiled ones. Then he went down and put the bowl of cherries in the center of the main table.

When the adults were called in for dinner, and the ladies started placing the pasta, sauces and vegetables on the table, Grandma Callaghan was the first to notice the surprise.

"Where did these come from?" She couldn't believe her

eyes. These weren't canned cherries, nor were they from a jar. She noticed that the cherries were split, and a bit small. She tried one. It was pulpy, but had a wonderful intense flavor.

As the adults took their places, they talked excitedly about the cherries. There were no frozen cherries in the food inventory, so it was a big mystery as to where they came from.

Then Grandma Callaghan started looking at the faces of the children, always wise to their ways. "Have one of you been out picking cherries somewhere?" she asked. Then it dawned on her. "Justin, come over here would you please, my dear." Justin had been waiting for this moment, when someone noticed him. "Yes, Grandma?" he said, innocently, as he walked proudly up to the main table. His face was as red as the cherries.

"Are those your cherries?"

"Nope. They're for everybody! I picked them from the orchard by making a tunnel." He glowed in the praise that was heaped on him. Everybody listened as he explained how there were still lots more cherries out there.

Without destroying his moment of happiness, Justin's father had to muster a very stern tone. "Justin, you know the rules about tunneling in the snow. No more than half a body-length. Never alone. And never without asking an adult!" Casey began.

"Yes Papa. But it was safe; the tunnel was a Quinzhee!"

"But nothing! True, you made a great discovery, but in the future you will abide by the rules all the time. Don't take any foolish risks. Understood? And I've told you before. You don't make a Quinzhee without an adult."

Later that evening when the children were in bed many of the adults gathered around the cooking wood-stove in the kitchen annex. The discussion centered on Justin's discovery.

"I would have thought that the snow and freezing-rain would have destroyed those cherries, but they seemed perfectly good to me," said Granny-G.

"They were fine. But they had been partly desiccated by

the wicking action of the frost," explained Nora. "It's kind of like how they prepared grapes for ice-wine in Eastern Canada. They leave them on the vine to freeze and that removes some water from the grapes, making them intensely flavorful. Then they harvest them while still frozen to the vine, and make ice-wine, with that unusual sweetness and delicate flavor. Justin's cherries have the same characteristics."

"So my Bing's should also be OK?" Granny-G asked, with growing excitement.

"Yes, in fact Justin's cherries were Bings, weren't they?"

"I think that he got them from the tree on the end, which was one of two Bing's we planted, so yes," said Casey.

"How many trees in your orchard?" asked Patti.

"I still had twenty four cherry trees, about 18 of them Bing and a half-dozen Reds," Granny-G said with pride. "And I had 24 Island Plums, 20 Frost Peach and a few Puget Gold's"

"What's a Puget Gold?" asked Nora.

"It's a new type of apricot, developed by Washington State University a few years back. It grows well in our cool, moist Pacific Northwest climate. Not anywhere near as prodigious as the apricots grown in the Okanagan, but very tasty little 'cots. But the mainstay of my orchard was the apples. I had fifty Aurora Golden Galas and twenty Ambrosias."

"WOW! That's a lot of fruit! I don't suppose you have any preserves back at your farm?"

"Nope. Sorry to say, Danny, I gave up canning a few years ago. The trees I could manage with some part-time laborers and seasonal picking-crews, but canning was just too much work for my arthritic old hands. So what little I had from the summer before last, Casey collected when he and Miles rescued me. I was all out of food. The farm's a wreck; the snow collapsed it. There's nothing of value there except, I suppose, the case or so of Certo down in the Cellar – that should be good for years."

"What was that Justin said about a Quinzhee?" asked Kevin Neumann, Geoff's 15-year old son.

"It's an Eskimo snow house!" replied his father. "I've never seen one. But Casey, isn't that what the Rangers use as emergency shelters on their Arctic patrols?"

"That's right, Geoff. I showed some of the kids and most of the adults how to make them before you got here. The heavy snow-base is perfect for making Quinzhees. All they are is snow caves. But up in Yellowknife, there was usually no more than a foot or so of suitable snow. You had to spend hours piling it up until you had a mound about eight feet tall. You smack the snow with your shovel as you build it up, to compress it. Then, when you have enough piled up, it takes about an hour to dig the inside snow out through the entrance tunnel. It's normally made just large enough for one or two people. When I did it, it was minus forty C outside, yet with just one candle burning I got it up to plus five inside. They're very strong. You can even stand on top of one if it's had a few days to glaze in the sun. It's perfect for a survival cave as long as you don't get snowed-in. I should have made sure you knew how to make one, but I guess I forgot about that when you arrived in October," Casey concluded.

"No problem, I had the Basic Winter Survival course in Edmonton, but we didn't demo the Quinzhees.

"I wonder, Granny-G, would you mind if we collected some of your fruit?" Nora changed the topic back to the fruit.

"I'd be delighted. I've already exchanged my twenty acres for a 1% share in the HOTH, and twenty new grandchildren to keep me busy. So the orchard is ours to do whatever we want with. It certainly would give our nutrition a boost. Let's get all we can before the freeze sucks all the juice out! And while we're at it, there're a few personal things I'd like to have."

"Justin has shown us the way. We'll tunnel down to a tree and make one of those Quinzhees around it," said JJ.

"But that's a lot of snow to move, JJ," said Amy.

"Actually, there may be a better way," continued Danny.

After Danny laid out his idea Amy joined in and made a few suggestions on how to get started. The two went on to develop a way to quickly gather the fruit from Granny-G's orchard.

After experimenting a bit, they determined that by making a Quinzhee at the base of a tree they could gather some of the fruit that had fallen off the tree. Then by placing eight or ten large candles in the Quinzhee the heat would expand the cavern to a much larger snow-cave without any additional labor. The fifteen foot snow-base made for excellent insulation and the glazed ice walls quickly hardened when the number of candles was reduced, leaving the fruit tree liberated from snow and ready for the bounty of fruit to be harvested.

Over the next two weeks they harvested over six thousand pounds of fruit. They stored some of it in the DFR, but most of it was just piled up on plastic sheets in the garage. It was soon processed in the canning and jam-making assembly-line that the two Grandmas and Tanya managed in the kitchen.

They also brought the Ring Families into the operation, inviting them to harvest fruit from the Granny-G orchard. However, the Ring Families were required to set aside 20% of what they collected, which the HOTH crews used for trading at the Errington market and donated to the food-aid center that Marty and Katy ran at the Qualicum Community Center.

They traded the fruit to those in need in exchange for things which the other traders could find by scavenging in abandoned homes. Danny and the Callaghan boys spent hours sorting nuts & bolts and other bits of hardware into jars. They stored the jars on shelves as they became available in the bunker. Other items, such as electronics and consumer goods, were squirreled away in other storage spaces around the HOTH.

The HOTH people, as they were now known, used these trading opportunities to help other survivors build their own systems for indoor food production. When trading fruit and other supplies at Errington Market, they gave out newsletters and advice on indoor food production.

Amy came up with a few designs for simple wind-power

systems which could be made out of commonly available components including the guts of skill-saws, bench grinders, bicycles, and auto parts like batteries and starter-generators. The helical wind paddle assemblies to drive these improvised generators could be put together from furnace ducts, various construction materials, and lots of metal-bashing. Amy's design worked well.

The sequence of events, starting with Justin's initiative and culminating in Amy's designs for improvised power-plants, made Casey proud of his son and confident that the HOTH was working out as he had envisaged.

33

BEEP

02 August: 15 Months After NEW

Casey awoke to the sound of Tanya drying her hair. The room was filled with bright sunlight, which was very hard on his eyes as he read 10:00 AM on the clock. Casey got up to close the window blinds. Suddenly, he realized: *it's sunny outside*.

He went up to the penthouse and walked out into a glorious sunny day with just a few puffy clouds in the sky. He heard the sound of his children playing, and walked over to the railing to look down. He saw his five children playing with a Frisbee while the family dogs, Abby and Limbo, chased after it. The enormous lawn was a vivid green. It was a perfect summer day.

Casey saw the cherry trees in the small orchard were in full springtime blossom. Looking to the horizon, Casey saw a cruise-ship plying the waters of Georgia Strait. Then he realized that it had all been a dream, *there had been no war*. He and his family could enjoy normal life in their beautiful home, and the end of the world had not come.

Casey felt elated that the world had not gone insane. He began to hear the "Beep, Beep, Beep…" of a truck backing up. He walked over to the other side of the roof-top deck and looked down to see the Dairyland milk truck backing up into the parking spot in front of the main entrance. The driver got out and carried a plastic milk-crate with a few milk cartons in it, heading towards the door.

The "Beep Beep" sound continued. "That's odd," Casey said aloud to himself as he watched the milk-man put down the new crate and pick up the old one from the front porch. *There should be no backing-up sound, the truck has stopped.*

Casey opens his eyes. He was back in the king-sized bed, and saw that it was exactly 10:00 AM. He shut his eyes against the brightness of the lights in the room. He rolled over and started to get up to close the window blinds, to cut off the bright sunlight. But by the time he reached the window he realized that something was wrong.

It was *dark* outside. The landscape was covered by a gloomy grey blanket of snow, dimly lit under a permanently overcast sky. He finally registered the "Beep Beep Beep" coming from the alarm clock, which had been set for 10:00 AM. Then he realized that there was no Dairyland truck. It is not sunny outside. The war really did happen and he and his family would not awaken from a bad dream.

In fact, he admitted to himself, things were probably going to get a lot worse.

34

ATTACK

20 December: 31 Months After NEW

Manfred found the camera. It was still attached to the branch that had broken off in the last storm.

"I found it, and the leads appear to be intact."

"Yea, Manfred, we're getting a clear picture now, but you've got it sideways," said Amy, over the XPR.

"I'm gonna disconnect it now to add more length."

"Make sure to mount it much higher this time," Amy said.

Manfred extended his ladder its full twenty feet and leaned it against a nearby tree while Peter slipped a wide plank under the ladder's feet, making a secure base on the deep snow. After climbing up to re-attach the surveillance camera under a thick branch, Manfred climbed back down and picked up the XPR.

"Are you getting a good picture now?"

"Yes, but who are those people? DANGER CLOSE! They're armed and moving tactically! Get out of there!" Amy said urgently.

"Hostile force! Run!" said Manfred, pushing Pete ahead.

Pete didn't have to be told twice. Ever since Pal's murder, Pete understood how fast an attack could take place.

Pete had been staying with Pal after Pete's family were killed in a home invasion a few months after NEW. The Walker gang had gone after Pete's boss, Mr. Palomar. Pal was killed before he even got to his gun cache in the basement. He had simply stuck his head out a second floor window so see who was banging at the door, when he was shot through the throat. With his hands trying to stop the blood pouring out of his throat, Pal told Pete to run. Pete got away that time by moving fast, diving out another window and running for his life.

This time, with Manfred a few paces behind, Pete wanted to fight back. He headed for the Gate House where he expected to find Duncan, the other man on gate duty. But when he rounded the corner of the brick structure he saw several men pointing guns at him from a few meters to his right, where the Gate House parking lot met the serpentine driveway onto the property.

He continued running, right past the Gate House, hoping to get around the next corner and make for the deeply-trodden trench-like path from the Gate House to the HOTH. Bullets whizzed by, making snappy puffs in the packed snow sides of the trench. Pete ducked low as he ran along the zig-zagging path, feeling like a First World War soldier in the trenches.

Seconds later Manfred rounded the first corner of the Gate House and saw Pete disappear around the next corner. When he saw the half-dozen men shooting at Pete from the right, he made for the Gate House door, yanked it open and ran inside.

The five hostiles inside the room were stunned to see Manfred, who had interrupted their torturing of Duncan.

Without missing a beat Manfred ran right past them for the rear storage room. Once inside, he slammed the steel door shut and threw a two-by-four into the steel clips bolted to the doorframe, securely barring the door. Manfred then went to the shelving unit at the far end of the room to uncover the hidden door into the panic room behind the storage shelf. Inside, he pressed the button to activate the emergency lighting inside and grabbed the 9mm from a shelf on the wall.

By the time he got back into the main storage room, someone was smashing the fire-door with something heavy, starting to bend the bottom corner inwards. The two-by-four held. Manfred fired a few shots through the bent corner, hoping to make them back-off a bit. His shots only infuriated the attackers. They smashed the fire-door even harder, at both top and bottom.

They stopped for a moment to deal with some trouble in the main room. The commotion ended when one of the attackers put a bullet into Duncan's brain, ending his valiant attempt to break free from those torturing him. Manfred heard the struggle and understood the finality of the single gun-shot.

With just a few clips of ammo for the 9mm he got from the panic room, and with no exit other than through the main guardroom, Manfred knew that he couldn't hold out for long.

Meanwhile, up in the HOTH, all available adults were arming themselves from the weapons vault in the lower level. As the men and women stuffed magazines and pistols into their pockets and slung rifles over their shoulders, Nora and Francis gave updates over the Public Address system. Watching the video feeds, they could see where almost every one of the attackers was.

With over thirty men, the attackers had come in force. Hope Callaghan thought one of them was a trucker who had turned down their offer for shelter and had chosen to take his chances in Port Alberni. He was one of the men in the Gate House, trying to break through to the storage room where it looked like Manfred was barricaded. They could also see Duncan's body on the floor.

There were other attackers in the forest near the Gate House and several were taking up firing positions along the snow-covered berm near the Gate House. The natural features had been created by Casey and Marc years ago; the OPs and cameras had been installed overlooking these "safe" places. The attackers would soon find how unsafe they really were.

The adults of the HOTH were divided into four groups. One was to remain in the HOTH with the children and elderly as a last line of defense, and to prepare the infirmary for casualties. The five people making up a second group had already left to take their position in the East OP. The cameras in this area hadn't picked up any movement, but if the attackers tried the HOTH's right flank they would find out the hard way that the East OP dominated the gully they found themselves funneled into.

The third group, with eight fighters led by JJ, was heading out the garage door for the North OP, close to the battle. Among them, Amy had a Super-Magnum sniper rifle, while Danny and JJ each had M-16s. The others had rifles, shotguns, and handguns.

The fourth group, a dozen men and women, had taken rifles and lots of ammunition to prepared firing-points on the rooftops of the HOTH and Barn, and began sniping. Casey was already in the Birds Nest setting up the Amalite while Jack was setting out the large 50-caliber rounds. Looking down from his firing table, Casey saw Pete running head-down along the trench, but he couldn't see any targets. The attackers had their heads down now, surprised by the intensity of the firing from the HOTH.

GT was firing at something in the tree-line, making satisfied noises that he had hit something. Meanwhile Jack, assigned as Casey's spotter and helper, carefully put a head-set on Casey and received a smile and thumbs up for his efforts. He then took a pair of binoculars, and scanned for targets.

"Zero this is Actual. What do you see in the Gate House?"

"Actual, Zero. There are eight hostiles inside. Looks like Duncan's dead, on the floor by the west wall. We have comms with Manfred now, he's prone in the panic room, firing at the store-room door. He's almost out of rounds."

"Roger. Listen, there are thirty bricks from west to east along the south wall of the Gate House, and fourteen from floor to ceiling. The first seven bricks from my right account for the panic room, so they are a no-fire zone. It looks like the snow has buried the back wall to the five foot mark, or about eight bricks high."

"I'm with you, Casey. We'll tell you which vector will

take out the most targets, reference Left and height, Roger?"

"Roger. Ready."

Using the live-feed from the two hidden cameras that every person in the HOTH knew were inside the main room of the Gate House, Francis worked out the best vectors for Casey.

"Eight bricks from left, standing."

To the ten attackers inside the Gate House, arguing about how to assault the well-defended prize, it seemed as if the entire wall exploded. The powerful 50-caliber round Casey fired into the designated brick made just a two-centimeter hole through the outside of the non-reinforced brick wall. The diameter on the inner side, however, was twenty centimeters. The shock wave and particles of brick formed an explosive projectile stream. Shards of brick and smaller particles fanned out, filling the room with white smoke. The high-velocity round hit the nearest man in his chest and tore a fist-sized hole through his body. As the bone, muscle and flesh blew out the other side, the internal shock-wave tore the man to pieces, throwing his head and torso to the left while his shoulder and right arm flew to the right. Francis had chosen the first vector well, as the bullet destroyed the pelvis of a second man, and carried on to destroy the ankle of a third man, standing behind.

The process was repeated three more times, killing another five men before the attackers realized that the defenders were firing right through the brick wall with a powerful weapon. Their leader got outside to call for a retreat and was about to shout out orders when his throat was sliced open by a shard of metal blown off the doorframe. Casey's fifth shot had missed but the power of the projectile striking the door-frame put so many metal splinters into the air that a clean hit wasn't necessary. The man fell to the ground spraying blood.

As he lay there dying, he saw his force being mowed down from a few tiny dark holes in a pile of logs and trees about a hundred yards to their right flank. Lined up like sardines in a tin along that little berm they had been sheltered behind, his men were killed right before his eyes. They hadn't even had time to figure out where the shooting was coming from.

The remaining attackers that had held back in the forest soon began to run for their lives. Many of them were taken out by the snipers firing from the rooftops. The rest were killed as they tried to cross Wainscott Crescent. It was unclear whether they were hit by fire from Group Two on the right, or Group Three on the left, as both parties had advanced to the edge of the forest in pursuit of the fleeing targets.

After the attackers were all dead, Danny led a recce to back-track. He soon discovered that the attackers had overcome the Gorton family. When Danny and his men got within site of the Gorton Farm, they reported what they saw. A large number of people had occupied the Gorton residence located close to the Port Alberni Highway. The Gortons were a small family of three who kept to themselves, and all had the same bright red hair. They were a Ring Family, but were barely hanging on.

Danny reported seeing someone throw a garbage bag out from the main entrance. Despite the SOPs, Danny just had to know. After sneaking in for a closer look, he reported that the bag contained fresh table-scraps of human bones and bright red hair. It was clear that the attackers had degraded into cannibalism.

It had happened time after time all around the world, Casey and the others had learned through the radio net. There was something particularly offensive in the idea that people were hunting people for food. The malnourished victims didn't offer their predators much nutrition anyhow, as the vitamin-containing fat was long gone. With human protein being difficult for humans to digest, and with the diseases and other deleterious effects, cannibalism is not only repugnant to civilized people, but it's also an ineffective survival strategy.

So is leaving cannibals free to kill. They will continue to hunt humans and therefore must be stopped. Any report of cannibalism in the Oceanside area resulted in armed parties heading out to exterminate them. The remaining members of the cannibalist gang realized that they were surrounded and that their attack on the HOTH had failed. They knew what was in store for them; they would fight to the death.

And death came swiftly for them, in the form of a two-liter pop-bottle filled with gasoline, dropped down the chimney. The explosion and subsequent fire was so intense that the thick snow around the farm melted all the way to the ground. The few people who made it out of the blaze were mercilessly mowed-down in a hail of gunfire. By burning the cannibals out rather than fighting their way inside, none of the members of nearby Ring Families, nor those from the HOTH, would have to suffer any grisly images of the horrors that must have gone on inside that farmhouse.

35

OOBLECK

17 May: 6 Years After NEW

Everybody was excited about the New-Year's celebration, just three days away, when seven year old Janie-Lee Arnott first saw the *Oobleck*. The survivors marked the NEW anniversary each year by spending the afternoon and evening of 20 May in candle-lit remembrance of the five billion people who had perished so far since the NEW. May 21st would be the first day of the next year ANEW, a time when people renewed their efforts to pull together to face the months and years of difficulty that still lay ahead. It was also a time to remind each other of why life was worth living and show their affection through gift-giving. In preparation, Amy and others were busy decorating the great room for the new year's eve banquet.

So when Janie-Lee kept saying: "King Derwin must have his crazy magicians working again, because *Oobleck's* falling!" Amy just laughed it off. Janie-Lee had a wonderful imagination, and loved the Dr. Seuss stories that Amy read to her at bedtime. With none of the adults interested, Janie-Lee tried to get Bartholomew Neumann interested.

"Hey, Bart, you can be Bartholomew Cubbins, and help me warn the kingdom about the Oobleck!"

"Thanks Janie-Lee, but I'm too busy to play right now. Go tell Bobby, he'll help you warn the Kingdom!"

"But Bartholomew, you're the only one who can make the adults believe me. It really *is* Oobleck, and it's *dangerous*. Please come see the Oobleck!" She put her little hand in Bart's. Even though he was twenty-one years old, he still loved the story which he had been named after.

"OK, Sweetie, I'll play Oobleck with you."

Amy heard this, and smiled. Young Bart had grown into a man in the six years he's spent in the HOTH, but he was still a boy at heart. With so few small children around the HOTH, little Janie-Lee had so few playmates.

About five minutes after Bart and Janie-Lee disappeared to the penthouse level, shouts came down the stairs.

"Dad! Amy! It's *true!* There really is Oobleck falling! We finally have something new coming down from the sky! Come look. I've got some here!" said Bart, excitedly holding up his hand as proof. It was covered with asparagus-colored slime.

"What the?" Amy said.

"Where'd you get that?" Geoff asked his son.

"Janie-Lee was right. There's Oobleck falling from the sky. We went to the upper deck; the snow is covered with it. It's sticking to everything! The sky is filled with it!"

It didn't take long for everybody to look outside and see

that the sky really was filled with a greenish mist. It also seemed that the Oobleck might be dangerous. It had a pungent odor, and made breathing difficult. Bart was quickly developing a skin rash, sore eyes and complained of a burning sensation in his throat. So Casey and Amy got everybody busy sealing off the HOTH and activated the Lung to filter out the mysterious liquid.

Zlata took charge of the analysis of the substance and, with Amy and Old Mr. Skinner, they carried out a series of tests in the laboratory next to the infirmary. Everybody was worried about chemical warfare. They waited with baited breath while the most qualified people worked on the problem.

While the initial tests were being run, Geoff and Manfred got on the radios to confirm that Oobleck was falling all over the Pacific Northwest. It soon started to be reported farther inland. It appeared that Oobleck was coming in off the Pacific Ocean, until Geoff got a report that a similar substance was coming down in North Africa. The name "Oobleck" stuck, as it truly was a new kind of weather with all the characteristics of Dr. Seuss's slimy Oobleck.

When Dr. Skinner confirmed that the substance was not radioactive, and Amy confirmed that none of the Biological and Chemical Warfare Detection Strips reacted to the green goo, there was a great deal of relief. It took a lot longer for Zlata to come out with her preliminary chemical analysis.

With only the simple resources of the small lab, all that Zlata could do was some alkalinity tests and a crude form of atomic emission spectroscopy. As she explained it, without a Mass Spectrometer or at least Gas Chromatography, all she could do was identify the elements present. When she first sprayed a fine mist of Oobleck into a flame, she was surprised at the extremely violent combustion that occurred. She tried again with a diluted sample and compared the spectral lines to color charts in some reference textbooks in the lab.

The results indicated that Carbon, Oxygen, Silicon, Aluminum, Calcium, Hydrogen, Iron, Sulphur and Nitrogen were the elements involved. It was definitely a volatile substance and seemed to be in the process of oxidizing. Samples brought in from outside turned from green to brown even when submerged in water. Zlata performed other tests and identified that the main component of the substance was an odorless crystal with a solubility of 118g/100g water at zero degrees C, pH of 5.4, and a melting point of 170C.

After the lab team provided a list of findings, Geoff and Manfred broadcast the information on the radio nets. They also asked if anybody had more sophisticated equipment to work with.

While they waited for more information, a white-board was brought from Ops to the lab, where those with any experience with Chemistry tried to work out what the Oobleck was. Zlata put the elements and relative proportions up on the white board, and listed the physical properties of the substance. Stumped, she looked at Amy and the others for ideas.

"Have you looked at it under a microscope?" Amy asked.

"Yes, but only briefly. All we can see is a core of colorless crystals being affected by a green substance which ultimately changes to brown as it oxidizes," Zlata said. "Our microscope isn't powerful enough to show us much more than that, but there are these odd cup-shaped objects mixed in with the green and clear materials."

"But, at its core, there is a colorless crystal right?"

"Yes."

"So we have two or more substances. One is green, and turns brown when it oxidizes, even under water. So it can't be getting its Oxygen from the clear substance, right? So it's a reducing agent. Let's assume it's associated with Iron, OK?"

"I'm with you, go on," said Zlata.

"Suppose it's Iron Sulphate? - $FeSO_4$," said Amy.

"Well." Zlata looked at a copy of the periodic table, and then looked something up in a few textbooks. "If it were the heptahydrate, melanterite, then it would be blue-green as long as it had all 7 water molecules. The Iron could oxidize, turning the agglomeration increasingly from green to brown," Amy reasoned, mapping the chemical reaction on the white-board. "So that works for one side of the equation, but what about all that Silicon, Carbon and Nitrogen?"

"I bet if you wash out those cup-shaped items you'll find they are aluminosilicates, and the clear substance is simply Ammonium Nitrate," said Amy.

"Ammonium Nitrate?" asked Zlata. "Wait a minute, that could work!" she said, as she mapped out the Al_2SiO_5 and NH_4NO_2 alongside the $FeSO_4$. "Yeah, Amy, that pretty much accounts for all the constituent elements. How did you come up with this?"

"Well, when you nearly blew yourself up in the lab I kept my mouth shut, but it made me think about all those warnings on the fertilizer bags we use in the green-house."

"You meant those '34-0-0' bags?" asked JJ.

"Yeah, it's great for boosting crop yield, but have you ever read the warnings and handling instructions?" asked Amy.

"No, I don't handle the stuff," said JJ.

"Well I do. If you don't use a mask and gloves when handling the stuff, as we do in the greenhouse when we mix up those batches of nutrient solutions for the hydroponics, you would get the same symptoms young Bart has after he started playing with Oobleck. Add that to Zlata's small-scale explosion, and voila!" said Amy.

"OK. So what's your theory about the silicon cups?" asked Zlata, working through some formulas on the white-board.

"Vesicles," said Amy.

"Why?"

"Because you said that green stuff, maybe Iron Sulphate, is oxidizing and changing brown. So before it falls as Oobleck it has to be cut off from oxygen, right?"

"Yes, it has to be in an anoxic state," said Zlata.

"So suppose that there was an aluminosilicate vesicle with Ferrous Sulfate and other reagents trapped inside. Somehow the vesicle breaks as it falls, and the Iron Sulfate begins to oxidize."

"That could be part of the puzzle. Vesicles would protect the reagents from the oxygen and dryness of the upper atmosphere, but would not account for the Ammonium Nitrate."

"Why not, Zlata?" asked Amy.

"The chemical process to fix nitrogen, to produce ammonia and to combine that with nitric acid, is technologically challenging. For this to occur on the scale we are seeing would be an impossible technological feat," explained Zlata.

As Amy considered this, there was a strange silence in the room. Everybody watched as Zlata began furiously writing symbols on the white-board that bore no resemblance to the inorganic chemistry that they had been exploring.

"Eureka! I've got it!" said Zlata, ecstatically.

"What is it?" Amy asked.

"Look, you guys spread the word that we think the Oobleck is made in vesicles, and contains Iron Sulphate and Ammonium Nitrate, and request confirmation from the UBC Profs. I have some experimenting to do to confirm my theory, but it works!"

By the time the university professors confirmed the chemistry, and asked for any theories about the origin of the substance, Zlata had it all mapped out. She called everybody into the great room to explain what she had deduced.

What she told them made them all very afraid. They didn't want to get their hopes up only to find out later that she was wrong. It seemed too good to be true.

"We'll get others working to test my theory, but I'm certain that this is good news. A wonderful new kind of weather is falling from the sky! Oh let the wondrous Oobleck fall!"

"Can you please explain what you mean?" said Granny-G.

"For something to be falling out of the sky, now, six years after the war, *it has to come from the stratosphere*. All the dust and debris in the Troposphere, the lower level of the atmosphere where liquid water is present, was washed out fairly quickly. Yet the sun remained blocked out by the billions of tons of dust up in the stratosphere. It has to be coming from the stratosphere, where all that super-fine dust has been trapped, blocking out the sunlight all this time.

We now know what the Oobleck is, and I think I know how it is being manufactured, *and by whom.*

"By whom?" Are you crazy, this stuff is falling all around the world. Nobody has the technology for this. It would be impossible even before the war!" said Amy, frustrated.

"OK, not exactly 'whom'," said Zlata. "But it's being made by little guys I call '*Nekataves'*. The Nekataves are bacteria in the stratosphere, and they make the Oobleck inside tiny vesicles that formed out of the materials injected into the stratosphere by the atomic blasts," she said with satisfaction.

"First of all, why are you so happy about this? And second, how can anything be alive in the stratosphere?" asked Mr. Skinner.

"OK, I can see you all looking at me like I'm crazy. So I'll slow down and take it step-by-step," Zlata said, calming herself. "First, the bacteria. In the decades before the war, scientists had confirmed that as many as twenty different types of bacteria and fungi were alive and well in the stratosphere. Russians, Americans and Europeans all confirmed it by sending up small rockets and high-altitude radiosonde balloons to take samples and return them for analysis. Some of you may not know this but, despite the low atmospheric pressure, the temperature in the stratosphere ranges from minus twenty to plus fifty C. So there are these vertical currents of air which tend to loft particles higher and higher, which partly accounts for how difficult it has been for the dust and debris to settle out of the stratosphere. Material from volcanic eruptions and forest fires is theorized as constantly populating the stratosphere with life. These organisms live, spread and rain down back down on us in microscopic quantities. But now, with billions of tons of material added to the stratosphere, these tiny organisms suddenly had a lot more material to work with.

The materials from the cities vaporized in the blasts provided, among other things, tiny grains of aluminosilicate and other materials which the air currents and a force atmospheric scientists call 'Gravito-photophoresis' lifts the materials higher and higher into the stratosphere.

Perhaps because of electrostatic charges, or for other reasons, these grains coalesced into larger clumps which included sulfuric acid and other materials in the toxic smoke. Then the stratospheric microorganisms got to work. Suddenly, protected from the dryness of the upper stratosphere, in the oxygen-free interior of these vesicles, new reactions began to occur." Zlata paused to make sure she was not going too fast. The blank look on people's faces told her that people were struggling to understand.

"Put another way, when you throw all sorts of food and energy into an environment, life responds to it. The life forms may be tiny but they have had six years to interact with the increased supply of materials. Now add the fact that the damaged ozone layer means that huge amounts of ultra-violet radiation cause these organisms to mutate, and you wind up with some unexpected life forms up there. At least one of them is a nitrogen-fixing bacteria, like the *Rhizobium* bacteria only much hardier. Anyhow, these vesicles wind up full of Ammonium Nitrate and Iron Sulphate. They agglomerate into larger and larger blobs which eventually become too heavy to stay aloft."

"And they fall down as Oobleck!" said Amy, suddenly as excited as Zlata.

"Right, and on their way down, they encounter the extreme cold of the Tropopause. The liquids inside freeze and expand, cracking the vesicles into the tiny cups we saw under the microscope -" Zlata had continued, until Amy interrupted again.

"And the Iron Sulphate leaks out and coats the vesicle

green. Soon after landing, it oxidizes, and turns brown!"

"Ladies! Amy! I see you share Zlata's excitement about the source of the Oobleck, but, other than the scientific breakthrough Zlata may have had and explaining where this stuff is coming from, why are you so damned happy about it?" asked Casey.

"Because, Boss, it's the beginning of the end!" said Amy.

"The Nekatave process, or whatever scientists will ultimately call it, has given the Earth a way to clean out the billions of tons of smoke and debris from the stratosphere. Without this mechanism, the material could stay up there for centuries. Now it's falling. We'll do calculations and communicate with other scientists but, I can tall you right now, that millions upon millions of tons of Oobleck are falling. The dust in the stratosphere has to be disappearing extremely fast now."

"You mean the sky will clear soon?" asked Granny-G.

"That's right! Whatever has been going on up there for the last six years has reached some critical point and has started a cascading effect. Nobody ever predicted it could happen, but here it is!" Zlata said, while Amy nodded in agreement.

"So you are saying that the nuclear winter is over?"

"Far from over, Granny-G. And I need time to analyze the rate of deposition, track the increase in solar insolation and the changes to the weather patterns. But yes, it will happen a lot faster now than we ever expected, or even dared to hope."

"So what will the effects be, on the ground?" JJ asked.

"I think we'll see sunshine within a month. With it will be dangerous levels of Ultra-Violet radiation, we'll need to track it, and come up with protective head-gear and goggles, but who knows whether the Ozone layer is repairing itself or not. I suspect that it will be manageable, but plants and animals will probably have more mutations and problems than in the past.

The jet-stream will migrate back north into Canada and we'll see the sea temps begin to rise gradually. This will bring increasing rainfall to the Island and begin to melt the snow in the lower levels. Snow accumulation in the mountains will increase again, but down here we'll see snow melting very fast. It may take a few summers, but we'll have above-zero temps starting this June, and lasting till September or so. After that, winters will be mild, but perhaps a bit snowy at times. In a few years, we'll have clear roads and things will really *explode* after that." Zlata said this with a whimsical expression that begged the question.

"Explode?" asked Tanya.

"Yes, in more ways than one. First, when soil meets sun again, with all of that Ammonium Nitrate fertilizer soaked into it, life will explode. Plants will grow like wildfire."

"And the other way?" asked JJ.

"Ammonium Nitrate is highly volatile. Oobleck that dries to dead vegetation will add an explosive quality to the inevitable forest fires. So the forests will also explode.

36

SNAKE HEAD

It took seven years to find where General Bing was. Even when found by western forces, they had no way to kill him. If they couldn't kill the Snake's Head, there would be no way to defeat the larger beast.

General Bing had been elevated to the post of Chief of PLA General Staff after General Wang's orchestrated heart attack right before the war began. Exactly as planned, General Bing was given emergency powers. He wasted no time in utilizing this unlimited gift, first arresting and executing the surviving members of the Communist Party, and then throwing the full weight of Chinese national resources into his global war effort.

OP PLAN XIALONG, Little Dragon, had been a strategic success. Little Dragons and follow-on Special Forces had seized control of the vast majority of their objectives worldwide. The local resistance had been a nuisance in some areas, particularly the Pacific Northwest, however additional follow-on forces were soon dispatched to reinforce those areas where Chinese forces were at risk of losing their foothold.

Under their new leader, China was fighting a very long war which would not be over until China had achieved total victory.

It would take years, but with the climate now warming rapidly back to normal levels, and a degree of food production becoming possible as the sky cleared, the food producing regions of the world were beginning to show hopeful signs. As long as Chinese forces could hang on long enough to be in a position to use food as a weapon, and to relieve the starving millions of Chinese at home, victory was theirs.

Recognizing that China was moving inexorably toward victory the few remaining allied military forces attempted to cut off the supply of personnel and materials flowing from China to their footholds around the world. Even with some success at interdicting Chinese reinforcements, however, American and British analysts could read the writing on the wall. China would win, and General Bing would be a global emperor. Unless, that is, the Snake's Head could be cut off.

American military strategists at DUMB One and their British counterparts spent futile months attempting to devise an effective strategy.

In England, a small team of analysts composed of a core of MI6 personnel from the short-lived OPERATION PANDA STING and a variety of defense personnel had evacuated to an improvised facility in Cornwall. It was initiated by Royal Air Force survivors who had been off-duty when their base at nearby St. Mawgan was destroyed. They moved into a university campus and organized a civil-military team to support the British war effort. It turned out to be a geologist among them who would turn the tide of the war.

Nobody asked the university professors to leave when the British military occupied a few floors in the Earth Sciences Department at the university. With so few military survivors, the intellectuals were a welcome addition to the collective effort: Survive to Operate.

The group in Cornwall had grown very close over the years, cooperating in their efforts to survive. Their location in the town of Penzance, jutting out into the Atlantic Ocean, meant they didn't have to contend with snowfall. They faired far better than other survivors around the world and were able to continue their work analyzing the Chinese war effort.

Albert Jones, now a Group Captain, was leaning over a large chart table, examining some satellite images, when Dr. Archibald Grant, a professor of geology, walked in. He looked over Jones' shoulder, intrigued. "What are you chaps up to with these old photos?"

"Oh, hello, Archie. Opportune that you should drop by. We're looking for underground complexes along China's northeast coastline. We've identified this region as being the likely 'home' of one General Bing, the Emperor of New China – and soon the world, if we don't find him and kill him first."

"Hmm, serious stuff! By the way, Albert, congratulations on your promotion."

"I'll say thanks, my dear chap, but I don't feel as pleased about it as I might have done. After all, it came at too heavy a price. You know, we military types have often referred to promotion by *'dead men's shoes'* but I never suspected how real it could turn out to be."

"Indeed," said the professor. He peeled off his half-moon reading glasses and tapped them on one of the photographs on the table. "I see that you're interested in a bauxite mine?" observed the geologist.

"Bauxite?" said Jones. "How can you tell that?"

"Well, this is one of those Canadian RADARSAT images. They're uncanny in the way that diasporitic bauxite shows up in this rather ghastly magenta color. This facility here, east of the Shihekou Delta, shows a perfectly clear rectangle of diasporitic bauxite. However, that must be an anomaly."

"Why?" said Jones.

"Well, there isn't a surface strip-mine anywhere near there."

Jones straightened up from the chart table and drew his shoulders back. "It may interest you to know, Archie, that this port facility became fully operational just a fortnight *after* the war started. See those tall cranes? They're crawler-type derricks normally used on construction sites. Here, they've been used to offload containers and food supplies in a manner that used to be done only with gantry cranes,"

"Why do you say '*used to*'?"

"Because our American friends took out this facility five days after this picture was provided by the Canadians," explained Jones. "It was one of over fifty facilities that the Chinese threw together to offload vessels they had seized to provide food and material for the Chinese War effort. We think General Bing has a large bunker somewhere in this region."

Jones showed Dr. Grant other data that he had been puzzling over for the past few years. With the sky now impenetrable, even to RADARSAT, there were no recent pictures. Intrigued by the challenge, Dr. Grant went to his office in the Geology Department and returned with disks containing data from the RADARSAT program going back to ten years before the war. Searching through the data using Jones' computer, the Geologist confirmed his hunch. "Well, Albert, I know precisely where your General Bing is."

"OK, Maestro; and where might that be?"

"500 meters below the top of this precise hilltop."

"How can you be so sure?" said Jones.

"Because this is the only deposit of diasporitic bauxite within 200 km. The geology in this area is highly anomalous, but there is this one concentrated deposit under that 800 meter hilltop. It's too deep for economical mining, even if it just jumps out at you from the RADARSAT data. Obviously the materials removed from the underground facility you are looking for in this region must have come from this deposit and then been used as fill for the cargo facility. And if you compare this older image to the most recent one you have, you can see subtle changes to this road, leading from your new container terminal there, east of the Chaohehe river, directly up into the mountains, east of the Shihe reservoir. And the road looks like it has seen increased load. There are new passing shoulders; see here - and here?"

After having the Geologist explain his logic to the Mr. Jessup, the intelligence team leader, Jones passed the data to the Americans. Two weeks later, the Americans flew a small Uninhabited Aerial Vehicle over the mountain-top north of the Shihe Reservoir. It confirmed the presence of unusually high-powered air surveillance radars in the region before it was downed.

Knowing where General Bing's lair was and how deeply it was buried under the mountain top had been an insurmountable challenge to the weapons-effects planners in DUMB One. Even the most powerful nuclear bunker-buster warhead, the Robust Nuclear Earth Penetrator, couldn't penetrate more than 200 meters into hard rock. With at least a 300 meter shortfall, there was no obvious way to kill the Snake Head.

At least, not until the same geologist was brought in on the weaponeering problem a few weeks later, when he was asked if there was anything in the local geology that could be exploited.

"No. It's very hard rock. If you're going kill this chap, you'll need to go there on the surface, with a diamond drill, and drill down into this layer of bauxite."

"Supposing we could get a team on the surface, how long would it take to drill that deep?" asked Jessup.

"Any exploration drill-crew worth their salt should be able to drill that deep in under two days."

"What diameter hole would they make?"

"About fifteen centimeters. What kinds of warheads do you have that could fit down a six inch hole?"

"None. The smallest the Americans have is the W-46, artillery shell for tactical use, almost sixteen millimeters in diameter - too tight to slide down a 500 meter long drill-hole."

"What about conventional explosives?" asked Preston.

"With the size of that facility, we wouldn't be able to assure destruction."

"And biological agents?"

"They would have effective CBRN equipment, and certainly be pre-warned by the sound of the drilling," said Albert.

"Well, what about this for an idea. It's rather simple, but it might work.."

Four weeks later, an armada of Chinooks and other helicopters operating from the decks of commercial ships landed drilling crews and ground personnel in the valley closest to General Bing's bunker.

They were supported by a Combat Air Patrol of ship-borne AV-8B vertical take off Harrier Jump Jets, with British and American pilots, and as many as two squadrons of Japanese Super-Hornet fighter jets. The Super-Hornets bore the brunt of the counter-air portion of the battle, as they were the first to arrive.

The heaviest losses occurred in the first two hours of combat. Many of the electronic warfare techniques employed by the allies had failed because they had long since been compromised by the methodical commercial and military espionage which the PLA had been engaged in throughout the decade prior to the war. Chinese air defenses took out more than half of the Japanese fighters before the Chinese air defenses were finally neutralized by the allies.

Were it not for the presence of two Russian manufactured Ilyushin Il-78M air-to-air tankers of the Indian Air Force, the CAP provided by the Japanese fighters would have been stretched too thin. With Group Captain Patel's tankers, the allies were able to maintain local air superiority, if not supremacy.

Lower down, while the Marines took heavy losses to their Harrier jump-jets and helicopters giving cover to the drilling crews, but they were able to hold off the Chinese forces for almost forty hours. SLCMs from a British Vanguard submarine were used sparingly, wiping out large concentrations of Chinese forces with small nuclear detonations in the transportation routes through the mountains to the battle area. Despite the heavy losses, the Chinese forces kept coming, intent on winning by attrition.

Inside General Bing's command center, as the drilling had become louder and louder, Colonel Hua had been one of the last men to don his CBRN suit and confirm that his gas mask was working properly. He had just finished going over the plan with the damage control parties preparing to deal with the drills.

He told them that the enemy would need at least two hours to draw the full length of the drill back up the hole, as each two-meter section of pipe had to be unscrewed and taken away on the surface before the drill could be withdrawn the next two meters. Until the drill-shaft was removed there was little danger of any devices being thrown down the hole.

Colonel Hua's plan was for the damage control team to attach a package of explosives to the last few meters of drill shaft. There would be a couple of minutes during which the shaft would not be rotating, as the drill crew on the surface re-rigged the drill for extraction. Then, as the drill was drawn up, the explosives package attached to the drill-bit would also be drawn up the hole. When the bomb was at least two hundred meters up the hole the explosives would be detonated, resealing the hole with rock fragments and rendering the drill rig useless. They would also stuff fire-blankets and other materials into the bottom of the hole, and brace their plug with timbers before the detonation.

Just in case the Americans had a trick or two up their sleeves, all personnel were to wear their CBRN suits and have their bio-warfare detector strips attached to their arms and legs to quickly spot any CBRN warfare agents.

With battle damage repair teams ready to carry out the assigned task, and key personnel ready to evacuate as far as possible from the penetrated areas, Colonel Hua believed that they had a good chance of survival.

Unfortunately, they couldn't use nuclear weapons against the Americans as they had expended their arsenal in the desperate five-year war against India, fighting for the Australian prize. But Colonel Ming's forces would soon brush the attackers out of the valley and destroy the drills before the drills could be withdrawn and a bomb thrown down the holes.

None of this helped reduce the fear that every person felt as the vibration from drilling got stronger and stronger.

Suddenly the first drill broke through the ceiling just a few meters above his head. Bits of concrete and rock-dust filled the Command Center, but Colonel Hua remained calm.

General Bing was monitoring events through closed-circuit video on the other side of the concrete wall separating his quarters from the Command Center. He was dressed in his CBRN suit and ready to evacuate if the enemy was not cleared from the surface soon. But he trusted Colonel Hua's plan, and from the reports coming from Colonel Ming's men on the surface, the enemy would be over-run in moments. He was surprised when the screen suddenly went blank and a strong concussion shook the facility.

Thankfully, it was not a nuclear detonation. Obviously something had gone wrong with Colonel Hua's plan with the tethered explosives. But General Bing was certain that he still had time, as the enemy would still have to withdraw the drill before they could drop a bomb in.

On the surface, once the drill-crews were certain they had penetrated the bunker with both drills, they set off their own high-explosives rigged to a collar welded on top of each over-sized 7" diamond drill-head. The explosion killed Colonel Hua and most of the damage control team. The secondary explosion caused by the detonation of Colonel Hua's explosives package blew a five meter hole in the concrete floor, killing dozens of personnel in the level below.

By the time the shock-wave from the drill-head explosion reached the crews on the surface they had attached a grappling-hook to the top of the drill shaft. When the Chinook helicopter took up the strain, the crew disconnected the drill rig from the shaft, and jumped clear. The aircrew applied full power and climbed the heavy helicopter as fast as it could go, pulling the 8,000 pounds of drill shaft out of the hole in two minutes flat.

The moment the metal pipe was clear, weapons' technicians dropped three W46 warheads down each of the holes, on two-minute fuses. The security troops, drill crews and technicians rushed for the waiting helicopters. They were spurred on by an intense series of explosions taking place all around as conventional tomahawk cruise missiles put up a protective screen around the valley, wiping out the leading elements of Colonel Ming's assault force.

After sliding down the seven-inch drill holes, the small warheads popped out of the drill holes and detonated inside the 110,000 square meter bunker.

General Bing had made it half-way to the evacuation tunnel when the first of the 0.3 kiloton warheads detonated. Any one of the modified artillery-shell warheads would have done the job, but six were used as this was a "no fail" mission.

The bunker complex was consumed in the small nuclear explosion, killing everybody inside. Two intense columns of flame jetted out of the drill holes, reaching thousands of feet into the sky.

From the vantage point of one of the Harriers videoing the

battle from altitude, the twin fire spouts coming out of the narrow end of the mountain looked like an angry snort from a fire-breathing dragon laying face down in the earth.

When this streaming video was transmitted to Penzance and Mount Weather, tremendous cheers broke out.

Word quickly spread around the world that the Yinglong Dragon had been slain; the Snake's Head had been cut off.

37

SCHNAPPS

30 May: 10 Years After NEW

Feeling the empty space beside her in the king sized bed, Tanya woke up. Casey wasn't there, and that made Tanya worry.

With only the three of them left now, the HOTH had become a strange place in many ways.

After tying the sash around her bright yellow dressing gown, Tanya went looking. First she checked Donny's room, and saw her fourteen year old son fast asleep. His room still had the bunk-beds and futons from when he shared it with his brothers, Grandma Callaghan, Zlata and Zlata's son Pavel. Donny had been unwilling to let Papa remove the other beds. So much had changed for him in the last few months, he seemed to need to keep a sense of normalcy at least in his bedroom.

Tanya looked into the four other large bedrooms, all completely empty save for some calendars and posters stuck to the walls, and some furniture that had been left behind when everybody left. As she wandered around the HOTH, the silence felt very strange. In her imagination she could still hear the round-the-clock sounds that had filled the HOTH, when as many as 74 people had lived there together.

It had been very close quarters, especially in the last two

years, after the Oobleck cleared the skies and the snow began to melt. Once everybody became excited at the rapidly improving climate they also began yearning to break out and make a new life on their own. Not so much to be free from the crowded HOTH as to rejoice in the freedom and opportunity that the restored climate now offered.

The reality had been a source of frustration and conflict. The frustration was because even with summertime temperatures of plus twenty in the months after the Oobleck fell, the snow couldn't melt fast enough. The warm summers allowed people to begin solar green-house operations outside, but large-scale agriculture had not been possible even by the next summer. Fresh accumulations of snow came again each winter.

By last autumn, however, it was clear that enough snow had melted from the agricultural land and the main roads were clearing up fast enough that the following year, this year, should be clear of snow by May or June - in time for planting.

This led to a predictable conflict. There were at least thirty opinions as to who should be entitled to what. Certainly, during the first six years ANEW, the HOTH had been the best place to be and having shares in the collective enterprise had been a source of optimism for all involved. But as people began to conceive of what they would like to do on their own once the snow finished melting, the trouble started.

Some of the arguments were rather mild, but others were heated. Some felt that they had contributed over and above what others had, and yet had essentially the same share of ownership. A few even called into question Casey's right to have issued the shares in the first place; however, this idea was quickly put to rest when someone asked if they had a better approach to offer.

Finally, two months ago, Casey came down with a decision. He presented it at a full meeting of the HOTH. The repaired Gate House was being manned by a few men from the Ring families, and Peyton Palaty had been brought in to hold the Ops Watch, so all the HOTH members were in attendance.

Nobody other than Tanya and Casey knew what Casey was going to say, but everybody hoped that it would be good.

"My Friends. My Family. My Saviors." Casey began, with a degree of sorrow and love that he had never shown before.

"My children, my wife, the Callaghan clan at large and I would not be alive today were it not for each and every one of you here today. Your effort, your cooperation, your sacrifice and your will to survive has saved all of us. You have also helped so many others in the Oceanside region to save themselves.

But now it's clearly time for you to go." Casey said this with a humorous look on his face that lightened the mood and provoked more than a few cheers.

"Each of you has ownership here, and most of you have some idea as to what you want to do with your newfound freedom. Zlata's data indicates that this summer will be warm enough for some serious outdoor growing, easier travel and access to the materials and other 'stuff' left behind after the war. So we need to sort out who gets what, how and when."

"Amen to that!" said one of the truck drivers.

"So tonight I am going to tell you what you will get. There will be no argument tonight, I guarantee it."

"I don't agree, Casey. You can't dictate to us!" said the argumentative Ryan Webber. He was the head of a family of four that had made it on their own for five years before begging to be rescued by the HOTH. Many long-time HOTH members had taken issue with the fact that he had been given a full share.

"Simmer down, Ryan. This is not one of those consensus meetings where we can argue for hours and hours. This is going to be *my prerogative*. You will kindly keep your questions and comments to yourself until I am finished."

Such a harsh, dictatorial tone from Casey was unusual, but everybody understood that the real savior here was Casey, with the foresight and energy to have put the HOTH together and generosity to welcome them all into its membership. So they kept silent and listened to what he had to say.

"What I am going to do now is go through a power-point presentation that will cover the following six topics: First, an overview of the shares issued. Some of you have a 0.5% share, others a full share, and a few have more than a full share. As these shares were issued out of my own holdings from the start, and I have your signed certificates of exchange, I am certain that there will be no squabbling about this. Second, I will go over what WE own together. Our holdings have expanded with each and every new member that was added, and from the stakes we have accumulated in other properties. Third, I will go over the equipment and supplies we have here at the HOTH. Fourth, I will go over the "accounts receivable", which lists favors owed to the HOTH by the city of Parksville, the town of Qualicum Beach, by other surviving landholders, and so on. Fifth, I will go over the landholdings and assets that Tanya and I own, exclusive of the HOTH. Our personal landholdings and gold coin may be relevant to some of you, and they are open to negotiation, but not tonight. The Sixth and final topic will be what I believe to be a fair and manageable system for the division of the assets or, if you will, the cash-out of your shareholdings," Casey paused, seeing the eager looks on the faces of many.

He then went on, with Tanya's help, to cover each topic. It was clear that Casey and Tanya had spent a lot of time and effort compiling the presentation. The landholdings and interests were clearly marked out on an electronic version of the Regional District map. The list of machinery, equipment and tools was exhaustive, as was the summary of livestock, food-stores and construction materials. Casey certainly was good with details.

But what was most interesting was the economic analysis. Casey had taken data from the trade records and established a system to convert the value of items into calories and from calories into ounces of gold, based on trading patterns over the last 12 months. He listed the value of each inventory item in terms of gold. The grand total was CDN $G 22,441,980, at a gold value of CDN $G 10,000 per ounce. This meant that each 0.5% share in the HOTH was valued at CDN $G 112,209.90.

Casey explained that only those property titles that had been registered with Judith, the district's property clerk, could be legally owned. The rule of law still applied. Casey explained that he had spoken with the newly acclaimed Governor of the Oceanside Regional District, Marty Penner, and gave his support to the notion that all the land abandoned by the deceased would revert to the ownership of the Oceanside Regional District, subject to a five-year right-of-succession consideration.

This meant that abandoned land could be purchased from the Regional District and that the only other available land in the area was that which had been formally registered and occupied by its registered owners, heirs or tenants. As Casey explained, this meant that members of the HOTH could choose land other than what the HOTH syndicate owned, and would have the $Gs to buy it.

Next, Casey explained that the valuation he had put against each item on the inventory was open to discussion over the "Pre-Market" period that was to start immediately and last one week.

"At the end of the Pre-Market period, we will begin the liquidation of the HOTH syndicate. We will proceed as follows: first, you will all indicate, on the white-boards I have prepared in OPS, which items you would like to buy at the listed price. If another name has been put against an item, just put yours there as well and that item will go into auction.

You are welcome to join forces with others, such as your family unit or those of you who are considering partnerships of some kind; however big-ticket items must be sold off as wholes, not carved up into little pieces."

"But that means only you can buy the HOTH!" objected Ryan.

"That's right. D'you think that you should have enough credit here to buy the HOTH?" asked Tanya, showing how much people had started to get on each other's nerves lately.

"Er, now, I was just saying…."

"By the way, Ryan, you are welcome to offer up your property on Grafton Road. It would make a nice addition to my own holdings," Casey joked.

"Sure, I'll list it, but I'll be asking… come to think of it, maybe I could buy some of that acreage that backs onto it…"

"Ryan, my boy, I think you are starting to get it." Casey concluded his presentation and the meeting broke into a free-for all discussion. There was a general consensus that Casey's mechanism for dissolution was fair; however, a few people wanted to discuss the valuation of some of the equipment. The more people engaged in debate, however, the more willing they were to talk about what they had their eyes on. In some cases this helped people recognize whose ambitions could go hand in hand with their own, and some strategic partnerships were started.

That had been three months ago. The price-adjusting went well, as had the auctions. As expected, Casey was left with the HOTH itself, much of the basic equipment he would need to operate his own green-house and some farming enterprises, and less than a quarter of his gold. What most people had been interested in were the land and equipment that would give them a means of generating their own income.

After the auction had been completed in late February, the items had been tagged with the new owner's name, and the property transactions were registered with Judith. She was now operating out of an office in town and had already demanded that Governor Penner provide her with more staff.

Many people had moved out by the end of March to get a head-start on repairing their new homes and preparing to get their enterprises started. Others, like Gwen Jenkins, April Mynarski, Gloria Neumann and both Callaghan girls wouldn't move out of the HOTH until their weddings, planned for early

May. This gave their fiancés added motivation to get their new houses in order and made the HOTH a hub of wedding-planning activities. But now even the young women had moved out.

When Tanya finally found Casey down in the Ops Centre, drinking, she had a sense of what he was going through.

"You're drinking alone. What's the matter?"

"It's all over. Everybody's gone. This place is so strange and quiet without them."

"But this is what you wanted, Casey." Tanya sat down on one of the well-worn chairs next to Casey and poured herself some of the Peppermint Schnapps Casey was drinking.

"What do you mean? I never wanted to be *so alone.*"

"But you wanted our children to make it to this point. You did all of this - the HOTH, the survival plans, the networking, the food storage – you did this to save their lives. Now they have their lives and the world is alive again. We have to let them go, to follow their own paths."

"Yea, I understand that. But they're going to be so far away. We won't see them a hundred times a day. They'll forget about us and we'll be all alone."

"That's the alcohol talking. They'll be right here in Oceanside. Well, all but Tara."

"That's my point. How do we know GT and Tara will be OK? - That they'll make it to Mazatlan in that little boat?"

"We don't."

"And how do we know that Liam and Justin will succeed in their building center idea?"

"We don't"

"And will Hope will be happy in town with Bart?"

"She'll be close to Francis and Keiko. Francis will be starting up the college and Hope will be at the school. He'll give her a lot of help, but you're right, we don't know."

"And how do we know that the Vogels will succeed with their flight centre? And that the Neumanns will make it to Black Creek? And that Mom and Mr Skinner will be able to take care of themselves in that little condo in town?"

"We don't." Finally Tanya saw that Casey was rattling off the disposition of former residents from a list on a white board, and took over the task.

"And we don't know how Miles, Patti, Andy and Allison will do down in Saanich. Or how Amy and Peter will do with the gun shop. Or how Roger, Sam, JJ and Gwen will do with the heavy equipment business. Or how Zlata and Ken will do with Zlata's salvage and recycling store, and Ken's new job as Sheriff.

Or how April and Danny will do with their farm. Or how Granny G, Don, and the Prakas will do with the orchard. Or how the Kellys will do with the bio-diesel business. Or how Yuri and Olga will do with their honeybees, winery and vodka business. Or how Ryan and his family will do with the Gorton farm – that was a strange purchase, by the way."

"OK, OK, I get it. Everybody is moving on to something good. They all have good prospects. But how are *we* going to cope? With just Donny here to help, I won't be able to get that algal-diesel plant going. We won't be able to run much of a garden on our own, let along your "U-Pick" berry business. And the animals; we won't be able to build up much of a herd, not without some helping hands." Casey sounded exasperated.

"Koochie-koo. You're almost sixty. Why don't you relax and enjoy your retirement? We'll have grandchildren soon. The kids will be dropping them off all the time. We'll have hours of 'ootie-pootie' with them every day. You can hire some helpers to look after the place. We could convert some rooms into a bed-and-breakfast. We could take in some refugees from Vancouver, for that matter."

"I suppose."

"You can't have it both ways. Our kids need to break out on their own and not be dependent on us to manage their affairs. Besides, haven't you had enough squabbling, tears, chaos, need, stress, hysterics and theatrics for one lifetime?"

"No. Never. *I want it all.*"

EPILOGUE

ICED TEA

15 March: 15 Years After NEW

He had the old man in his sights, but hesitated for a moment. Something seemed strange. There was just one old man, digging in the dirt at the edge of a large vegetable garden. As he looked around the well-fortified structure, he couldn't believe that there were not other people around.

Just before squeezing the trigger, he saw an old woman carrying a tray with a pitcher of some iced beverage. Seeing only two glasses on the tray, he opened fire, taking the two old people out with two short bursts from his automatic weapon.

They showed no fear as they went down. The old man crawled to the old woman, and she reached her hand out to touch his. Then there was no more movement. Casey and Tanya were dead.

Moments later, the soldier was passed by his squad of soldiers, eager to storm the fortified structure. The only gunshots that Captain Ng heard were easily recognized as coming from his own men's AK47 assault rifles. There had been no others inside, and soon the Chinese flag flew from the rooftop.

As he walked by the dead couple, he saw a look of peace in the old man's face, as though he had welcomed the end.

Suddenly, Casey reached up and grabbed the Chinese soldier's leg, pulling him down on top of him. As he started to torture the soldier with tickles, the child broke out laughing. Other "soldiers" soon dog-piled on top of Grandpa Callaghan and joined in the fun.

Casey had over-acted his death scene and couldn't stop laughing at Tanya's own overly dramatic final scene.

"Don't you children ever tire of playing 'Chinese Commandos'?" asked Tanya, getting up off the ground.

"But the war isn't over yet! They could attack us at any moment!" said one of the children as he re-loaded the forked stick he used as an assault rifle.

"They may still be fighting in Australia and Africa, but with the new military bases up and running now, they'll never threaten North America again," Casey said, thinking about a discussion he had listened to on the subject from the popular radio show hosted by Ron Jasmine, in Astoria, Oregon.

"Go on now; get yourselves cleaned up and join everybody else down on the lower deck," said Tanya. "Grandpa Callaghan and I will be down with the veggies in a few minutes.

As Tanya watched Casey drink his iced tea, she had a tremendous feeling of satisfaction. With so much going on in Oceanside, with reconstruction in full swing, Casey had regained his vigor and energy.

With daily visits of friends and family, and hours of ootie-pootie with the grandchildren, Tanya and Casey enjoyed every minute of their retirement.

The End

ABOUT THE AUTHOR

Gene has served as both a civilian and a military pilot from 1988 to 2011. He has studied an eclectic range of subjects, and has a degree in Philosophy from UBC in his home town of Vancouver. Father of four, Gene has taken up writing books as his retirement activity. Gene is also a founding member of Flea Circus Books. To find out more about Gene, explore his page through Flea Circus Books. www.fleacircusbooks.com

THE WINTER KILL STORY CONTINUES

Gene has begun working on a parallel Winter Kill novel, centered on how the war plays out in Australia. The North American sequel to Winter Kill, with just a bit of overlap, will also be completed. Post your opinions about whether you would like to see the sequel or the parallel next, at Gene Skellig's blog www.winterkill.blogspot.com, or through Flea Circus Books.

Of course, making Winter Kill into a major motion picture or perhaps a miniseries would be a great deal of fun, but so far nobody knows about this book. If you really enjoyed this book why not clip out one of the coupons, post your honest review of the book on Amazon, or put your tattered old copy of Winter Kill into the hands of someone important.

As a self-published author, Gene "the flea" Skellig could use all the help he can get!

INVITATION

With millions of self-published titles released each year, the book buying public are overwhelmed. By promoting royalties-based collaboration on books, so that authors can improve their content without investing large sums of money, Flea Circus Books has made it possible for this author to publish and market this book at a relatively low price. You are invited to explore www.fleacircusbooks.com to find out how to get involved as a content collaborator, an author, a niche marketing entrepreneur or as a book buyer. Help us re-brand the self-published author under the Flea Circus TM brand, where interesting books of the highest quality can be discovered. Embrace the diversity and passion of what is really going on in the flea world - get involved!

"Flea Circus" is a registered trade mark. All rights reserved.

When you enter code: FJEHR84S at
www.createspace.com/3537111

When you enter code: FJEHR84S at
www.createspace.com/3537111

When you enter code: FJEHR84S at
www.createspace.com/3537111

WINTER KILL by Gene Skellig
THE RESPONDING DRAGON WAR HAS ALREADY BEGUN

In Winter Kill, one man's carefully prepared plans for the security of his loved ones is put to the test by the effects of another man's ambition for world domination.

- military technothriller / 393 pages
- also available as an e-book [Kindle]

A Flea Circus™ Book

Earn royalties writing, editing, illustrating and marketing books at   www.fleacircusbooks.com

WINTER KILL by Gene Skellig
THE RESPONDING DRAGON WAR HAS ALREADY BEGUN

In Winter Kill, one man's carefully prepared plans for the security of his loved ones is put to the test by the effects of another man's ambition for world domination.

- military technothriller / 393 pages
- also available as an e-book [Kindle]

A Flea Circus™ Book

Earn royalties writing, editing, illustrating and marketing books at   www.fleacircusbooks.com